A Time OF Discovery

A NOVEL

MINDY LAWRENCE

SILVER THISTLE
PUBLISHING

To my husband, who quietly goes about making my dreams come true.
I love you.

A Time

OF

Discovery

A NOVEL

CHAPTER I

ENGLAND, 1947

D aniel Carter was late.

By his own fastidious standards, anyway. He had promised himself faithfully that he'd arrive no later than seven this morning, yet his inability – or perhaps unwillingness – to decide between volumes one and two of *Trade Tyrants: Masters of the Silk Road* had significantly delayed his start.

Checking his watch for the dozenth time, Daniel swore under his breath. It was now 7:15, and he was still poring indecisively over the two heavy volumes. A mourning dove landed on a branch outside the window of his rooms and cooed throatily, as if to goad him. *First day of term*, it seemed to cry. *Must be on time, early even!*

Giving up all deliberations, Daniel stuffed both books into his already crammed leather satchel. Why not? he thought with a wry smile. After all, a little light reading never hurt anyone.

He soon deemed that proverb to be false, however; "a little light reading" bumped very awkwardly at his side as he began his trek to campus. Perhaps he *had* been a bit overenthusiastic in his packing after all. Thankfully, the sights and sounds of the morning soon distracted him from the cut of the heavy satchel into his shoulder. The slow rise of the sun, the gentle warming of the air, and the clear, thin wind at his back all swirled in familiar heraldry: summer's grip on the earth was slipping away, pushed aside by the cooler hand of autumn.

Each year it was the same. The air chilled, the leaves withered, and the flora died away. He loved it. Ironically, what many labeled a season of death and dormancy was, to Daniel, a rebirth. It meant the start of a new year, of countless challenges, of unnamed adventures still to come. Anticipation was building steadily within him, and his feet thumped the cobblestones accordingly.

The sleepy little university town was only just awakening on either side. Belmont, as it was called, was one of those quaint English villages that looked as though it had been frozen in time over a century ago. There was a decent market district, anchored by several worn-out pubs and shops with peeling storefronts. A string of bakeries piped the mouthwatering smell of hot bread into the air, and even now a few students were drifting sleepily between them in search of coffee and pastries. A portly old woman in a strawberry-printed apron wheeled a cart directly into the street, clearly determined to tempt customers inside her own tiny establishment.

"Good morning, young man!" she called out, seeing Daniel approach. "Care for a spot of breakfast? I've got muffins with marmalade, pecan buns, lemon scones, and apricot hand pies, all yours for the asking."

"That's very kind, but I'm afraid I haven't time to stop."

"What, no time for a fresh-baked muffin?" The woman arched her greying brows. "Oh, that's a shame, sir. Can't think of a better way to start a term, indeed I can't."

Daniel nodded blandly, unmoved by the woman's salesmanship.

"It's just like my mum used to say," she continued, hastily wafting the scent of hot buns in his direction. "She'd pop me in my chair with an 'Eat up, Effie my love, because you can't learn your letters on an empty stomach, and in school a grumbling belly is worse than a giggle.' Perhaps I could tempt you with a sweet roll, sir? Or a raspberry popover?"

"I'm afraid I …" Daniel's voice trailed off uncertainly. His feet were itching to resume their journey, but upon glimpsing the limp state of the woman's coin purse, and the outstretch of her weather-beaten hand, his breath had unexpectedly caught.

This still happened, occasionally, but it was never something he could become used to. There was a dull, numb feeling spreading throughout his skull, coupled with a sudden sealing off of his lungs. His mind wrenched to an altogether different scene as a fragment of memory flashed before him, its coloring and detail as sharp as life. It was the image of another empty hand, this one gnarled and cracked and hauntingly frail as it clutched at his clothing, begging him for coins or a crust of bread.

For the smallest instant, Daniel was back on that street with toppled stones and sooty air. He was back in that place where children knew only need, and where abundance was so distant a memory, it was recounted by the elderly in reverent, fabled tones.

Gratefully, the image was trickling away as quickly as it had seized him. He took a slow, steadying breath, forcibly returning himself to this smaller matter of the woman with her cart full of buns. Beset by an ache of guilt over dismissing such plenty, he reached into his pocket for a few coins.

"On second thought, I'll take a lemon scone. If you please."

"Ah, you won't regret that choice, sir," the old woman trilled, shoveling the largest one into a paper bag. "My scones won the prize ribbon at our church fete the year before the war broke out." Her eyes twinkled kindly as she handed it to him. "First day at our lovely university, then?"

Daniel accepted the bag with a weary smile. "Afraid not. I'm actually—"

"Morning, Professor Carter!"

The woman's husband, whom Daniel vaguely remembered as

the hard-of-hearing but affable baker, Archie Boswell, was limping towards them. "Off to impart some learning to these young rascals?" he asked, dusting copious amounts of flour off his apron.

Daniel nodded pleasantly. "I certainly mean to try."

"Pr-professor?" Mrs. Boswell gasped, glancing between the two gentlemen. "*Professor?* Oh, my goodness, I do apologize, sir! I had no idea you were—"

"Not to worry, Mrs. Boswell." Daniel handed her a generous fistful of coins. "Thank you very much for the scone. Good day to you both."

The old baker cheerily raised his cap. "We appreciate your custom, Professor."

Sinking his teeth into the pastry, Daniel resumed his walk. He could hear poor Mrs. Boswell stammering behind him in embarrassment, but the woman's mistake had been forgivable. He was quite used to that sort of blunder, for he was an unusual specimen in the town: too old to be labeled a student, and too young to be immediately considered a teacher.

His clothing did nothing to help passersby in their judgments, for though meticulous in other ways, Daniel had never felt the need to project seasoned authority through his dress. It had been three years since he'd worn a suit to lecture, and today was no exception. Oxfords, tan trousers, a collared shirt, and a dark green sweater were all that he had reached for. The fine leather satchel bumping at his side was his only truly professional accoutrement.

This in-between appearance, combined with his considerable height, meant that he often attracted curious looks – particularly from the town's female residents. Only this morning, several young ladies had slowed upon seeing him, and one had lingered hopefully in his path. But Daniel's dark blue eyes were fixed only on his beloved school.

Browning University was now visible through the tree line, and he ambled through its stone archway with the comfort of someone coming home after an arduous journey. Unlike the sleepy little town of Belmont, the university's two-hundred-year-old campus was buzzing with activity. A crush of students roamed between the stone buildings, chatting loudly and embracing old friends. The autumn air was thick with start-of-term excitement.

It was impossible for Daniel not to be amused at how easily he could distinguish the languid upperclassmen from the anxious first-years. The latter were desperately studying maps and searching for their lecture halls. Despite his lateness, Daniel troubled to point a group of nonchalantly terrified young men in the right direction. He had only just finished that good deed when a familiar, jolly voice filled his ear.

"Professor Carter! Daniel, over here!"

He turned to see the dean of the Archaeology department, Dr. Antony Miller, trotting towards him with his pipe in hand. Dr. Miller had been his undergraduate mentor, and following Daniel's own appointment at Browning, had quickly become his closest colleague and friend. Though the old dean was nearing retirement, he looked as giddy as a first year that the term was beginning.

"Good morning, Professor." Daniel shook his hand warmly. "How was your summer?"

"Excellent, my boy, just excellent!" Dr. Miller replied, with a gleeful puff of his pipe. "We had a very productive season, you know. Uncovered quite a few things in Crete. Stoneware, a few gold rings, beads of course, but also some evidence of glassworks."

Daniel smiled and nodded. "I read about that in *Archaeologist's Weekly*. Congratulations, Antony."

"But you must tell me all about your own find!" Dr. Miller thumped Daniel jovially on the shoulder, accidentally tipping a quantity of pipe ash onto his sleeve. "I simply couldn't believe it when I heard the news. Will you be allowed to do the conservation work here? And is it true that the Minister of Antiquities himself has become involved in your case? Well done, my boy, very well done indeed. I must say, the number of articles you've catalogued since taking up that site—"

"What do you say we meet for lunch," Daniel suggested, brushing the ash off his sweater before it singed, "and I'll tell you all about it?"

"Splendid notion. Shall we say eleven?"

"Can't, I'm afraid. That's my first lecture. Half-past twelve?"

"Perfect. The professor's lounge? My treat."

The two men fell into step beside each other.

"How are your courses shaping up?" the old dean continued, puffing out one of his trademark, perfectly formed smoke rings. "As rigorous and demanding as ever, I trust?"

"The assignments are appropriately challenging, I think."

Antony burst out in a hearty chuckle. "I doubt your students will agree, if your past curricula are anything to signify. Still heavy on translations and original texts? Dear me, I do feel for those students."

Daniel shrugged. "Anyone who is serious about this field should get used to slogging through original texts."

"True enough, I grant you." Miller rubbed his hands together eagerly. "What are you teaching this term, then?"

"Cross-Culturalization and Trade, Advanced Theories of Excavation, and Paleography."

"Goodness! All upper-level classes, then? That will certainly make for a demanding term, Daniel."

"I prefer to keep busy."

"Of course, of course," Dr. Miller answered, though he looked a little dubious.

They had nearly reached the large, gothic-style Archaeology building. "I ought to set up for my first lecture," Daniel remarked, crossing the stone courtyard and alighting the steps.

"Already?" the old man said. "I thought your first lecture wasn't until eleven?"

"That's right, but I've made a few additions to my reading lists. I'll see you at lunch, Antony."

"Very well, then. And Professor Carter?" Dr. Miller raised his pipe in farewell. "Bonam fortunam, eh?"

"*Etiam tibi,*" he called back with a half-smile as he entered the hall.

CHAPTER 2

At eleven sharp, Daniel walked into his full and anxiously buzzing classroom. It fell silent.

He nodded calmly in greeting. "Good morning, ladies and gentlemen."

This distinction was only barely necessary. There were perhaps six or seven female students in this class of fifty, and far fewer proportionally in the department overall. Setting his satchel upon the desk, he began scrawling information across the chalkboard.

"I am Dr. Carter, Assistant Professor of Archaeology. It's my very great pleasure to welcome you to Paleography: the study of ancient writing systems." He turned to face the group. After a brief pause, he smiled. "There's no need to look so frightened."

Nervous laughter rippled throughout the room.

"I don't know what you may have heard about this class," he said, taking up his position behind the lecture podium. "But I can assure you the rumors are only mostly true."

Here the students laughed more heartily.

Excellent, Daniel thought with satisfaction. A lively bunch.

"It's good to see you have a sense of humor," he continued, dusting chalk off his hands, "because you're going to need it this term, that much is certain. Levity, confidence, and grit: these are the qualities you'll need to stay afloat in this course, to say nothing of the field. You'll need levity when you're awake at two in the morning, writing a thirty-page paper on the evolution of ancient alphabets. You'll need grit to learn to read Aramaic as well as you can English. And you'll certainly need confidence when deciphering, on sight, an obscure original text for your final exam."

There was a slight groan and shuffle about the room, which Daniel had anticipated.

"I know what you're thinking," he said quietly. "And I can assure you, there will be times this term when you'll curse the Phoenicians, or the Egyptians, and wish the science of writing had never been invented. But I can also assure you that by the term's end, if you've put in the effort, you'll be able to decipher ancient symbols better than half the men I've worked with in the field." He slowly looked over the silent, riveted room. "Hard work is nothing to be afraid of, and I'm here to help you succeed."

A young lady in the front row let out a garbled little sigh. Daniel glanced at her. The woman, a voluptuous redhead, was leaning on her hand and regarding him with starry eyes. He ignored her. Daniel had become quite used to his female students giving him this sort of doting attention, at least during the beginning of term. When he was a new professor, it had somewhat flattered him. After three years of teaching, it only encouraged him to plow back into his lecture as quickly as possible.

"First things first," he announced. "We'll review the syllabus. You will note that your first paper is due this Friday."

The class let out another collective groan.

"None of that feeling sorry for yourselves," he scolded them good-naturedly. "It's a short one. I'm not a barbarian, after all."

Several students chuckled, and again Daniel had the thought that this would be a responsive, pleasant group. He continued describing the various elements of the course, making it halfway through the syllabus before the door to his left creaked open once more.

Daniel paused his lecture as a young woman shyly poked her head through the doorway. She was of unremarkable height and build yet carried an armful of books and a satchel that rivaled his own in terms of its heaviness. A pencil had been stuck jauntily through her dark, sideswept hair, though she seemed unconscious of its protrusion past her forehead. Daniel guessed she was a fourth year, and that in addition to being late, she was lost.

"Pardon me, but is this ...?" Her voice trailed to nothingness as she read the words he'd scribbled on the chalkboard. "Oh yes, I can see that it is," she continued, her cheeks a bit pinker now. She wrinkled her rather snub nose, clearly unsettled by having the attention of the entire room upon her. "Excuse me for being late, Dr. Carter. I've just been speaking with Dr. Miller, and—"

"I'm afraid there must be some kind of mistake," Daniel said, masking his irritation that a well-flowing lecture had been derailed. "This class is full, and our instruction period began over twenty minutes ago."

He moved to resume his lecture, but saw out of the corner of his eye that she'd stepped determinedly forward.

"Yes. Again, I'm very sorry to disrupt, Professor. But I was just speaking with Dr. Miller. He approved an add slip." She pulled a piece of paper out of her skirt pocket and held it uncertainly in front of him.

Daniel inwardly groaned, calculating the hours of extra work this student's addition would mean over the term.

"Take a seat, please, and we'll sort it out after class."

Every desk in the room was occupied, as Daniel well knew, but his lingering irritation over this intrusion made him not very disposed to assist her further. One lad chivalrously offered her his seat, but she refused it. Instead she opted to pull a loose chair to the side of the room, near the window.

With the interrupter out of his view, Daniel got the lecture pretty well back on track. Indeed, he had almost forgotten the incident by the time the old campus bell rang out once more.

"All right, that's enough for today. Turn in your syllabus agreements, if you please, and be sure to pick up a copy of your first assignment: prehistoric murals and pictographs. Goodbye then, goodbye," he added, bidding the students farewell as they drifted to the door. A few young ladies hovered foolishly near his desk. Daniel busied himself with cleaning the chalkboard, as there was no question they could ask him at this point that had not been covered by the syllabus. Small talk, whether benignly intentioned or not, was simply not of interest.

"I'll see you at lunch, Margie," a low voice whispered to the group behind him. There was a pause, a step, then a gentle clearing of the throat. "Professor Carter? Is now a convenient time to discuss this paperwork? I dearly wish to join your class."

The add slip. Daniel had almost forgotten. He turned halfway and held out an impatient hand.

"Give it here, then."

She passed over the form, fixing a pair of keen dark eyes on him while he reviewed her course list with growing discontent. It was positively crammed with advanced subjects.

"I can't approve this," he said, shaking his head. "We recommend a workload of four to five classes at a time. You have *seven* listed here, and I see that you're enrolled in Classical Languages as well. It's unwise to take that course at the same time as Paleography. Both subjects are extremely challenging."

"Yes, it's a lot to take on," she reluctantly admitted. "But Dr. Miller thinks that it might be done. He's given me his approval."

Daniel made a mental note to discuss this arrangement with Antony at lunch. His frown deepened as he read the list once more. Human Origins, Structural Conservation, Islamic Art – it was truly a nightmarish amount of work.

"I need to catch up this term," the young woman said more firmly. "I'm willing to put the time in. I'll do whatever it takes. Anyway," she continued amusedly, "it would be a bit backwards to study prehistoric writing *after* I'd learned Greek and Latin, wouldn't it?"

He shot her a glance, and her smile faded ever so slightly. Hastily removing the stub of pencil from behind her ear, she said, "I know your course is full, Dr. Carter, but I hope there might be some way of adding it. I've read all your recent papers. Your work in Egypt over the summer was—"

Daniel signed the carbon copy form, still somewhat impatiently. "If Dr. Miller has approved this, then so will I. But you're in for a lot of work, make no mistake about that." He tore off the bottom sheet for his records and handed the rest back to her. "Good luck to you, then."

She appeared a bit stunned by his abrupt dismissal, but accepted the form with a steady hand.

"Thank you, Professor Carter."

As she retreated softly from the room, Daniel finished cleaning the chalkboard and locked his materials in his office. It was time to meet Dr. Miller for lunch, and the old dean certainly had some explaining to do.

His walk to the professor's lounge was swift and brisk, enabling Daniel to clear his head. When he arrived at the lunchroom he found Antony loading up a table with an assortment of white paper packages.

"Sit, my boy!" the old man beckoned, pulling off his tweed coat. "I've ordered up a smorgasbord. Sandwiches and pickled eggs, some apples, biscuits of course, and even some vanilla fizzy pop." Dr. Miller snapped open a bottle and took a sip. "Ah," he murmured dreamily. "This tastes right. Oh, how I missed these during the sugar-rationing days of the war. But on to more important topics. How was your morning lecture?"

"Excellent, until a student arrived twenty minutes late with an add slip." Daniel casually unwrapped a sandwich. "Now how did that happen, I wonder?"

Dr. Miller shook his head with stately gravity. "Students are getting very good at forging documents these days. Highly troubling. It is a concern across all departments."

"The thing is, as a language and writing expert, I'm quite good at detecting original works from forgeries. So, I can tell," he said, pulling the crumpled add slip from his pocket, "that this is your actual signature."

"Really?" Dr. Miller took an innocent sip of pop.

"Yes, really. What's even more troubling is that I recall sending you a message explicitly detailing my wish not to add any more students this term. Particularly ones whose course loads are already full."

"Hmm." Dr. Miller frowned, but there was a merry twinkle in his eye. "I must not have seen that message. Or if I did, I did not understand it. It's all Greek to me, as they say!"

Daniel wearily rubbed a hand over his forehead. "And how is it, may I ask, that the world's foremost expert on ancient Greek cannot comprehend a simple interoffice memo?"

"Perhaps it was poor handwriting. Doctors and professors, you know!" Setting down his bottle, Antony engaged him more seriously. "Can you blame the student for wanting to join? Your classes have been at maximum capacity every term for the last two years." He leaned forward, lowering his voice to a murmur. "I tell you plainly that you are one of the finest educators in our department. If a student values their instruction too highly to settle for less than the best, I must applaud them. I must help them where I can."

Daniel grunted.

"There. I knew you'd see it my way, when it came to it." Dr. Miller sat back comfortably. "Which student was it? I've signed several add slips this morning."

He looked down at the name, which he now realized was faded in portions. Whoever the young woman was, she had not pressed the pen down hard enough when writing her name.

"Jennifer ... Elliot, or something."

"Ellison?" Dr. Miller raised his brows. "Jenny Ellison? Oh, you'll have no trouble with her. I taught her last year. Bright young thing. Sharp as a tack, and particularly gifted with languages. Marking her papers will take you no time at all, I assure you."

"Let's hope so," Daniel groaned, "because I signed this." He moved to stuff the add slip into his pocket, inhaling sharply as his lower back contorted. He winced, biting his lip and trying to straighten before Antony could notice anything amiss. Unfortunately, the old man's sharp blue eyes were fixed on him with predictable concern.

"It's still bothering you, then?" the dean asked, with a quiet nod to Daniel's torso.

"No," he said hastily, lifting his own bottle of pop. "Now hear this, Antony. No more additions. No more. If my memo was unintelligible, is my elocution at least clear?"

Dr. Miller threw back his snowy head and chortled heartily. "Perfectly clear, my boy. Very well, very well." He raised his drink. "To your health, Professor Carter. To life, ancient and present. And to a prosperous schoolyear!"

"I'll drink to that," said a more cheerful Daniel, clinking his bottle against the old professor's.

"Now." Antony set down his pop after a long gulp. "Tell me about Abu Simbel."

CHAPTER 3

A cross campus, a dark-haired young woman waded through a sea of heads in the student dining hall. In one hand she clutched a brown-bagged lunch, and in the other a pile of notes from her morning classes. They weighed her down uncomfortably as she traversed the crowded room, but at last her gaze fell upon a group of young ladies huddled around a corner table.

"Jenny! Jenny, over here!"

Jenny Ellison smiled and nodded at the beckoning Marjorie Payne, her flatmate and closest friend at Browning. Margie sat next to Jillian Stewart, a fourth year and one of the only other female students in the department. The sight of Jillian was less cheering; she and Jenny were not the closest of friends, if truth be told, but as there were so few ladies in the Archaeology program, they tended to stick together whatever their feelings.

"Hi, Margie." Jenny strode past Jillian and took the open seat near her friend. "Where's Nyra?"

"She's just coming. She's getting an apple or something." Margie squeezed Jenny's arm warmly. "Golly, it was such a nice surprise to see you in class! I had no idea you were taking Paleography."

"Neither did I, until today."

"Still trying to catch up, are we?" Jillian asked.

"That's right."

"Did you hear the news?" Margie excitedly dashed salt over her potatoes. "Billy Cavendish got taken on at a site in Jordan."

"Yes!" Aside from the pressing task of adding Paleography, little else had occupied Jenny's thoughts all morning. "Does anyone know where, exactly?"

"Petra," Jillian reported, staring into a compact mirror and smoothing her bright red hair. "He'll be studying the water conduit system."

She let out a low whistle. "Lucky tyke. To get something so soon after graduation ... how is that even possible?"

"Because Billy's uncle is third cousin to a lord," Jillian snorted. "How else does one get anywhere?"

"Well, I haven't got any lordly cousins, so I'll just have to hope my parents' loyalty to Browning will be enough to get me something," Margie said, absently oversalting her potatoes.

Jenny gently pulled the saltshaker away from her as Nyra Patel returned with her apple.

"I think I'm in love," Nyra sighed, plopping down in an open seat. "Why did no one warn us that Dr. Carter was such a dish?"

"Because most of the students in our program are men." Margie chuckled. "Why should they care? Besides, he's only just got back from Africa."

"Southern Egypt," Jenny specified, through a mouthful of chicken sandwich.

"That's right, Egypt. But I couldn't agree more, he's an absolute dish." Margie giggled. "Jillian and I have been doing reconnaissance all morning. His name is Daniel. He started teaching just before the war broke out, and he's been back at Browning for almost three years now. He's thirty, or thirty-one, Barbara Danvers wasn't sure. He was the youngest ever recipient of the Bowman Fellowship—"

"What's that?" Nyra interrupted.

"It means he completed a dual program for his doctorate," Jenny said, now studying her course schedule. "At Cambridge, then Harvard."

"Anyway, he's a genius," Margie finished importantly.

"And so *tall*." Nyra slumped dreamily over her lunch, apparently having lost her appetite. "He's almost *too* tall. I swear, my forehead wouldn't even reach his chin. However can they expect us to focus on pictographs?"

Here Jillian took over the report. "He served in the war, of course. Barbara said he was made a captain by the end of it, but he came back early, in '44. Nobody knows what he did, or where he was stationed. And he never talks about it."

"None of them do," Jenny reminded her.

"Yes, but this is different." Jillian waved her hand dismissively. "The rumor is that he can't talk about what he did. Which almost certainly means he was a secret operative. A spy for Churchill himself, perhaps? Or maybe even an assassin, working undercover for the government?"

"Jillian," Margie said with a nervous laugh, "you can't be serious. An assassin, or a former assassin, walking the halls of boring old Browning? That's absurd."

"Maybe they hired him to keep the vole population in check?" Jenny suggested, suppressing a laugh.

"All I know is he has a murkier reputation than one might expect," Jillian whispered, leaning in towards the group. "There are rumors. Violent ones, at that. Tales of a fight that broke out two years ago between Dr. Carter and a student."

"*What?*" Nyra gasped.

"It's true. It was all hushed up immediately, but Barbara Danvers said it was almost certainly an illegal boxing match in a pub somewhere, and that a man even ended up in hospital. I wonder if Dr. Carter went to jail! That would certainly explain—"

"Jillian," Jenny groaned. "Stop rumormongering. Margie's right, Browning couldn't employ someone with a criminal record. He's probably just—"

"Oh, what would you know about it anyway?" Jillian snapped. "Were you in that pub?"

Jenny bit back a retort. The feeling of restrained dislike between them had always been mutual, but she had learned it was rarely worth rising to Jillian's taunts.

"Simmer down, all," Nyra the peacemaker chirped. "Remember, ladies, we're scientists. We're in the business of gathering *facts*. What did you think of him, Jen?"

She bit into a carrot stick thoughtfully. "Nothing, really."

"Nothing?"

Jenny shrugged. "I was surprised that he was so young. But I don't think we could ask for a better teacher. He's already an Amity Scholarship chair, and his site's very highly rated in the program. Besides, I've read his papers, and he certainly seems experienced."

"Oh, let's hope so," Jillian murmured slyly, as Nyra began giggling again.

"Do you think he's handsome, then?" Margie whispered with a blush.

Jenny couldn't quite recall the details of the young professor's face just now, outside of the furrowing of his dark brow and the strong clench of his jaw in response to her petition. Laughing, she said, "To be honest, I was more focused on getting him to sign my add slip. He clearly didn't want to."

"Oh! But did he, in the end?"

"Yes, thank goodness."

"That's a relief." Margie speared a salty potato. "You can help me with that pictograph assignment. I haven't the faintest idea of where to begin."

"Why not ask me?" Jillian said, arching a brow.

Margie shrugged. "I guess I didn't want to hear you moaning

and groaning about how easy all of our assignments are. I wouldn't be asking for help if *I* thought they were."

"Look alert, here comes Anders," Nyra whispered sharply, kicking them under the table and flashing a brilliant smile. A slim, very good-looking young man was approaching their group. He was a Manwaring, one of the fabulously wealthy blue bloods that owned the great estates outside of Belmont. Generations of Manwarings had matriculated at Browning, and this latest model was something of a celebrity among the female students. He was blonde-haired and blue-eyed, with a perfectly respectable jawline and the confidence of someone who knew he was attractive. Three of the girls straightened up, beaming. Jenny, however, pulled out her pictograph assignment and began to work.

"Anders, darling!" Jillian cooed. "How was your summer?"

"Swell, thanks." The young man grinned. "We spent most of it on The Riviera."

"Oh, how lovely," Nyra gushed. "But hang on – weren't you supposed to go on that dig with Dr. Chilcott?"

"I couldn't, in the end." He sighed and slapped his right hip. "Old war wound flared up at the last moment. They gave my Amity Scholarship to John Timmins."

Jillian and Margie simpered in sympathetic unison.

"You'll just have to try again this year," Margie consoled him.

"Although this time," Nyra said, "you just might have to beat Jillian for it. I keep telling her she should apply, now that she's a fourth year."

"Perhaps I will," Jillian said loftily. "You never know."

Anders seemed to pay little heed to these comments. "You ladies all look well. None of you broke your backs working sites over the summer, I'm pleased to see."

"We are a little less pleased," Margie answered, though she batted her lashes. "It would have been nice to get something. Golly,

I'd have been dead chuffed just to take pictures of Hadrian's Wall. Thanks all the same though, Anders."

"What's this?" Anders asked, now looking down the long table at Jenny. "Hard at work already, Miss Ellison?"

"That's right." She heaved a textbook out of her satchel, grateful her dark curls obscured most of her face. "Loads to do."

"I'd be more than happy to tutor you, if you need catching up?"

"I'll be fine, thanks."

Anders paused, shrugged, and shoved his hands into his pockets. "Suit yourself. I'll see you in class, then. So long, ladies." He winked as he departed, presumably well aware that most of the table was watching him walk away.

As soon as he was gone, Jillian threw her napkin on the table. "I don't know why you're always so rude to him. He's a perfectly lovely chap. What's the matter with you?"

"I was not rude, and it's none of your business," Jenny returned coolly.

"Don't you remember, Jilly?" Nyra whispered in her ear. "Barbara told us. Anders took Jenny out last year, but when he asked her out to dinner again, she wouldn't go."

"Her mistake to make. Thank goodness I'm not as cold-hearted," Jillian said with a little toss of her head. "Mark my words, ladies. By the end of this term, I'm going to have a new boyfriend. Either Anders Manwaring ... or Dr. Carter." She grinned wickedly as Margie and Nyra gasped.

"Jillian Stewart, you take that back!" Margie cried.

"Why should I?"

"Because you can't have flings with teachers, everyone knows that! It's against Browning's code of conduct!"

Jenny was certain Jillian did know, but did not care. She was forever in and out of relationships, of all shapes and sizes.

"What's the harm if no one finds out?" Jillian retorted.

"But of course someone would find out, eventually!" Margie,

who loved a cause, dropped her fork in a fit of passion. "Dr. Carter is one of the most respected professors at this university, and if you go after him you'll be expelled, and he'll lose his job, or be blacklisted from future positions, or—"

"Let's just hope Jillian settles for Anders, then," Jenny soothed her. She threw Jillian a reproachful look, but the young lady merely lifted a brow and stole one of Margie's salty potatoes.

"Anyways, we all have a much more pressing problem," Nyra muttered.

"Oh?" Margie frowned. "And what is that?"

"How on earth are we going to learn hieroglyphs with the great distraction of Dr. Daniel Carter before us?" she moaned.

The ladies all burst into laughter, and this time Jenny happily joined in.

CHAPTER 4

On the second day of Daniel's course, students filed in more excitedly than nervously. It was gratifying to see they had retained some enthusiasm for the material, even after signing his daunting syllabus. He couldn't wait to finally dig into the work with them. Being in high spirits, he had even begrudgingly brought in an extra desk for his late addition and placed it under the far window. To his immense satisfaction, every seat was filled by the time the opening bell chimed.

"Good morning, class. I'm relieved you all came back, as I would rather like to keep my job."

A slight murmur of laughter rolled throughout the classroom.

"Today, we go back to the very beginning of the written word: prehistoric pictographs." Daniel drew several symbols on the board. "Like nearly every civilization that came after them, early man left records, the most famous of which were painted in the Cave of Altamira, in northern Spain."

He turned to face his audience. "Bison, deer, horses, hunting scenes, handprints, other images that are over 35,000 years old. At first glance, these pictographs seem obvious in their messages. 'Ancient people hunted,' one might say. 'They ate oxen and sheep.

Their daily lives were about survival, and little else. There is nothing more to the story.' Do you agree?"

The class hesitated, not wanting to misspeak. Daniel had expected this.

"Let us challenge ourselves to think deeper," he prompted them. "Altamira, for example, is a system of caves, inhabited over many generations. As such, we can reasonably assume these drawings were a record intended to be passed on to descendants, linking the groups together. Our task is to analyze why these were the messages they passed on. Why were these symbols, these scenes, so important that prehistoric peoples would painstakingly collect and tint bat excrement just to have some medium in which to record them?"

Several students chuckled at the mention of excrement. Another moment Daniel had been expecting.

"Clearly these images were significant. Perhaps even sacred. We must look for messages beyond the perfunctory and analyze what they tell us about life in prehistoric times. Most of all, we must avoid the naïve assumption that these glyphs were no more than a diet recommendation or menu."

Daniel now had the rapt attention of the entire class. Well, nearly the entire class. His extra student, who sat in the front row, had not looked up from her notes since the hour began. She was bent over her papers, busily writing and paying no heed to the lecture.

Homework for another class, Daniel guessed. Annoyance at this blatant inattentiveness washed over him, but he pressed on with his presentation.

A young woman a few seats away raised her hand. "Have you ever seen them, Dr. Carter?"

The speaker was a redheaded, heavily made-up fourth year wearing a skirt suspiciously ill-suited for the cool autumn weather. Her question was innocent enough, but the hungry look on her face implied that she was anything but.

"The cave drawings?" Daniel replied evenly. "Yes. I did some preservation work in Serra da Capivara, when I myself was at Browning."

"Under the Amity Scholarship, sir?" asked another chap. At this point – finally – the extra student looked up from her notes with interest.

"That's right." Daniel cast his eyes over the very full lecture hall. "On that subject, please remember that all Amity Scholarship applications are due by the middle of term. Any qualified third or fourth year may apply for the opportunity, and I strongly encourage each of you to consider doing so. Recipients will gain real field experience on an active archaeological site."

"With you, sir?" The short-skirted student in the front row was speaking again. "In Egypt?"

"Perhaps. The three scholarship recipients will be sponsored for a summer of work in Egypt, Iran, or Crete. I currently supervise the Egyptian site."

"Excellent. My name is Jillian, by the way." She smiled and crossed one sheer-stockinged leg over the other. A few people giggled uncomfortably. Daniel, being used to overtures from his older female students, nodded blandly and continued with his lecture. With another flash of annoyance, he noted that the other young woman in the front row had returned to her absentminded scrawling.

The rest of the class flew by, as it always did in the beginning of the term. As soon as the bell chimed, the air was pierced with chatter and the scrape of desks against the tiles.

"And remember, your first paper is due this Friday!" Daniel called into the din. The students ignored his warning, as eager gossip about the Amity Scholarship coursed throughout the room. The thought made Daniel smile as he turned to erase the chalkboard.

"Excuse me, Dr. Carter?"

Daniel suppressed a groan. Yet again his questioner was the bold girl from the front row, Jillian.

"Yes?" he answered politely. "How may I help you?"

"I'm afraid I'm having trouble with my pictograph paper," Jillian simpered. "I don't know which periodicals are the most reputable. I wondered if I might schedule some time to go over our readings with you?" She widened her eyes ever so slightly, then lowered them until they were half-shut. Daniel supposed this was meant to be seductive.

"Hopefully today's lecture will have helped you with your outline," he replied. "If you're still confused, however, you're more than welcome to sign up for one of my teaching assistant's office hours. Max Caldwell will be happy to assist you." Looking behind Jillian, Daniel saw that his extra student had finished packing up her satchel.

"Miss Ellison," he called to her, "I need a word. If you wouldn't mind staying behind a moment, please?"

The young woman looked a bit alarmed but nodded. As Jillian walked off in a huff and the room emptied, Miss Ellison approached his desk with a questioning air. Daniel folded his arms and took a calming breath.

"I can appreciate, Miss Ellison, that you have a great deal on your plate this term. But I must ask that you refrain from doing your other coursework in my class."

Her dark brown eyes widened. "I wasn't doing other course-work, Professor Carter. I promise."

Daniel took another steadying breath. Though he loved teach-ing, he never would get used to students lying to his face. Still, he attempted to keep his tone light. "May I ask what you were working on during our lecture, then?"

She looked down at her notebook and began reading off it: "We will look for messages beyond the perfunctory and analyze what they tell us about life in prehistoric times. Most of all, we will avoid the naïve assumption that these glyphs are no more than a diet recommendation or menu." Her eyes skipped upwards. "I was taking notes. It's well-known that you don't pass out copies of your lecture outlines. I thought that if I wrote down everything you said, then I might ..."

"You copied my lecture word-for-word?" This was surely impossible, but the young woman nodded fervently.

"Yes. Or, almost. I had to approximate when you spoke particularly fast."

Daniel frowned and held out his hand for her notebook. "May I see it, please?"

After an uncertain pause, she handed it over. What Daniel saw was an unintelligible mass of squiggles, symbols, and roots of various languages – French, German, and a little Latin. He glanced up at her skeptically.

"It's a shorthand system I developed as a first year," Miss Ellison explained in a rush. "I didn't much like the other systems that existed, so ..."

Daniel regarded her more curiously. "You made up your own?"

"Well, yes."

She said this so matter-of-factly that Daniel almost laughed out loud. He turned back to the paper with interest. Though he did not have her key, he was a skilled enough linguist to detect traces of his lecture among the patterns. Again, Daniel's gaze flitted upwards. Miss Ellison was watching him carefully, hugging a textbook to her chest and tugging on a wavy brown curl. His eyes returned to the paper. Feeling slightly foolish over his accusation, Daniel cleared his throat and handed back the notebook.

"Thank you, Miss Ellison. That will be all."

"Oh. All right, then." Her rigid posture softened at this turn of events. She walked briskly to the door, stopping and calling back brightly at her halfway point.

"I meant to say, that was a fascinating lecture Dr. Carter. Thank you."

Daniel nodded, not looking at her. Yet he glanced to his left as she slipped out the exit, catching a flash of blue skirt and the briefest glimpse of a slim, pretty leg. He strode to his adjoining office, puzzled by this odd student who would trouble to write a lecture word-for-word. He found his teaching assistant already in there, hard at work.

"Hello, Dr. Carter!" Maximilian Caldwell spun around in his chair and grinned widely. Max was a ginger-haired, bespectacled fourth year. A bit exuberant, perhaps, but a dab hand when it came to paperwork.

"I've finished filing all of your syllabus agreements," he announced with almost comical jubilance. "I could start on the pictograph worksheets now, if you like."

"No, I'll mark them myself, Max, thanks. You can come back next week."

"Really? Excellent," he replied, looking very cheery at this unexpected time off. "I'll be going, then. See you next week, Dr. Carter!"

"Max," Daniel stopped him. "Have you filed the student information sheets for this term?"

"Yes, sir. They're in the lower drawer, just there."

"Thank you."

Daniel diligently marked worksheets while the boy put on his coat. As soon as Max left the office, however, he pushed his chair near the filing cabinet. Per university requirements, Daniel had an information sheet on file for each of his students in case of emergencies. He thought them a nuisance and almost never used them; indeed, he was bothered by the circumstance which drove him to do so now. But Miss Ellison's unexpected responses today, and Dr. Miller's high praise of her abilities, had made him undeniably curious. He thumbed slowly through the files.

Elliso █ J.

He pulled out her sheet and began to read.

Jennifer Celine Ellison. A third year. She had enrolled at Browning in 1944, taken a gap year in 1945, and resumed her studies in 1946. Strange. Daniel thought he remembered Miss Ellison saying something about needing to catch up in her coursework. Yes, she had definitely mentioned something to that effect while trying to add his course, though he could not recall any explanation as to why.

Major areas of study: Archaeology and Linguistics. A double major, then. And a minor in Art History, besides. Her heavy class enrollment was making much more sense.

Hometown: Brookfield, England. Since he'd never even heard of it, he could only presume it was a small village.

Age: Nearly twenty-three years old. Daniel closed Miss Ellison's file, feeling slightly discomfited at how he had noted this point particularly. Shoving the drawer closed, he locked it for good measure and began marking worksheets in earnest.

"I am in desperate need of tea," Jenny groaned as she entered her flat that evening. She found her roommate Margie lying on the sofa in her dressing gown with both ankles propped comfortably upon the radiator.

"Well, hello to you, too," Margie said with a smirk. "The kettle's just boiled, and you can help yourself to some Bakewell tart if you like. My mum keeps sending me boxes of it."

"You're an absolute saint." Jenny wearily cut herself a slice. "Mmm. Lovely," she murmured, holding a steaming cup of tea near her face. "That walk home is getting colder every day."

"Have you been at the library all this time?" Margie asked.

"Yes. How was your evening, Marge?"

"You mean you were there for five hours?"

Jenny swallowed thickly. "Yes. And I intend to go back tomorrow night, and the night after. I'd still be there now, if I'd remembered to bring dinner."

Margie stared at her, her mouth slightly agape. "That's it. As self-appointed mother hen of this flat, I am putting my foot down. You cannot study every night this week. You'll work yourself to death."

Jenny only laughed. "I may starve to death, if I forget to pack supplies. But I'm not in danger of overwork. To be honest, I'm rather enjoying it." She took another satisfied bite of Bakewell.

Picking up a copy of *Wonders of the Ancient World*, Margie said, "You're a lost cause, Jenny Ellison. I wash my hands of you."

"That's a good girl," Jenny answered, cheerfully refilling her teacup.

Margie shot her a reproachful glance from behind the book. "May I ask what has prompted all this frantic studying? It's only the first week of term! You've always been a bit over the top when it comes to homework, but this is extreme even for you. What in heaven's name is going on?"

"I wonder if you might guess," Jenny said quietly. "Two words."

After a brief pause, Margie smiled. "Amity Scholarship. You're trying for the Amity this year, instead of next."

"Yes."

"But why?" she demanded. "Jillian said they hardly ever award it to third years. Why not look for a different internship, one that's not so competitive?"

"Oh Marge, just think about it," Jenny murmured longingly. "Dr. Miller, Dr. Chilcott, and Dr. Carter. Three highly respected professors, leading three magnificent sites. Crete, Iran, Egypt — what better internship could there be for any hopeful archaeologist?"

Margie acknowledged this with a grunt.

"Rumor has it Dr. Miller could retire any day," Jenny said

gravely. "There are three Amity spots open this year, but in the next there might only be two." She took a deep breath. "If I ever want to become more than a telephone operator, this is my best chance. I have to try."

Margie sighed. "Oh, very well. If you must, you must. But you're not working next weekend. It's your birthday, remember?"

Jenny smiled. "Yes, I remember."

"Are you excited?"

"For what?"

"Your *party*, of course!"

"Oh – right."

"Don't tell me," Margie said with a roll of her eyes. "You forgot."

"No, I ... yes, I did. Sorry, Marge."

"You've been forgetting a lot of our get-togethers lately," her roommate grumbled. "Peter's rugby match was yesterday, and he was really quite gutted when you didn't show up."

Jenny winced. "I'm sorry, it's just ... I've been busier than I expected. On that note, I *was* looking forward to my party, but I have a project due next Monday, and—"

"This is your twenty-third birthday!" Margie cried in indignation. "The only twenty-third birthday you will ever have. We're *not* canceling. Just leave it all to me. We'll have a magnificent celebration, one that I am not going to tell you anything about, and that you must go along with no matter how many term papers you have due the next day. Are we understood?"

"Time ... thou ceaseless lackey to eternity," Jenny intoned melodramatically. But she winked.

CHAPTER 5

Two weeks into the term, Jenny's friends were still pursuing intel on Dr. Carter with unflagging zeal.

"He's single," Nyra whispered euphorically one day. "I know for a fact because I've just been talking with Mrs. Perkins, the department secretary. I was casually asking questions about his background and home life, nothing too obvious, you know, and she told me that although he's been in and out of relationships for years, she hasn't heard anything at all about a current girlfriend!"

This news was met with relief on the parts of Jillian and Margie. While this amused Jenny greatly, she had to admit that on some level she, too, was beginning to understand why they found him so particularly magnetic.

He was handsome, of course. Anyone could see that. Extremely tall, athletically built, with dark blue eyes, thick brown hair, and (when it showed itself) a delightfully warm, wide smile. But Jenny was more impressed by the manner in which Dr. Carter spoke and taught.

He was different from her other professors, and not only because he was so young. When he lectured, it was as though he were having a conversation with each of his students. He never referenced notes. At the beginning of each class, he would set his materials on his desk, lean against the podium, and launch into an effortless discussion of cuneiform or Aramaic. Often he would recall a field experience relating to the topic of the day and divert into thrilling tales of pitch-black cave explorations or scalding desert digs.

During these outbursts, Dr. Carter would become swept up in professional passion. He would clutch at his hair, pacing the room and gesturing while the class hung on his every word. He described, almost reverently, the feeling of being the first human in thousands of years to read messages left by ancient peoples. Over and over, he emphasized that the work of Archaeology was a gift: an honoring and an offering.

"It is an honoring," he would say, "of those who have gone before. The lives they lived. Their relationships, their triumphs, their struggles and humanity. It is an offering," he continued, "of knowledge. Of wisdom, and warning, to generations still to come."

With these as his guiding principles, Dr. Carter demanded that his students treat the subject with utmost respect. At the start of term, Jenny had wondered whether her classmates might take advantage of Dr. Carter's youth and "assistant professor" status. But she needn't have worried. He had a powerful presence, both physically and intellectually, and he made it very clear that he expected the highest levels of both work and conduct. When three young men talked loudly during the first bit of a lecture, he'd stopped the entire presentation. Walking up to them, he had asked curtly that they leave the classroom until they were ready to stop wasting his time and their parents' hard-earned money.

There was very little side chatter after that moment.

Jenny liked best the rare times when he was relaxed, leaning against the front of his podium and telling funny anecdotes with his hands in his pockets. He dressed much more casually than her other professors. Dark slacks, a collared shirt or sweater (often with the sleeves rolled up), and Oxfords seemed to be his standard uniform. Overall she found him to be a fascinating instructor, and because he was so young, a deeply motivating example of what hard work could accomplish.

On the second Friday of term, Dr. Carter walked into the buzzing classroom with a stack of papers underarm.

"Good morning, everyone. Today's lecture is one of my favorites. We're moving from petroglyphs to hieroglyphs. But first – a quiz."

The class groaned. Dr. Carter let out a pleasant, throaty chuckle.

"There's no need for such a fuss. It's only ten questions, and it's more for my benefit than yours. I need to assess what you've learned and see if there are areas we ought to cover again. You will have" – he checked his wristwatch – "eight minutes. Good luck to you."

❦

Daniel handed out stacks of quiz papers and watched as they circulated the room. Once each student had a copy, he sat behind his desk to monitor. It was his habit to watch, like a lifeguard, for students who struggled with the assessment, for although he had a reputation for designing difficult courses, he truly did want his pupils to succeed. Never did their experience in his course become more transparent than when they took an unexpected test.

He saw expressions of fear – these were the students who didn't understand what they had been taught and required extra help. There were looks of frustration – from those who were insufficiently prepared and skipping readings. Then there were the causal, unconvincing expressions of students arching their gaze towards other papers to cheat. These were the students Daniel took aside for private conversations after class.

Suddenly remembering his chat with Miss Ellison, he glanced

her way to see what she made of the quiz. As was her habit, she sat on the right side of his classroom under the window. Truthfully, Daniel expected her to struggle. Her impossible course load would surely prevent her from completing readings as she ought. Yet her expression was pleasant, and mildly interested. She wrote swiftly, tapping her chin with her pencil between answers. At one point she smiled to herself, seemingly remembering some hard-to-trace fact at the perfect moment.

He turned back to the general classroom. Paul Corvellian was stretching suspiciously, and Daniel realized he needed to keep a sharp eye out. The Corvellians, along with some of the other notable families in the area, were known among Browning professors for their feelings of privilege in the classroom. Daniel was determined that privilege should not extend to cheating in his class.

Yet within a few minutes, his eye had inexplicably drifted to the right side of the classroom once more. It took a moment for him to register what had drawn his attention. A young man near the front was gazing absently into the distance, chin in hand. Daniel realized the lad was staring at Miss Ellison – though judging by his smitten expression, this was not with the intent to copy her work. Daniel felt a surge of amusement, for a single glance towards Miss Ellison confirmed she was ignorant of this nearby admirer.

Again, he observed her with a questioning eye. She was mouthing silently and writing down a complicated response, paying little attention to anything else in the room. She opted against the fashionable red lipstick the other young ladies were sporting. If she wore a lip color, it was much closer to her natural tone. Softer, and deep pink.

Suits her, Daniel thought, to his own mild surprise.

He took in the rest of Miss Ellison, soon concluding that he could comprehend the poor fellow in the front's distraction. Though not stylish in the curled, pinned, and powdered ways of the other girls, Miss Ellison was decidedly pretty. Short, but pretty. She was willowy more than shapely, a fact that was emphasized by the straight-cut skirt that hit just below her knee. Her legs – again, very smooth and pretty – were crossed at the ankles and tucked neatly under her desk. Her olive skin, slim neck, and open countenance were all gracefully suited to one another. The simple arrangement of her dark hair, however, suggested that hers was a raw sort of beauty, the kind the wearer either didn't perceive or did not care to accentuate.

As she shifted in her seat, a few wavy tresses fell onto her shoulder and obscured her face. His observations being thus halted, Daniel turned to face the rest of the classroom. Just in time, he realized the eight allotted minutes had passed.

"Time's up," he called. "Pass your quizzes to the end of the row, please."

There was a general murmur and a clatter of pencils falling onto desks. Once the papers had been collected, Daniel launched into a forty-minute discourse on his specialty: Egyptian hieroglyphs. Chiding himself for his earlier distractibility, he kept his gaze fixed on the center of the classroom for the balance of the lecture. It passed all too quickly, as it always did when he was speaking about the land he deemed his second home. The campus bell chimed to end the hour, and as students swarmed out, he occupied himself by rifling aimlessly through their quiz papers.

"Professor Carter?" a voice sang out from nearby.

Daniel sighed gruffly. It was Jillian Stewart. Again. Evidently she had not given up her efforts to ensnare him.

"Yes, Miss Stewart?"

"That was a very difficult quiz, Dr. Carter," Jillian pouted. She rested her weight on one leg and tilted her head coquettishly. "I did all my reading, but there seemed to be a few questions on material we haven't covered."

"Which ones in particular gave you trouble?"

Jillian started in on a vague complaint. Behind her, Daniel could see Miss Ellison's admirer visibly plucking up his courage. She was packing up her things nearby, still quite unconscious of the young man's pining efforts. While nodding at Jillian with carefully disguised boredom, Daniel allowed his ear to take in the more interesting goings on behind her.

"Hi, Jenny," the lad said, waving a bit too grandly given his short distance from her. "Wow, that was a scorcher of a quiz. What did you make of it?"

"Oh, I thought it was all right." She slung her satchel heavily over her shoulder. "How was the rugby match?"

The young man grinned at the question, rocking back and forth on his heels with conspicuous pride. "Glorious. We won 38-7. Shame you missed it."

"Well done, Peter," she said smilingly, but her foot tapped softly on the tile floor. Daniel surmised that she was waiting for an opportune exit point.

"I was wondering," the boy called Peter continued, reddening slightly. "If you're free this evening, perhaps you might – care to see a film? There's a new one showing in town, *The Ghost and Mrs. Muir*. There are still plenty of tickets."

Miss Ellison pinned up a loose curl distractedly. "Oh? Are you getting up a group to go? I'm so sorry, Peter, but I can't this evening."

"Ah! I see." Peter tried, and failed, to hide his disappointment. Daniel suspected the young man's plan had certainly not been to get up a group.

She hugged her notebook to her chest. "I know what we can do. It's my birthday this weekend, and Margie's planned some sort of celebration. Why don't you come?"

"Why, I'd love to!" Peter looked elated. "What time? Where?"

"Actually," Miss Ellison replied, laughing, "I don't know. Margie won't tell me any of the details. You'll have to ask her. But if she's planning it, I'm sure it will be a lovely time." She waved a cheerful goodbye as she walked past him. "See you then!"

Peter looked wistfully at Miss Ellison's retreating back. Daniel felt a slight surge of pity for the lad, who was clearly besotted. Evidently Miss Ellison was blind to that fact, though whether this was a conscious choice or not, he could not say.

"Professor? Do you think I scored highly, Professor?"

Jillian's question brought Daniel back to the present. She arched her brows at him suggestively, adding, "If not, may I ask for a bit of extra help? Perhaps during an office hour?"

"I advise you to wait until your quiz results have been posted, Miss Stewart." Daniel calmly gathered the rest of his materials. "I'm sure you did just fine. If you did struggle, I'll ask Max to go over any missed questions with you next week. Excuse me, but I have another lecture to prepare for." Nodding politely, he walked into his adjoining office and barred the door.

CHAPTER 6

That evening Daniel attended the Archaeology department's annual social. It was the professors' custom to celebrate the start of term with food and drink and a game or two of Machiavelli. Daniel had always liked the professor's lounge. It was a good-sized room, with a large stone fireplace, a generous hearth, and plenty of plush green armchairs. A white banquet table stood at one end of it, laden with platters of cold ham sandwiches and tinned biscuits. Post-war provisions at Browning had not quite caught up to their pre-war plenty.

Despite the warmth and cheer of the fire, the gathering was not a lively one. A few professors smoked cigars and talked politics in a corner. Others somberly sipped Scotch from paper cups or played rummy. Daniel, having no affinity for cards, was content to chat with his old mentor Dr. Miller.

"What a cheerful party," Antony jested with a wink. "Will the coroner arrive soon, do you think?"

"It'll warm up," Daniel consoled him, looking around. "Just give it time."

"I'm not so sure. I overheard Dr. Christiansen grumbling about tonight's meager fare. If he only knew what it took to get even the smallest discretionary budget from the administration. There simply aren't enough funds for a banquet, I'm afraid. Not after the war." He took a pensive sip of Scotch. "Even if there were, it would take more than a feast to brighten up this sorry old bunch. For a group of people that go about studying life, we don't seem to live very much of it, do we?"

"Do you think so?" Daniel raised his brows. "The men in this room have traversed the furthest corners of the earth. I'm not sure I'd agree with you."

"Ha! But you should." Dr. Miller set down his cup with a flourish. "Take you, for example. A spry young fellow, only twenty-eight—"

"Thirty."

"Yes, as I said, only thirty, in the prime of his life, yet he chooses to spend all of his days and nights cooped up in a study."

"Not this again," Daniel groaned, refilling Antony's cup. As fond as he was of his friend, the old dean was all too prone to harp on about Daniel's social life (or lack thereof). "Don't worry about me, Antony. I go out nearly every weekend, like a good boy."

"The occasional pint at The Belmont Arms with Charlie Russell doth not a social life make, my boy. What about your other connections?"

Daniel shook his head with a shrewd look. "I know what you're getting at, Antony. And no, I'm not seeing anyone at the moment, but before you object, you should know that I'm quite content that way."

"Why is that?" Antony said with surprising sharpness. "Most young men your age couldn't wait to settle down after the war ended. Why not you?"

"I haven't ruled it out, you know."

"You always were a bit of a hermit, even as a lad. But a young man of thirty should at least be *thinking* of reading the banns one day. What about that nice secretary on the first floor? Corinne, I think her name was. She's a lovely girl."

Daniel nodded patiently. "I'm sure she is. I'm just focusing on other things at present. My Amity site, for a start."

Antony leaned forward. "Daniel. Take it from an old man, who has lived a whole life. There is more to this world than the work. People. People are what truly matter. And I don't mean only studying them. I mean living among them, really living. Connecting. Having your heart broken. Giving it again anyway. *Love.* That is the true education. That is where the greatest learning of our lives takes place."

Daniel cleared his throat, unsure how to respond to this unexpectedly sincere speech. "Wise counsel. I'll be happy to turn my mind to it, once the term is over. As it is, my courses are keeping me busier than I had anticipated."

The old man sat back, looking vaguely disappointed. He took another sip of Scotch. "Speaking of your courses, how is Miss Ellison faring?"

Daniel feigned a sudden interest in the carved legs of his chair. "Who?"

"Miss Ellison. Jennifer Ellison, the late addition to your class. Is she keeping up? How are her papers and assignments?"

"All excellent," he reported begrudgingly.

"Aha! I told you they would be. She's a clever girl, that one. Top of her class and no mistake. I expect great things from her."

"Look sharp," Daniel said, changing the subject. "Here comes Chilcott."

"Oh, not again," Antony muttered. "Would that he would give me one day of peace."

"Dr. Miller!" called a rather reedy voice from across the room. Dr. William Chilcott, the third chair in the Amity program, was forty-something and thin as a rail, a trait that his love of pinstriped suits did nothing to soften. His long nose ended in a surprisingly bushy moustache, and he wore an expression of perpetual smugness. Daniel stiffened as he approached; there was a faint sense of rivalry between the two men, though he had always felt this was unjustified. They specialized in different regions, after all. Whatever the reason, he avoided the man when he could.

"Good evening, gentlemen," Chilcott said with a grin. "Dr. Miller, I hope you've had a good start to your term?"

"I have, thank you. This cohort of students is one of the brightest I have ever taught, and the crop only seems to be improving each year. I wonder what the next will bring."

"The next?" Chilcot's smile faded slightly. "You – you plan to return next year, then?"

"But of course."

"Good heavens, Antony. What ... inexhaustible stamina you have when it comes to education!"

"That I do, William." Dr. Miller's blue eyes twinkled mischievously. "Are you sorry to hear it?"

Chilcott quickly recovered from his blunder. "Of course not. I am relieved. There have been rumors, of course, of your impending retirement, but I am pleased to hear it is not yet upon us. And when it inevitably does come ... well, we shall celebrate, even more grandly than we are this evening, your many, *many* achievements as the department's head."

"How very kind. Thank you for that, William."

Chilcott nodded curtly and excused himself. Daniel watched as the man immediately refilled his cup to the brim with alcohol.

"Well," Miller chuckled to himself, "I certainly hope my farewell will be more elegant than an evening of cheap spirits after thirty-eight years of dedicated service to Browning."

"He's all bowing and scraping to your face," Daniel murmured. "But Dr. Christiansen told me it's another story behind your back. He's the one spreading rumors about your retirement."

"Yes, I know. Truth be told, I'm rather enjoying plaguing him by refusing to give the date of it. I'm determined no one should know it but myself."

"Will you endorse him, then? As the next dean? You know it's what he's after."

"Chilcott?" Dr. Miller grunted. "I'm not overly concerned about his chances. I have no good opinion of his interactions with our students."

This piqued Daniel's curiosity, but noticing the time, he quickly informed Antony that he had to be going. "I have to pick up a book from the library before it closes."

"Daniel," Dr. Miller reproached him, "it is the weekend! A time to rest and make merry! To rejuvenate!"

"I'll go out to a pub or something tomorrow," Daniel placated him. "I promise. Goodnight, Antony."

"Goodnight, Daniel. And please, my boy. Think on what I said."

Daniel brushed off his friend's words and headed outside, fortifying his collar against the brisk October air. Far in the distance, the library's windows glowed invitingly with comfort and warmth. It was one of the oldest buildings on campus, and Daniel's favorite of all Browning's structures. Curved stone arches set off an exterior corridor punctuated by exquisite stained-glass windows – scenes of Galileo studying the stars, of Sir Isaac Newton under an apple tree, of Edward Jenner administering the first vaccine.

He breathed a contented sigh when he finally entered the place. A wall of warmth washed over him, for in sharp contrast to its gothic exterior, the library's insides had been renovated for comfort. A cozy fireplace and lounge were just off the entrance, and the sunken main hall was lined with deep, plush reading chairs. Several pieces of valuable art graced its oak-paneled walls. The university could even boast an original Rembrandt.

More impressive to Daniel was the five-million-strong collection of books. Shelves of brightly bound volumes wound through the room like a labyrinth. At the entrance of the main hall, a commanding mahogany desk monitored all goings in and out. It was staffed by Amos Prewett, a wiry and wrinkled old fellow with a sharp chin and even sharper eyes. He had been the head librarian since Daniel's own days at Browning, and seemed almost as permanent a fixture as the Rembrandt. Few goings on in the library escaped his notice.

"Young Dr. Carter!" Mr. Prewett wheezed. "Good evening to you!"

"And to you, Amos," Daniel said as he walked over. "I've come about that book I ordered."

"Ah, yes!" Prewett rubbed his gnarled old knuckles. "*Tamil, The Oldest Living Language in India*. Author, Sir Richard Walter Evans, Publisher, Pumphouse Press, Oxford, August of 1936. I have it just here." Amos reached below his desk and pulled out a thick leather-bound volume.

"Thank you." Daniel thumbed through it eagerly. "How has your start of term been, Amos?"

"Oh, very bad sir, very bad, as it always is," Mr. Prewett rasped. "For the students consistently test the limits of our library rules, especially when it comes to food and drink. Why, only yesterday I caught two young men sneaking in a bag of apple hand pies. Can you imagine? In this temple of learning?"

"Astonishing." Daniel did his best to keep a straight face.

"Indeed, it is!" the old man cried indignantly. "Suppose they had got crumbs in our first edition of *Candide*? The absolute impudence. I had half a mind to – but what's this? Is that a chocolate wrapper I see?" Mr. Prewett's nostrils flared as he spotted another piece of contraband across the room. "Excuse me, Dr. Carter, but I must drive some sense into the thick skulls of these miscreants. You, there! Yes, I am talking to you!"

As Mr. Prewett hurried after the offenders, Daniel smiled and gazed around the library's main hall. By now, most of the students would be "making merry," as Antony put it, at the local pubs and cinema. Only three or four people remained amongst the shelves this late on a Friday evening. One young man snored loudly in an armchair with a book over his face. Two others were packing up satchels and preparing to leave for the night. And in the center of the room, to Daniel's astonishment, sat Miss Ellison.

She was alone at a round table, with piles of books and papers spread around her like a fortress. Her chin was propped in her hand, and she was deeply engrossed in a volume entitled *Decoding Egyptian Hieroglyphs*. Daniel glanced at the clock. It was now past nine, yet Miss Ellison seemed to have no immediate intention of leaving. He cautiously approached.

"Miss Ellison?"

She started.

"Pardon me for interrupting, but—"

"Good evening, Dr. Carter."

Daniel thought she looked simply exhausted. There were dark shadows under her eyes, as though she had been burning the candle at both ends for some time now. Looking over her colossal stacks of books, he felt a flash of genuine concern.

"It's getting late, Miss Ellison."

"Yes," she replied absently, closing her volume and searching out another. "But I believe the library is open until ten this evening."

This was not exactly what Daniel had meant. "I expect the heavy course load is catching up with you, then?"

He had not intended to be quite so direct in his questioning. Miss Ellison seemed to assume some sort of judgment on his part, for flushing slightly she replied, "I'm managing." Without looking up at him again she opened a second volume, *Latin in a Modern Age*, and began to read. Daniel was not sure if he had just been dismissed, and so lingered awkwardly for a few moments. Shaking his head, he moved to leave, but not before another question escaped his lips.

"If I may ask, Miss Ellison ... why have you so overloaded your schedule? Why not put off some of these courses until next term, or next year? You'd have a much easier time of it."

There was a brief pause, in which she wrinkled her nose with thought.

"That's true, of course. But I'm pretty far behind the rest of my classmates due to my gap year. I'd like to graduate with them if I can."

"Why did you take a gap year?"

Daniel immediately regretted asking. It was none of his business, after all, but his curiosity was getting the better of him. Though Miss Ellison looked surprised by his continued questioning, she answered him.

"I worked as a nurse for a time. During the war."

Daniel felt a stinging pang of guilt. He had done his best to prevent her from joining his class, while privately (well, perhaps not so privately) disapproving of her choices. Yet all this time, her crammed schedule was a concerted effort to catch up after personal sacrifice. He dearly wished he had posed these questions earlier.

"And where did you serve?" he asked, much more pleasantly this time.

"In France. Offranville. They were short on volunteers, so ... I went."

Daniel had to admit, that kind of gumption was admirable. Clearing his throat uncomfortably, he remarked that this was a very brave thing to have done, considering the dangers of occupied France.

Miss Ellison shrugged. "It wasn't so bad, really. I arrived in '45, after the Nazis had already gone. My mother is French, so I stayed with relatives while I worked in the village hospital. It was well-equipped, and the director was kindly. I was lucky."

"Offranville." A memory stirred. "Wait a moment," Daniel said.

"I know it. A tiny town in Normandy, isn't that right? Famous for a tree?"

She smiled. "That's right. A thousand-year-old Yew, twenty-three feet in diameter. It's really quite something." She opened her book once more, but instead of reading, she looked up at him with interest.

"You ... you also served in the war, I believe, Professor?"

"Yes."

"And where were you stationed?" Her tone was piercingly curious.

"Oh, you know, sort of ... all over the place." He gave a brief, tight smile. Miss Ellison nodded, her brow furrowing with unspoken questions. Daniel gestured towards her mountains of books.

"Quite a collection you have here. A few of these aren't even on our course lists."

Miss Ellison bit her lip. "No."

He glanced over the stacked volumes. Among the textbooks were outside readings on Iran, Crete, and Egypt. She clearly intended to try for the Amity Scholarship. Daniel was on the verge of asking which site interested her the most, but at the last minute decided against it. Strangely, he found he did not wish to know.

"Well, try not to burn the midnight oil too often. And be sure to have some fun, once in a while. That's also part of the university experience." Again, Daniel hated how paternal he sounded, particularly on a subject that was none of his business, but Miss Ellison only brightened at his words.

"Oh, I mean to. In fact, tomorrow's my birthday. My friend Margie's planned ..."

She stopped and shook her head, as though thinking she had said too much.

"Planned what?"

Miss Ellison gave a merry laugh. "Actually, I don't know. She won't tell me what we're doing. I'm rather worried about it."

Daniel cleared his throat once more. The conversation had strayed too long into personal details. As a younger teacher, he was especially vigilant of professional boundaries. It was time for his departure.

"Sounds like fun. Have a happy time."

As Daniel moved to leave, he noticed an open bag of peanuts hidden in Miss Ellison's satchel. Seeing what had caught his attention, she flushed and looked uncertainly up at him. Mr. Prewett was even now swooping through the shelves in search of contraband.

Stifling a little smile, Daniel put a finger to his lips and walked quietly away.

CHAPTER 7

R iiiiiiiiiiiiiiing.

    "Carter, look out! Carter, they're coming!"

"Nils, get the men out of here!"

"No, sir, I'm not going to—"

"Get out, I said! That's an order, I told you to—"

Riiiiiiiiiiiiiiing.

"Get out of here, get out! All of you move to shelter, NOW! They're in range, they're—"

Riiiiiiiiiiiiiiing.

"AAAAUGH! No, my leg, I can't – HELP ME! Please, sir, help me! Help—"

"Daniel! Daniel, behind you! BEHIND YOU!"

Daniel shot upright, his chest heaving and his hand grasping wildly at his side. For a moment he scrambled to find his rifle, but his fingers clutched blindly at thin, empty air. The weapon he sought had not hung by his side for nearly three years. All around him was silence, until once again he heard a sharp, shrill:

Riiiiiiiiiiiiiiing.

A cold bead of sweat trickled down Daniel's neck and onto his bare chest. Not a raid, he told himself, forcibly exhaling. The telephone. Just the telephone.

Screams of pain and fear still reverberated between his ears. Suppressing a shudder, he shut his eyelids tightly against the remnants of his nightmare – murky visions of blasted buildings, of screaming civilians, of scarlet blood blossoming from the limbs of a young man. Daniel could still picture the unnatural limpness of the boy's body, the sickening contortion of limbs. The ghost of his last, terrified scream still etched on his face.

Riiiiiiiiiiiiiiiing.

Daniel searched for his bedside clock and tilted it to catch the moonlight, swearing under his breath when he saw the time. Evidently the person on the other end of the telephone did not care that it was nearly midnight. The blasted thing kept ringing incessantly. Flipping on his bedside lamp, Daniel threw a robe over his bare torso and trudged to the tiny kitchen.

Riiiiiiiiiiiiiiiing.

"Yes?" he said gruffly into the receiver. "What is it?"

"Good evening, sir," a flat female voice replied over the line. "I have a long-distance call for you from a Mr. Charles Russell, Chisholm, 2-2-5-0."

Daniel blearily rubbed his temple. It was only Charlie Russell, one of his oldest school friends. Charlie had also settled in Belmont, and the two men often got together for a drink or a round of billiards on weekends. What had possessed him to call at such an ungodly hour, however, remained a mystery.

"Put him through, please."

"Connecting," the woman said sleepily. There was a little pop and a click on the line.

"Daniel? Can you hear me? It's Charlie, Charlie Russell."

"Hello, Charlie."

"Did I wake you?"

"No," Daniel lied, forcing aside the last chilling images of his dream. "What's this about, then?"

"Awfully sorry to call so late, chum, but the fact is we'll be getting back to Belmont a day earlier than expected. After six days of supervising obnoxious fifteen-year-old boys, I find myself in desperate need of some rational conversation. Care to get a drink tomorrow, around sevenish?"

Daniel smirked, and the tension lingering about his shoulders eased somewhat. Charlie was a cricketing coach at a local school and had just finished taking his team on a tour of the northern counties. If he was calling long-distance to set up something as trivial as a pub visit, it must have been a very trying week indeed.

"All right. Tomorrow at seven it is."

"Excellent." Charlie sounded enormously relieved. "The Belmont Arms?"

Daniel hesitated. It was their usual haunt, to be sure. Perhaps it was the desire to distance himself even further from old, familiar memories that made him reply, "No, I don't think so. I'm in the mood to try something new. What about Damion's?"

"I don't recall seeing ... oh, you mean that new restaurant in the main square? That might do. It looks terribly swank, though. Won't it be overrun with students on a Saturday evening?"

Daniel pursed his lips. "Maybe. But we don't have to dine. They have billiards."

"Well!" Charlie exclaimed. "I'm always up for a game of snooker! You're on. I'll meet you there at seven. Can't wait."

There was another crackling click on the line. Setting his own receiver down, Daniel took a deep breath and walked through the suffocating darkness back to his bed.

CHAPTER 8

"Where are we going, Marge? The Blue Dragon?"

"Ah-ah-ah!" Margie tutted, practically pushing Jenny into her tiny Austin Devon. "That will remain a secret until we arrive."

"Happy Birthday, Jenny!" Nyra Patel chirped happily from the back seat. "Twenty-three, and all the lovelier for it I say."

"Thanks, Nyra." Jenny slid across the empty front row.

"How long is the drive?" Jillian grumbled as Margie climbed behind the wheel. "We're packed like sardines back here."

"Patience, patience," Margie said. "I promise, you'll all love it."

Jenny nodded encouragingly. It seemed kindest not to press Margie any further, now that they were on their way. "I'm sure it will be worth the wait."

"Easy for you to say, being up front," Jillian muttered.

Despite the crowding, it turned out to be a very merry drive. Margie's car had a radio, and the girls sung along loudly to tunes by Perry Como and Frank Sinatra. As they neared the main square, Margie veered the car away from town and over the dark village roads. They were cutting through a part of the county Jenny had never before seen. After twenty minutes of bumpy travel, curiosity spurred her to break her resolution of silent support.

"Margie," she ventured. "What is your plan? A midnight picnic in the woods?"

"You'll see, we're nearly there. Look, just ahead!"

The car pulled into a winding lane lined bordered by a dozen ancient-looking oaks. At the end of the drive was a magnificent wrought-iron gate, looking like something out of a Brontë novel in the darkness.

"There are the boys," Margie said, pointing to a second vehicle parked on the side of the road. "Peter and Sagan. Nyra, would you be a darling and push open the gate for us? It's unlocked."

Nyra scurried to obey. Squinting slightly, Jenny noticed that there was a coat of arms and intricately cast golden 'M' at the gate's center.

"Margie ... is this ..."

Jillian gasped. "This is the Manwaring estate! I'm sure it is, I recognize that crest!"

"Hush!" Margie urged.

"Oh, why keep it a secret now," Jillian snapped. "We're here, aren't we?"

Jenny stared at Margie. "You brought us to Anders Manwaring's estate?"

"Yes," Margie said hastily. "I did, but hear me out for a moment. Anders overheard me agonizing about what to plan for your party, since there's nothing to do in boring old Belmont. He offered me the use of the house tonight, just for a change of scene."

"Margie, I—"

"Anders isn't here. I promise. None of the family are. They're visiting friends in Grassby, but Anders left the butler to help with our party."

"Well, I call that lovely of him!" exclaimed Nyra.

"Yes," Margie happily agreed. "That is, so long as this is all right, Jenny? I was determined your birthday should be better than a pub dinner and a trip to the cinema. I know you don't much like Anders, but it's supposed to be a lovely house. And he isn't here, after all. Do you ... do you want to stay?"

Jenny took a deep breath. "Why not? It could be fun."

"Oh good," Margie sighed, looking relieved as she put the car back into gear. "Because I already had the butler set up our food inside."

They rolled over the gravel drive, soon pulling in front of the most opulent home Jenny had ever seen. It was a monstrous structure of marble and stone, with a grand entrance flanked by columns. Iron torches blazed regally on either side of the door.

"Blimey ..." Jenny whispered as the boys and girls climbed out of their respective cars.

"Happy Birthday, Jenny!" Peter called to her across the darkened stone courtyard. "Twenty-three years young, eh?"

Sagan neglected his birthday wishes, as he too was looking up at the house in awe. "Get a load of this place, Pete."

"Amazing," he whistled. "I can't believe places like this still exist after the war."

"Where does the money come from?" Sagan asked. "Does anyone know?"

"They own a chain of slate mines in Wales," Jillian answered, checking her hair in her compact mirror. "Oh I *knew* it, my fringe has been flattened."

"Stop fussing, Jilly. Come on, everyone!" Margie grabbed Jenny's hand and pulled her up the marble steps. The rest of the group followed, laughing nervously as they approached the mansion's double oak doors. Drawing herself up to her fullest height, Margie knocked.

The entrance creaked open, revealing a thin, balding man in a crisp black uniform. Looking down his nose at the group of youngsters, he cocked his head and addressed Margie, who was foremost in the cluster. "Miss Payne, I presume?"

"That's me." Margie swallowed. "Anders said we ... that is, Mr. Manwaring told me I could ..."

"Do come in, Miss Payne."

Wide-eyed, the group entered a two-story hall crowned with a crystal chandelier. Statues and faded tapestries lined both sides of the wide entry. The walls and floor were clad in a highly burnished red stone, making Jenny feel as though she had just walked into some lavish cave. A grand staircase constructed of the same reddish material rose commandingly before them.

"My name is Branwell," the butler said. "I believe you'll find that everything has been set up according to your specifications, Miss Payne. Changing rooms are down the main corridor and to your right."

"Thank you," Margie replied, with an equally imperious nod.

"If you need anything, I shall be in the library." Without a bow or a backward glance, Branwell retreated into a side room. He clearly didn't care if this undignified group of guests would be able to locate him again, whether in the library or not.

"Changing rooms?" Jenny asked dubiously.

"Look!" Nyra said, giggling and pointing. "On the table, over there!"

Jenny's eyes fell upon a crystal vase stuffed with at least two dozen plump, red roses. A gilt-edged card poked out from between them. Nyra ran to the flowers and popped it open with a squeal.

"They're for Jenny, from Anders! For '*Dear Jenny, on her birthday*,' it says. Well, don't you want to read the card?"

"Nope."

"I swear I didn't know about the flowers," Margie whispered in her ear. "He told me he would leave the empty house, and I assumed—"

"Never mind, Margie," Jenny replied, eyeing the staircase's sleek marble railings with interest. "As you said, he's gone. Now that we're here, I mean to enjoy myself."

"Not planning to slide down the banisters here, too, are you?" Margie said, elbowing her playfully in the ribs.

"I only did that once!" Jenny protested, rubbing the sore spot with a laugh. "I was late for Paleography!"

Her roommate clapped to get the group's attention. "All right, everyone, gather round. In honor of our darling Jenny, we're going swimming."

"What?" Jenny exclaimed, as her friends nodded comprehendingly. "But it's October. How will we—?" She stopped, only just noticing that each of her friends had brought a small satchel with them.

"The Manwarings must have an indoor swimming pool, of course." Jillian hitched her bag over her shoulder. "I must say, Margie, when you told us to bring our bathing suits, I thought you'd finally cracked. I half expected you to drive us to some muddy little pond in the forest."

"Marge, this is *excellent,*" Jenny said with a grin. She loved swimming, as her friend well knew.

"Glad you think so. And don't worry, I packed your suit." Margie took her hand and pointed to a shadowy hall ahead of them. "Courage, friends. Girls on the left, boys on the right. Last one to the pool has to kiss Peter!" With another shriek of laughter, the party split to change.

❧

Apparently thinking better of condemning anyone to the fate of kissing Peter, Margie suggested the girls link arms and walk out of the changing room together. The boys howled in disappointment at this turn of events, but Jenny paid no heed. Her eyes were fixed on the rare scene before her.

It was her first time in a private pool house, though she wouldn't have admitted it for the world. She suspected such a thing was less novel to her wealthier, more established friends. The water didn't look very deep, but the pool was beautifully paved and long enough to do proper laps. A glass domed roof let in slicing shafts of moonlight, while underwater lamps cast an otherworldly green hue over the room. The warm air was thick with the scent of chemicals.

Dipping a toe in the water's glassy surface, Jenny tried to forget that all of this belonged to Anders. Being in his home distressed her more than she would ever confess, but yet again, she resolved to enjoy herself. Margie had worked so hard on this evening. Besides, to a girl from Brookfield, an October swim in a heated pool was something out of a fairytale.

"A toast!" called a voice from behind her. Turning, Jenny saw each of her friends accepting a small paper cup from Margie. Taking her own, she was touched to see that it was filled to the brim with her drink of choice: a sparkling mix of peach juice and ginger ale.

Margie raised her cup exuberantly. "To our darling Jenny on her twenty-third birthday. Though she is a nut, she is our nut, and the brightest, funniest friend a girl could ask for. We wish you the very happiest of years ahead, Jenny." Margie's voice cracked with emotion at these last words.

"Cheers!" Nyra and Sagan cried in unison.

"Cheers," added Peter, a little more softly. The group downed their drinks.

"Ugh." Jillian wrinkled her nose in disgust. "What is this?"

"Some sort of ... peach something?" Sagan laughed. "I might liven mine up a bit, if it's all the same to you, Jenny." Winking, he pulled a small flask from the pocket of his swim shorts.

"Give it here," Jillian ordered, snatching the liquor from him and pouring a sizable amount into her own cup. "Not all of us like baby juice."

"What *is* the matter with you this evening?" Jenny asked wearily. She'd had quite enough of Jillian's bad temper.

"Oh, pay her no mind," Margie said. "She's been in a rotten mood all week."

"She's just sour because Dr. Carter won't give her the time of day," Nyra added, crumpling her paper cup.

Jillian scowled. "Shut it, Nyra."

"What's this?" Sagan asked with a smug look. "You mean Mr. Prettyface hasn't fallen for the wiles of Queen Jillian?"

"Well, this is an outrage!" Peter gave an exaggerated bow. "What punishment shall we inflict upon Mr. Prettyface, your Majesty? Send him to the tower with the rest of those ungrateful, good-for-nothing boys?"

Jillian crossed her legs haughtily. "A boy, you say? *Professor* Daniel Carter is more of a man than you will ever be, Peter Collier. One has only to note his arms – as strong and wide as tree trunks. Rather unlike yours," she finished, tweaking Peter's nose, "my little sapling."

"Play nice, Jilly," Nyra warned, tucking her hair into a swim cap.

"Well, I for one am counting the days until *Professor* Prettyface's course is over," Peter said, straightening up. "I can't wait to be shot of him."

"How can you say that, Peter?" Jenny asked with astonishment. "He's one of the finest professors I've ever had. I love his course."

"Oh, he's a decent teacher, to be sure. But I'm sick of hearing all the girls mooning over him. How is a fellow supposed to hear through all that endless sighing in the front row? Even you lot have gone soft on him."

"Not everyone," Nyra said, still adjusting her swim cap. "Barbara's engaged, remember? And I don't think Jenny has looked twice at Dr. Carter."

"Yes, that's true, Nyra, excellent point." Peter knelt near Jenny, who was sitting by the water's edge. "Why haven't you fallen under his spell, Miss Ellison? Is your heart so very impenetrable?" Peter stuck out his lower lip in a suggestive pout. Jenny's only response was to push him into the pool.

Sagan spoke more loudly as a laughing and spluttering Peter resurfaced. "The truth is, none of you ladies should waste your daydreams on him. He may be a good professor, but there are some things about him that just don't square. Why did he come back early from service, for example? Then there was that fight with the student last year."

"You think it really happened?" Jenny asked him curiously.

"Of course it happened," Sagan scoffed. "Billy Cavendish was there, he told me about it himself. The university should have fired Dr. Carter for something like that. Why didn't they? Then there was his work during the war ..."

"What work?" Jenny broke in. "Do you know what he did?"

"Well, no, not exactly, but I know that it was all very hushed up and sinister. They say he speaks about a dozen languages. I wouldn't at all be surprised if he turned out to be some sort of double agent, or hired gun. We came across people like that in every branch of the force, you know. Useful in a tight spot, to be sure, but" – Sagan's gaze slid to vacancy – "loyal to no one. People who bought favor by pawning secrets and cutting deals with the War Office. "

"What?" Jenny cut in, laughing. "A traitor? A double agent? You've been listening to Jillian for too long, Sagan. Now come on, let's go for a swim. All in!"

Jenny dove headfirst into the pool, and her friends soon joined her. The water was colder than she'd expected, but after a few lengths it felt quite pleasant. She splashed and swam and flipped for nearly an hour before wading, out of breath and gasping, to the pool's shallower side where Margie, who was not a strong swimmer, sat on the pool wall and chatted with whomever happened to be near her.

"Do you know," Jenny said, hoisting herself onto the slick tiles to join her, "as much as I chide Jillian for her theories, I think Dr. Carter *may* have been some sort of undercover operative during the war. I was talking to him yesterday, and—"

"Really?" Margie's brows shot up her forehead. "Where?"

"In the library. I asked him where he'd served during the war, and he was quite evasive. He didn't even mention which branch of the force he served in. He just ... changed the subject."

"Hmm. Well, it's like you said." Margie shrugged. "Most of the men don't talk about the war, if they can help it."

"True," Jenny mused, rubbing her sopping curls with a towel.

"Miss Payne?"

Branwell the butler reappeared at her elbow, causing both girls to jump.

"Are you in need of any more refreshments?" he asked glumly.

"No," Margie gasped, clutching at her heart. "I think we're all right. Thank you, Branwell."

"Very good, ma'am. If there is anything more you require, you may tell Mr. Manwaring. He should arrive within the hour."

"I beg your pardon, did you say Mr. Silas Manwaring?" Margie asked, looking rather pale.

"No, ma'am. Young Master Anders just telephoned to say that he has been released from a family engagement and would like to pay his respects. I bid you good night."

Jenny stood the moment Branwell had exited the pool house. "Time to go," she said somberly.

"What?" Jillian cried. "You can't just leave. It's his house. He's our host."

"He's not our host," Jenny said firmly.

"But we're his guests! It would be abominably rude to leave now."

"Stay if you want. I'm not his guest, and even if I were, I could certainly leave whenever I wanted."

"I'll come with you," Nyra said as she climbed the pool's ladder. "I'm not much for swimming, anyway."

Jillian chewed the inside of her cheek and watched the girls gather their things. "Oh, I wish you'd just tell me once and for all," she snapped. "Why don't you like Anders? What has he ever done to you?"

Jenny paused with her towel wrapped about her waist. For a long while she stood, a dozen half-formed explanations rising to her throat but losing themselves on their way to her lips. At last meeting Jillian's eye, she proffered: "He's ... well, he's ... chauvinistic. I don't think coming here was such a good idea for me after all, Marge. I don't wish to break up the party, but I'd like to go home now." She looked around apologetically. "You all should stay, if you like. I can get a cab."

"If you're leaving, I'm leaving," Margie said in stubborn solidarity. Nyra walked arm-in-arm with Jenny to the changing rooms, whispering a stream of rapid questions under her breath. The boys glanced at each other in confusion, but dutifully hoisted themselves out of the pool, and with much huffing and scowling, Jillian at last gave in and followed suit.

CHAPTER 9

Daniel felt rather off when he lectured the following Monday. He kept losing his train of thought, and even had to refer to his notes twice. This was most unlike him. He chalked this lack of focus up to a long weekend of grading, broken up only by a night of billiards with Charles. Although that evening had been a welcome escape from marking essays, Daniel hadn't stayed at the restaurant very long. Damion's was one of the newer dining establishments in town, and by ten o'clock it had become uncomfortably packed with students.

"Are you worried you might run into some of yours?" he recalled Charles asking him with a boisterous laugh. "You're a deer in headlights every time that door opens."

It was a comment Daniel had nonchalantly brushed off, leaving twenty minutes later under the pretense of a headache. Perhaps he had a headache in earnest this morning. Rubbing his temple to regain focus, he announced, "During Wednesday's lecture we'll move from Egyptian hieroglyphs to the Phoenician alphabet. The Phoenicians created the writing system that was the foundation for Greek, Hebrew, Aramaic, and Roman alphabets, among others. We will revisit—"

The classroom door burst open. In ran his teaching assistant Max Caldwell, red-faced and gasping for air. The lad had obviously been sprinting as fast as his gangly legs could carry him. In one hand he clutched a large, official-looking envelope.

"Excuse me, Dr. Carter," Max wheezed, brandishing the letter. "I forgot you have a lecture at this time. But you told me to bring it as soon as it arrived."

"Give it here," Daniel said urgently, forgetting he had a classroom of fifty – well, actually, fifty-one – students watching him in confusion. He tore open the envelope and devoured its contents.

"Brilliant." Daniel let out a huge sigh of relief as he finished reading. "Students: I would like your attention please."

Fifty young men and women sat up with interest. Daniel glanced at Miss Ellison, who was still bent over her desk, scrupulously writing notes in shorthand.

"And I do mean everyone's attention," he repeated quietly.

She slowly lifted her eyes – two chocolate-brown eyes, fringed with dark lashes. Putting down her pencil, she gave him a shy smile. A tiny, darling smile. Daniel's stomach inexplicably lurched. With mild distress, he snapped his head back to the center of the classroom.

"As you may know, I spent the summer directing a conservation site in Egypt, near the temple of Abu Simbel. While excavating some ancient clay pits in a nearby valley, my team and I stumbled across a very unusual find."

The class sat forward eagerly. Gratified, Daniel continued. "We uncovered a large slab of semi-petrified earth. It soon became clear that this was *not* a piece of naturally occurring stone, but an oblong piece of limestone or alabaster."

"An *artifact?*" a young man near the center squeaked, wide-eyed.

"Yes." Daniel tried not to mind that this revelation had been pre-empted. "It is the first novel discovery to have been made in that region for some years."

A few students began to clap in admiration, but he held up his hand to silence them.

"As such, the rights to the cleaning and preservation of it were hotly contested. Though my team had uncovered it, we could not begin our work without approval from the Egyptian government." He gave a half-smile. "You will soon learn that Archaeology is five percent fieldwork, ninety-five percent paperwork. Our discussions have been taking place for weeks. But I've just received notice" – he held up the letter in his hand – "that Browning University has been given permission by the Egyptian government to clean and archive the find. The slab has been crated and shipped to England as a gesture of goodwill between our governments. It's on its way even now."

The class erupted into cheers.

"How big is the stone, sir?" one lad shouted over the din.

"A little more than six feet across, and about half that in height." By now, Daniel's carefully harnessed excitement was bubbling over. "I've been authorized to put together a team of up to four students to clean, photograph, and archive the find. This research team will be supervised by me, of course. If you are interested in taking on extra work this term, I invite you to put your name forward." He hesitated. "You should know that due to severe budget cuts after the war, these research positions will be unpaid."

Several students groaned audibly.

"But very rich in experience," Daniel emphasized, with a slight frown.

The bell rang, and a shuffle of textbooks and desks drowned out his voice.

"If you wish to participate, come and see me now," Daniel called into the clamor, reaching for a pad of paper. Although most of the classroom emptied, a group of about fifteen students drifted excitedly towards his desk. Predictably, Jillian Stewart was the first to put her name forward. Joining her were several young men Daniel did not know by name, and a very eager-looking Jennifer Ellison.

"Come forward one at a time to discuss your availability," he instructed. Jillian advanced, and Daniel politely took notes as she described her schedule. A little to his right, Peter Collier was yet again seeking out Miss Ellison.

"Hello, Jenny." The lad stopped rather close to her side, by the standards of friendship. "I looked for you at Nyra's breakfast do this morning. Did you ever pop in?"

"What? Oh, no, I was in the library. Isn't this exciting?" she whispered.

"Very." Peter studied her intently. "You're going to work with Dr. Carter, then?"

"Yes. At least, I hope so. I can't believe he's giving us this chance!"

"What do you mean?"

She lowered her voice, but not to a register that prevented Daniel from hearing the exchange. "He could have done the work on his own, couldn't he? And taken sole credit? But instead he's arranged for it to be sent to Browning, just so we can take the lead and get field experience. I think it's just lovely of him."

Daniel would not have minded more of this talk, but Peter did not seem to want to converse along those same lines. "I had a nice time last weekend," he said, with a significant look. "At your party."

"Yes, it was great fun. And much warmer than the pond at Brookfield."

"Ha! I can only imagine. Anyway, I was wondering—"

Daniel was now interviewing his sixth student, but even through his notetaking he could predict what was about to happen. He felt a slight surge of annoyance. Was he going to be forced to listen to the maneuvers of lovesick boys at the end of every class?

"—if you'd like to go to dinner with me next Friday?" Peter said. "And perhaps see a film after?"

"Oh." Miss Ellison's cheeks pinked a little. "I don't know, Peter, I've got loads of reading to do for Dr. Miller's class."

"But it's important to have a little fun too, isn't it?" Peter countered hastily. "Make the most of being young?"

Miss Ellison simply shrugged.

"Besides, Talbot Cinema has excellent banisters for sliding," he added with a wink.

"*Shh!*" she hushed him, laughing and blushing deeper still.

"Come on, you haven't been anywhere in ages," he urged. "Even you need to relax once in a while. What do you say?"

Again, she hesitated.

"Think it over," Peter said with a decided nod. "I'll telephone you later this evening."

"Wait, aren't you going to be part of Dr. Carter's research team?"

"Ha! Not a chance. Just hoped to talk with you, that's all."

He backed out of the classroom, leaving behind a pensive Miss Ellison. Daniel, who had finished interviewing the other students, watched as she silently brushed off this exchange and stepped towards his desk.

He shook his head. "No, Miss Ellison."

Her eager face fell. "But why not?" she almost demanded. "Professor," she added quietly.

"Why not?" Daniel looked around in exasperation. "Because you're taking seven courses, that's why not. You don't have time for this, Miss Ellison. It will be too much."

She waved a hand impatiently. "I dropped French. I didn't need it anyway. I have time now."

Daniel had just enough time to register his amusement that a young woman presumably fluent in the language had even been taking French before objecting with, "The work will be painstaking. I need a dedicated team. I can't afford to have my researchers distracted by …"

Young men, he thought privately.

"Other coursework," he finished audibly.

"Dr. Carter." Miss Ellison took a deep, steadying breath. "I have been captivated by Egypt since I was nine years old. I've been planning a trip to Cairo since I was eleven. I've read every book I can on Egyptology, and if you'll forgive me for saying, I've received top marks on every hieroglyph translation you've assigned." A strange gleam came into her eyes, and her mannerisms gained energy as she made her argument.

"This is a once-in-a-lifetime opportunity," she stated firmly. "I have to do this. I promise I'll work hard, harder than all your other researchers combined. You'll never have cause to doubt my commitment or my availability." Her brow wrinkled with an unspoken worry. "I know I'm only a third year," she raced on, "but I promise I'm ready for a chance like this." She paused, waiting on him with bated, uncertain breath. "Please, Dr. Carter. Please give me this chance."

Daniel chewed the inside of his cheek. He had no doubt that it would be as she said. It was true. Miss Ellison had outperformed even his fourth-year students on every examination. His other objections he could not voice. They were yet half-formed in his mind. Though he hated to admit it, he had a sneaking sense it might be inadvisable – dangerous even – for him to spend too much time in her company.

Still … she was looking at him so eagerly, so hopefully, that he could not help relenting. He sighed. "Very well."

She beamed. "Thank you, Dr. Carter."

"Put your availability here, if you please." Daniel pushed the notepad into her arms and turned towards nothing in particular.

"There," she said, scrawling rapidly. "That's everything, I

think." Glowing with happiness, she laid the pad upon the desk and moved to depart. "Have a good afternoon, Professor."

A question burst unexpectedly from Daniel's lips. "And how was your birthday?"

She stopped, turning back with a puzzled air. "It ... it was fun. Thank you."

"The entertainment was meant to be a surprise, wasn't it? What did you do, in the end?"

For some reason, Miss Ellison looked embarrassed. "Just ... juvenile things," she laughed. "Nothing to trouble you with."

"Well." He cleared his throat. "Happy birthday, Miss Ellison."

She shot him another quizzical glance.

"Thank you." With a little smile, she turned and left the classroom. Daniel kept his eyes on the floor, but listened intently to the click of her pumps against the tiles. Within seconds, she was gone.

CHAPTER 10

J ust two days later Jenny received notice of the team's first
  session. Dr. Carter's brief memo had directed the students to
  meet in the third-floor Archaeology lab that same evening.
Jenny had readily confirmed her attendance; unfortunately, the
class she attended just prior was located all the way across campus.
It was that unhappy circumstance that found her walking between
Browning's buildings at top speed, her satchel bumping against her
thigh with every step.

"Please," she had said to him. "Please give me this chance."

With her stout reassurances to Dr. Carter flashing through her
mind, Jenny began to sprint across the courtyard. Her pumps clattered against the stones and her ankles wobbled treacherously
beneath her, but at last she reached Milton Lecture Hall. Wrenching
open its double doors, she took the stairs two at a time, cursing
when one of her ankles buckled at the top step.

Far in the distance, the campus bell's sixth chime was fading to
nothingness. She adjusted her heel and checked her watch, grinning with satisfaction.

Perfect.

Still panting heavily, Jenny pushed open the lab door. The team

– which, to her very great surprise, included Jillian – had already assembled. Two other fourth-year fellows stood near a large workbench. Spencer and Howard, if she remembered their names correctly. Max, the omnipresent teaching assistant, manned the door with a clipboard and a look of great self-importance. Dr. Carter, however, leaned casually against a desk at the room's end, the very picture of calm and leisure.

"Ah," Max greeted her. "Here you are at last, Miss Ellison. If you'll just sign in here? Excellent. Each of you students must sign in and out every time you work in the lab. Please note the duration of your stay in the second column, here. Is that understood?"

The students all nodded. Jenny smothered a laugh at Max's pompous manner. He seemed to have forgotten that he, too, was a student. She slipped off her coat and looked around in awe. This place was not so much a lab as it was an eclectic library. The shelves were laden with lumps of purple and blue geodes, old reference books, dusty maps, jars of delicate beads, and even a fractured human skull. The far end of the room held equipment: crates of brushes, heavy paper, cameras, and glass beakers next to shining bottles of chemicals.

In the center of the room, and taking up most of the space, was a large work bench surrounded by wooden stools. Lying on the bench was a slab of pale, solid earth. Jenny's heart lurched at the sight of it. This was surely the stone artifact, still shrouded in thousands of years of ancient sediment. It was about six feet wide, and not quite that in height. Poking out from one of the slab's earthen edges was a stone corner, light and sandy red in color.

A queer, otherworldly sensation overtook Jenny; the tiny piece of stone that was visible had an almost ghostly presence in the room. She could so easily picture a warm, suntanned hand moving over that same surface millennia ago. She could practically *see* the fingers smoothing the limestone to perfection. This unnamed craftsman's work, the endurance of their skill and artistry, so undimmed by desert and time, sent a jolt through her heart as surely as if she'd seen an apparition. With a slightly shaking hand, Jenny smoothed her hair and waited longingly for instruction.

"All right then." Max rubbed his hands together. "Let's begin. This stone was found—"

"Thanks, Max," Dr. Carter calmly interrupted, standing with his hands in his pockets. "I'll take it from here."

"Oh. Right." Max looked a little wet-blanketed, but he stepped back obediently and watched the proceedings with interest.

"Welcome, everyone," Dr. Carter said. Jenny had the fleeting thought that his voice was very pleasant to the ear. Steady and even. Unintimidating.

"First things first," he continued, gesturing over their small group. "Do you all know each other?"

The students nodded dumbly in response. Each seemed too stunned by the sight of the stone to speak, or in Jillian's case, too distracted to bother. She sat examining a hangnail, occasionally looking up at Dr. Carter with a saccharine smile.

"Good." The young professor rubbed his palm over the back of his hair, as he always did when he was concentrating. "First of all, I appreciate your volunteering for this project. I believe what you learn will be worth every sacrifice of your free time. But before we get into the vast amount of work before us" – he inclined his head towards the stone slab – "we have a few house rules to go over."

"Please refer to the protocol sheets beneath your research agreements," Max broke in, distributing forms.

"Yes, thank you, Max," Dr. Carter said patiently. "First and foremost: please understand that this stone slab is not Browning's property and never will be. I expect you to treat it with the utmost caution. The Egyptian ministry has given us until mid-December to complete the restoration, and it is imperative that we meet that deadline. To do so, you may need to fit in extra hours during the week."

"But how will we get in?" Howard asked anxiously. "The lab door was locked when I came. I had to wait until Max got here."

"You will each be given a key." Dr. Carter suddenly looked a bit stern. "We are trusting you to use your access *only* for preservation work. Understood?"

Again the students nodded placidly, but Jenny's serenity was forced. Despite her assertions of competence, she hadn't the faintest idea of where to start on an artifact restoration. The idea of being left alone in the lab, working without any guidance whatsoever was nerve-wracking, to say the very least. What if she were to damage this priceless relic by mistake?

Perhaps Dr. Carter sensed her worry, because, glancing her way he continued, "Since this stone is an object of international significance, you won't be cleared to handle it on your own until either Max or myself has observed your work and determined that you have been appropriately trained."

"Oh, good." Howard sighed with relief.

"Perhaps you'd like to tell them about the paperwork, Max?" Dr. Carter turned the floor back to his research assistant, who flushed with genuine delight.

"Yes!" Max's chest puffed slightly. "Each of you have been given a non-disclosure agreement. Before we begin, you must agree not to discuss the contents of your work with *anyone* outside of this research team. That includes other professors and staff at Browning. If you cannot abide by these terms, you will be asked to leave the project."

"This is all very hush-hush," Spencer muttered, signing his paper with a frown. "Why all the secrecy? What's on this rock, anyways?"

Dr. Carter shook his head. "We don't know. But we don't want anything to leak to the press—"

"The press?" Howard cut in excitedly.

"—until we know exactly what we're dealing with," Dr. Carter finished. "And, of course, until we've reported the findings to the Egyptian government. They deserve to be the first to hear what it contains, if anything. It was one of the provisions they most insisted on in giving us this chance."

Jenny signed her paper without hesitation. "Will you tell us more about the excavation, Professor? How did you find the stone?"

Dr. Carter walked slowly around the workbench. At first Jenny thought he hadn't heard her, but then he replied, his back still turned against her.

"We were photographing some ancient graffiti that had been carved into a ridge a few leagues from the temple. We broke for lunch on top of the rocks and spotted a mud pit on the outskirts of the camp. There are holes like that all over Nubia. Clay wells, used to make bricks for the temples. But this one seemed ... I'm not sure, just different, somehow. It had a strange depression in its center." He lightly tapped the frozen earth. "After a few hours of digging, we hit the slab."

"How old did you say it was?" Jillian asked, at last looking vaguely curious.

"We'll know more once it's uncovered, but if I were to hazard a guess ... I'd date it from at least 1300 B.C."

Spencer let out a long whistle. "Blimey."

Dr. Carter nodded amusedly. "Our task is to clean and photograph it. We've also been authorized to copy the contents, if there are any, onto archival paper – that heavy stuff, on the shelf over there – and complete an initial translation."

"You really think there are hieroglyphs on there, Dr. Carter?" Howard squeaked.

"I think there's a good chance, yes. The size of the slab, and its proximity to the temple site, suggests that it *might* have been some kind of marker for the region."

"When do we start?" Jenny asked happily.

"Tonight." With his back still turned to her, Dr. Carter pulled a handful of brushes off a nearby shelf and held one up for their examination. It was small, only about eight inches in length, but even from across the room Jenny could see its bristles were thick and incredibly soft.

"Our first step is to sweep off the sediment and brick mixture, one layer at a time. Be very gentle, as we really don't know what state the stone is in underneath all that earth."

"If the mud is too hard in places, use a spray bottle with distilled water to loosen it," Max blurted out, seemingly unable to keep quiet any longer.

Jenny glanced at her professor, who was nodding patiently.

"Again, thank you, Max." Dr. Carter set a box of white cotton gloves onto the workbench. "You'll wear these gloves each time you work. No one may move the stone on or off the table. Absolutely no food or drink is allowed in the lab, and ladies must pull their hair back before beginning work. Agreed?"

The students murmured their assent.

"Excellent." Dr. Carter's dark blue eyes crinkled with a warm smile. "Now, enough rules. Let's have some fun."

Jenny tied up her hair, chatting excitedly with Howard and Spencer as they slipped on the tight-fitting gloves and selected brushes.

"Partner up, and begin at the edges," their professor directed.

The students tentatively approached the workbench. Jenny found herself paired with Howard, while Spencer worked with Jillian. The group began brushing off the clay with slow, timid strokes. After watching them work for a few minutes, Dr. Carter let out a loud burst of laughter.

"You can be a little firmer than that. This stone's already been covered up for three thousand years. Let's not take another three thousand to clean it."

The group chuckled foolishly and began to work with more confidence. Jenny was thrilled to see that with stronger strokes, the earth on her side of the stone began to crumble. It was chalk-like in some places, and extremely satisfying to rub away. Other areas were more stubbornly caked. Jenny did not mind; these remnants of clay were the closest she'd come to touching Egypt itself, and the mere thought of it sent another thrill through her heart.

The room was very quiet as they worked. Dr. Carter walked behind Spencer and Jillian's partnership, observing them and giving advice. After circling twice between them and Max, Dr. Carter approached Jenny and Howard's side of the table. Jenny shifted nervously in her seat, keenly aware that she was the only third year in the room. It was vital that her work tonight made a good impression. The young professor seemed more preoccupied with her companion's progress, however, and after a minute or two of silent observation, he focused his feedback there.

"A bit more gently, Howard," Dr. Carter instructed. "Sometimes pressing the brush in softly and rotating it will get you further than sweeping from above."

"I've uncovered a whole inch!" Spencer yelled in disbelief. "A huge chunk of dirt just fell away, I hardly touched it, look!"

"Where? Where?" squealed Howard, nearly overturning his stool in his excitement. "Can you see anything?" He ran to join Spencer, ducking under Max's outstretched arm in the process.

"Move over, ninny," Jillian cried, elbowing him in the ribs for a better view. "I want a look."

Jenny craned her neck, desperate to see their progress but unable to do so from her seat. As there was no room for her at the opposite side of the workbench, her own glimpse of the stone would have to wait. She brushed away in disappointed silence at her section, which was far more reluctant to give up its secrets.

"Very wise, Miss Ellison," Dr. Carter observed in a low voice. He was watching the crowded students with a frown. "For it's best not to move too exuberantly. In a small room. Among three-thousand-year-old artifacts."

Jenny smothered a laugh. "They're just excited, that's all. Inside I'm elbowing them out of the way myself."

The corner of his mouth lifted. "So am I, to be honest. Well. You'll uncover your own section in no time." He nodded to her work. "That's a good touch you have there."

"This bit here is very solid, though. Should I ...?"

"You need water. I'll get you some."

Dr. Carter walked to a sink along the far wall and filled a small spray bottle. Though he seemed exhausted, Jenny could tell how much her young professor was enjoying this evening's work. He was clearly in his element.

"How is your shorthand holding up?" he asked, handing her the bottle. "Still catching everything?"

She nodded. "I am, thank you. Although I must say, you've been using an awful lot of five- and six-syllable words in your latest lectures."

A sly smile crept up Dr. Carter's face.

"Have you been doing that on purpose?" Jenny whispered, wide-eyed. "To test my system?"

Dr. Carter did not answer, but there was a mischievous twinkle in his blue eyes as he moved away from her bench.

"Back to your seat, Howard. You can't let Miss Ellison have all the fun."

CHAPTER 11

Later that evening, Daniel heard a loud rap on his office door.

"Come in," he called, reaching for the stack of term papers he was meant to be grading. After a full night of conservation work, motivation to complete his more mundane tasks eluded him.

Dr. Miller poked in his snowy head. "What's this? Still here, my boy?"

"Antony! Come in, come in," Daniel beckoned, cheered by this unexpected company.

"It's nearly *nine*, Daniel. What are you still doing in your office?" Dr. Miller shook his finger with a scolding look. "All work and no play make Jack a dull boy, you know."

"I'm just catching up on a few things. We started the conservation tonight."

"Did you?" Dr. Miller's sternness was replaced by an almost childlike enthusiasm. He took a seat by Daniel's desk. "And? How is your team?"

"Pretty good, I think." He smiled a little in remembrance. "Very enthusiastic, at least."

"Have you found out what the stone is, then?"

76

"You're as bad as the Egyptian ambassador," he chuckled. "Remember, Antony, it's caked in earth and plaster. Cleaning it will take more than one night, perhaps more than one *term* if my students play truant."

"I see." A strange, unsettled look crossed Dr. Miller's features. "On second thought, Daniel, you'd better not tell me anything too specific about the project. William's been bothering me about it."

"Dr. Chilcott? Why? What's he been saying?"

"Oh, you know. Asking whether the local papers will pick up the story, and if this will put you in line for more Amity funding." Antony stroked his chin thoughtfully. "You two don't get on, do you?"

He shrugged. "Not really. Though I couldn't tell you why."

"Couldn't you? I could. He's jealous. It's plain as the nose on your face."

"Nonsense. Chilcott has no reason to envy me."

"Of course he does. Here you are, barely three years into your career, and yet you are a popular professor, an Amity chair, and the finder of this bumper of a discovery to boot."

"But he's *also* an Amity chair," Daniel objected, "with his own site to manage. He has no cause to be jealous of mine."

"That site is picked over, Daniel. It's an open secret that Chilcott hasn't found so much as a shard of pottery in nearly five years. Then *you* turn up, an assistant professor but a rising star if ever there was one." The old dean pulled at his bowtie, as he often did when he was in distress. "The longer I ponder it, the clearer the root of his dislike becomes."

Daniel shook his head and went back to his paperwork. "If he does dislike me, then so be it. I have more important things to worry about."

Dr. Miller did not press him further, but it was clear the matter was far from resolved. Antony's expression was much too grave for Daniel's liking.

"Antony?" he probed. "Was there something else you wanted to say?"

The old man sighed roughly. "Perhaps. Chilcott has officially put himself forward as a candidate. For my replacement."

"*What?*" Daniel flushed indignantly. "Of all the brazen, disrespectful—"

Antony held up his hand. "Peace, my boy, peace."

"To not even wait until you've officially announced your—"

"Well, he can't do much publicly until I resign, but I suspect he's rallying supporters. I think ... " Antony cleared his throat. "I fear that my influence here may be waning, Daniel."

"It's not," the ever-loyal Daniel objected. "You're the true captain of this ship, Antony, and everyone in the department knows it. Chilcott's campaign will founder on the rocks, you'll see."

"I thank you for that." The old dean suddenly looked very tired. "It's a cheering, if inaccurate thought. The prospect of Chilcott heading things does wrinkle my spirits a bit."

"Because he'd be rubbish," Daniel said flatly.

"Do you have a better candidate in mind? The truth is, I'd rather hoped that you might be interested in the deanship, Daniel. After you're tenured, of course."

"Antony, that's—"

"It's not," the old professor said firmly, anticipating Daniel's words. "It's not ludicrous. You're gifted, Daniel. You're a favorite with the students. Your research is of the highest caliber, *and,*" he added, nodding to the chiming clock, "your work ethic is clearly unparalleled."

Daniel shook his head for the second time. "It's kind of you to even suggest such a thing, but I'm happy where I am, Antony. I want to teach, and I want to research, and I want to run my site in Egypt. That's what's right for me."

"I suppose it's always the way," Dr. Miller grumbled, standing with the assistance of his cane. "Why, oh why, must exceptional talent and ability consistently fall upon the least ambitious among us? Oh, very well. I shall leave you to your meagre aspirations. But don't think for one minute this lets you off the hook, Daniel Carter," he added more severely. "I may have relinquished my concerns over your professional goals, but I still maintain that you need to find yourself a lady. Heaven knows a handsome young man like you could have your pick. In the last three years you have taken to dinner, by my count, nearly a dozen different women. Why haven't any of them suited?"

Recognizing that Dr. Miller had fallen back into his scolding mood, Daniel held up both hands in surrender.

"I just haven't met the right woman for me, Antony. But I will. Someday."

The old professor's eyes brightened. "What about that Tregardner girl, the one you met at the bring-and-buy sale last year? Rachel, or ... Rebecca! Yes, Rebecca. Any chance you might rekindle things with her?"

"No, I don't think so."

"But why not?" Dr. Miller rapped his cane impatiently on the ground. "She was beautiful, and clever, and rich ..."

"And small-minded, and vengeful, and unkind," Daniel finished quietly. "In the end."

"Was she?" Dr. Miller's face fell. "Pity. I liked her."

"You liked her yacht," Daniel reminded him.

"Ha! So I did." Antony chuckled and shoved on his hat. "Well. It's your life to waste, as they say. Don't stay up too late, my boy."

Daniel cocked an eyebrow in amusement. "Out of curiosity, what would you say to me if I were out on the town with some ravishing young woman on my arm?"

Old Dr. Miller grinned and flourished his cane above his head. "Why, in that scenario, I would say 'don't come home too soon,' of course!"

With a parting wink, he closed Daniel's door softly behind him.

CHAPTER 12

"Margie, are you home? Sorry I'm late, I've just been – agh!" Jenny shrieked and stumbled backwards, having bumped directly into her roommate. Margie's physical appearance was startling, to say the very least. Her auburn hair was piled high in rollers, and her face was caked in cold cream. Her towering hairnet and long green bathrobe made her look more like a creature from the deep than a young woman.

"Golly!" Jenny gasped, clutching at her heart. "You startled me!"

"Likewise!" Margie chuckled, adjusting her mountainous hairdo. "Why were you running in like that? Is something wrong?"

"I'm just cold, that's all. I forgot my gloves." Jenny held her hands over the radiator, moaning with satisfaction as her fingertips smarted with heat. "Oh, it's lovely over here. I might never leave."

"You may want to in a minute," Margie cautioned. "Jillian's in the kitchen. We've been working on that project for Chilcott's class. She's just getting a cuppa."

"Right." Jenny straightened, bracing herself for what would inevitably turn into some sort of confrontation. Things had been especially frosty between the two ladies recently, although Jenny really couldn't name a particular incident that had escalated the tension.

"Peter called earlier," Margie said. "He's invited you to his next rugby match."

"I'm busy that evening," Jenny replied, still warming her hands.

"I didn't say which night it was." She chuckled.

"Oh, right. Well, just tell him I'm busy if he calls back."

"He'll only call again," Margie grumbled, "and I'm getting a bit tired of coming up with your excuses. Why not just go out with him once and have done with it? You haven't been on a date at all this year. It might do you good."

Before Jenny could answer, Jillian emerged from the kitchen with a steaming cup of Earl Grey in her hand.

"Oh," she said, wrinkling her nose at the sight of Jenny. "It's you."

"Hello, Jillian," she replied lightly.

"Don't tell me you were at the lab again. Why don't you just sleep there, for goodness' sake?"

"Because I live here," Jenny replied through gritted teeth. She took a deep breath, determined not to spar with Jillian if she could help it. It was late, and above all she wanted to go to sleep with a clear head. "So! You two were working on the project for Chilcott? How's it coming?"

Jillian ignored her question and plopped on the sofa, folding her legs tightly beneath her. She appeared to be in an especially contrary mood this evening, and within moments had laid into Jenny again.

"If you're putting in extra hours to try and impress Dr. Carter, you're wasting your time. The man is an absolute block. Not a scrap of human feeling in him."

"You've changed your tune, Jilly," Margie said amusedly. "You were half in love with him a week ago."

"Yes, well I've seen the light, as they say. He may be a handsome ex-assassin, but when it comes to flirting, he's unforgivably obtuse."

"I *told* you he wasn't a rogue," Jenny said, thumbing through her agenda for tomorrow. "He's quiet, and serious. He seems so kind."

"He seems like a thumping bore, you mean. Undeserving of my attention," Jillian added rather slyly. Jenny rolled her eyes and walked to the kitchen for a cup of her own.

"There are far more generous and attractive men in this world," Jillian called, seemingly determined to make Jenny hear her. "Dr. Daniel Carter is simply not worth my time."

Margie turned to Jillian with interest. "Are you implying you've found a new beau?"

She coyly sipped her tea.

"Who?" Margie begged.

"Not telling."

"Is it Anders? Has he asked you out at last?"

"Again, I'm not telling," Jillian insisted, but she was giggling furiously now.

"Leave it there, Margie, I beg of you," Jenny entreated wearily as she returned from the kitchen. She was in no mood to listen to Jillian boast of her conquests. "Hang on ... is that why you've stopped coming to the lab? Because you've finally given up on Dr. Carter?"

"So what if it is?"

"Poor Jilly," Margie chuckled. "After all the trouble she went to, bribing the other applicants to withdraw."

"Yes." Jillian scowled. "What a waste of my coppers. After three weeks of work, the only move Dr. Carter's made is to correct the way I hold my brush. I'm moving on."

Jenny sucked thoughtfully on her teaspoon. "At least you got some kind of feedback."

"What do you mean?" Margie asked her.

She shrugged. "Dr. Carter's an excellent lecturer, but he's not as accessible as one might hope. I have to agree with Jillian on that point."

"There," Jillian said triumphantly. "I told you."

"When we're in the lab for our group meetings," she continued, "he won't answer any of my questions. If I get stuck in the work and ask him for help, he just shuffles me off to the teaching assistant. Max is a nice enough chap, but he doesn't have any practical experience. There's only so much he can advise on. It's incredibly frustrating," she finished, bitterly stirring her tea.

Jillian rolled her eyes. "You just want to butter up Dr. Carter before submitting your Amity application."

"That's not true," Jenny rebutted. "This is a once-in-a-lifetime opportunity, Jillian. Dr. Carter's an emerging leader in the field. We ought to—"

"You're wasting your time, anyway. They'll only choose men for the Amity, as they always do. Why even bother submitting an application?"

Jenny was about to retort when Margie, sensing danger, interrupted with a timid, "And, erm ... how is the preservation work coming? Have you cleaned off all the, erm ... mud?"

A sour-faced Jillian stood to put on her coat. "We're getting there, thanks to dirt-fanatics like Jenny."

"We're archaeologists!" Jenny said, abandoning her patience entirely. "It's our job to care about dirt, and everything that lies above and beneath it."

"We are not archaeologists, Jenny Ellison," Jillian said flatly. "We never will be."

"Of course we will!"

"Ever the activist," she muttered, buttoning her coat.

"We have to make the most of these chances," Jenny argued. "If you put in just a little more time and effort, it could open so many doors for you. I know it could."

"You're wrong," Jillian snapped with sudden ferocity. "You know as well as I do that women never get hired on sites. So tell me, what's the point of wasting my university experience on a fever dream? Better to have fun, I say, and distract oneself from the disappointments that will inevitably follow graduation."

There was a heavy silence, in which the two ladies stared dumbly at each other until Jillian turned to Margie.

"I have to go. I have Advanced Theories first thing tomorrow. Such a bore. Goodnight."

"Goodnight, Jillian," Margie mumbled sadly.

"Wait." Jenny stopped her on her way out. "You don't really mean all of that, do you?"

Jillian hitched her bag over her shoulder impatiently. "And if I did?"

She swallowed hard. "You mustn't talk like that, Jillian, you really mustn't. The situation is … not ideal, I grant you. But we can find positions, I know it. There have to be some site directors willing to hire us. If there aren't, well, then we'll just have to open our own agency. We can be the first. Who's stopping us?"

Jenny attempted to smile bravely, but her eyes were filling. "Listen, Jillian. I know we don't quite get on, but you know what you're about. I've seen your work, and you're *so much* cleverer than Anders, and Peter, and Sagan, or any of the others put together. You'd make a fantastic archaeologist." Her voice wavered treacherously. "You cannot give up."

Jillian's face was varnished with a strange mixture of coldness and sympathy. "If you were to look up from the dirt once in a while," she murmured, noticeably without a sneer, "then you might understand how the world really works, Jennifer Ellison. Goodnight." Without another word, she walked into the biting November air.

CHAPTER 13

Jenny's eyelids shot open, releasing her from the grip of a nightmare. Her limbs were still frozen with the heaviness of sleep, yet even in her half-conscious state adrenaline was surging. She strained her ear to the most minuscule sounds about her, trying to eliminate the possibility of danger. The apartment was deathly dark; nothing could be heard besides the rustle of her quilt and the eerie scrape of a branch outside her window. Margie's snores thundered loudly from beyond the thin wall. All else was still.

A quick glance to the frosty panes told Jenny it was not quite dawn. She unwound herself from her tangled sheets and settled flatly onto her back, trying hard not to glance at the bedside clock. Anxious awakenings were nothing novel to her, and she knew from experience it would be easier to fall asleep if she couldn't calculate the remaining time until her alarm rang. Pressing her eyes shut, she instead tried to recall her quickly fading dream.

It was a nightmare she'd had many times before. In it, Jenny had been strolling peacefully through Browning's campus only to discover that the Archaeology building was on fire. She'd screamed for help as a scarlet blaze engulfed the building, but no one came to assist. She had tried to rush in and put out the blaze herself, but the doors had morphed into gleaming black bars. No matter how hard she had pushed or how loudly she had shouted, she couldn't enter. The metal of the gate had instead burst into red-hot flames, searing her hands so painfully she had awoken in an instant.

Jenny rolled onto her side and breathed deeply for several minutes, enjoying the delicious sense of relief that always accompanied realizing a dream was just that – a dream, and nothing more. No matter how much she willed sleep to return, it wouldn't. The nightmare, and Jillian's acrid words from last evening, had sparked a cascade of troubling thoughts that would not be quieted. One pressed more firmly on her heart than the rest.

Today was Monday.

Today was *Amity* day.

After a few more minutes of tossing and turning, Jenny relented and glanced at her bedside clock. It was now five in the morning. As there was little point in falling back to sleep, she threw off her quilt and stole a reassuring glance at the application packet lying on her bureau.

It was quite impressive to look at: thick, precise, and painstakingly bound. Jenny surveyed the contents with pardonable pride, flipping one last time through the forms and essays she had spent so many hours preparing. A painful lump formed in her throat. Years of sacrifice and the triumph of will over experience had led her to this point. Now Jenny's future rested on these humble papers. She murmured a prayer, or perhaps a plea, that her plans might have at least some chance of succeeding.

As today was the dreaded "day of judgment," Jenny dressed with special care to honor it. She pulled on a navy-blue blouse and pleated gray skirt, braiding her curls loosely at the side of her head for an effect that was both professional and pleasant.

It was time.

Too nervous to eat a proper breakfast, she shivered into her coat and locked her apartment behind her. The outdoor railing was furry with frost, and a few leaves blew bitterly about her feet. The sun's pale light did little to warm the morning. Fortunately, campus wasn't far – just a twenty-minute stroll as the crow flew. With her adrenaline still surging in waves, Jenny barely heeded her surroundings as she walked. She nearly crashed into the wall surrounding Browning's grounds. Luckily, the only people about to witness her blunder were the school gardeners, who were picking up branches broken by the frost.

"Blast these trees," one older gentleman muttered to another as he stooped. "Belmont, the finest forestland in England," he pantomimed shrilly. "The only county that's not had the hand of man on every acre. Well, I say, or rather me back says, any tree that drops its twigs at the first sign of frost deserves to be chopped up for kindling, in't that right, Ted?"

Jenny didn't linger to hear Ted's response. Pushing her way into Milton Lecture Hall, she steadied her nerves by forming a plan. Submissions were to be collected in Dr. Miller's office, just down the hall from the Archaeology lab. After dropping off her application, she would soothe her jitters by fitting in some brushwork before class.

Unsurprisingly, the third-floor corridor lay empty at this hour. Dr. Miller's office was bolted shut, but a lockbox sat on a chair outside his door with an arrow pointing to a wide slot labeled "Amity Scholarship Applications." Taking a deep breath, she dropped in her packet.

It was done.

A wave of calm rippled through Jenny. She had done all that she could. She knew that much. Now fate would decide, and she dearly hoped fate would look kindly on her. Touching the lockbox once more for luck, she turned towards the Archaeology lab and learned that she was not the only one in the hall. Dr. Chilcott hovered just outside the lab door, reading a posted bulletin with both hands clasped tightly behind his back.

Jenny cautiously approached him. "Good morning, Dr. Chilcott."

"Hmm?" Chilcott jumped slightly, his moustache twitching as he struggled to place her. "Yes, good morning, Miss ...?"

"Ellison."

"Of course." He pressed his thin lips together in a frown, as though searching for something more to say to her. "A bit early to be on campus, isn't it, Miss Ellison?"

"I was submitting my Amity application, sir."

"Indeed?" Dr. Chilcott looked surprised, but not pleasantly so. "Well. Very ambitious, I must say. Good for you. Very aspirational."

"Thank you," Jenny replied curtly. Though his words were encouraging, his tone reeked of disapproval. It was a sad truth that few Browning professors encouraged their female students to pursue fieldwork. Jillian's words from last night echoed again in Jenny's ear, and she began searching for her lab key to hide her annoyance. Dr. Chilcott watched as she fumbled grumpily through her satchel.

"Pardon me, Miss Ellison, but am I correct in assuming you are part of Dr. Carter's research team?"

"I am."

"Splendid." The man smiled in earnest now. "And, erm ..." Dr. Chilcott jerked his head towards the lab. "How's it coming in there?"

"Very well, sir."

"Excellent, I'm glad to hear it. Do you think you'll meet your deadline?"

"I don't believe I—"

"To have been given only one term," Chilcott lamented, ignoring her, "to do all of that cleaning and archiving? To say nothing of shipping the artifact back! I do feel for Dr. Carter. Indeed, I feel for you all. What a strain your team must be under."

Jenny frowned. Dr. Chilcott's expression seemed too carefully arranged to be considered truly sympathetic. "I'm sorry, Dr. Chilcott, but I'm afraid I'm not at liberty to discuss the project. We have strict instructions."

"Yes, of course. Confidentiality and all that. I quite understand." Dr. Chilcott smiled, but his gray eyes remained rather cold.

"I should be going," Jenny murmured. "I'd like to fit in some work before my first class."

"You intend to work now?" he asked, his eyes widening. "Dr. Carter allows you to handle the artifact on your own? Unsupervised?"

Jenny hesitated. "Some of us, yes." She felt a sudden need to defend Dr. Carter. "But only after we've been fully trained to do so."

"A novel approach." Chilcott stroked his chin thoughtfully. "Very novel."

"Yes, well, he trusts us. If you'll excuse me, Professor, I really should get started." Jenny stepped in front of him and unlocked the lab door. To her dismay, Chilcott immediately craned his neck to see inside the room. She opened it just wide enough to slip inside and bolted it behind her with a loud "click."

"Odious man," she whispered, taking off her coat.

"Who is?" came a voice from the other side of the room.

CHAPTER 14

J enny nearly jumped out of her skin. Dr. Carter was calmly sitting at his desk along the far wall. He appeared utterly relaxed, a book in one hand, a cup of very dark coffee in the other.

"Professor Carter!" Jenny gasped. "I had no idea you would be here this early."

"Nor I you," he replied, snapping his book shut. Despite the earliness of the hour, Jenny thought he looked rather pleased to see her. Or at least he seemed as though he were in an especially good mood this morning. As he set down his coffee cup, Jenny noticed a half-eaten pastry near his elbow.

The young professor followed her gaze to the plate. "Ah. Yes." He looked a little abashed. "I know I said absolutely no food and drink in the lab, but ... I was particularly hungry this morning."

Jenny simply smiled as she hung up her coat and white beret.

"So, are you going to report me to the rest of the team?" he asked, raising his brows.

"I can't. I've signed a non-disclosure agreement." She tried to hide her smile, but Dr. Carter was already laughing. Once he'd started, she found she couldn't help but join in. He had such a warm, full-throated laugh.

"No, I'm not going to tell them," she continued, pulling on her gloves. "You saved my peanuts from Mr. Prewett, after all. Besides, you'll be no good to any of us if you wither away and join old Nigel over there." She nodded to the fractured skull on the shelf, which Howard had fondly christened last week.

Dr. Carter smiled. "Thank you, Miss Ellison."

"It's a good thing you did make us sign that agreement," Jenny muttered as she took her seat at the workbench. "Dr. Chilcott was just—"

"Ah. So that was who you meant by 'odious man'? I'm relieved."

Jenny furrowed her brow. "Did you think I—"

"So what is Chilcott up to now?" Dr. Carter interrupted. He was still smiling.

Jenny sifted through the details of that strange conversation. "He asked if I thought we would finish on time, and if you ever let us work in here alone."

"Hmm." Dr. Carter's jaw clenched slightly, but he didn't say anything more. After a moment of silence, Jenny left him to his pondering and began work on the partially exposed slab.

Brush, brush, brush. Jenny shaved off mud silently for several minutes. It was satisfying work, the kind one could quickly become absorbed in – especially if one got caught up in dreams of the markings that might lie underneath all the earth.

"Miss Ellison, why are you here so early?"

The question jarred her from her imaginings. Dr. Carter had evidently been watching Jenny work, though for how long she wasn't certain. For some reason, it was a mortifying thought.

"I ..." She shifted uncomfortably. "I suppose ... well, I wanted to turn in my application early, and I couldn't sleep, so ..."

Jenny didn't hold his gaze long. It was a little too understanding for her comfort.

Dr. Carter drained the last of his coffee. "I'd almost forgotten. It's Amity day. Well. I'd better go and offer Dr. Miller some support, then."

Despite his declaration, Dr. Carter slowed as he crossed the room. Jenny kept working, wondering with mild distress whether her professor still watched from the corner of his eye. Any level of monitoring from him came as a great surprise. He had been largely absent as her supervisor, redirecting her questions and preferring to coach the other students. This sudden change in attention unnerved her. Had she selected the wrong brush this morning? No, she was using a number four, just as he'd instructed.

Seemingly deciding against leaving, Dr. Carter walked to the workbench and sat across from her. To Jenny's increasing surprise, he pulled on his own pair of gloves to help her. She noticed, before the gloves slipped on, that his knuckles were scarred – like those of a laborer, or a fighter. For the hundredth time, Jenny thought of his rumored brawl with a student last year. Could there be any truth to it?

She stole an upward glance at the young professor. He was certainly mercurial, and very private. Secretive, even. But she had only ever known him to be kind and serious. He clearly loved his profession and respected his students. A fistfight with one of them seemed laughably out of character.

And what of the other rumors? With a deepening frown, Jenny tried to imagine him as an undercover agent. He certainly had the intellect for it. More than that, the well-cut muscles beneath his white shirt suggested he could hold his own in a fight. But his personality was just so ... bookish. Could he really have been a spy, or an assassin? A dangerous one at that?

Dr. Carter met her eye. Jenny snapped her gaze back to the stone, uneasy that she had been caught studying him. Both brushed and worked in silence for several more minutes.

"Why nine?" Dr. Carter asked.

"Hmm?" Jenny said distractedly. A particularly satisfying chunk had just fallen off her side of the stone.

Dr. Carter paused in his work, his eyes fixed on the table. "You told me you've been fascinated by Egypt since you were nine years old. Why nine? What happened then?"

Jenny stared at him in amazement. Despite his inattentiveness as a supervisor, he had a remarkable memory when it came to their short conversations.

"I found a book on Egypt," she replied simply. "At the library."

"Which book?" Though he still did not meet her gaze, he sounded sincerely intrigued.

She shrugged. "I don't even remember. But my mother tells me I checked it out over and over again. Then I started buying books about Egypt with my own pocket money, and I've been trying to get to Egypt ever since." She studied Dr. Carter's downcast eyes, his quietly set jaw. It was not typical of a Browning professor to be so personable, apart from Dr. Miller perhaps. This line of questioning puzzled her, but if he truly wanted to know her better, she would happily return the favor. Smiling pleasantly, she asked, "What about you, Professor Carter? How did you settle on Egypt as your specialty?"

Dr. Carter let out a warm, full laugh. "Oh, that was almost fore-ordained. I visited on holiday with my father when I was a boy. Our guide took us to Saqqara to see the step pyramid of Djoser. It's one that almost no tourists visit, so he let me climb all over the place." His wide grin faded ever so slightly. "He probably shouldn't have, from a conservation standpoint. But you can imagine how tales of mummies and buried treasure would fire up a young boy's imagination."

Jenny could well believe it. Even now, her professor was speaking with an almost boyish energy. She found it … endearing.

"I decided then and there to study hard and return to Egypt someday. And so I have," he finished modestly.

"To find some buried treasure of your own," Jenny added, gesturing to the stone.

"Maybe treasure, maybe trash. We'll know more tonight."

"We'll know what it is by *tonight?*"

"Oh yes." Dr. Carter gently stroked away a chunk of earth. "We're close to the limestone. One more evening of work should clear enough of it for us to make out what this is."

"Brilliant. I've been *dying* to know."

"So have I. You've ... everyone's been working so hard. It troubles me that we can't pay you. Funding is still so very tight, after the war."

"We understand," Jenny assured him.

Dr. Carter shrugged. "You might. I'm not sure the whole team does. But no matter. I've pulled a few strings. We've been given enough funds to do an outing, or host some kind of celebration. It'll be something, at least."

"Where university students are concerned, a tin of biscuits and a bowl of punch will cover a multitude of sins." Jenny's response felt much more animated than she had intended, and she quickly resumed her work. What was the matter with her? Their conversation this morning felt unusually frank and collegial, but there was certainly no need for such a lack of inhibition, such openness on her side.

Dr. Carter didn't seem to mind her joviality, however. "It must be quite a relief to have finished your application," he said, gently misting the slab with water. "I don't think I slept for a full week before submitting mine."

This seemed a kind admission on his part, given her earlier confession. A surge of gratitude evaporated the last of Jenny's formality. "What is the review process like?" she implored him.

Dr. Carter didn't answer for a moment. When he finally did, his words were slow to come and very deliberately spoken. "We take two weeks to read all the applications. Then Dr. Miller, Dr. Chilcott, and I meet in a committee to discuss the best candidates. The three winners are assigned to their top-ranked site, insofar as that is possible."

"I see," Jenny whispered.

He glanced up at her, his expression unreadable. "Which ..." Roughly clearing his throat, he asked, "I believe you're fluent in French? You said your mother is French, is that right?"

Again, his memory showed itself to be impeccable. "She is. And yes, I'm fairly fluent. I can get by, at least."

"That could be helpful at any of the three sites. We interact with scholars and officials from all over the world. How did you learn? Did your mother speak only French at home?"

Jenny had to think for a moment, as those kinds of particulars were hard for her to recollect now. "She spoke it, yes, though not exclusively. I suppose we mostly learned it through music. All the little songs and nursery rhymes she sang were in French."

"Alouette, gentile alouette," Dr. Carter chanted, with such a funny expression that Jenny laughed out loud.

"Yes, that one. But also Dodo, l'enfant do, or Pomme de reinette et pomme d'api."

"Your accent is lovely," the young professor said, locking his gaze properly with hers for the first time. Jenny's smile warmed and deepened. The little compliment pleased her enormously. Dr. Carter's eyes moved gently over her face. He opened his mouth to speak, then stood and roughly cleared his throat.

"I ought to prepare for my first class," he murmured, stripping off his gloves.

A tinkle of keys in the lab door announced they were to have a visitor. A moment later Howard walked in, proclaiming his own entrance with an enormous sneeze.

"Oh! Good morning, Jenny. Good morning, Dr. Carter." He trumpeted noisily into a handkerchief. "Excuse me, Professor, I find the dust rather works up my – achoo! – allergies." Dabbing at his watering eyes, he asked, "How goes the work?"

"It's coming along." Dr. Carter moved stiffly away from the bench. "Will you help Miss Ellison finish up? I have a few things to prepare for my first lecture. I'll see you both this evening."

Without another word or glance towards either of them, Dr. Carter crossed the room and left. Jenny watched him go, her thoughts softening for the first time all morning.

"I'll join you in a minute, Howard."

While her friend hung up his coat, Jenny walked to Dr. Carter's desk. Once she was sure Howard was not looking, she quietly hid her professor's coffee cup and pastry from view.

CHAPTER 15

The hours dragged by, but at last six o'clock came. Daniel Carter waited restlessly for his team to assemble. After weeks and weeks of painstaking work, a large section of the stone was ready to yield its secrets. Only the lightest layer of earth remained on the top-left quadrant. It had taken everything in Daniel's power to resist finishing the clearing of it on his own. As impatient as he was to know what exactly this artifact was, he also knew his students would benefit the most by leading out on the work. Far better for him to be their guide than their ruler.

That being said, Daniel didn't see any point in waiting longer than was needful. It was past six now. Howard, Spencer, Max, and even Jillian had already taken up their positions around the workbench. Miss Ellison, however, was late, which was unlike her.

"All these weeks of brushwork," Spencer groaned, ruefully rubbing a blister on his thumb. "Why couldn't we have just doused the lot in a hot water bath?"

"Or some acid?" Howard chipped in hopefully.

"Because acid might dissolve the stone, dummy," Jillian said with a roll of her eyes.

"You're not a dummy, Howard. But Jillian's right," Daniel

absently confirmed. "We occasionally use acid to remove oxidation from metals – statues, tools and the like – but it should only rarely be applied to stone." A moment later, Daniel heard the dull rise and fall of voices outside the lab. He strained to catch them more accurately, without success.

"Wait here, everyone. I'll be back in a moment."

Stepping into the hallway, he noted with a start that Miss Ellison was engaged in a terse conflict with Anders Manwaring. Daniel took a step backward, observing the pair from afar. Neither person noticed his presence, as whatever they were discussing had engrossed them completely. Miss Ellison's cheeks looked strangely flushed, and she was shaking her head firmly as Anders talked over her protestations. Daniel felt a flash of concern that something might be wrong, a feeling that only intensified as he began to overhear their conversation.

" … said no, Anders. How many times do I—"

"Come on, Jen." Anders moved closer, until his chest was only inches away from hers. "I've already made all the arrangements. You'll love it, I promise." He moved to place a finger under Jenny's chin, but she flinched and stepped backwards with a scowl.

"For the last time, *no*. I have to go, Anders, I'm late for my meeting. You really shouldn't have followed me here."

As Jenny started to walk away, Anders caught her elbow in a vice-like grip. The boy's self-assured grin faltered for the first time, and his lowered voice took on a strange new edge. "You know … I'm getting rather tired of asking, Jenny."

Jenny snatched her arm back, her brown eyes narrowing. "*I'm* getting rather tired of you asking, too. Now leave me alone, Anders. I'm warning you."

She turned on her heel, scarlet-faced with emotion. Seeing Daniel, she straightened her satchel and walked quickly past him. "I'm sorry I'm late, Dr. Carter."

Daniel was too busy glaring at Anders to respond. Something

lingering in the boy's expression was making his blood boil. He took a few steps forward as Anders leaned casually against the wall and lit up a cigarette. Finally noticing Daniel's approach, Anders blew out a cloud of smoke.

"Hello, Dr. Carter. I didn't notice you there."

"Obviously."

He took another long draught of tobacco. "Sorry to delay your meeting. I was asking Jenny for some help with Dr. Miller's class."

"Is that so?"

"Yes. Jenny's a brilliant Latin tutor, you see, but she's far too busy now to take me on. It's a shame, for I'm quite behind." Anders shrugged and tipped the ash off the end of his cigarette. "Oh, well. At least I can tell my parents I tried. Goodnight, Professor."

"Anders?"

"Yes, Professor?"

Daniel's dark eyes flashed. "No smoking in the building."

For the briefest moment, a look of sinister defiance crossed Anders' face. But he quickly recovered, hitching back his trademark jaunty smile. Dropping his cigarette butt, he ground it under his shoe until it singed the carpet.

Looking down in false dismay, Anders muttered, "Blast. That might have left a mark." He snapped his fingers cheerfully. "Not to worry, Professor. Let me know the cost of damages, and I'll have my parents add it to their annual donation to the department. It should be a very sizable one this year, I'm happy to say. Goodnight, sir."

Before Daniel could say another word, the boy slid down a stair railing with a tuneless hum. Glowering at this blatant manipulation, Daniel turned to re-enter the lab. Jillian stood like a sentinel in the doorframe. Her arms were crossed, and she was raising a single thin eyebrow. The girl had clearly watched this entire encounter – a realization that made Daniel feel strangely defensive.

"Poor Anders," Jillian said with a dramatic sigh. "He's quite moony over Jenny. I've tried to tell her to cut him loose, but she's such a tease. Loves playing hard to get. I suppose stringing him along is just too much fun."

"I think you'll find I've interpreted this scenario differently, Miss Stewart," Daniel said in a low voice. He strode past her. "Inside, please. We're about to begin."

❧

It took all of Jenny's willpower to shut her exchange with Anders out of her mind, but nothing was going to distract her from the all-important work of this evening. Nothing. She took her seat next to Howard, who she had become quite good friends with over the last month, and squeezed his arm excitedly as Dr. Carter rejoined the group.

"It's finally time!" she whispered.

The limestone slab lay before them on the workbench, still shrouded in a thin layer of earth. The air was filled with a nervous energy. Howard kept trumpeting into his handkerchief, Spencer snickered at odd intervals, and Max alternated between barking useless instructions and picking anxiously at a wart plaster on his finger. Even languid Jillian wore an expression of begrudging interest.

"Shall we begin?" Jenny asked briskly.

She thought Dr. Carter looked unusually somber given the excitement of the task ahead, but after a brief pause, he launched into a set of instructions. "Listen, everyone. We're nearly to the stone's surface now. With luck, we should be able to discern the contents within the next half an hour." Dr. Carter handed out several spray bottles. "Begin," he directed.

"Blimey, this is something," Spencer murmured.

The group picked up their brushes. Taking a deep breath, Jenny began clearing away this last, thinnest layer of debris. Except for the occasional crumble of earth onto the workbench, the room was deathly quiet. Not even a grandiose correction from Max broke the silence. It seemed none of the students wanted to mar the first moment of seeing what lay beneath the shroud of earth. Ten minutes passed, then twenty. Then, without warning or fanfare, as Spencer misted the light-colored slab once more, a vibrant swath of red appeared upon the stone.

Several things happened at once: Jillian actually shrieked, Max began swearing fluently at the top of his lungs, and Dr. Carter held up a halting hand, his face pale and intensely focused. Jenny mouthed wordlessly, over and over, staring down at what had been revealed, but no sound exited her throat. She could do no more than clutch Howard's hand at her side and press it, white-knuckled with shock.

"Paintings," Howard murmured dreamily.

"Not just paintings," Dr. Carter said triumphantly. "*Carvings*. Painted relief carvings."

"Red, and yellow," Jenny croaked, finding her voice at last. She pointed to a ridge of stone that was still steeped in gold pigment. "You can see the coloration, there, and there, and *there*!"

"Yes! Yes! Proceed," Dr. Carter directed excitedly. "But gently ... gently!"

The partnerships brushed in tandem for another twenty minutes, misting and dabbing and holding their breath as more relief carvings were revealed. Most of the colors had long been ravaged by time, but the occasional hint of a red ox or gold cobra would set them all chattering excitedly. Two hours later the team had cleared several feet of the limestone, revealing a breathtaking scene of shallowly carved figures uniformly draped in white linen. They were walking in solemn procession, with baskets of grain and fowl in their arms and bundles of green rushes atop their heads. Rows of precisely cut hieroglyphs lay beneath the processional figures.

"This is incredible," Jenny whispered, her eyes brimming with emotion.

"These people, lining up here," Jillian said, gesturing with uncharacteristic energy. "What are they doing? What does it mean?"

"Only one way to find out," Dr. Carter said, grinning as he rolled up his sleeves. "I hope you all have been paying attention during our lectures this term."

"We're translating the glyphs *now?*" Howard squeaked. "Oh dear. But can't glyphs be read in any direction? How will we even know where to start?"

"Follow the vulture," Jenny and Jillian began in unison. Jillian met her eye for a split second before resuming an inspection of her nails.

"The bird is facing left," Jenny finished. "So, these glyphs are meant to be read left to right."

"It's a funeral procession," Spencer said eagerly. "It *has* to be. The workers are lining up to fill the tomb of the pharaoh!"

A royal tomb?

She cast Dr. Carter an exhilarated glance, but his face was slack with disappointment. He had evidently been reading ahead. Apprehensively, Jenny turned back to the stone. Her eyes moved slowly over the glyphs, painstakingly connecting the images to phonetics.

"A sacred ... honor ..." she murmured aloud.

"It's approximate," Dr. Carter prompted, watching Jenny translate. "Go on."

"To the ... Son of Horus, Son of Nekbhet, Son of Wadjet ..."

"How can you be the son of three different gods?" Spencer muttered.

"An ... an offering," she continued steadily.

He nodded. "Or tribute."

"Oxen, sheep, honey ..."

"Cardamom, dates," Spencer took over with a frown. "This is a shopping list. What's it mean?"

Jenny bit her lip. "Professor, is this … have we uncovered a tax record?"

Dr. Carter sat down wearily. "It would appear so."

"What?" Jillian sniggered scornfully. "You're joking." When no one answered, she looked from Jenny to Dr. Carter in disbelief. "No. Taxes? *Taxes?*"

"A record of tribute," Dr. Carter corrected. He pointed to the row of white-clad figures. "These workers are collecting raw goods on behalf of the nomarch – the regional governor of Nubia – for delivery to the pharaoh."

"What? *Taxes?*" Spencer choked back a laugh. "And here I thought we'd uncovered a record of a royal tomb! All of us working with bated breath, and this is nothing more than the same old, 'Hear ye, hear ye, give all your goods to the king!' that mankind has been hearing since Adam was a boy!" By now Spencer was nearly doubled over with laughter.

"I just can't believe this," Jillian groaned over Spencer's snorts. "A tax record? Weeks and weeks of work, for *nothing.*"

"It's not nothing," Jenny contradicted her, annoyed by Jillian and Spencer's flippancy. "This is still an ancient artifact, isn't it? And the carvings are beautifully preserved. Come on, everyone. Chin up."

She took in Howard and Max's gloomy faces. Jenny secretly shared their disappointment at the blandness of the record, but she couldn't bear for this long-awaited moment to be categorized so harshly. Her admonition did little to rouse her friends, however; Howard nodded uncertainly, Max picked at his teeth, and Jillian's scowl softened to a frown. Jenny's sole encouragement was from Dr. Carter, who nodded with a little smile. Suddenly the dull find did not seem so wholly unjust.

"Actually, the produce listed here sounds similar to what you would need for making sweetmeats," Spencer offered, wiping mirthful tears from his eyes.

"Sweetmeats?" Jillian repeated dubiously.

"It's an ancient Egyptian treat, still sold in the markets today," explained Spencer. "My dad tried them once. They're sort of like a fig and date ball, sweetened with spices and honey. They're supposed to be very good," he finished, trying – and failing – to hide his amusement.

"They are." Dr. Carter stood up, his hands in both pockets. "Unfortunately for us, sweetmeats and taxes are not very novel discoveries." He exhaled slowly. "I'm sorry, team. I know you were hoping for something more interesting or valuable. But this is how the work goes sometimes. We must appreciate all finds, both large and small."

"We're just lucky so much of the pigmentation has been preserved," Jenny said under her breath. She gazed in wonder at a slim line of cerulean sky, as hauntingly bright as if it had been painted two days ago. "This blue is rare. It's just lovely."

After a long moment Jenny looked up, only to find Dr. Carter's blue eyes on hers. With a start and an abrupt nod, he turned to face Howard, who had squared his shoulders and was proclaiming stoutly, "Well, if all we've accomplished today is to learn that the people of ancient Nubia liked sweetmeats, then I for one am glad to know it."

"There are no unimportant finds," Dr. Carter agreed. "Tributes to a pharaoh may be nothing new, but we might learn more about Nubia's goods and trade by reading these records. It's possible, anyway. We'll start the transcription next week." He began sweeping dried mud off the far end of the table, seemingly recovering some of his enthusiasm. "You'll be duplicating the markings on archival paper, precisely as they appear. The copies must be exact, since these transcriptions will eventually be stored in the archives of the Cairo Museum."

"Blimey," Howard croaked, looking rather pale.

"Professor," Max cut in. "It's nearly seven. You wanted me to remind you?"

"Oh, right." Dr. Carter checked his watch. "Blast. I'm sorry to run, team, but I have a call with the Egyptian ambassador. He's anxious to hear what we've uncovered tonight." Smiling wryly, he added, "I'm afraid all he'll learn is the ancients had a sweet tooth. Good work, everyone. Max, will you take it from here? Mention the event."

"Right." Max rose importantly as their professor exited. "Dr. Carter would like to thank you all for your hard work over the last month. We know it's been a tough slog, and that you've sacrificed a great deal of your personal time without any – erm – financial compensation. In recognition of your efforts, the Archaeology department has kindly agreed to foot the bill for a team outing. It will be held next Friday evening, and we hope that most of you can attend."

"What kind of outing?" Spencer asked happily. "A rugby match? A trip to the cinema?"

"Damion's?" Howard guessed.

"You'll find all of the information posted on that bulletin over there." Max pointed to a flyer tacked on the opposite wall. The students rushed over to read it.

"No. You're joking," Spencer groaned.

"He can't be serious," added Jillian.

Jenny read the announcement, smiled, and quickly turned away to hide her face.

"What is it?" Howard puffed, hopping up and down behind them as he was too short to see over the group. "What's the event?"

With another groan, Spencer answered, "Browning University Orchestra Presents: An Evening of Classical French Music."

CHAPTER 16

D aniel had arranged to meet his students in the center of Browning's concert hall lobby. It was a lovely space to wait, with its lush red carpet, dramatic oil-painted murals, and carved staircases that reminded him so strongly of an opera house he'd visited in Vienna. A colossal rendering of Browning's coat of arms adorned the upper balcony, and a twinkling crystal chandelier bathed the entire place in a soft, yellow glow. There was ample beauty to take in, but Daniel's eyes were fixed only on the hall's double-door entrance.

Though his outward appearance radiated calm, the incessant tap of his foot against the carpet betrayed a frantic energy. Where was his team? Most of tonight's concertgoers had already settled into their seats. He was in great danger of being left here alone, a thought that bothered him almost as much as the fact that he *was* bothered about it. When a red-coated usher at Daniel's left announced there were but five minutes until the curtain rose, he tugged anxiously at a cufflink and debated whether to abandon the evening altogether.

He had just begun worrying whether he had overdressed for the occasion when a young mother dragged her loudly protesting son into the hall, providing Daniel with much-needed distraction. The harried woman was clearly determined the lad be exposed to the finer things in life.

"But I want to go to the cinema!" the red-faced boy sobbed. "I don't like vio-violins! It will be bo-bo-boring, mummy!"

Poor chap. No doubt Daniel's students felt the same.

Most of them, anyway.

With a jolt, his eyes fell upon the sight of Jenny Ellison walking in alone. She gazed around the hall in wonder, lingering for a moment in front of a large mural of Orpheus with his lyre. When her eyes finally met Daniel's, she waved and walked swiftly over. He assumed what he hoped was a professional yet pleasant expression.

"Good evening, Miss Ellison."

"Good evening."

Her smile was far warmer than he'd allowed his to be. Daniel noticed she was a little pink-cheeked from the cold and that she wore no hat. A moment passed. He searched for something else to say and had almost settled on asking how her walk over had been when she spoke again.

"Thank you so much for planning this, Dr. Carter. I've really been looking forward to it." She looked with interest at another large mural behind him. "This place is so lovely. I've never been here before," she whispered confidingly.

"May I take your coat?" Daniel offered. He immediately regretted doing so; it seemed too intimate of a gesture, but almost as immediately he shook himself. This was mere politeness, after all, and there was nothing wrong with being gentlemanly. Jenny had already started unbuttoning her wrap. As Daniel helped her shrug out of it, he wished for a second time he had not offered. Underneath she wore a red dress, attractively cut and straight skirted. A single glance told him it was fitted perfectly to her curves, and that it would be best to keep his eyes on the carpet.

He quickly left to check the garment at the front desk. While walking back, he managed to take in the rest of her from a respectable distance. It struck him that there was something different about her tonight. A lightness of her bearing, perhaps the natural result of an evening away from books and studies.

Or perhaps it was the fact that she, too, had deemed this occasion grand enough for special ornament. A tiny gold chain sparkled at her throat, and a smaller version of the same adorned her wrist. Miss Ellison's brown hair flowed gently over her shoulders, and her dark eyes strained upwards as she admired the huge chandelier. Her entire being glowed with the anticipation of delight. Were Daniel not a professor, he might be able to admit that she looked, well, *stunning*. As it was, he distracted himself by readying another talking point.

"I'm afraid Spencer canceled on us," he announced as he rejoined her. "I think there was a rather tempting indoor rugby match going on across campus."

"Jillian isn't coming either," Jenny said quietly. "I think she had a prior engagement."

This was good news for several reasons, not the least of which being it saved him from Jillian's overtures.

"That just leaves Howard and Max," he tallied. "But there's no sign of either of them yet, and the performance is about to start ..."

Daniel felt more comfortable with their absence than he would let on, but he cast Miss Ellison a questioning glance. He wasn't certain whether she would want to stay in such circumstances. To his surprise, she appeared completely at ease. Cheerful, even.

"Shall we take our seats, then?"

He nodded and was dangerously close to offering his arm when the front door of the hall burst open. With a flash of – what was the feeling, irritation? No, not so strong as that. Disappointment, perhaps – Daniel saw that the latecomer was Max. The boy ran frantically towards the pair of them, gasping for air.

"I'm sorry I'm late, Professor." Max winced and clutched a stitch in his side. "We had cleaning inspections at our flat today, and I had to re-do the kitchen. Took me almost two hours."

"Don't worry, Max," Daniel replied in a voice that was perhaps less welcoming than it ought to have been. "We should take our seats now."

"Right!" Max responded, rubbing his hands together cheerily. "Music. Excellent. In we go!"

The three of them entered the concert space and made their way slowly to seats 111, 112, and 113. The inside of the hall was even lovelier than the foyer. Twelve smaller versions of the lobby's crystal chandelier hung overhead, and the red upholstered seats looked surprisingly plush. Daniel hung back as they neared the chairs. To his immense satisfaction Jenny ended up in the middle. He settled in comfortably at her left.

"So, uh, how long is this meant to be?" Max asked Daniel, a little too casually.

"Shh ... it's starting!" Jenny whispered as the house lights dimmed and the curtain rose. Browning University's orchestra was greeted with thunderous applause, as was the fluffy-haired conductor who waltzed onstage. Bowing deeply in thanks, the maestro launched his players into a lively rendition of George Bizet's *Carmen* overture. Daniel thought it the perfect opener for tonight: the strains were energetic, rousing, and cheering in a way this post-war community still sorely needed. The audience clapped along appreciatively until its end with very un-English exuberance.

Debussy's "Prelude to the Afternoon of a Faun" followed, hauntingly beautiful and serene.

"I love this one," Jenny murmured. "So peaceful."

Daniel privately agreed and found himself wondering what else they might mutually enjoy. The orchestra moved seamlessly from one piece to the next, performing a surprisingly robust repertoire: Satie, Fauré, and Poulenc, among others. Ravel's "Boléro" came next, seventeen minutes long and monotonously repetitive. He bent his head a fraction of an inch nearer Jenny's.

"This one's fine, for the first ten minutes," he mumbled to her. She stifled a laugh, filling Daniel with an odd sense of triumph. Max was less amused; he had long since fallen asleep and was snoring loudly. Daniel supposed dozing was understandable. Despite the glare of the stage lights, the concert hall was surprisingly black. He could barely see his concert program, let alone Jenny's outline to his right. Yet for the first time in a long while – the end of the war, to be precise – the darkness didn't feel as though it might smother him. Instead it felt private. Intimate, even. It was as though all of Daniel's senses had suddenly been heightened. He became keenly aware of every movement Jenny made, every shift of elbow or leg, every contented sigh at the end of a number.

When a cello and piano struck up Saint-Saëns' beautiful "Le Cygne," she leaned forward in rapture and closed her eyes. So fixated was Jenny on the piece that Daniel could watch her in no danger of being caught. So, he did. He slowly took in her smile, her shining face, her complete attunement to the beauty of the music.

Somehow the swelling, resonant notes of the cello unbridled Daniel's own defenses. Militantly repressed feelings stirred poignantly in him, and for once he did not fight them. He examined them with interest. He let them breathe and have their own life.

She was lovely. She was interesting.

... And he cared.

For the first time all term, that thought did not frighten him. In this space – this tiny moment of music, and magic, and madness – there could be no danger in acknowledging that truth.

The music stopped, and a crash of applause jerked Daniel back to reality, and Max out of his nap.

"Wha'?" the lad grumbled, sitting bolt upright. "Is it over?"

"Yes." Jenny patted his arm consolingly. "It's over."

"Oh, thank goodness." Max let out an enormous yawn and checked his watch. "Two hours. Blimey."

Guests had already begun pouring out of the concert hall. "Let's try to beat the crowd," Daniel suggested. The three of them strode to the lobby, where Daniel left to fetch Jenny's coat. When he returned, he found his assistant taking his leave.

"Well!" Max ran a hand through his tousled hair. "That was – uh – long. But it was marvelous, Professor Carter, just marvelous. A resounding success. I'm afraid I have to run, though. Some friends of mine are catching a late-night showing of *Dark Passage*, and I don't want to miss it." He gave a comical jerk, almost a bow, in Daniel's direction. "Goodbye, Professor! Goodbye, Jenny."

Max sped off, leaving Jenny and Daniel alone once more. She looked up at him with something akin to curiosity, but said nothing. Daniel covered the moment of silence by helping her shrug on the coat. His earlier thoughts lingered like a lovely fragrance, and it took considerable restraint not to let his hands rest gently on her shoulders as she buttoned it. He cleared his throat and stepped back.

"Thank you, Professor," Jenny said, turning to face him. Her eyes sparkled in the dim chandelier light. "That was exquisite. I loved every minute of it."

"Good." Daniel smiled. "You deserved it. You've put in more hours at that lab than the rest of the team combined."

Jenny gave a merry little laugh. "I don't know about that."

"It's true," he insisted. "I've seen the time logs, you know."

She shrugged. "Maybe. But it hasn't felt like work. I've enjoyed it." She watched the exiting guests, now not quite meeting his eye. "Well, thank you again, Professor. This was simply wonderful. But I suppose I ought to get back too. Goodnight."

"How did you get here?" Daniel called, taking a short step after her before his thoughts had fully collected themselves.

Miss Ellison turned back very quickly. "I walked. I live close to campus."

Concern stirred within him. "You're not planning to walk back alone, are you? At this time of night?"

"Oh, no. I'm taking the bus."

"Do the buses even run so late?"

She nodded. "Every half hour until midnight."

"But the station is on the other side of campus," he objected. "You'd be waiting in the cold, alone."

"Oh, I really don't mind."

Daniel had made up his own mind. "May I walk you back?"

Blushing and stuttering, she began to protest. "Oh no, I couldn't possibly—"

"Please, it's no trouble," he said. "It's nearly ten. The next bus won't be along until half past. This was a school event, and it's my responsibility to make sure you get home safely. Walking would take much less time." He strode a few paces towards the door, which felt reckless considering she'd not yet agreed to the plan.

For a moment Jenny hung back. But at last, she nodded. "That's very kind of you. Thank you, Professor."

Daniel gestured politely towards the door. Jenny hesitantly joined him, and feeling happier than he could confess with the arrangement, he fell into step beside her.

CHAPTER 17

Though Jenny's apartment lay only a mile and a half from campus, the tree-lined route that led to it felt as threatening as a minefield. The explosive risk here, of course, was being seen in Dr. Carter's company. Agreeing to let him walk her back was seeming more foolish by the minute. What if they should run into someone she knew? What might they think?

What might they wrongly assume?

She soothed herself with the knowledge that few people were out at this hour. Casual passersby could not speculate anything out of the ordinary. He was only thirty, after all, and she was twenty-three. Nothing untoward could be said about their coupling (at least in the walking sense). Still, the potential for gossip and unwarranted judgment troubled her, and Jenny made sure to keep at least a few feet away from him during the entire journey.

Dr. Carter did not seem to share her concerns. By all appearances he was utterly contented. Indeed, he'd hardly spoken to her at all since leaving the concert. After exchanging a few pleasantries about the music, he seemed more than content to walk in calm, companionable silence.

With her thoughts as occupied as they were, Jenny had no

objection to the quiet. Outside of the classroom and lab setting, she couldn't think of a single word to say to the handsome young professor. Twice she had considered commenting on the weather, or the unusual solitude of the lane, but just as swiftly she dismissed the topics. Far better to endure a heavy silence than to bore them both with mindless chatter.

She hugged her coat more closely around her, wishing she had worn a thicker one. Though it was only mid-November, the night air made it feel more like January. Sneaking a sidelong glance at Dr. Carter, she noted that he was far better outfitted for the temperature. He wore dark slacks, a long wool coat, and a green plaid scarf. His gloved hands swung cheerfully at his sides as he walked.

"We're nearly there now," Jenny murmured, just for something to say. It was true. The journey was more than halfway over.

"All right."

Silence fell between them again. Jenny stared up at him as they walked, this time making no effort to conceal that she was doing so.

Professor. Professor Daniel Carter.

It was hard to believe he had already been teaching university-level courses for three years. Many times over the term, Jenny had pondered how someone so young had achieved a professorship. Since there was no better topic of conversation at her fingertips, she made up her mind to find out.

"How did you do it?" she asked, the question bursting suddenly from her lips. "How did you become a professor so early in your career?"

Dr. Carter chewed the inside of his cheek. "Dumb luck, I suppose."

"Truly. I'd like to know."

At first, he didn't answer her. Their silence was punctuated only by the crisp crunch of leaves underfoot. But then ...

"I entered university early," he said simply. "At fourteen."

So that was it. He had enrolled in school as a youth, practically as a boy. She examined his well-cut profile, paying particular heed to his intelligent brow and dark, thoughtful eyes. Jenny could easily picture the teenage Dr. Carter: brilliant, gifted, and prematurely thrust into the adult world. His serious nature was even more understandable now.

"You attended Browning?"

"Yes."

"Where you studied under Dr. Miller?"

"Yes."

"And then you went straight into your doctoral program? The dual program at Cambridge and Harvard?"

Dr. Carter looked at her curiously. Jenny realized with embarrassment that she sounded suspiciously well-informed. She silently cursed Jillian and Nyra for the thoroughness of their research.

"Yes," he confirmed. "With a bit of interruption, but ... yes."

"Because of the war?"

Dr. Carter nodded grimly and once more fell silent. Jenny knew it would be best to drop the subject – she remembered from Jillian's report that he either would not or could not talk about the war – but there was something so lovely about asking him these questions openly. She could not help but enjoy the prospect of unraveling campus gossip.

Her earlier discomfort was quickly fading. Walking side by side in this moment, it felt almost as though she were talking to a friend. After his kindness tonight, and his gallantry in walking her home, she was tentatively starting to regard him as such. Could a professor be both a teacher and a friend? Would Browning allow it?

Would he?

"Dr. Carter, what did you do during the war?"

He stopped. Turning slowly, he faced Jenny head-on. Again, he did not speak.

She held her breath as his dark blue eyes scanned every inch of her face. Dr. Carter seemed to be slowly studying her, as though looking for malintent. Though she shivered, Jenny held his pene-trating gaze. In some vague corner of her mind, she realized the two had drifted closer together as they walked.

"Intelligence," he said at last, his breath forming clouds in the night air. "But beyond that ... I'm not sure I should say."

Jenny's face broke into a smile. "Then you *were* a spy."

To her great surprise, the young professor chuckled and scratched his jaw. "I'm really not sure how to answer that. I don't think I was."

She resumed walking, treading more cheerfully this time. "That's exactly what a spy would say."

Still laughing, Dr. Carter overtook her in a few steps.

"I promise to keep this private," she assured him as they walked. "There are enough rumors flying about."

"Hmm." Dr. Carter nodded gravely. He had clearly caught wind of a few of those rumors himself. "That I was a double agent, for example. A hit man for Mussolini. Or that I single-handedly shot down a fleet of German BF-109s."

"Or that you were an assassin," Jenny spouted off. "And a weapons broker, and a captain, and—"

"Hang on," Dr. Carter interrupted, looking almost offended. "I was a captain."

Turning away to hide her laughter, Jenny realized with a jolt that they were arriving at her building.

"We're here," she announced, feeling inexplicably nervous as they approached the two-story block of flats. "Thank you so much for – for walking me back. It was very kind of you."

He nodded and gave half a smile. "You're welcome. I'll" – he motioned awkwardly at his side – "I'll just ... wait here. Until you get inside."

"Goodnight, then."

" ... Goodnight."

Jenny sped lightly up the apartment steps and through her

door. She did not look behind her as she closed it. But once inside, she couldn't resist peeking out from behind the parlor curtain to see if he had remained.

Dr. Carter stood looking up at her landing. After lingering for a moment, he began slowly backing away from the building. Shrugging his collar over his neck, he turned on his heel and started the cold trek to wherever he lived.

"Captain," Jenny whispered into the darkness.

CHAPTER 18

"What the devil are you whistling for?"

"Mmm? What's that?" Daniel replied, stopping his merry tune.

"Are you hard of hearing now?" Antony chortled. "I thought that only happened to us elderly folk."

The two men were walking down the third-floor hallway, each with stacks of unread Amity applications under their arms. It was true that Daniel felt most unlike himself this morning. Despite it being a Monday, the day ahead seemed especially bright. There was only Palaeography and Advanced Theories of Excavation to teach, and that light schedule was reason enough to be cheerful. More-over, a thick blanket of snow had fallen over the weekend, which he had decided was a good omen. Though he still had hours of Amity reading to slog through, Daniel had never felt more unburdened.

"You were whistling," Antony repeated. "Have been all morn-ing, as a matter of fact. Why?"

"No reason." Daniel shifted the stack of applications under his arm. "Just the ... joy of being alive, I suppose."

"Good heavens," Dr. Miller chuckled. "I hope it isn't catching."

"Hope what isn't catching?" called a familiar reedy voice. Dr.

Chilcott was approaching from the other end of the hall, sporting yet another pinstriped suit and a garishly purple tie.

"The joy of living," Dr. Miller answered with a good-humored wink at Daniel. "Our Dr. Carter is feeling rather merry this morning."

"Really? Well, I'm relieved to hear it, Carter. I feared you might be a bit downcast after the disappointment of the artifact."

Daniel smothered a groan. So much for non-disclosure agreements. "And what disappointment might that be, Chilcott?"

The man innocently held up both hands. "I don't know any of the particulars, of course. Your students have all been very discreet. But – forgive me – I gathered that the contents of the stone were not so very groundbreaking after all, judging by the disappointed faces going in and out of the lab. Such a shame. It seemed so promising."

"A find is a find, William," Dr. Miller said, hoisting up his slipping stack of files. "Any contribution to our field is valuable, be it large or small."

"I'm just encouraged that my site is still yielding," Daniel added. "Not everyone can say the same. The ancient world is shrinking, is it not?"

Chilcott's gray eyes narrowed at this subtle jibe over his own lifeless plot. Another time Daniel might not have gloated, but he harbored a growing resentment towards his colleague, and not merely on his own account. It was hard to forgive Chilcott's shameless campaign to replace Antony as dean.

"You're right, of course," the man replied calmly. "You are fortunate to be so happily placed." His expression shifted to one of pitying concern. "But is the transcription proceeding on time? I'd be more than happy to lend my assistance, if you find you're at risk of missing your deadline."

"Thank you, but that won't be necessary."

"Are you certain? I advise you to accept my help, Dr. Carter. Consider that an unpaid student team will not stay engaged in the work for long. I've seen it time and time again. They'll stop coming in when their exams begin to pile up, or when the holidays approach, mark my words. It would be a shame to return a half-finished project to the Egyptian government. Why, they might never trust Browning again!"

"As I said, Chilcott. We'll be fine."

Chilcott's concern faded into a mild snarl. "Very well. I only wish to be of service. You'll let me know if you change your mind, of course?" He paused. "Just one more question, Dr. Carter. Is it true that – of course, I might have misunderstood your student – is it true that you permit your assistants to work alone?"

"That's right."

"Unsupervised?"

"Yes. Once trained. Why?"

Dr. Chilcott laughed silkily. "What progressive ideas these young professors have, don't you think, Antony?"

Daniel's dark eyes flashed with anger, but he controlled his irritation well. "Are you making your way to a point, William?"

After a dramatic pause, Chilcott sighed. It was all masterfully done, Daniel thought – the careful wheedling, the manipulative sympathy, the false concern.

"It's just that your practices have sparked some interesting discussion among our colleagues," Chilcott murmured. "About whether such an artifact could truly be safe in the hands of an unsupervised twenty-something."

"How interesting, Chilcott. I find my students rise to the challenges I set before them and flourish best in an environment of trust."

"Is it really wise to stake your reputation on that, Carter? Let them practice in our simulated lab, it will be education enough. Bring some faculty onto your project, real professionals who can be trusted with the work."

Daniel's suspicions that Chilcott wanted to derail – or worse, annex – the conservation project were now confirmed. "Thanks for the advice," he replied coolly, "but I have no intention of dismissing my team." He nodded to the clock above the man's head. "Five minutes past. You're late for Human Origins, Chilcott."

The professor scowled. "So I am. Good day, gentlemen." With a cold jerk of his head, he departed for his classroom.

"Pompous, preening, presumptuous," Antony muttered under his breath, still struggling with his stack of papers. "If there is a more arrogant, self-absorbed man to be found at Browning, I'll eat my hat. The fellow's insufferable."

"Odious," Daniel muttered. The word stirred a memory, and he smiled.

"He'd love nothing better than to take your project over," Antony warned. A large chunk of his files finally slipped to the floor.

"So I gather," Daniel replied, stooping to collect them. "Don't worry, I can manage him."

"Yes, but Daniel …" Dr. Miller paused before whispering, "I need a word. Come into my office for a moment." He shuffled away, leaving a very puzzled Daniel to follow close behind.

The dean's office was not far. Together they entered the well-lit space, which was surprisingly humble given Dr. Miller's status at the school. It was little more than a desk surrounded by shelves of books, beautifully bound in colors of scarlet, indigo, brown, and green. An intricately carved cuckoo-clock ticked dutifully above the window, and some Greek banners had been draped clumsily over the panes by Antony's own hand.

The old professor plopped his files unceremoniously upon the desk. "Chocolate?" he asked, brandishing a small gold box.

"Thanks, but I'd much rather know what's on your mind, Antony."

The dean picked out a caramel cream. "Well, my boy," he began. "I've said it before, and I'll say it again. You need to watch your back where Chilcott is concerned."

Daniel sat down wearily. "What's he done now?"

"It's not what he's done, it's what he's *doing*," Antony warned through a sticky mouthful. "Spreading rumors about your project, trying to sabotage you in the eyes of the rest of the department. He's ruining any chance you have of becoming a leader here."

Daniel let out a short, barking laugh. "He's wasting his time. Me, a department leader? I've only been teaching for three years. I'm not even tenured."

"Nevertheless," Antony muttered, "whatever his reasons, it seems William has marked you out as his most dangerous rival."

"What's he been saying to the other professors?" Daniel asked. He had always got on rather well with the other men in the department, and as ridiculous as Chilcott's undignified smear campaign was, it rankled him.

"He's touting your relative inexperience, and your – forgive me, Daniel – your tendency to keep to yourself." Antony grimaced. "Despite his flaws as an educator, Chilcott has great pull with some of the more established professors. He's trying to convince them that letting your students work on this project is a clear sign of your juniority, your naiveté."

"Antony," Daniel said firmly, "you know as well as I do that if we don't give the students opportunities for practical training, they'll be rubbish upon reaching the field. It's our job to set them up for success, and if we—"

Dr. Miller held up a hand to silence him. "I do not question your methods, my boy. Indeed, I wish more of the old hats in our field would follow your lead. The world has changed since the war, I fully admit, and it couldn't hurt to modernize. But I want you to keep a low profile from now on, do you understand? Don't engage with Chilcott, do not engage. Warn your team off talking to him. I don't want him finding any more ammunition to use against you."

Daniel regarded him with growing unease. Though the old dean's cautions were pragmatic, his last words, and the heaviness with which they were imbued, made him suspect a deeper trouble simmered beneath them.

"Antony, what aren't you saying? What aren't you telling me?"

There was a heavy pause. Then the old man sighed. "Oh, bother. I wasn't going to make anything of this, Daniel. I really wasn't. But given Chilcott's scheming, it seems I shouldn't just dismiss it out of hand."

With a grave look, he reached into the drawer of his desk and brought out a blank white envelope.

"As I opened my office this morning, I found *this* stashed under the door." Dr. Miller opened the envelope and pulled out a single sheet of paper, typed but not signed.

"What is it?"

"An anonymous note of complaint," Antony murmured. "Against you."

After a few moments of silence, Daniel pressed his fingertips together and leaned them softly against his mouth.

"What sort of complaint?" he asked, with a gentle clearing of his throat.

"It alleges that you were seen in the company of a young lady last Friday evening. The note claims that the meeting was a ... a late-night tryst of some kind." Dr. Miller glanced up apologetically. "Normally I would be overjoyed upon hearing such news. But this young lady is reported as being a student at Browning." He crisply folded the paper. "That's it. No other information is given."

Daniel lifted his gaze, his fingertips still pressed together.

"Well?" Antony prompted expectantly.

"Well?"

"My dear boy, is there any truth in it?"

He gave a tiny, almost imperceptible nod.

"You mean – oh dear." Pulling out a dull silk handkerchief, Antony mopped vigorously at his brow. "Oh dear, oh dear. I thought this might have been a prank of some sort, but—"

"There is *some* truth in it, Antony," Daniel interrupted, dropping his hands. "You'll recall that last Friday was the planned outing for my research team. A trip to Browning's concert hall, sanctioned and paid for by the Archaeology department."

"Yes." Dr. Miller sounded more than a little relieved. "Oh, yes. I'd forgotten that."

"One student who attended planned to walk home alone. I escorted her back for reasons of safety. That is all."

"Oh, but Daniel, think how easily this has been misinterpreted," Dr. Miller reproached him. "It was very good of you, to be sure, but—"

"I couldn't let her walk home alone, Antony." Daniel stood and paced the tiny office. "Three to five young women are attacked at Browning every year."

"Daniel, my boy, I do not doubt your intentions. I have absolutely no doubt that everything was above board and as it should be."

"It certainly was."

"But why didn't you just call a cab for the girl?"

Daniel stopped his pacing. "I-it honestly did not cross my mind."

"Well perhaps it should, next time," Antony said somewhat crossly. He threw the letter onto the desk and interlaced his fingers with a huff. "Dr. Carter. I intend to keep this incident out of the department's earshot. But make no mistake. Chilcott is working against you."

Daniel sat down heavily. "I know."

"And he could absolutely use something like this to his advantage," Dr. Miller said, thumping his finger repeatedly upon the letter. "Daniel, you know how much I hate sounding ... well, paternal. But as your mentor, and your friend, I really feel I must put you on your guard. You are our youngest professor. One of our best and brightest, it is true, but the youngest, nonetheless."

His expression softened. "The students will naturally be drawn to you. They may even try to befriend you. But a young professor must work twice as hard to maintain his authority. Unfair as it may be, you must hold yourself to a stricter standard of conduct than our other teachers. You must be always above, always apart – always at arm's length. Escorting a young woman home, or any other act of kindness towards the fairer sex, could easily be misconstrued. I don't want you giving Chilcott any reason to exploit you." He paused before ascertaining gravely, "Do you understand this?"

Daniel kept his eyes on the carpet, not wanting to betray the tangle of emotions behind them. He was at once angry, remorseful, humiliated, and defiant. Of course his actions had been unusual, but they could never be called inappropriate.

And neither were his intentions. After all, he had only meant … but no. Here Daniel could not afford to deal honestly with his intentions. With brutal urgency, he snuffed the subtlest, tenderest suggestions that had begun to creep into his brain. He labeled them as foolish, selfish, dangerous even.

And not just for him.

Slowly, he looked up at Antony.

"I understand."

☙

Daniel felt almost numb as he lectured later that morning. He kept his eyes on the classroom's back wall, describing Incan Khipu with the same level of passion he might use if reading out a local telephone directory. His flat affect quickly rippled through the class. Several young men snoozed languidly in the back of the hall, and the rest of his students were becoming visibly less engaged by the minute. All except the young woman in the right-hand corner of the room. Even without looking, Daniel knew she was copying his every word with rapt, unnerving attention.

The chime of the bell was a merciful release. He mechanically gathered his materials, heart racing as a clump of students pushed towards the exit. Snippets of conversation filled his ear – debates over the last rugby match, and reports of an adder that had been spotted in the courtyard this morning. He shut out the sound, keeping his eyes dutifully fixed on the tile floor. To his great distress, a pair of familiar green pumps soon appeared in his view.

"That was a fascinating lecture, Professor," her voice sunnily intoned, causing his heart to somersault painfully. "I'd always assumed Incan knot records were used only for accounting purposes. Can you recommend any outside readings? Perhaps with photographic examples?"

With excruciating determination, Daniel turned his back. "I should ask Mr. Prewett if I were you. It's safe to say he has our department's catalogue memorized. Good day to you."

Though several other students were approaching him, Daniel marched rapidly to his office and barricaded the door against their questions, their prying eyes, and most of all, the image of one bewildered and slightly hurt Jenny Ellison.

CHAPTER 19

That was the start of a very long week for Daniel. Dr. Miller's words had shaken him more than he cared to admit, and to atone for his lack of judgment he reverted to a highly professional, distant, and, he might add, dull presence over his students. No longer did Daniel walk the halls and public spaces. When he wasn't lecturing, he scrupulously marked papers in his study. His nights he spent at home, reading through dozens of Amity applications.

The lab he entirely avoided. He sensed it wouldn't be safe to return there for some time.

After two days of such isolation, Daniel was understandably eager for his next Paleography class. He had prepared a particularly good lecture on a fascinating subject: Mayan glyphs. They were the only Mesoamerican writings that could still be substantially translated, and as such were a rare treat to study. During the tedium of the last evenings, Daniel had found his mind drifting constantly to how she – that is, how they – might adore the material.

At long last, the two weary days were over and Wednesday came. By five minutes to eleven Daniel was in position at the front of the lecture hall. Most of his class had already taken their seats, but the front right corner of the room remained notably empty. Odd, he thought. What could be—

"Professor Carter!"

A rather hoarse voice disrupted Daniel's thoughts. Howard rushed towards him, a look of utmost penitence on his face.

"Professor!" he croaked. "I'm so, so sorry I missed the team outing last week. I meant to come, but I caught a terrible cold that morning, and I almost came anyway, but then I was sneezing so often that I thought it best ..."

"It's quite all right, Howard." Daniel gave the lad's shoulder a rough pat as he walked to the podium. "These things happen."

Relieved, Howard trotted away to his seat. The classroom buzzed with excitement over the hour ahead, and Daniel's own anticipation was rising. When the bell chimed at eleven, however, Miss Ellison had still not arrived.

Her chair was the only unfilled seat in the room. After five minutes of pleasantries and stalling for time, Daniel was forced to begin the lecture without her. Ten minutes passed, then twenty, then thirty, and still Miss Ellison did not come. It was the first lecture she had missed the entire term, and her absence disrupted Daniel's focus completely. He even had to correct his drawing of a jaguar.

When the bell rang to end the hour, he cleared the podium with irritable speed. Miss Ellison had missed the entire presentation. She now risked falling behind in her coursework.

And there were two whole days until the next class.

As he chided himself for his weakness, his childish disappointment, a fragment of conversation wound its way to his ear.

"Hiya, Margie," someone said cheerily. "Where's Jenny today?"

Daniel glanced upwards. The speaker was the lanky fellow who sat in the second row of his class. Peter Collier, if Daniel remembered correctly. A fourth year, and a professed admirer of Miss Ellison.

Margie shrugged. "Not sure. I haven't seen her all morning. Knowing Jenny, she probably just got stuck in a textbook somewhere. Must have lost track of time."

"Let's look for her together," Peter suggested. The two left the classroom, taking all talk of Miss Ellison with them. There was nothing for Daniel to do but wait impatiently for the next class, but when Friday came, Miss Ellison still did not attend.

He began to feel rather worried. It was most uncharacteristic of her to be absent for one class, to say nothing of two. If she kept this up, she would miss the entire Mesoamerican segment of the course. After a twenty-minute tangent on Isthmian scripts, Daniel had made up his mind. He would get to the bottom of this. Something was clearly amiss, and whatever Dr. Miller had cautioned, it was surely the minimum of Daniel's responsibility (as Miss Ellison's instructor) to find out why she was short-changing her education.

At the end of Friday's lecture, Daniel posted himself like a sentinel at the exit.

"Yes, my pleasure. Thank you, same to you, have a nice day," he said distractedly to the students bidding him farewell. When an auburn-haired girl with freckles and a long, good-natured face approached, he gently held up a hand to stop her.

"Excuse me, Miss ... Payne? Marjorie, is that right?"

"M-me, sir?" The girl's green eyes widened. "I ... yes, that's me, but everyone just calls me Margie." She giggled, fumbling nervously with the strap of her bookbag.

"May I have a word, Margie?"

She let out another shrill giggle, then swallowed as heat rushed into her cheeks. Her features contorted with concern. "Is this about my last paper, sir? My reference page? I wasn't sure about that final source, but I checked with Max, and—"

"What? Oh, no, not at all, I'm sure it was fine. You're a friend of Miss Ellison's, I think?"

"Yes, sir."

Daniel put his hands in his pockets, arranging his features into what he hoped was a neutral expression. "I noticed she's missed quite a few of our classes, which puts her at risk of falling behind in our course. Do you know where she's been? Is she – is she sick, perhaps?"

"Oh, no sir," Margie quickly replied. "She's fine, I saw her just this morning. We live together, you know – that is, we share a flat – and she did say she'd be in class today, but she won't fall behind, you can be sure of that. She's been borrowing my notes to keep up."

Daniel chewed his tongue and stewed over this new piece of information. "I see. Thank you, Miss Payne."

"You're welcome, Dr. Carter," she replied faintly, hurrying away before any other question could be asked.

So. Miss Ellison was skipping lectures. Daniel could easily guess the reason why. Once the lecture hall had emptied, he climbed the stairs to the third-floor Archaeology lab. When he arrived outside its door, he slid the time log off its hanging clipboard. A single glance confirmed his suspicions.

Jenny Ellison – Monday – 8am–6pm
Jenny Ellison – Tuesday – 3pm–10pm
Jenny Ellison – Wednesday – 11am–7pm
Jenny Ellison – Thursday – 2pm–6pm
Jenny Ellison – Friday – 7am

She had been spending entire days in the Archaeology Lab. Daniel's lectures could not have been the only ones she was skipping. If the log was to be believed, she was hard at work there even now.

Alone.

Setting his jaw, Daniel turned the doorknob.

The lab's layout had changed dramatically since the last time he'd entered. His team had been carefully photographing and copying the glyphs, and equipment covered every available surface. Huge sheets of archival paper were draped over the furniture, making the place look like an estate shrouded for auction.

In the center of the room sat Jenny, leaning over the workbench. She was studying the fully cleaned stone with a camera in one hand and her chin in the other. A little wrinkle in her forehead indicated a state of the deep concentration; so deep, in fact, that she didn't notice Daniel had entered.

With Dr. Miller's warnings about student-teacher propriety ringing in his ear, he left the door wide open as he approached the bench. Still, Jenny did not look up. Daniel was barely an arm's length away from her now, yet something in the carved slab had completely absorbed her attention. After an awkward moment of silence, Daniel hemmed and hawed.

Jenny's eyes snapped up, glazing with surprise. "Oh – good morning, Dr. Carter." She looked at the clock. "Blast, noon already? Good afternoon, then."

Daniel did not reply as he assessed the shadows under her eyes, the weary smile lingering about her mouth. It was clear that, yet again, she had been burning the midnight oil.

"Miss Ellison," he began, in a tone that was unexpectedly flinty given his concern over her absences. He held up the telltale time log. "I couldn't help but notice that you have logged twenty-nine hours at the lab this week alone."

"Hmm?" Jenny had returned to studying the stone. "Oh, yes. Something like that, I think."

"You've been skipping classes to do so, I presume? Mine, Dr. Miller's, and Dr. Valverde's, I can assume from this log."

"That's right," she confirmed. Her eyes remained fixed on the slab, one finger hovering above a carved cobra.

Daniel stared at her, not knowing whether to laugh or to reproach. He settled for a solemn warning somewhere in the middle. "Miss Ellison. I appreciate how much you are doing to help us meet our deadline. I really do. But you cannot let your work in the lab detract from your other coursework. Skipping classes will only—"

"Dr. Carter?" Jenny interrupted. She had clearly not been listening to a word he'd said. "Could you come and take look at this glyph, please?"

"What?"

"This glyph here. Something is very ... odd."

An odd glyph?

He hadn't noticed anything out of the ordinary during the preservation work. With his irritation melting into curiosity, he pushed aside all warnings from Dr. Miller and sat beside Jenny at the workbench.

She turned to face him with a frown. "It's been bothering me all week. The same thought, over and over again. Why would this stone have been buried like that, in a brick-making pit? So far away from the temple?"

Daniel nodded. The thought had occurred to him as well, but having worked on ancient sites for years, he knew how common it was to find refuse holes like this. "Dumping grounds have always existed, even in the ancient world," he explained. "This stone was probably debris from prior builds."

But Jenny only shook her head. "I just don't think it was debris. Look at the edges. They're all beautifully smooth and expertly fashioned, except for this one." She pointed to the right-hand corner of the slab, which, now that Daniel looked properly at it, was much more roughly shaped.

"There are chisel marks here." She pointed to several deep gouges in the stone. "It's almost as if this mural had once been part of something larger, like a wall or building, but had been pried off. Hurriedly. And intentionally discarded."

Daniel approached the carvings with greater interest. Having had ... *other matters* ... on his mind the last few weeks, it had completely escaped him that the stone bore any signs of intentional damage.

"Pried off?" he murmured to himself.

"Then there's this." Jenny pulled a large sheet of archival paper towards them both. "I noticed it when I started transcribing the glyphs. The markings are ... well, they're very strange. Look at the shepherd's crook in the third line. It's supposed to face left, like the bird. All the glyphs face left, so they should be read left to right. But this one is right-facing."

"It could have been a mistake in the copying," Daniel suggested. Still, his eyes moved rapidly over the stone. Even without reading it in its entirety, he could see what Jenny meant. Something was off. Something looked wrong.

"I thought so too," Jenny continued, pulling on a curl in frustration. "But that's not the only deformed glyph. The nebu is upside down. The eye is backwards. The cobra's tail is truncated. And the fold of cloth curves sometimes to the left and sometimes to the right. It doesn't make any sense; it makes the line almost impossible to read."

There was a long, silent interval.

"Miss Ellison," Daniel said, so quietly that she had to lean in to understand him. "Shut the door."

After a stunned pause, she jumped up to do so.

"What is it?" she whispered urgently.

"Lock it."

"Why?" she said, clicking it shut. "What's wrong?"

"This is a code."

CHAPTER 20

J enny stared at him blankly.

A code? No. Surely, she must have misheard him. When her blood began to soar through her veins, however, and her heartbeat matched the frantic energy of Dr. Carter's movements as he cleared away equipment, she knew she could not have done.

"A *what?*" she whispered, nearly choking on the words. "How ... are you *sure?*"

"Positive." Dr. Carter snapped his fingers. "Hang on."

He rifled through the workbench drawer until he found a small white placard. Jenny could see that it read "Lab Closed for Cleaning" in dingy letters. He tossed it to her.

"Put that on the outside of the door. I don't want any interruptions, not until we know exactly what we have here. We'll wipe down a shelf or two, so it's not a lie," he added with a lopsided grin.

Jenny immediately hung the placard and bolted the door.

"Who did these transcriptions?" Dr. Carter asked, pulling several archival sheets towards him.

"I did," Jenny said, her voice still sputtering with shock. "No one else came in this week."

Dr. Carter looked around at the many transcribed sheets and crisply developed photographs. "You did all this work alone?"

"Yes. Well, most of it, anyway."

Dr. Carter's mouth twitched. "Right. Well done." He walked to his desk and picked up the telephone receiver. "Chicken or tuna?"

"I beg your pardon?"

"Sandwiches," he answered matter-of-factly, spinning the rotary. "I can order some in from campus dining."

Jenny stared at the young professor in amazement. After jubilantly announcing there was a three-thousand-year-old encoded message on the stone, his next priority was ... lunch?

"Forgive me, Dr. Carter," Jenny murmured. "But are you sure now is the right time for ... ?"

He glanced up at her with the receiver still pressed against his ear. "We're going to need our strength to crack this, Miss Ellison."

"We?"

"Of course. You don't think I'd try to solve this on my own, do you? It was you who found it, after all."

Jenny gave a reluctant smile.

"Chicken *and* tuna, then," Dr. Carter continued, resuming his dialing. "And a huge pot of tea. Who knows how long this will take."

"You truly want me to help?" she asked, beaming.

He set down the receiver. "Truly."

The depth and sincerity of his expression caught her off guard. "Thank you," she managed to reply. "I wish I could, but" – her face fell – "I can't stay. I have an exam for Dr. Miller's class in twenty minutes."

Dr. Carter chewed his lip for a moment. When he did speak, the short, bursting comment seemed almost wrenched from his lips.

"Tonight, then. Meet me tonight."

Jenny nodded happily. "When?"

"Six o'clock, but only if you don't have a lecture."

"I don't."

Dr. Carter studied her face shrewdly. "You do have a lecture, don't you?"

"Well ... yes," Jenny admitted. "But it's only Dr. Chilcott's. I can miss it."

"Miss Ellison—"

"My coursework is my responsibility, and my business," she objected. "If you're inviting me to help you, then I'm coming. As you said, I'm the one who found this."

Jenny hadn't meant to speak so firmly, but Dr. Carter did not look at all offended. In fact, he appeared mildly impressed.

"All right, then. Six o'clock it is."

"I just can't believe this," Jenny whispered almost reverently, her finger hovering a few inches over an inverted vulture. "I've been staring at those symbols for days! I knew they were important, I could just feel it. But I didn't know why."

"We'll soon find out," Dr. Carter said, clearing more materials away from the workbench. He paused while shifting a crateful of camera equipment. "Miss Ellison, have any of the other team members mentioned anything unusual about the glyphs?"

"No. Or if they did, they didn't say anything to me about it."

"And did you mention them to anyone? Student or faculty, even by chance?"

"No."

"Miss Ellison, could I ask ... may we keep this newest development private? Just for the time being?"

Jenny's heart secretly thrilled with the intrigue of it all, but a question rose stubbornly to mind, one that wouldn't be squashed not matter how she challenged it.

"Shouldn't you alert the Egyptian ambassador?" she cautioned. "Wouldn't he want to be kept informed?"

The young professor set down the crate and folded his arms, lost in thought. "Yes. He would."

"But you don't want to tell him?"

"Not quite yet, no."

"Why, please?"

Dr. Carter hesitated. "Let me put it this way. If I tell the ambassador that we *may* have found a hidden message concealed in a three-thousand-year-old artifact, he'll demand it be sent back to Egypt on the next plane." He rubbed his stubbled chin thoughtfully. "That's understandable, of course. But Browning still has two weeks left with the stone, and the archaeologist in me—"

"—wants to try to unravel its secrets before handing it over," she deduced.

He nodded somberly. "If only because I've never seen anything like this crop up in the ancient world. Ever. It may be selfish of me to want to puzzle this out first, but I'd deeply regret not trying."

Jenny felt the same, and told him so. "What about the rest of the team? Shouldn't we involve them too?"

The young professor shifted his shoulders restlessly. "Probably."

Jenny studied Dr. Carter's face, which had become strangely ruddy – almost flushed.

"You don't think it wise?" she prompted him. "You're worried they might leak information to the press somehow?"

Dr. Carter cleared his throat uncertainly. "Something like this could be hard to keep a secret. Of course," he quickly added, "if it would make you uncomfortable to work here without other company, we can certainly—"

"Chicken sandwiches for me, please," Jenny interrupted. "I'll be back at six." She moved cheerfully towards the door, stopping for just a moment in its frame. "Ask if campus dining has sweetmeats. You never know!"

They studied the slab for variations in pattern. Daniel had taken it upon himself to jot down a list of all the manipulated glyphs. The flax knots, snake, vulture, folded cloth, crook, nebu, and eye had all been distorted. As Miss Ellison had indicated, these distortions were arranged at random throughout the tablet.

"All codes have a key, don't they?" she said, tying up her wavy brown hair and settling in behind the bench. "A central text to help the reader decipher it?"

"Often they do, but I doubt we'll find one here," Daniel replied, wrenching his attention back to the stone.

"Why not?"

"Less than five percent of the ancient Egyptian population would have been literate," he explained. "Only nobility could read hieroglyphs. Scribes, doctors, priests, royalty, that's it."

"No key? Then how will we even begin to crack this?" she said, the shine in her eyes dimming somewhat.

"By looking at motives," Daniel said with an encouraging nod. He pulled one of her transcription sheets between them. "Let us assume that a secret message, nine times out of ten, conceals malintent."

"A conspiracy, then."

Daniel looked at her curiously. "Quite a conclusion to draw."

"Also quite a stretch, isn't it?" she said with an arch look, though her cheeks pinked a little under his gaze.

"Not at all," Daniel said with a laugh. "Conspiratorial groups have existed in all societies, ancient and modern."

"But why would someone put a conspiratorial message in a public carving?" She frowned. "Wouldn't that be terribly foolish?"

"Not necessarily. It could be a case of hiding in plain sight. Which would be quite clever, actually," Daniel continued with resurging interest. "There were no real mail services, no telegrams of course. Putting a coded message in a carving like this, one that you'd see every time you passed the temple, would have been a good way to reach a lot of people at once. If those people knew what they were looking for."

"Still, the creator of the message might have been anyone," Jenny anguished.

"Well, the stone mason and scribe were definitely in on it," Daniel said, swallowing far too much tea and wincing as it burned its way down.

"What makes you say so?" she asked, reaching for a triangle of pistachio baklava (the closest thing to sweetmeats campus dining could offer).

"No official edict would ever contain malformed glyphs. The deviations were definitely intentional."

"Again, how can you be sure?" Jenny intoned softly, raising her brows. Noticing for the first time the dimple in her chin, Daniel answered the question a beat or two later than propriety dictated. Shaking himself, he cleared his throat and replied:

"Because the ancient Egyptians prided themselves on precise aesthetics. Their style of art, of dress, of writing didn't change for thousands of years. All their beliefs and choices centered on the concepts of permanence, symmetry, and perfection. Scribes and masons had significant status in Egyptian society. They would have prided themselves on their work far too greatly to let mistakes like that stand. Not unless those mistakes were intentional."

"You really understand them," Jenny murmured, studying his face so attentively that Daniel's lungs seemed to temporarily forget their purpose of moving fresh air into his body.

"I have to," he said, somewhat lamely.

"And you were a codebreaker."

He flinched. "What?"

"During the war," she replied calmly. "You worked as a code-breaker."

Daniel stumbled through a misdirection. "I ... I'm afraid I don't ..."

"Of course," she sighed. "It's all so clear now." She tucked her legs underneath her on the bench, not seeming to notice (or care) that one of her pumps had slipped to the floor. Daniel saw that there was a hole in the toe of her stocking and a disarming run up the back of it.

"The Allies would have needed all kinds of experts, wouldn't they? To help encrypt messages, and analyze code? I've heard rumors that defunct languages were sometimes used for internal communiques." Jenny looked at him with penetrating concern. "Was it dangerous work?"

He cleared his throat and pulled the archive sheets towards him for what seemed the hundredth time that evening. "It certainly wasn't as hard as this is proving to be."

A rattle of the doorknob silenced him.

Daniel jumped to his feet, reacting more from instinct than thought.

Another harsh rattle of the doorknob split the air. Someone was trying to enter the lab, and whoever was outside of it did not care that it was after hours or that the entrance to the room was dead-bolted. The assailant twisted and shoved, shaking the door violently in and out with their full weight.

Jenny, who was white with fear, half-rose from the bench. Daniel held a finger to his lips to signal quiet, his entire body rigid with attention.

After a few more fruitless attempts, the would-be intruder abandoned their goal. The two stared at each other in petrified shock.

"Go," he whispered, at last drawing a proper breath. "I'll lock up here."

She nodded steadily, though her face remained ashen. "Same time tomorrow?"

"Yes. Tomorrow."

CHAPTER 21

Walking Jenny home was out of the question, however much the prospect appealed. Daniel called a cab and escorted her to it, but did not linger after it departed. The attempted break-in had put him on high alert, and he wouldn't leave the lab undefended for a moment longer than was needful. Once Jenny's car pulled safely away, Daniel vaulted to the second floor to confront his prime suspect.

But Chilcott was not there. His office door had been bolted, and the room was pitch dark. Daniel paced the hallway, scanning left and right for any signs of activity or scuffle. A fluorescent bulb flickered overhead, bathing the corridor in a cold white glow. Maddeningly, nothing looked out of place or suspicious to a degree that might give him any leads.

For good measure Daniel ran behind the building to check the footprints in the snow, but hours of students traipsing between buildings had made any sort of track identification impossible. Whoever the assailant had been, they had gotten away undetected.

Daniel swore under his breath. Though he couldn't be certain what the intruder was after (he reassured himself that no one could *possibly* have known about the stone's hidden code), he felt certain they would be back. The surest way to thwart them was to crack the artifact's secret and ship it back to Egypt, as soon as possible. This was yet another reason to resent the intruder. For reasons he could not yet voice, Daniel would have preferred to take his time.

They met again the next evening for a comparatively uneventful decoding session. No trespasser attempted to force the lab door, though Daniel and Jenny kept a chair shoved under the handle for good measure. Likewise, no members of Daniel's research team came in to work. Spencer and Jillian had reportedly given up interest in the project after the stone's bland message had been revealed. Even Howard and Max's hours had dwindled as final exams loomed large on the horizon. Jenny assured Daniel that they were unlikely to sacrifice a whole Saturday evening here at this stage of the term.

He was grateful for the privacy their preoccupation afforded. Decoding the stone was a process he wanted only capable and trustworthy eyes seeing. Currently, Jenny's brown ones best fit that description, though admittedly the two of them were making little progress in the decryption. Trying to match the symbols to their phonetic equivalents had yielded no coherent message. No matter which direction the symbols were read, the result was unintelligible gibberish.

The atmosphere in the room, however, was not one of tension or boredom. Daniel was frankly in awe at how comfortably he and Jenny got on together in such conditions. Of all his partnerships in the field, this was easily becoming the most collegial he'd enjoyed. Suggestions and ideas flowed freely between them; they almost seemed to sense each other's theories.

This was in part because Jenny was such a transparent compan-ion, one moment shining with enthusiasm, the next groaning in frustration. Comically, she remained her own best cheerleader. Just when a look of despair would overtake her, she would buck herself up and declare stubbornly that the answer was there, waiting for them, and with a little more time it would be known. These were the moments when Daniel's focus was rather less focused on the glyphs and a little more focused on the company.

At his suggestion, they had taken several long breaks to simply talk. Daniel had brought in a slab of very dark chocolate, and as he broke off squares she asked more about his life in the military. He didn't share much, but spoke a little of a harsh and hungry time during his last year of service, when bars of chocolate were even more valuable than gold. Jenny understood such things, having seen many a starving soldier come through her hospital in France. With her typical vivacity, she had connected the topic to happier memories – ones of begging her grandad for a penny to buy candy, only to be given a whole half crown. She had immediately put it into a fund, she said, to save for her trip to Cairo.

Jenny shared many family stories, often with great warmth and alacrity. It was clear her home had been a happy one, if not particularly prosperous. When Daniel asked if their family had traveled much, she simply replied that her parents had done their best to give them memories, even if that meant a trip to the local lake was their only summer holiday. A notable anecdote was a childhood camping trip, in which her older brother had tasked her with staking down the family tent. It had blown away during a hurricane-level storm, and the entire family had been forced to sleep in the footwells of their tiny car.

The picture she had painted, of snoring brothers and dangling feet all over the place, had made Daniel laugh until tears came to his eyes. She kept doing that: making him laugh. To his great delight, he'd returned the favor at least four, maybe five times that evening. He found himself quite impatient for the next opportunity to do so.

After two hours of exhausting, but by no means unpleasant, work, they had parted with a plan to meet again on Sunday. Daniel arrived hours early, as he had taken to haunting the third-floor corridor in defense of the lab. Thankfully the hall seemed as empty as one would expect on a weekend. While searching for his jangle of keys, Daniel spotted Dr. Miller's office door standing open down the hall. There was a strange scuffle of noise from within it, and a dull murmur of speech pervaded the air.

"Antony?"

Daniel poked his head inside the tiny office. The old dean sat behind his desk, thumbing through a stack of papers and swearing fluently.

"Antony, what are you doing here?"

The old professor shot up from his chair. "Daniel, my boy!" He pulled his pipe out of his mouth with a chuckle. "Well, there goes my last shred of credibility as a professor. I've been caught red-handed. Despite years of scolding students for doing so, I, my boy, am cramming. I still have eighteen Amity applications to read."

Daniel smothered a laugh out of respect for his mentor. "Will you finish in time?"

"Of course!" Dr. Miller scoffed. "The committee meets at – what, three o'clock tomorrow? That still gives me" – he referenced a pocket watch – "twenty-one hours. God created the fish and fowl in less time than that, you know," he said with a wink.

Daniel smiled. "An ambitious comparison. I won't keep you, then."

Dr. Miller stopped him. "And what brings you here on a weekend, Daniel? Not behind yourself, I hope?"

"No, I finished all my Amity reading last night."

"What, then?"

Daniel hesitated. "I'm here to work on the stone."

"Indeed? I thought the conservation was all but finished."

Again, Daniel hesitated. "The transcription is done, yes, but I thought we might as well keep it until the deadline."

"Why? Ambassador Nassar would welcome an earlier delivery I'm sure, and oh, how I'd love to see the look on Chilcott's face when you return the works ahead of schedule." The old dean giddily popped in his pipe. Daniel, on the other hand, fidgeted as he searched for words truthful enough to satisfy his conscience and vague enough to satisfy Antony.

"We're – well, yes, we're nearly ready to send it back. I just need to be sure we didn't miss anything in the translation. Then we have to pack up the photographs in archival tubes and settle the stone into its crate, so it will take a few more days at least."

Dr. Miller eyed him shrewdly. "Well. You know best, Daniel. No one likes a rush job, as they say."

"On that note, I really should get to work. We have quite a bit to get through today. Good luck with the reading, Antony."

"Daniel?"

"Yes?"

"We?"

After a brief pause, Daniel nodded. He had never lied to Antony and had no intention of doing so now.

"One of my researchers is helping me."

Dr. Miller's expression was unreadable. With some speed he turned his back to Daniel and plucked dusty books off the shelves at random.

"Well, as you said. You'd better get started."

Feeling a surge of relief at this dismissal, Daniel left for the lab. Had he stayed within earshot, this relief would have been short-lived. Moments later, Antony let out a low whistle, and a murmured, whispered entreaty:

"Be careful, my boy. Be careful."

CHAPTER 22

"Have we tried ordering the glyphs from largest to smallest?"

"Twice," Jenny confirmed, swallowing a large yawn that popped uncomfortably between her ears. She tilted her face away from Dr. Carter to conceal her exhaustion. The last thing she wanted was to give him a reason to gallantly dismiss her and insist she rest.

"Did we try arranging them by symbolic importance? Starting with the Nile?"

"Yes," she repeated, reaching for a cool glass of water in the hopes it would revive her energy. "Also twice."

"Hmm." Dr. Carter frowned. "But did we try standing on our heads?"

Jenny nearly snorted water out of her nose in laughter. There it was again: his delightfully dry, delightfully silly sense of humor. Over the past three days she'd become increasingly familiar with that facet of him so rarely seen in the lecture hall. She loved his lighter moments, and there had been a delightful cluster of them this evening alone.

Having spent most of the weekend in his company, Jenny was learning to read all of his expressions, silly and somber, as well as she could any ancient symbol. The subtle clench of his jawline, she knew, indicated a deep frustration. If his forehead smoothed, he'd been inspired with a new idea, which would reliably spill a moment later from his wide, quiet mouth. Less discernible were the piercing expressions of his dark blue eyes, sometimes shining in contentedness and curiosity, sometimes twinkling with mischief and a hint of something else, as now.

He leaned his trim torso over the ancient stone, as if he were trying to spot some new detail he'd missed before. His hair, she saw, was quite disheveled after an evening of chasing failed theories. Both of his hands pressed softly into the workbench surface. The sleeves of his dark green sweater had been carelessly pushed up over his elbows, the left of which rested not far from hers. In Jenny's weary, depleted state, there was something immensely comforting about having it so near.

Sensing her gaze, Dr. Carter stopped scanning the length of the stone. He slowly turned his face towards hers. For once, Jenny was not the least bit embarrassed at being caught observing him. And for a moment – just a moment – she let her eyes linger in his.

The moment grew. A strange, swooping feeling overtook her stomach and sent her striding to the opposite end of the workbench. Something inside her warned it might be best to remain there for the rest of the evening.

"We haven't tried that," she said, taking up her new position. "I'm too tired to stand on my head, but this is the next best thing."

"Worth a shot," he said, reaching for a fresh pencil. As his lower back twisted, he let out a sharp grunt and swore under his breath. The pencil he'd been holding clattered to the desktop.

"Dr. Carter?" she asked urgently. "Are you all right?"

"Fine, I'm absolutely fine," he said, smiling tightly. His pallor suggested otherwise, but he nodded pleasantly towards her. "Better than you're about to be if you *do* stand on your head."

She let out a hesitant laugh and nodded, uncertain whether to press him further. The crease of his brow betrayed a lingering unease, but the speed with which he broke from her gaze suggested the subject had just been closed. Instead she looked helplessly at the stone, which now lay upside down in front of her. As she studied the markings under this new orientation, her agitation faded.

"Dr. Carter ..."

"Hmm?" He was busily jotting down a new arrangement of symbols.

"I think ..."

"Yes?" Dr. Carter cast her a puzzled look. "What is it?"

"I don't think it's a message," Jenny mumbled, her eyes widening. "I think – I think it's an image."

Dr. Carter shot up from his seat and ran around the workbench to join her. His eyes darted frantically between the glyphs. Seizing a pencil and the nearest archival drawing, he traced a faint line between the manipulated symbols, connecting the cobra to the cloth, then the vulture, then the nebu, eye, and Nile. The resulting shape was a mountain-like outline, with a steep front and a long, sloping back.

"What the ...." Dr. Carter's voice trailed off to nothingness.

"It's not a message!" Jenny repeated in stunned disbelief. "It's an image!"

"It's *genius*."

"It is, it really is! A hidden image doesn't need a *key*! Its meaning is self-contained!"

"*Exactly*." Dr. Carter re-traced the outline triumphantly. "This could have been read by anyone, literate or not, if only they knew where to look!"

"But what could it be?" Jenny cried. "That shape could be anything!"

"It could." Dr. Carter straightened with a deeply satisfied look. "Luckily for us, I have spent a great deal of time in southern Egypt."

"You're saying you know what it is?"

"Oh, yes."

"*What, then?*" Jenny demanded.

"That," Dr. Carter said, running his finger softly over the penciled shape, "is a side profile of Abu Simbel. The great temple, built by Ramses the Second." He smiled happily. "It's part of my site. I'd know that layout anywhere."

"This – this is unbelievable!" Jenny exclaimed, dizzy with joy. "An outline of Abu Simbel!"

"Concealed in a carving stripped *from* Abu Simbel."

"Yes! But *why?*"

He grinned. "I imagine something's there. Hidden."

Jenny gasped. "*Buried?*"

"Possibly."

"What makes you say so? How do you *know* that?"

"The wadjet glyph, just here." Dr. Carter pointed to the elaborate carving of an eye, positioned to one side of the temple's outline. "It was an ancient symbol of protection. There's nothing there at the actual Abu Simbel, it's just an outer surface of solid rock. But putting that kind of marking here could indicate a hidden cargo of some kind. Tribute money, spices. Perhaps even the remains of a smuggling operation."

"Then this is a *map?*"

"It's possible." He clutched his hair thoughtfully. "It could also mean nothing of the sort, but I'd bet my shirt that if anything's there, we'd find it underneath the temple."

Jenny barely heard his last words. She had been studying the wadjet carving, and stood abruptly with her face draining of all color. "*Dr. Carter!*" she cried. Wringing her hands speechlessly, she ran to his desk at the end of the room and rifled through a box of equipment. At last she located a large rectangular magnifying glass and ran back with it to the stone. She pushed it into his hands before Dr. Carter could even form the question hanging on his lips.

"Just look!" she ordered him, trying desperately not to clutch his elbow and shove his face into the glass. "Look at the eye. *Look!*"

He took the offered tool in confusion and squinted over the glyph. A moment later his face had likewise paled; his hand, still clutching the glass, began to shake uncontrollably.

"Oh my ..."

There, resting in the pupil of the wadjet, lay a tiny, almost imperceptible etching. The lines were incredibly faint and fine, but they formed a distinct oval with a line at one end.

"A cartouche," the young professor croaked in disbelief.

"Vulture, flax, Nile, crook ..." Jenny quickly translated the glyphs enclosed within it. "Ah-rn-*run*-set? *Ahrunset.*"

"A royal name, if it's inside a cartouche. Yet it can't be," Dr. Carter said with a shake of his head. "There's no pharaoh of that name. I've never heard of him."

"Because this stone was pried off and thrown away, remember?" she said in exhilaration. "Buried!"

"Yes. Yes! Why? *Why?* Ahrunset. A forgotten royal name. *A forgotten royal name?*" he repeated, as though trying to convince himself of its veracity.

"A name hidden in a stone from a temple —"

" — hidden in a *wadjet*, the symbol of protection — "

"— meaning — "

"There could be a royal cache down there, or even a tomb!" Jenny rejoiced. "You're going back this summer, you can look for it!"

"Yes! Yes, I can!" he said, jubilantly stepping forward before pinning his arms to his sides, looking stiff and suddenly rigid.

"Oh, Dr. Carter! A *tomb!*"

"I know, I know," he said with a shallow breath. "This is ... I mean ... but we mustn't get ahead of ourselves. The only way to know for certain is to mount another excavation. I'll apply for an additional dig permit tonight. I mean, of course not tonight, I ... first thing tomorrow." Dr. Carter marched aimlessly about the room, as though he could not bear to wait even until then to get started.

"You'll have to tell the ambassador what you found," she whispered.

"What we found," he insisted, facing her. "None of this would have happened without you." Dr. Carter's dark blue eyes softened. "You're incredible, Jenny."

She blushed violently at the little compliment. His pronouncement was not unwelcome, but it was wholly unexpected. Something about the words struck her as odd, and it would be several more hours before Jenny realized he had used her first name.

Having no idea what to say to him in response, she moved towards the hat rack and pulled on her long wool coat. "This is *all* incredible, but ... I'm afraid I have to go. It's much later than I thought, and tomorrow is a very big day."

"Yes." Dr. Carter put his hands in both pockets, looking very grave. "The Amity Scholarship."

Jenny fumbled with her scarf, tying a double knot to avoid meeting his eyes. "When does the committee meet?"

"Three o'clock." He took a deep breath. "Announcements will be made by six."

She paused, looking up at him through a flutter of nerves. Biting her lip, she steadied herself and recited the message she had rehearsed many times but hadn't yet found the courage to deliver.

"Dr. Carter, I want to say that ... although it's true I want the Amity Scholarship more than anything I've wanted in my life, I hope you know that I haven't been doing this work in order to ... to increase my chances."

The corner of his mouth lifted. "I know, Jenny."

"Good." She nodded once. "Well then. Right. Good luck to all, of course."

A relieved and slightly mortified Jenny pulled open the lab door.

As she walked into the empty corridor, she could see from the corner of her eye that Dr. Carter was still smiling.

CHAPTER 23

The Amity meeting took place in Daniel's office. Despite his being the most junior of the three co-chairs, his study was by far the largest. It adjoined his lecture hall and was a coveted location among instructors for that reason. Some might have scratched their heads at an assistant professor enjoying such luxuries, but at Browning, practicality often surpassed seniority. Of the three men, Daniel's classes had the highest enrollment. A capacious study was necessary, if only to fit his many cabinets of student papers.

It was a pleasant room: paneled, rectangular, and well-lit by an arched window at one end. He had a lovely view of an old whitebeam tree, which bloomed beautifully during the warmer weather. The campus bell beyond it chimed three, warning Daniel that his companions would soon arrive. He dragged a round table to the center of the room and plopped down his shortlist of applications.

The tick of the wall clock seemed unusually loud this afternoon, and Daniel's foot tapped nervously in time with it. He glanced again to his stack of files. Feeling more than a little uneasy about the name that rested on top, he strode to a cabinet near the door to make a calming cup of tea.

At two minutes past Dr. Chilcott sauntered in. The man's thin lip curled as he took in the commodious space. He muttered churlishly under his breath, "To have given this to a—"

"Good afternoon, Dr. Chilcott," Daniel said from behind the half-open door.

Chilcott nearly jumped out of his skin. "Goodness, Dr. Carter," he said in a clipped, accusatory tone. "Standing guard, I see?"

"Not quite. Care for a cup?"

"What? Oh." Chilcott wrinkled his nose. "No, thank you."

Daniel shrugged. "Suit yourself. It could be a long meeting."

"All the more reason not to waste any time." The professor sat down with surprising weight for one so thin. "No Miller yet, I see."

"He's finishing up a class," Daniel answered, plugging in the kettle.

Chilcott's fingers rapped impatiently against the table. Neither man spoke until Daniel casually prompted, "How was your weekend, Dr. Chilcott?"

"Fine, thank you."

"Do anything fun?"

Dr. Chilcott shot him a skeptical look. It wasn't typical for Daniel to engage in this kind of small talk. At least not with him.

"My wife and I spent the weekend at our cabin," he answered shortly. "In Blythe."

"How luxurious." Daniel assumed a carefully light, disinterested tone. "A whole weekend in the mountains. Must have been nice, with all the snow and everything. When did you leave?"

"Friday."

"Really? What time on Friday?"

Chilcott merely checked his watch. "What can be keeping Antony?"

The kettle's indicator popped upwards. Daniel poured himself a steaming amber mugful of tea, keeping his eyes fixed on Chilcott's rapidly drumming fingers. "We had quite the eventful weekend here. I don't know if you heard, but someone tried to break into my lab on Friday."

"Is that so?" Chilcott stood and irritably poured his own mugful. "Then you'd best change the locks out. Where the devil is Miller?"

"Here I am, here I am!" Antony puffed, walking in at top speed. The old dean mopped his glistening face with a handkerchief. "A thousand apologies, but I couldn't shake a student. He wanted points back on his last test, due to my 'unfair phrasing on questions seven and nineteen.' Never mind that this same student has also chosen not to attend my last four lectures ..."

"Ghastly," Dr. Chilcott snorted. "I hope you wrote him up for insolence."

"Tea, Antony?" Daniel asked, searching out another mug.

"Love some, thank you." Dr. Miller continued mopping his face as he collapsed into a chair. "And no, William," he said with a sharp look. "I did not write him up. My students are welcome to question and challenge me, for that is an excellent way to learn. I like a healthy debate. Though," he chuckled, "perhaps not right before an Amity meeting."

Chilcott flushed, but the timbre of his voice remained civil. "Well, I hope I shall remain as open-minded when I approach my retirement."

Dr. Miller let out an audible groan, which he quickly turned into a cough.

"Shall we get started, gentlemen?" Daniel suggested, handing Antony his cup.

"Certainly." Dr. Chilcott straightened his papers and called them to order. "Gentlemen, it is my very great pleasure to welcome you to the twenty-seventh annual Amity Scholarship committee meeting, Browning University chapter, unit identification number three-six-two-nine-zero."

Daniel and Antony exchanged an uncomfortable glance. It was

normally Dr. Miller who convened their meetings, but neither man said a word at this overt takeover. Taking no notice of their distress, Chilcott continued his pompous speech.

"Established in 1920, the Amity Scholarship has grown to be one of the most prestigious and competitive scholarship programs in all of Europe. Its sacred mission is threefold: to promote goodwill among nations; to engage the brightest young minds in archaeological work; and most importantly, to add to our shared body of knowledge. Today, the active sites within Browning's Amity chapter include Iran, Crete, and Egypt."

"Yes, we know, Chilcott," Daniel replied calmly.

"Our task today is to select the three most exceptional, qualified, and promising students from our scholarship applicants. These fortunate recipients will be sponsored by the Amity program during a summer of fieldwork at each of our respective sites."

"We know, William," Antony replied more impatiently.

"Given our tendency to disagree on candidates," Chilcott pressed on undeterred, "I propose that together we compile a shortlist of five names. Then, per Dr. Miller's 'love of healthy debate,' we can discuss the merits and potential of each of those five students. Are there any objections?"

"None from me," Daniel said politely. His interrogation about Dr. Chilcott's weekend had not yet concluded. He felt it best to keep the man in a good mood.

"Very well," Antony grumpily conceded.

"Excellent," Chilcott said. "For a start, I—"

"I propose Mark Phillips," Antony cut in. He seemed eager to reclaim the meeting. "He's a fourth year and a top student. This past term he's worked as my teaching assistant for Classical Languages, and he spent two weeks last summer analyzing soil samples in Lithuania on his own ticket, just to get field experience. That shows initiative."

"I've no objection," Daniel replied. "I was impressed by his application."

"Mark ... Phillips ..." Dr. Chilcott scribbled down the name. "Very well. We have our first." He looked up at his colleagues. "I follow with Andrew Hastings, also a fourth year. The lad shows a particular interest in Farsi. This is a rare inclination that ought to be encouraged."

"His marks are low." Dr. Miller looked over the application uncertainly. "Dr. Carter? Your thoughts?"

Daniel frowned. "I wouldn't equate attending one Farsi symposium to an all-consuming interest, Dr. Chilcott. If it's Farsi you need, you ought to consider Solomon Jannati. He's a native speaker, and he's in the top five percent of the class."

"He's also a very fine young man," Dr. Miller said.

Daniel nodded. "I'd like to see how he does in the field."

Chilcott bit his lip. But for now, he too seemed to want to keep the peace.

"Very well. Solomon ... Jannati." He stiffly scrawled out the name. With a somewhat challenging glance, Chilcott countered with, "Amos Ballantyne."

Daniel nodded. "Agreed. He's a hard worker."

"And kindly," Dr. Miller added. "Very kindly."

"Jennifer Ellison," Daniel put forth.

Predictably, the room went silent. Dr. Chilcott's fountain pen hovered over his paper, and a drop of ink fell upon it with a splat. Antony, on the other hand, interlaced his fingers and intently studied his thumbs.

"I beg your pardon," Chilcott said with a mild sneer, "But did you suggest a Miss—"

"Jennifer Ellison, yes."

He snorted. "A fine joke, Dr. Carter. But let us get back to the matter at hand."

Annoyance was gnawing away at Daniel's resolution of civility, but with some effort he kept his expression serene. "It's not a joke. I propose Jennifer Ellison."

"She's a third year," Dr. Chilcott objected. "She's not prepared for an opportunity like this."

"You've read her application, I assume?"

Chilcott glowered. "Yes?"

"Then you'll recall that she would have been a fourth year, were it not for her voluntary service during the war. You may also recall that she'll have completed the requisite coursework by the end of this term." Daniel folded his arms, mentally digging in his heels for a fight.

"That may be so, but I fear the girl lacks the relevant experience to—"

"She's double majoring in Linguistics," Daniel interrupted. "She's fluent in French and conversational in German. She's worked as a nurse. She can translate hieroglyphs upon sight without referencing a manual. With no promise of payment, she logged 150 hours of conservation work in my lab. This was more time than any other member of my team. Her effort in my class is unparalleled, and she's had the top score on nearly every test and paper I have assigned. Miss Ellison deserves to go."

Dr. Chilcott looked incredulously at Dr. Miller.

The old man nodded. "Oh, she's brilliant. There's no denying that."

Shaking his head in disbelief, Chilcott muttered that he would at least add her to the shortlist.

"Miss Jennifer ... Ellison," he penned. "And, in the last slot, of course, Anders Manwaring."

Dr. Miller shifted uncomfortably at this name and Daniel scowled, but neither man objected. The Manwaring family had made a sizable donation to Browning just this week. Daniel could not help but scoff at the obviousness of this timing, but even he was forced to acknowledged that not putting Anders on the shortlist, at the very least, could be consequential.

"Now the bloodbath begins," Chilcott said with apparent relish. "Two names must be eliminated, and the remaining three assigned to each of our—"

"We *know*, Chilcott," Dr. Miller said, now making no effort to hide his annoyance.

"I'm afraid Amos Ballantyne is out," Daniel observed, referencing his application for a second time. "He has acute asthma and weakness of the chest. Unfortunately, the work required at any of our sites would aggravate those conditions."

"And for similar reasons," Dr. Chilcott replied while crossing out Amos's name, "we can eliminate Miss Ellison."

Daniel's eyes snapped upwards. "And why is that? Miss Ellison has no health problems, as far as I am aware."

"Because the work would be too taxing for a lady," Chilcott replied, as though this should have been obvious. "These sites are rough places, Dr. Carter. No running water, sleeping in tents for months at a time, no gilt mirrors to powder one's nose in." He snickered. "These are only a few of the reasons we don't award the scholarship to girls."

"Women," corrected Daniel. "These conditions alone are not grounds for cutting Miss Ellison. She knows the circumstances. She's as ready to face them as any man."

Dr. Chilcott waved a hand dismissively. "Even if that were true, it would be foolhardy to waste such considerable resources on her."

"What utter nonsense, Chilcott."

"It's not nonsense; it's the truth." Chilcott dropped his pen on the table. "Gentlemen, I am all for the education of females. It is the mark of any civilized society. But we must be pragmatic. You know as well as I do that in a post-war world, with limited positions available and project funding being cut right and left, no prominent agency will ever employ a woman over a man, no matter how impressive her work ethic."

"They might if that woman had the Amity credential behind their name," Dr. Miller offered, at last breaking his silence.

Daniel's temper flared in earnest now. "As long as we're talking about work ethic, we can start the cuts with Anders Manwaring."

Chilcott scoffed. "Certainly not. He ought to go. It's his time. Remember that he was slotted to join me in Tehran last year. Unfortunately, he had to drop out at the last minute due to a war injury flaring."

"Yes," Daniel fumed, "most unfortunate. Though I do find it unusual that he often can't remember which leg he wounded."

"You dare doubt him?" Chilcott spat. "I'm surprised at you, Dr. Carter. After everything young Anders has given for our country, and after all that his family has done for—"

"Anders Manwaring is an entitled sot," Daniel cut in firmly. "His marks are mediocre at best, and he hasn't bothered to attend my lectures for the past two weeks. He has absolutely no interest in becoming an archaeologist, and from what I've observed he spends more time down the pub or on his yacht than with his textbooks."

"Mmm. Just like his father," Dr. Miller remembered, nodding in agreement.

Daniel took a calming breath and adopted a steadier tone. "The Manwarings are an important part of the Browning community, that I can't deny. As a potential next dean, Chilcott, it will be on you to keep Browning in the graces of all our prominent families. I'm sure you wouldn't want your department openly accused of favoritism. Or worse, bribery. What might our more conservative donors say to that?"

Dr. Chilcott sputtered with pleasure and indignation. "As a potential next ... well, of course I ... to be sure, appearances are ..."

Dr. Miller slowly lifted his head. "Anders is out."

"But—"

"Miss Ellison will be an Amity recipient."

Daniel stifled a triumphant cry. "All right then," he answered soberly. "Mark Phillips, Solomon Janatti, Jennifer Ellison. We have our three."

Dr. Chilcott looked helplessly from one professor to the other. After an icy pause, he pulled out an official-looking bulletin. "As it seems I have been overruled ... I hereby decree that the three recipients of this year's Amity Scholarships will be Mark Phillips, Solomon Janatti, and *Miss Jennifer Ellison.*" He wrote the names very slowly, a slight curl lingering about his upper lip as he formed the last one. "Now for their sites. I suppose I shall take Janatti, as he does speak Farsi."

"No objection," Daniel replied, his heart beginning to pound.

"Mmm, yes. Highly logical," Dr. Miller added absently.

"As for the other two?" Chilcott prompted. "Their assignments?"

Antony went back to inspecting his thumbs. "You know, gentlemen, I always find this the most difficult part of the Amity deliberations. It's a tremendous responsibility to make these kinds of judgments. When one considers that the sites we assign have the potential to influence a student's entire life – the trajectory of their career, their reputation, their safety, their opportunities – I'm reminded that we have an obligation, nay, a solemn duty to make these decisions with our students' best interests in mind." Antony turned somberly to Daniel. "Dr. Carter? What are your own thoughts?"

He glanced briefly at his friend. The old dean's expression was one of mild, polite interest.

But his eyes warned.

Daniel fixed his gaze on the back wall. For several moments he did not look at either of his companions. Finally, with a deep, shuddering breath, he gave his answer.

CHAPTER 24

After the meeting, Daniel shut himself up in the Archaeology lab. He needed quiet. He needed to get away from the bustle of students crowding the Amity bulletin. Most of all, he needed to escape the sinking disappointment that he knew, quite positively, was pervading the corridor.

Despite the wintry weather, the third-floor lab felt uncomfortably close and hot. Its radiator had always been temperamental, and tonight was no exception. Daniel tugged crossly at the collar of his shirt, unfastened his top two buttons, and shoved his sleeves roughly up his forearms.

The place was an absolute mess of equipment; he and Jenny hadn't bothered tidying it up after their breakthrough last evening. With a gruff sigh, he began rolling up scattered papers and drawings. The stone would be sent back to Egypt this week, along with the fully developed photographs and renderings. The project was truly finished now.

Oh, how dearly he wished it weren't.

The doorknob shook. Daniel froze at the sound, one hand on an archival tube, the other reaching aimlessly at air. The lab door creaked open, and a quick, light step approached steadily from behind. His pulse roared in response to it. Blood pounded in his ears, temporarily deafening him and slowing his thoughts, but even without those senses he knew who this evening visitor was. With considerable effort, he fixed a cordial smile.

"Miss Ellison." Daniel turned slowly about. "Congratulations."

"Thank you," Jenny said hastily. She looked windswept and flushed, as if she'd been running as fast as her pump-shod feet could carry her. "It's a great honor, and I'm fully aware of that. But Professor Carter – why am I going to Crete?"

The agony in her voice was a fresh stab to his heart. Avoiding her gaze, Daniel stepped past her and picked up a camera. "Dr. Miller is an excellent supervisor, Miss Ellison. I studied under him myself. You're lucky to be working with him, since he may retire any day."

Jenny stepped between him and the camera bag, putting herself directly in his path. "You've given Egypt to Mark Phillips. Why? He's far more interested in classical studies, and he's been working with Dr. Miller for months now. I've spoken with Mark, and he's just as confused as I am. It makes no sense. I'm trying to understand, I truly am, but—"

"The Amity assignments do not always work out as students might wish," Daniel replied evenly, but his panic was building. Turning away from her, he scooped up loose brushes and camera bulbs at random. "In these situations, we hope students will seek to maximize their learning and apply what they—"

"But we found the Abu Simbel map together!" Jenny cut him off with a look that was equal parts beseeching and infuriated. "I can help with the new dig. I'm sharp, and quick, and I'd work twice as hard as any man on your site, I promise I would."

"I know that," Daniel said, still not meeting her eye. Emotion was rising dangerously close to the surface now. "There's no denying we've worked well together, but—"

"Yes, we have!"

"It's just that—"

"Professor Carter," Jenny broke in, her voice thick with feeling. "Why did you pass me over? Egypt is all I've ever dreamed of, all I've ever worked for. If I was good enough to get an Amity Scholarship, then I'm good enough to go with you. I know I am."

"It's not a question of being good enough," Daniel replied, more forcefully than he'd intended. He took a deep breath and started sorting brushes. "I have no doubt that you'd be a great asset to my team. You'd be a blessing to any team, in fact. In my opinion, you're the best of the lot."

This only deepened her air of pain and confusion. "Then why?"

"I know it isn't fair." Daniel abandoned his feeble attempts to pack and turned to face her, his stomach churning with guilt. "You deserve to go to Egypt. And you will go, someday, I'm certain of it. But it ... it just can't be this year, Miss Ellison. It can't be with me."

"Why not?" she demanded, stepping nearer. Her dark eyes sparkled with tears of defiance. "You're the best chair in the Amity program, and I want to work at your side. We can find the hidden tomb together! We *have* to find it together."

"Jenny," Daniel began desperately.

"You're the finest professor I've ever had, and if you think—"

"Jenny—"

"—that I'm going to let this opportunity go by without a fight, then—"

"*Jenny, I can't!*"

The words had been spoken loudly, in a burst of intense, uncontrollable feeling. Daniel's chest heaved unevenly as he stared into her widening eyes. She took a single, faltering step backwards. Looking down, Daniel registered with horror that his hand was resting gently against her waist.

He snatched it back in a panic. "I'm s ... I'm sorry," he whispered. Stumbling backwards, he shook his head in agony. "I didn't mean – I'm sorry. *I'm so sorry.*"

Without another word, he fled from the room.

CHAPTER 25

Had the atmosphere of the earth evaporated and every particle of air been sucked out of the room, Jenny could not have been more in want of breath. She longed to cry out and stop him, but no exertion would animate her vocal chords. The door slammed shut. Her hands immediately began to tremble at her sides, while her throat seared with the thousand questions she could not hurl after him.

Breathe, she thought frantically. Don't faint. Breathe, breathe, just breathe.

Resting a hand on the workbench, Jenny summoned all the calming tactics she'd once practiced as an anxious young girl and continued to employ as an anxious young woman. She tapped her right thigh, counting slowly to fifteen in French, then in Latin. She mentally recited one of Shakespeare's sonnets. When these efforts failed, she cast her eyes about the workspace in a last, desperate attempt to ground herself.

This tactic proved more effective, as it successfully drew her out of her thoughts. There in front of her were the comfortingly familiar books, the maps, and the old, cracked skull grinning crookedly on the shelf. Its smile appeared strangely mocking, as though it had witnessed what had occurred and was daring her to deny it. This was all foolish imagination, of course; yet in her current state of bewilderment, Jenny almost wished the skull could speak and confirm that what had happened was reality.

Dr. Carter. Over and over, the young professor's name raced through her brain. Dr. Carter, Dr. Carter.

Daniel Carter.

No more calm could be gathered here, that much was certain. Jenny left the lab and locked its door behind her. The corridor was deathly silent, as it was now past eight in the evening. Hordes of disappointed Amity applicants had left hours ago, eager to drown their sorrows in the local pubs. A custodian grumpily buffed tiles on the stairs leading to the floor above, but no other companion could be seen.

She stood in front of the lab door for a full minute, forcing her lungs to inflate with unnatural, deliberate breath. It was no good. Her entire being was tingling with a strange new energy. For all she knew, her veins might have been emptied of their lifeblood and filled again with fire. Try as she might, Jenny couldn't calm the swell of feeling coursing through her, or persuade her more logical self to take over and veto the plan of action at her feet. After debating the consequences of her next choice for what seemed an hour, she moved quietly, soundlessly, to the second floor.

She knew without question where he would be.

Walking slowly down the second-floor hallway, she positioned herself in front of Dr. Carter's empty lecture hall. Silently, she turned its knob.

The door creaked open, revealing a completely darkened classroom. Her pumps clicked softly upon the tile as she entered. For a moment she let herself gaze at the rows of shadowy desks and the hall that seemed so much larger when vacant. In the darkness this space was as eerie as a tomb, but Jenny was hardly intimidated by the comparison. She hoped to make an entire career out of exploring such spaces, after all.

Her eyes fell upon a triangular shaft of light on the floor. Dr. Carter's office, just off the lecture hall, was lit. The door was ajar.

Taking a steadying breath, she pushed it fully open.

She found him sitting in the center of his office, his head resting in both of his hands. Everything about the young professor's posture suggested acute sorrow and distress. His form was subdued, slumped – even anguished. He was so distracted that she might have approached unnoticed, had the door not swung heavily on its hinges. As Dr. Carter heard its telltale creak, his dark head snapped upwards.

Jenny entered, and he bolted upright. For a long moment he paused, staring at her in obvious shock. Crossing to the window in two steps, he pulled down its shade and turned to face her once more. His expression was peculiarly energetic; the workings of his dark eyes were almost wild.

"You shouldn't be here," he said.

"I know."

"You should go."

" ... I know."

She closed the door firmly behind her.

Silence hung between them. Dr. Carter opened and shut his mouth repeatedly, teetering on the edge of speech. She read a second apology in his furrowed brow, a deep embarrassment in his flushed countenance, and dread in his darting eyes. He was clearly terrified they would be discovered here, and Jenny was scarcely less so. But so busy was she making discoveries of her own, she found she was quickly able to push away that fear.

Tilting her head shyly, she at last gave herself permission to view Dr. Carter not just as a young, accomplished professor, but as a man. Seeing him in that light, she again felt as if the air had been sucked out of the room.

His skin was still tanned from his summer fieldwork. His arms were strong and well sculpted, as was his chest, the top of which was just visible beneath one or two unfastened shirt buttons. He was tall – nearly a full head taller than she. This was a towering difference she had barely noticed when they sat together at the workbench. His eyes, so dark and kind and wonderfully expressive, were fixed on her now with intense feeling.

And remorse.

Seeing it, she stepped closer.

"Why didn't you tell me?" she whispered sadly.

He pocketed his hands stubbornly. Biting his lip he muttered, "I'm not sure what you mean."

"You should have told me," Jenny repeated. "You should have said something." To her great humiliation, a tear dropped onto her cheek. Hoping he had not seen it, she brushed it back and steeled her expression.

Thrillingly – terrifyingly – she watched as Dr. Carter's defenses crumbed. It was now the man, Daniel, who stepped forward.

"What could I have said?" he whispered throatily. "I'm – I'm your professor, Jenny."

Anger sprang up like a weed inside of her, and she let it bloom, hoping it would crowd out her more complicated emotions. Astonishment, of course. Pain at knowing he had voted against her Egypt placement. Dread at what the dangerous, unspoken truth between them might mean if voiced. And most poignantly of all, a desperate urge to admit (both to him and herself) the extent of her own attachment.

"If you'd only told me," Jenny protested, "I might have withdrawn from your course, and—"

"I never planned to speak," Daniel insisted, pacing the short end of the office. "I swear it. At least not yet."

But Jenny could hardly hear him. Her temper was truly sparking now. In some corner of her brain, she knew this outsized reaction was a cover for deep embarrassment at her own ignorance, her own blindness.

"You might have at least stopped me from joining your project or suggested I transfer classes," she continued fiercely.

Daniel stopped his pacing. "Do you truly wish that?" he asked, looking painfully deflated. "That we had never spoken, or worked together?"

Against her will, Jenny's anger melted like hoar frost in springtime.

"Don't you?" she whispered.

"No," he answered at once, his chest rising and falling with tortured breath. "Not for a moment."

Jenny cast her eyes to the floor, desperate to conceal the rapidly shifting feelings behind them. Her heart had leapt at his last words, and the cavity of her chest was again filling with that strange, flame-like energy. He stood so close to her now; Jenny could see his hands hanging gravely at his side. A blaze of yearning consumed her, as potent as it was frightening. She longed for those hands to reach for her, to strongly grasp her waist, to pull her into his firm, unyielding chest.

A second surge of common sense crowded out those longings. *No.* It was madness even to have come here. This was *ludicrous,* this was reckless. There was no chance of happiness here, none. No future, no possibilities, nothing but concealment and worry and scandal. The barriers and obstacles were too great to even consider her own wishes. There was nothing to do but run and escape his searching eyes forever.

Jenny was about to flee, when quite unbidden, a memory of the French concert surfaced. She recalled the quiet way he'd smiled at her during their walk home, and the readiness with which he'd answered her very personal questions. No amount of logic could make her forget the hours he had spent at her side in the lab: the shared breakthroughs, the frustrations, the laughter and split sandwiches, the chocolate bar and private jokes as each moment together felt more wonderfully comfortable than the last.

They'd spoken with a sincerity that had been all too easy to dismiss as mutual respect; but no more. Feelings bloomed rebelliously in her heart, no longer content to be suppressed as mere admiration. She raised her head. The word floated from her lips before she was even conscious of it.

"Daniel."

His forehead gently wrinkled in response. Suddenly it smoothed, and a flash of understanding crossed his features. With a sharp intake of breath, he closed the distance between them.

"Jenny," he whispered. He cupped her face in both of his hands, leaning his head gently against hers. "I ..."

His touch was warm and beautifully comforting. She closed her own hands about his, finding they barely spanned his wrists. Shyly, she brushed her lips against his cheek. Daniel pulled back in astonishment, which she found highly amusing given how closely they were standing. His dark eyes scanned her face, searching – questioning. Then his gaze moved slowly to her lips and lingered there. A deep, unnamed something twisted deliciously in the space behind Jenny's navel. It dove and swooped and blazed, somersaulting violently in anticipation of what was to come.

She gave the slightest nod.

They kissed.

Ever so gently, once. Then twice.

Daniel's frame was very taut at first. His entire body seemed rigid with apprehension, poised to flee at the first sign of discovery. But when they kissed a third time, his shoulders slackened. After their fourth kiss, he exhaled heavily and swept her towards him. Slipping one hand beneath her curls, he caressed the back of her neck as his lips moved over hers with warm, disarming eagerness. She quickly matched his intensity, her heart pounding thunderously as Daniel's free arm encircled her waist.

A hazy, blissful sensation overtook her being as he held her fast. Jenny was no stranger to romance (though Jillian had often goaded her otherwise). She had spent time with, and embraced, and even kissed several young men. But in this moment, she was realizing with dizzying effect the difference between kissing a boastful boy versus an experienced, intelligent, and powerfully attractive man. The response Daniel elicited was palpable. A delicious hunger had awoken in her skin, which ached beautifully for more of his searching, tentative caresses. Her own limbs were restless against his, eager to test their newfound strength and daring.

For a minute, or perhaps an hour (time seemed suddenly robbed of meaning), they kissed in slow, beautiful synchrony. Then, in a moment of boldness, the next time Daniel's mouth laced through hers, she tugged playfully upon his lower lip and splintered their shared rhythm. Daniel's response was immediate; a burst of excitement overtook him, as though weeks' worth of pent-up wishes were at last being expressed.

He began energetically walking her backwards. After a few short, willful steps, he pressed her against one of the bookshelves and moved both hands down her back in a glorious dance between freedom and self-control. A rough stone figurine toppled off the bookshelf as a result of his enthusiasm, but neither party seemed to notice or care. Jenny's fingers slid to the bare patch at the top of his shirt and the skin beneath his collar. At her touch, Daniel's breathing shallowed. His chest rose raggedly, becoming uneven in its draws, and a moment later he seemed to try and ease out of their embrace. Not yet ready to relinquish the joy of being held by him, Jenny again pulled his lower lip between hers.

His arms tightened their hold about her form, but their kisses were delicately slowing. In a haze they broke apart, trembling together in the lamplight.

"Jenny Ellison," he murmured. His exhale was warm upon her

cheek, reminding her pleasantly of peppermint. "I fully confess ... you are unlike any woman I have known."

"Thank you," came her faint little reply. She, too was steadying her breathing and could think of no cleverer response.

"I mean it." Daniel's gaze was unexpectedly tender. "You're funny. And kind. And brilliant, and beautiful. So, so beautiful."

Joy temporarily robbed her of speech. She yearned to respond in the same vein, but before she could muster the courage to express her own shy feelings, Browning's campus bell began to chime nine. The muffled peals broke the spell holding them both, and they sobered.

"Daniel, what will we do?" she whispered.

"I don't know. But right now, I ..." He closed his eyes, as though willing time to stand still. "I can't think about any of that yet. I just ... need to stay in this moment. Just a little while longer."

Jenny leaned into his chest. As Daniel's head bent protectively over hers, she thought privately that despite the risk and uncertainty of their fate, nothing had ever sounded better.

CHAPTER 26

They stayed in his office for nearly an hour, huddled on the floor by the radiator's warmth. Jenny leaned comfortably against Daniel's chest with her pretty legs crossed at her side.

"I just can't believe this is happening," she whispered softly in his ear. "And that all this time ..."

"I know." Daniel closed his eyes. "There's a decent chance I'll be fired tomorrow. But in this moment" – he gave a tiny nod – "I feel it will have been worth it."

"Why would you be fired?"

He studied her face in surprise. "Because Browning has a strict policy against instructor and student relationships. There are about a dozen regulations forbidding it."

"Yes, I guessed as much," she said, nervously smoothing her hair. "That's not what I meant. You made it sound as though someone knew we were here. There wasn't anyone in the hallway when I entered. I made sure of it."

When he made no response, Jenny tilted her head to catch his eye.

"Daniel? What is it?"

Letting out a rough exhale, he said, "Someone saw me walk you home. After the concert."

"What?" Jenny's cheeks took on a deep shade of scarlet. "Who?"

"I don't know. Whoever it was reported it to Dr. Miller via an anonymous note, and I received a warning about teacher-student boundaries from Antony shortly thereafter."

Still a little flushed, Jenny settled back into his arms. "Oh."

"A warning," Daniel continued with a chuckle, "that I have apparently discarded." Helplessly, he rubbed a hand over his face. "I can't believe I've done this. I swore to myself when I took the job that I never, *ever* would. I was distant, I was careful. But the truth is … I never saw you coming, Jenny."

"Nor I you." Though Daniel couldn't see Jenny's face, the warmth of her tone suggested she was smiling. "I suppose I shouldn't be surprised," she added. "Half the girls at this university are head over heels for you, after all."

"Is that so?" he asked, playfully resting his chin atop her head.

"Yes, it is so!" She laughed and shrugged him off. "A fact that only served to slow my feelings. I was bound and determined not to be one of the 'sighing six' in the front row, as Peter calls them." She began pensively tracing the hair on his arm. "So that's why you voted against me?"

"Hmm?"

"For Egypt. You recommended me for Crete."

Daniel paused. "Yes."

"Because you thought it would be dangerous to work together?"

"Not just for me, Jenny," he said slowly. "Think about it. You're the first woman in more than twenty years to win the Amity. The last woman's work was more ceremonial than legitimate. I think they allowed her to take photographs during an Amazonian River cruise."

Jenny acknowledged this with a deepening frown.

"I didn't know what else to do," he agonized. "You're going to be under a great deal of scrutiny as it is. Chilcott expects you to fail. He thinks you'll buckle under the harsh conditions, or struggle with the workload, or at the very least fail to keep up Browning's high standards. If we had gone to Egypt together, and anything happened to cause gossip, anything at all, he wouldn't hesitate to discredit us both."

Jenny's lips pressed together in a thin line. "I don't much like Dr. Chilcott."

Daniel let out a short burst of laughter. "Neither do I, for several reasons. I'd bet a pound to a penny he was the one trying to break into our lab."

"Dr. Chilcott?" Jenny's brows drew together. "Why would he do such a thing?"

He shrugged. "He wants the deanship. A novel discovery would certainly put him ahead of the pack. He's been trying to weasel his way onto our project for weeks."

Jenny let out a low whistle. "That's despicable."

Daniel of course agreed, but his thoughts took a sharp turn as long-simmering regrets poured unstoppably from him. "Jenny, I'm sorry. I'm so, so sorry about the Amity assignment."

She looked down, suddenly very quiet.

"You've worked so hard for this," he continued bitterly. "Just because one ruddy professor fell for you—"

"I'm not exactly impartial to you either," Jenny reminded him.

"All the same," Daniel said firmly, determined not to excuse himself on even the smallest point. "I was the deciding vote. It's my fault you're not going to Egypt."

The little teasing smile she'd worn was fading now. She bravely hitched it back, but not before Daniel had caught the wistful look dimming her beautiful eyes. It was enough to compel him to hunt for a solution, however far-fetched.

"I could exchange sites with Chilcott," he suggested. "For a single summer, nothing more."

"No," Jenny said flatly. "I refuse to work with a man I don't trust. Would you want him to discover the tomb of Ahrunset, and take all the credit for your—"

"Our," he corrected.

"Yes, our discovery? I don't think so." Jenny took a deep breath. "I ... I will go to Crete. That is my decision. But ..." She winced. "I can't deny that my feelings towards you are fairly complicated at the moment."

"I know that feeling well." He meekly kissed the dimple in her chin. The bluntness of her admission had bathed Daniel's heart in a fresh wave of guilt. He posed the question that hung like a sword over their heads. "What happens now?"

"I don't know." Jenny closed her eyes, as if shutting out the world. After a long while, her dark lashes fluttered open. She smiled faintly as she realized he'd been watching her ponder.

"A penny for your thoughts, Miss Ellison?" Daniel tried to tease, but fear over what he might next hear was seeping through his words. His nerves were as frayed as the woven rug on which they sat.

"They are not long, the days of wine and roses," Jenny quietly recited. "Out of a misty dream ..."

"... our path emerges for a while, then closes," Daniel finished, his heart sinking. "You think that will be our fate? That's what you want?"

"I don't know. I want ... I think I want *this*, Daniel. I ... I want what I feel now, with you." She shivered in his arms, though Daniel suspected this was due to emotion rather than cold. "Yet not at the expense of your job. You love teaching, and the students adore you."

Daniel said nothing. There was a strange lump in the back of his throat, and he couldn't yet trust himself to speak.

"I won't graduate for a year," she whispered. "But perhaps ... at that time?" Heat began to pool in her cheeks. Perhaps she was embarrassed by the suggestion that his attachment might continue for that long. Daniel, on the other hand, inwardly rejoiced. She had landed upon the very solution he'd crafted for himself, days ago. Hearing her suggest it now, however, he felt extremely impatient with that timeline.

"Suppose we were cautious," he began to say, but Jenny was already objecting.

"If what you said about Dr. Chilcott is true, then we are both under surveillance as it is."

"What then?" he anguished. "We wait a year?"

"Not in the sense of putting our lives on hold," Jenny said with endearing determination. "We'll keep busy. Then, at that time, if we feel the same?" Her voice trailed off uncertainly. The plan was logical and pragmatic, but even as she spoke it her hand had tightened around Daniel's. He loved the feel of it: small, but stubborn as the day was long.

Giving her a melancholy smile, he said, "If I were a student, or some chap who worked at a local shop ..."

Jenny settled deeper into his arms, joining him in his world of make-believe. "What would you do?"

"I'd take you dancing. Or stargazing, high atop Mont Belle."

"How lovely that would be," she murmured wistfully.

"Then we'd split a chocolate malt," he said.

"From The Blue Dragon?"

"Where else?" Daniel chuckled. "They have the finest ice cream in all of Belmont."

"They do, they really do!" Jenny heartily agreed. "I've always said so. Margie prefers Damion's, but ..." She stopped. "Oh no. *Blast,* I forgot all about ... I have to go, Daniel, I have to go right now. Margie, my roommate, she's expecting me, and she'll be worried sick that I never came home. She's definitely the type that would send out a search party." Jenny began reluctantly unwinding herself from Daniel's arms, but for a moment he held her fast.

"Have dinner with me," he said.

"Wh – *what?*" she laughed in disbelief. "I ... why?"

"To talk this all over again. We need a clearer plan. Meet me somewhere, anywhere. Not in Belmont, some other town perhaps. Grassby, or Blythe, or Alwynshire."

"Those villages are only miles away, Daniel. I know people who live there and dine out regularly. We just can't."

Daniel hesitated, certain his face was reddening. "Meet me at my flat, then. Just for dinner," he added hastily, disguising his own anxiety with a playful smile. "I'll do all the cooking."

Jenny missed this jovial moment, as she was too busy looking shocked by his dangerous suggestion. "Suppose someone *sees* us?"

"There are no other faculty or students in my building. Even if there were, you could get home quickly, without their noticing."

She hesitated.

"Dinner. Just dinner." Daniel repeated. "And a chat. I'll stay ten feet away from you the whole time if you prefer."

To his great relief, Jenny agreed.

"Friday?" he suggested.

She nodded. "And until then?"

"Covert intelligence," Daniel whispered, kissing her for what he dearly hoped was not the last time.

Jenny saluted. "Aye, Captain Carter."

"That's the navy," he said in mock offense. Teasingly pulling on his collar, Jenny whispered a parting sweetness in his ear. Her scent was wonderful: delicate and faintly floral, like orange blossoms. He helped her rise and stumbled over his own farewell, trying to make sense of what on earth had just happened.

"Until Friday," Jenny whispered, slipping into her pumps and running into the night.

CHAPTER 27

J enny managed to catch the ten o'clock bus. The only other
rider was an elderly woman, sitting and gently snoozing with
a bag of dirty potatoes in her lap. Relieved to find relative solitude, Jenny took a vacant seat across from her. As the bus lurched
into motion, she stared out the frosty window and escaped into her
swirling thoughts.

I've just kissed Professor Carter. Oh, my goodness, we kissed. I
kissed him.

Now that Jenny was out of Daniel's arms, that fact induced a
mild state of panic.

I kissed a professor, she repeated. Oh my goodness, I kissed my
professor.

She pressed her fingertips into her throbbing temple. It had
been such an adrenaline-filled day, from the intense joy of winning
the Amity to the devastating grief of losing Egypt (and of course,
the exhilaration of everything that had happened afterwards).
Mercifully, somewhere along the dark drive her panic subsided.
Anxious thoughts were replaced by calmer ones, far sweeter ones –
thoughts that swelled her heart with quiet hope and happiness.

Daniel Carter cares for me.

He truly cares for me.

And I'm seeing him on Friday.

The bus halted to a stop, and a few potatoes popped out of the old woman's bag. The lady let out a rattling snore, but did not stir. Jenny absentmindedly collected the produce, replacing it quietly so as not to wake her. The driver wearily asked, "Getting off, Miss? Last call for Haxby Lane."

"Thank you," Jenny stammered, hurrying to the front and dropping a token into his till.

"Night, Miss," the man said gruffly as the bus door creaked shut. Jenny trudged through the two snowy blocks to her apartment building. She climbed the exterior staircase quickly, anxious to assure Margie that she was safe and that she'd been, well, nowhere in particular, as she would surely have to say.

Upon opening the door, she was met by a cacophony of whispers and cheers.

"She's here!"

"*Oi,* she's here!"

"Finally!"

"Jennifer Celine Ellison, *where have you been?*"

"At last, the woman of the hour! Congratulations, Jenny!" Peter whooped, clapping heartily.

"Well done, Professor Ellison!" a boisterous Sagan added.

Nyra and Margie started up a badly tuned chorus of, "For she's a jolly good fellow!" which the lads (and a reluctant Jillian) joined in singing. All four of them were crowded into her tiny parlor wearing paper hats and brandishing cups of what was unmistakably peach juice and ginger ale. A few limp, salmon-colored balloons hung from the ceiling, and a tray of half-eaten pastries lay askew on the coffee table.

"What's all this?" Jenny exclaimed, unbuttoning her coat. "Have you been waiting for me? Oh Marge, I'm so sorry I'm late, I completely forgot to phone you, and I—"

"Ah, not to worry, isn't that right, Marge? Hail the conquering heroine!" Peter cheered, picking Jenny up by the waist and spinning her above his head. "The first female Amity winner in over twenty years! And very deserving too, don't you think, ladies and gentlemen?"

"It's just marvelous, Jenny," Nyra said, beaming.

"Thank you." Jenny pried herself from Peter's hands, conscious of another embrace she had just enjoyed. "All of you, thank you so much. Oh, just look at this!" She beamed, then winced. "It looks like you've been to so much trouble."

"We waited for a few hours," Margie said quietly. "But then we got rather hungry, so I'm afraid we've eaten most of the meat pies. I think there are some cherry tartlets left, and there's a bit of vanilla ice cream in the icebox. Shall I go and fetch it?" Her roommate stalked away rather stiffly.

"She's a bit miffed you blew her off again," Nyra whispered to Jenny from behind her hand.

"She only said to be here at seven," Jenny groaned. "I thought she was taking me to dinner. I swear, I had no idea you all were here."

"Well, it was meant to be a surprise," Jillian said, examining a nail. "Where were you, anyway?"

"Just ... just dawdling."

"Come in and tell us all your news!" Nyra ushered her to the couch. "It's so *thrilling*, Jenny! Crete. Although, I know you had your heart set on Egypt. I'm so sorry if you were disappointed. Were you, Jenny?"

"Yes," she admitted.

"That's rotten luck," Sagan said with a sympathetic nod.

"What are you talking about?" Jillian said. "Rotten luck, my ... she's an *Amity winner,* isn't she?"

"Oh, shut it, Jilly," Peter snapped. "There's no need to be sour, not on Jenny's big day."

"No, Jillian's right for once," Jenny interjected. "I'm going. So many people hoped to, and I've been given a tremendous chance. I'm really very grateful."

"That's all tickety-boo," Nyra said with a frown, "but you do look odd, Jenny. Almost feverish. Are you sickening for something?"

"No," Jenny said hastily. "I'm just tired, that's all. Let's finish up the cherry tartlets, shall we? I'll help Margie with the ice cream."

"I know just the tonic for you, Jenny," Peter called as she retreated to the kitchen. "A night on the town with me!"

"Give it a rest," Nyra hissed. "She's not interested, I've told you before."

Peter took no notice of this. Under his breath he stubbornly replied, "I'll take my chances, Nyra, thanks very much."

CHAPTER 28

On Wednesday morning Daniel was whistling again. In just two hours he would see Jenny. The previous day of teaching had felt like the longest of his career, but with no established way to communicate with her, there was nothing to be done but wait for their next lecture. And walk the campus between classes, of course, on the off chance they might meet. So far, they had not. Fortunately Jenny's attendance on Wednesday was assured. Even now, Daniel was devising inconspicuous ways to start up a conversation.

He was well into the chorus of "It's Magic," a tune he'd recently heard in some silly Doris Day film – *Romance on the High Seas*, if he remembered correctly – when Max walked in, his trusty clipboard clutched at his side.

"Good morning, Professor Carter."

Daniel stopped his whistling at once. "Max. You're in early today."

"Yes, sir. I've just been checking your mail. You've got another telegram from Ambassador Nassar." He held out a small yellow envelope. "The ministry wants to confirm the date of the stone's return. How would you like me to respond?"

"I'll take care of it." Daniel unfolded the short message and began to read. Max hovered eagerly near his left shoulder.

"Dr. Carter," the lad said slowly. "I was doing some filing yesterday, and I couldn't help but notice that you've applied for an additional dig permit."

"That's right," he confirmed, still reading the telegram.

"Well?" Max prompted.

"Well, what?"

"Do you think you missed something over the summer, sir?"

"It's just a routine inquiry, that's all." He reached for his sweater. "The ambassador sounds impatient. I'd better go and answer him. Look over the Cyrillic assignment while I'm gone, will you? We can discuss the rubric later."

Daniel moved towards the door, but Max, blithely unaware that he'd been dismissed, readied further questions.

"Where are you planning to dig?" he asked, speaking very quickly. "How extensively will you excavate? When will you begin?"

"I don't know, Max."

"You don't have the funding for another dig," the boy objected, pacing just behind him. "You'd need to hire more men, and all of your project funds have been allocated; you told me so yourself."

"Let me worry about funding," Daniel said, now losing his patience. "For now, just—"

"But Professor," Max persisted, overtaking him, "if I may say so, Ambassador Nassar isn't likely to approve a new dig until the original conservation work is finished. That is, unless you were extremely confident of finding something new. Are you, sir?"

"I'm asking for permission to look," he said firmly, "as a matter of routine. That is all. Now, let me get on."

"Does this have anything to do with the stone?" Max stared at him with a look that fell short of greed, but came to near it for Daniel's comfort. "You have some leftover leads from last summer, is that it? If you need any help with the permit paperwork, I can—"

"I'm handling it, Max," Daniel said in a tone that closed the conversation. He tossed his assistant the telegram. "File that with the rest of the ambassador's correspondence, all right? I'll be back in a few minutes."

Max's face fell. "Yes, sir."

Daniel swept out of the room, disgruntled by the lad's incessant probing. He was starting to regret ever having given Max a key to his study; with Chilcott sniffing around, he didn't want to draw more attention to the new permits than was necessary. A little extra paperwork on his plate seemed a small price to pay to avoid that possibility.

He took the long route to the professor's lounge in an attempt to clear his head. As he walked to the mail room, he noticed the door to the Dean's office was, yet again, slightly ajar. Daniel checked his watch. Antony had a class in five minutes. Was the old man holed up in his room and smoking again? He grinned, relishing the chance to goad his old mentor, but was halted in his approach by the clear sound of an argument coming from within. Antony was engaged in a terse discussion with none other than *Dr. Chilcott.*

"... true that he's more liberal-minded than most of our faculty when it comes to work placement, but I for one view that as a strength. You're making too much of this, William," Dr. Miller said, sounding weary.

"But why this particular girl?" Chilcott blustered. "Why a third year, why now? What makes her more qualified than the rest of our applicants?"

Realizing that Jenny was the subject of this debate, Daniel ducked into a small alcove to the left of Dr. Miller's office and strained his ear towards the conflict.

"William," – Daniel imagined Antony plucking at his bowtie impatiently – "Jennifer Ellison is one of the brightest students I have ever had the pleasure of teaching. I would have put her name forward myself, had Dr. Carter not beaten me to it, and I'm enormously proud to have her working on my site. I have no doubt she will be one of the hardest-working assistants I have ever coached. Such a gracious little thing, she even sent me a note thanking me for the opportunity. What young man would have thought of doing that, I ask you?" Antony chuckled.

The sound of Chilcott's pacing faded as he snapped the door shut. Daniel knelt and opened a ventilation grate near his foot, willing the garbled conversation to become clearer. Mercifully, it did.

"... and then I thought, what if there is something ... *untoward* going on? Eh?"

For a moment Antony did not answer. "I'm afraid I don't have the pleasure of understanding you, William."

"Well, she's a pretty girl, isn't she?" Chilcott railed. "Dr. Carter's young, and as far as I know completely unattached. An easy target for any opportunist." He lowered his voice. "Suppose Miss Ellison found a rather more – shall we say – surefire way of strengthening her application? It would certainly explain the vehemence of Dr. Carter's arguments."

"I assume you have some evidence to present in defense of this claim?" Miller cut in sharply. "For I will not tolerate idle slander, William Chilcott. You are not to sully the name of any Browning professor or student without probable cause. What is your proof?"

Chilcott resumed his pacing. "I have none. Yet."

"Indeed," Antony returned coldly. "In light of that fact, I think you had best give up your weekly complaints against Dr. Carter and get out of my office. I have work to do."

"What sort of complaints might these be, Dr. Chilcott?" Daniel said, walking directly into the office and facing the two men with folded arms. Chilcott's face paled at the sight of him, and Antony appeared scarcely less stunned.

"Dr. Carter," Chilcott stammered, "I—"

"Another effort to discredit me, Chilcott?" Daniel glared at him. "I would have thought you tired of that by now."

"Poppycock!" Chilcott spat, in a rather lame defense. "You misheard me. I was—"

"Accusing me of accepting sexual favors to further a student's career." Daniel's dark eyes flashed. "Do I have that right?"

Chilcott straightened up haughtily. "Not accusing. Just ... questioning."

"In the future," Daniel said through gritted teeth, "you will bring your 'questions' directly to me. I think you'll find me more than able to answer them."

Dr. Chilcott suddenly looked uneasy. "Come now, there's no need for all this fuss. I'm only seeking to uphold the good name of the Amity program. When suspicious activity such as this occurs, I feel I am honor bound to—"

"Honor would compel you to give up spreading rumors. If you won't, then I insist you face the consequences like a man."

Chilcott's nostrils flared. "Are you threa—"

"Stay away from me, Chilcott." Daniel unfolded his arms and strode out of the office. "And my lab. That's a warning."

CHAPTER 29

The goal was to keep her eyes fixed on the page. That was Jenny's plan, her intent: to keep taking notes as calmly and carefully as she always did, without raising her head during Daniel's lecture even once. It proved very difficult, however, now that she was actually in his lecture hall. Jenny longed to make even the briefest eye contact to see if he, too, might betray signs of significant feeling. Somehow she managed to keep her eyes on her notes, letting his warm, deep voice wash over her like an embrace.

It was almost as comforting.

Despite the fascinating subject matter – Cyrillic, a precursor to Slavic alphabets – the sixty-minute period passed by at a glacial pace. At long last the bell tolled, and she heard Daniel call out over the crowd, "Worksheets are due this Friday, ladies and gentlemen. By the beginning of class, remember that!"

The worksheet was the least of her concerns as she slid out of her seat, plotting a casual question to ask about the assignment. Before she could approach Daniel, a cheery voice at her right interrupted her thoughts.

"Hiya, Jenny!"

It was Peter.

"Great lecture today!" He grinned and stuck a pencil behind his ear. "Cyrillic. I'd never even heard of it before."

"You've changed your tune," Jenny said, pinning up a loose curl. "Are you a supporter of Dr. Carter's now?"

"Yes, well." Peter shrugged. "Only two weeks left of term. What's the use in holding a grudge? He seems like a decent enough fellow. Poor chap, it's hardly his fault all the girls are soft on him, is it?"

"Right," Jenny quietly agreed. Feeling that now-familiar swoop behind her navel at the mention of his name, she snuck the tiniest glance in Daniel's direction. It was the first time she'd taken him in since they'd parted. He looked as handsome as ever, today sporting a dark blue sweater and tan slacks and trying, unsuccessfully, to smooth his hair. It was always endearingly untidy after a demanding lecture. He was listening with kindly attention to a student's concerns, but his shoulders were strangely stiff, almost rigid. She wondered if he, too, was watching her out of the corner of his eye.

Peter launched into a string of jokes and campus gossip, but Jenny's mind remained fixed on how best to approach Daniel. His conversation with the student was ending, and the hall was emptying fast. Ironically, it seemed the least suspicious to speak to him when the room was full – casually, on subject matter, and in plain sight. She was running out of time.

"Jenny? Are you listening?"

"Hmm?" She turned back to Peter. "What?"

"I swear, Jenny, I don't know where you go sometimes." Peter laughed. "I said, we never got to properly celebrate your Amity win."

"Oh?" She raised her bows. "We had a party, didn't we?"

"That wasn't a proper celebration, was it. Let me take you out to dinner. How does this Friday sound?"

She hesitated. "I—"

"There's a nice little place in Grassby," he continued hurriedly. "A Greek restaurant. I thought, since you're going to Crete, we might—"

"Peter, why are you asking me?" Jenny blurted out before he could continue.

"I'm not sure what you mean?" he answered with a chuckle. "I just thought we could celebrate."

"Peter," Jenny said with a deep, agonized blush. She'd have given anything in the world not to say her next words and stumbled to find them. "You're a good friend. But ... I'm ... trying to keep it that way."

His expression froze, then soured. When he next spoke, his voice betrayed an uncharacteristic tremble.

"I don't understand you, Jenny. I want to spend time with you, as more than a friend, I admit, and I've had to edge out quite a few fellows for the chance. But you're never around."

"I ..."

"Even when you are, you're so focused on your studies that you can't see anything or anyone else."

"Peter, I've just been busy this term, with the Amity and everything. I really haven't had time to—"

"I know you're busy, I know that," he cut her off. "Yet it's more than that. You don't show up to any of our outings. You brush off your friends, you push us away, all of us. Me, Sagan, Nyra, even Margie." He gazed at her wistfully. "I used to admire your drive, I really did. You're spunky, you're different. You always seem to be thinking about the things no one else is, and making plans no other girls would even dream of making, and I find that so very ... but now I can't help thinking you're the one missing the point of it all. If you stepped away from your books for a moment, just a moment, you might realize there are people around you who care." He swallowed painfully. "You might find that you could care for some of them too."

His sincerity might have been touching, had Jenny's offense not crowded out such feelings. "I'm sorry you feel that way," she said, bristling. "I've always been entirely honest with you. We're good friends, and—"

"Maybe Anders is right," Peter grumbled, staring at the wall behind her. "Maybe you *are* a trophy hunter, dangling a string of fellows off a loose end. You're not interested in anything real, are you?"

"How ... how dare ..." she stammered, too stunned by this insult to form a proper response.

"Goodbye, Jenny." Peter backed away mournfully. "I hope you have fun in Crete, I really do. A word of advice, eh? Pick up a souvenir for Margie while you're there. She's been a bit down in the mouth lately. Not that you'd notice."

Jenny swallowed drily and tried again to defend herself. "How dare you?"

"If you do change your mind about Friday," he said, turning on his heel, "you know where to find me."

Jenny nodded curtly to conceal how severely this rant had rankled her. Guilt and embarrassment writhed within her like dual-headed snakes, and to add injury to insult, there was now no chance of speaking to Daniel. Dr. Miller had entered the class-room, and just now he and Daniel were engaged in a rather heated exchange. Jenny could hear him protesting as she walked by.

"You'll just have to find someone else, Antony." Daniel shot her the briefest glance, causing Jenny's heart to leap into her throat. His gaze was intense, penetrating. Stay, his eyes seemed to plead. She slowed her pace.

"My dear chap, I would not be asking you if there were anyone else," Dr. Miller huffed. "Chilcott has something he can't get out of, Painswicke will be traveling to a conference in Cannes, and none of the other professors are bothering to return my memos. I know it's a big favor to ask, but the fact is I simply cannot attend. You must go in my place."

"Antony," Daniel said firmly, "if it were any other weekend I would, but I can't. I've already made plans."

"Well I'm certain Charlie Russell wouldn't mind if you push your billiards off a day or two," Dr. Miller chuckled. "The annual gala is a cakewalk, it's almost formulaic. Step one, greet President LaTrell and find a subtle way of reminding him we are *well* within our departmental budget. Step two, shake hands with three or four of the visiting dignitaries, extolling the virtues of the university and, I might add, Browning's contributions to archaeological research over the past two decades. Step three, thank Patricia and Silas Manwaring, the Tregardners, and Lord and Lady Corvellian for their continued generous support of Browning. Step four—"

"Antony, I'm not meeting Charlie for billiards. I have an important engagement, and I can't break it. I'm sorry."

"Ah!" The dean leaned forward with interest. "Did you finally ask that first-floor secretary out to dinner? I thought I noticed a little spark between the two of you at our last faculty meeting. Or perhaps you've rekindled things with Rebecca Tregardner at last?"

"No," Daniel replied hurriedly, though not soon enough to spare Jenny's feelings. Her heart had sunk at the mere suggestion of his interest in another, and her plan to linger was replaced with a passionate desire not to overhear this conversation. She kept walking past.

"Daniel," Dr. Miller murmured. "I'm truly sorry to ask this of you, especially after the nastiness with Chilcott this morning. Whatever you have planned, I'm sure it's … very important to you. But my sister is still recovering from her surgery, and I promised I would be with her this weekend. For support. I leave for Blythe tomorrow."

"Antony—"

"Someone has to represent the department," he insisted. "You know how tight funding has been after the war. A strong presence at the gala is critical for our future needs. I don't want our funding requests to be shuttered in favor of some newfangled electrical panel for engineering." He wrinkled his nose in disgust at the very thought. "Please, my boy."

Jenny had reached the door. Though she was not looking at Daniel, she felt instinctively that he was watching her. She nodded her head once, and walked out. As she leaned sadly against the outer wall, he let out a rough exhale and said, "All right. I'll try and move my plans to Saturday."

"Thank you, Daniel," Dr. Miller sighed with relief. "Actually, it's a two-day event. The gala dinner is on Friday – black tie – and the charity auction is Saturday afternoon, followed by a concert at the music hall. Some of the vocal majors are performing operatic pieces. Heaven help us all. I'll send you the details this afternoon. Again, a thousand thanks, Dr. Carter!"

Jenny heard Dr. Miller's heavy footsteps approaching and tripped down the hall so as not to be caught eavesdropping. She had not got far when she heard a jolly, "Miss Ellison!" resounding from behind her.

"Good afternoon, Dr. Miller," she said, smiling bravely.

"What a fortunate meeting, Miss Ellison." Dr. Miller beamed at her. "I've just finished preparing some materials to get you up to speed on my site: six or seven of my published papers, some charts, a map of the area, a few other odds and ends. I also have a wonderful book on the islands of Greece. We work on several of them, you know, not just Crete."

"Yes, I'd heard that," Jenny replied politely.

"They're in my office," Dr. Miller continued. "I was hoping you might spend a good part of this weekend reviewing them. We should also make an appointment to discuss this summer's work. Perhaps Monday morning?"

"Oh." Jenny worked to keep her expression neutral. "It's ... it's a bit early to start preparing for this summer, isn't it?"

"Well, there's a lot to know." He chuckled. "But you're right, of course. No need to run before you can walk. I'll just lend you the articles for this first weekend, shall I? We can fetch them together."

He gestured towards the staircase with a kindly smile. Jenny began helplessly walking to the third floor. As she reached the stairway's curve, she realized with a jolt that Daniel was watching them climb, his arms folded and an utterly determined look on his face.

CHAPTER 30

The gala that Friday was a nightmarish bore, as Daniel had predicted. Hundreds of stuck-up Browning boosters crowded into the large ballroom, drinking cheap champagne and gushing about their latest trips abroad. Daniel had shaken President LaTrell's hand, made the necessary promotions for the department, and left as soon as he could. It had proven nearly impossible to extricate himself from the grasp of Lady Corvellian.

"Are you quite sure you're a professor?" she'd crooned, pinching his cheek. "Why, I simply cannot believe it!" she'd giggled, leaning so near to him that his eyes burned with the stench of her perfume. "You're just too good-looking a boy to be one of these broken-down gargoyles!"

It was a miracle when he managed to escape her clutches and slip out the exit. After the stuffiness of the Browning ballroom, the cold night air felt as restorative as the Balm of Gilead. A light snow fell, gently frosting his tuxedo and muffling the swoosh of a passing bus. He had completely forgotten his overcoat in the cloakroom, but wild horses couldn't have dragged him back to retrieve it. Better to freeze than to be spotted again by Lady Corvellian.

Despite the cold, Daniel pulled off his black tie and shoved it roughly into his jacket. He *hated* fancy dress, and that article of clothing was an irritating reminder of the last three hours. Determined to blow off some steam, he wrestled open his stiff collar and walked into the night.

A sharp pang of hunger only added to his discomfort. He'd snagged three or four salmon puffs off a passing tray at the gala, but had been too occupied with leaving to invest time procuring a full plate. He debated whether to ring Charlie and suggest they go out for a bite, but decided against it. Somehow it seemed too late to dine, and too early to go home. Having no set destination, he wandered aimlessly through the streets of Belmont without much caring where his feet took him.

The streets of the little town were quiet; the pubs in the main square, however, were brightly lit and crammed with students drinking away the weekend. Daniel could hear a rowdy chorus of "No, Nay, Never," spilling out of The Blue Dragon. He wondered if Jenny were among the revelers, although he thought he remembered her saying she wasn't much of a drinker.

Jenny.

He kicked at a stone in frustration. He hadn't spoken to her all week. He had tried to this morning, after class, but she'd walked out of his lecture hall without so much as a backwards glance. The memory of it had troubled him all day. What could have been behind such avoidance? Where did things stand between them? When would he next get the chance to ask her?

These matters were uncertain, but of one thing Daniel was sure.

Dr. Miller knew.

The thought filled Daniel with a strange mixture of relief and dread. There could be no other explanation for Antony's odd behavior. He had very neatly given Jenny extra work, roped him into a full weekend of commitments, and purposefully brought up women from his past in her presence. A pang of guilt struck Daniel's heart at that last point. There simply hadn't been time to explain Antony's romantic prodding or defend himself against it.

One matter truly plagued him. If Dr. Miller suspected, then why hadn't he said anything to Daniel outright? Was he giving him the space to find a solution? Or was the dean merely thinking how best to act and keeping Daniel on his guard in the meantime?

He let his mind drift to the scenery of his walk, needing to escape the crush of too many questions without answers. Since he'd paid little heed to his surroundings, Daniel was actually lost – an impressive feat in a town that was so very small.

Turning to get his bearings, he watched for a moment as a lone dog barked at the falling snow. White-plastered blocks of flats lined each side of the road, looking ghostly in the moonlight. There was a militant row of hawthorn trees to his left, and a single streetlight burned dimly at the end of a sidewalk. Daniel squinted to observe the lamp more closely. There was something distinctly familiar about it. It was more elaborately designed than most corner lights, with an odd crown-like piece of ironwork adorning its top. Haxby Lane, the signpost beneath it said.

With a start, Daniel recognized the two-story building that lay across the street. It was Jenny's. He had unconsciously traced the path they'd walked after the concert.

Chiding himself for being a foolish, lovesick Romeo, Daniel turned before he could be noticed. Yet the sound of a scuffle in the distance made him pause. It was coming from the north, the direction of her building. Glancing back at it, Daniel saw two people stumbling about the exterior landing and pounding heavily against the central flat's door.

Her door.

Without hesitating, without thinking, Daniel ran at top speed towards the building. As he approached, he heard a hiccuping male voice complaining loudly.

"Amity winner ... *hyup* ... brilliant little Jenny, always ... *hyup* ...

stuck in a book."

With a burst of fury, Daniel realized one of the lurkers was Anders Manwaring. A blindly drunk Anders Manwaring. The boy shook her doorknob roughly. "Don't be such a spoilsport ..." he drawled. "Peter told me about the Amity. I only want to congratulate you. Isn't that right, Petey?"

"S'right," Peter Collier slurred. Stumbling backwards, he brandished a bottle of whisky high overhead. "Here's to the queen of de–Nile, Jennifer Celine Ellison!"

Daniel silently climbed the exterior stairs, keeping out of sight and watching as the boys downed more enormous gulps of whiskey.

"Let's go," Peter said with a yawn and a belch. "We can talk to her tomorrow. She's not home, Anderssss."

"Oh, she's home. It's Friday night, isn't it? She'll be in there *studying*. Come on ... open up," Anders barked, kicking loudly at the door.

"*No!*"

Daniel's heart missed several beats as he heard the muffled voice from behind the curtained window.

"Go away, Anders! I've telephoned the police!"

"Mr. Manwaring!" Daniel bellowed as he reached the top of the stairs. He strode menacingly forward. "I think you'd better go home now."

Anders jumped at his sudden appearance, while Peter frowned and swayed back and forth on his heels. Both young men seemed unable to place him in their drunken state.

"And who might you ..." Peter drawled.

Jenny's curtains flitted open.

"Keep the door locked," Daniel muttered to her.

Anders took a fortifying swig of whisky. "Why it's Mr. Pretty-face, of course. Have you come to ... *hyup* ... tell little Jenny she's not going to the pyramids? Oh, she already knows. We told her. Serves her right, I say. Ungrateful girl. It's a little late for a … *hyup* … a social call, isn't it Mr. Prettyface?"

"My thoughts exactly," Daniel growled as Peter squinted at him in confusion. "Go home, gentlemen. You heard Miss Ellison. She's called the police, and they'll be here any moment."

Anders let out a short, barking laugh. "That doesn't *matter*," he replied, with surprisingly good enunciation for one so inebriated. "They're my old friiiieeeends. And my parents wouldn't tolerate—"

Daniel would hear no more of this nonsense. He pulled roughly on the boy's arm and steered him away from the door. Roaring in indignation, Anders broke free from Daniel's grip and swung his bottle wildly overhead. Daniel only narrowly escaped it; it shattered against the outdoor railing, and with a look of drunken rage Anders stabbed the fragments wildly upwards. One edge caught Daniel hard on the shoulder.

With a roar of triumph Anders swung for Daniel's nose, but this time he calmly ducked, stepped right, and grabbed the boy's dominant hand. With a single sharp twist, he pinned it behind Anders' back and smashed the boy's chest over his knee. With a dull thud, Daniel shoved him to the ground. Anders curled his knees to his chest and gasped for air. Though he coughed and whimpered, he did not attempt to get up. Peter, meanwhile, had long since fled the scene, swearing and crashing into the side of the landing as he fumbled his way down the stairs.

The apartment door burst open.

"Daniel!" Jenny whispered in a panic. "What are you doing?"

Sirens split the night air as a police car with flashing lights pulled in front of the building.

"Get inside," she ordered him. *"Now."*

Daniel hesitated. "Is—"

"Margie's not home," Jenny said impatiently. "Now get inside."

Daniel obeyed and closed the door firmly behind him. He stayed pinned against it, not daring to move or even breathe. His pulse, so calm and steady during the familiar act of fighting, was racing in its aftermath. A bead of perspiration trickled down his forehead as the police lights cast long shadows on the opposite wall.

"Are you all right, Miss?" one of the men asked.

"Good evening, gentlemen," Jenny replied hurriedly. "Thank you so much for coming. This young man has been trying to force entry to my flat for the last twenty minutes. He's a student at Browning University. His name is—"

"Oh, we know who this is," the second officer replied wearily. "Anders Manwaring, isn't it?"

"Phiiil!" Anders yelled out happily. "Thank goodness you're here. Mr. Prettyface just hurt me. You should lock him up, ssssstraight away."

"He's completely drunk," Jenny explained. "Possibly even hallucinating."

"You don't say," Phil groaned. "All right. Let's get him up, Connor. I want to get home to the wife."

"Come on, Mr. Manwaring. Up you go." The two officers grunted as they heaved Anders between them. "You're going to have a nice long sleep in the jailhouse, and in the morning we'll call your parents."

"Oh, they're going to love this," Phil muttered.

"But I'm not the bad one," Anders moaned as they dragged him off. "It's Mr. ... *hyup* ... Prettyface you should throw in the bucket. He's a bully and a traitor, and he *hurt me*, and I hate him. Jennnnnny, tell Phil you hate him, too!"

"There was another boy," Jenny said, more reluctantly. "He's run off somewhere, but he can't have got far. I doubt he even knows where he is."

"Not to worry. We'll find him."

"Goodnight, Miss." Connor tipped his cap. "Sorry these lads have been bothering you. Won't happen again."

"Thank you, officers," Jenny called after them. "Goodnight!"

CHAPTER 31

Jenny slammed the door behind her and locked it.

"What are you doing here?" she demanded. She was so upset that she barely registered the fact she was wearing her old blue pajamas and robe, while he was in his gala tuxedo. "What were you *thinking,* thrashing Anders like that?"

"What was I thinking?" Daniel rebutted, the tips of his ears reddening. "You mean what was Anders thinking, or Peter? Jenny, they looked as though they were trying to—"

"I'd called the police, hadn't I?" she broke in, still too distressed to listen. "Everything was in hand. You're lucky the officers came when they did and not a moment sooner. Think what might have happened if they'd seen you, Daniel! You, a Browning professor, in another fight with a student!" she fumed.

"But I couldn't just—"

"Come with me," she ordered. "You're getting blood on the carpet."

"What?"

He reached up to feel his neck and shoulder. A steady stream of blood flowed from the edge of his open collar. Anders' broken bottle had unfortunately proven effective. Jenny took Daniel's hand and led him to the kitchen, trying to ignore the way his fingers closed immediately around hers.

"Wait here."

Jenny left him sitting at the table while she fetched her nursing kit. She had barely touched it since the end of the war. It took a full minute to search it out in the back of her dark closet, but at last she felt its familiar shape: oblong and medium-sized, with two worn leather handles at the top. Hoping she had left it well-stocked, Jenny hoisted it out of the room and into the kitchen. Daniel had taken off his coat and was attempting to stem the flow of blood with his fingers.

"Keep the pressure on it," Jenny instructed crisply, rolling up her sleeves. For the first time in two years, she was using her "nursing tone." It felt like hearing the voice of an old friend.

"Unbutton your shirt, please," she asked, pulling a vial of antiseptic out of the bag.

Daniel managed the task surprisingly well one-handed; in fact, he began unabashedly slipping off the whole thing. Jenny's brisk nursing manner faltered as his well-cut chest was revealed. For the briefest of seconds she became keenly aware that they were alone, in her apartment, completely unchaperoned, with her bedroom door only a few steps behind her. Steeling her nerves she mumbled, "Could you ... could you possibly keep the right sleeve on, please."

Daniel made no reply, but after a little pause, he shrugged it back over one shoulder. From the corner of her eye, Jenny could see that he was smiling.

"Hold still," she said, wetting a cloth with antiseptic. "I'm going to clean the cut."

She gently removed Daniel's fingers from the wound to inspect it. It was about two inches long, jagged but not deep.

"You're lucky," she said. "It's small. But this may sting a little." Daniel watched with interest as she dabbed the area with disinfectant.

"What are you doing here?" she repeated, though the anger had long since evaporated from her voice. "I thought you were at the gala."

"I was. Then I went walking, and I just … sort of ended up here. I was going to leave, but then I saw Anders and Peter."

She kept cleaning the cut, not quite meeting his gaze.

"Jenny?"

After dabbing quietly for several more moments, she said, "They just showed up twenty minutes ago. I was asleep, and I heard a pounding at the door. I saw at once that they were drunk, so I didn't let them in."

"Very wise," he said, looking relieved.

"They wouldn't leave, so I called the police. Hold this, please."

Daniel obediently pressed the cloth against his neck while Jenny cut a length of bandage. "Where is Margie, anyway?" he asked, quite calmly for someone who was bleeding freely.

"Skiing in Blythe with her parents. It's the students' weekend. Most of my building went up there."

"Right." Daniel watched her intently. "Now tell me about Anders."

"What?"

"What happened between you and Anders? I heard the way he spoke to you, Jenny. The night we first translated the stone, he cornered you outside of the lab. He was threatening you. Why?"

Jenny didn't answer. While cleaning Daniel's shoulder, she had noticed something strange on his lower back. To the left of his spine was a long, ragged scar, about the length of her hand. Judging by its gruesome scarring pattern, it had been hastily and poorly treated. She glanced up at him in alarm.

"Where did you get that?"

"Get what?"

"That scar. On your lower back."

"Oh." Daniel assumed a light expression. "Appendicitis."

Pointing impatiently to the right side of his abdomen, she said, "*That's* your appendix."

" ... Right."

"Daniel, where did you get that wound?" Jenny repeated, ignoring his amused expression. "It looks awful, and painful. Is it from your fight with the student?"

"That's another thing," Daniel said, his countenance darkening. "What did you mean when you said, 'Another fight with a student?' What are you talking about?"

"The student you got in a brawl with last year," Jenny said sharply. She trimmed the bandage, as her first attempt had been too large. "The one where a man ended up in the hospital."

After staring blankly at her for a moment, Daniel threw back his head with a bursting laugh.

"These students," he muttered, swearing under his breath. "Yes. I was in a fight, but not with an undergraduate. Although, the fight was at a pub, so I imagine there were some students there. That's probably how the rumor mill got started."

"What happened?" Jenny demanded, determined to finish her interrogation.

A far-off look came into Daniel's eyes, and he scowled. "A local man was saying stupid, ignorant things about the war. About the Nazi death camps, and Jews and Gypsies and who knows what else. I took exception to what he was saying, and I let him know it."

"By punching him," Jenny concluded.

"Well ..." Daniel looked a little ruffled. "I attempted to talk with him first, but when he got riled it just, sort of, happened. A few other men got in on the fight." He shook his head. "I'm really not sure who threw the first punch."

"And Browning didn't do anything about it?" Jenny said in disbelief.

He shrugged. "I got a formal warning. Most of the administrators were on my side. The war had ended not long before. Emotions were still running very high."

"Did a man really end up in hospital?"

Daniel laughed hollowly. "Oh yes, someone ended up in hospital. Me."

"*You?*"

He nodded. "Unfortunately, the fellow I mentioned was a much better fighter than Anders. I won, but got a badly split lip in the process."

Jenny thought about the sharp, snake-like way Daniel had twisted Anders' arm behind his back. He had been completely calm, anticipating his opponent's movements and restraining him just enough to incapacitate, but not seriously wound him. It had been like watching a lethal sort of dance.

"Where did you learn to fight like that?" she asked, putting surgical tape over his bandage. "I've never seen anything like it."

"The army," Daniel replied simply. He flexed his fingers, as though remembering some deeply engrained training.

"I only hope Anders and Peter were too drunk to recognize you," Jenny mumbled. "One moment more and they might have said your real name."

He winced as Jenny pressed the bandage against his wound. "Back to the subject of Anders ..."

"Hold still. I'm nearly finished now."

"Jenny?" Daniel's dark eyes found hers. "Anders?"

Again, she avoided the question. "How was the gala in the end?"

His brows knitted together, but though he looked distressed by the change of subject, he went along with it. "It was fine. Well, no, it was dreadful. Unless you like bad champagne and salmon puffs."

She smirked. "There. Finished."

He inspected the neat bandage with a curious smile. "You're a skilled nurse. Thank you, Jenny."

"You won't need sutures, though I'm afraid it'll scar," she cautioned.

He shrugged, re-buttoning his shirt. "I've known worse."

"So I see." Jenny gestured to the wound on his back, her breath catching as she waited for him to share the gruesome story behind it.

Daniel opened his mouth to speak, then stopped. He pressed his lips together firmly, and in that moment Jenny knew he was either readying another excuse or preparing to explain that he *couldn't* explain. Though he likely had good reason for such ambivalence, something inside of Jenny hardened. All of the strain and uncertainty of their situation – the unspoken questions, and the distance, and the hesitancy between them – made another secret seem too much to bear just now. With a stony look, she snapped her bag shut and began to stalk woodenly towards the bedroom.

Daniel caught her hand before she had gone two steps. She looked at their entangled fingers, then slowly up at him. His countenance was agitated, and most of the blood had drained from his face. The hand that so firmly grasped hers, however, was warm and steady. A look of quiet resolution entered his eyes.

"I had an assignment."

CHAPTER 32

There was a tremendous pause.

"In Telemark," he continued, filling the void.

"No," Jenny whispered hoarsely. "No. You said you had an intelligence job. A desk job. Safely cracking codes from some London warehouse."

Daniel shook his head very slowly. "I never said that."

After another strenuous bout of silence, Jenny walked back to him. "Tell me what happened," she murmured. "Please."

He said nothing, but drew her to his knee. Despite the grimness of the moment, Jenny could not help but smile a little as he snuck one arm about her waist.

After what seemed an eternity, he took a deep breath and said, "I – well, we – I had a partner, you see. A contact in the Norwegian resistance." The words seemed to strangle him. With great effort he continued, "We were dropped behind enemy lines. It was a difficult landing, very difficult. The wind was strong, and ... well, it was the dead of night. We couldn't see our hands in front of our faces, so we overshot our drop point. My partner gashed his knee pretty badly during the landing, but there was no option of going back. We had a chance to cripple their waterworks, to try and derail the

German advanced weapons program. I can't tell you much more than that."

"That's all right," Jenny said quickly. She had a feeling Daniel was telling her too much already, yet she couldn't stop herself from seeking further details. "What happened? Did they catch you as you landed?"

Daniel swallowed. "No, we reached our target easily enough. But a couple of soldiers spotted us on our way back to the extraction point. We hadn't brought any firearms since we had to travel silently. It was that kind of mission: do it right or don't come back. Those were the instructions. We disarmed them, and then it was hand-to-hand combat."

Jenny stifled another little cry. She could guess what had happened to the Nazi soldiers.

"And the ... the scar?" she prompted, her voice trembling slightly.

He winced. "Knife wound. I didn't see when – anyway, it wasn't as bad as it looks. My partner patched me up pretty well."

"What happened to him?" Jenny whispered.

He shook his head. "I don't know. We met another Nazi patrol over the ridge, and we got separated. But I hope he got back all right. I've tried to find out if he survived, but ..." he shrugged. "I don't even know his real name."

Jenny buried her face in the uninjured side of Daniel's neck. The war was long since over, yet it was still finding ways to terrify and possess those that it left behind. In this moment, she wanted nothing more than to hold him and ensure he was never in such danger again.

Judging by Daniel's cautious response, he was surprised by her sudden show of affection. She supposed this was understandable. After all, her manners towards him this evening had been more brusque than demonstrative. To borrow one of her grandfather's colorful turns of phrase, she had been "about as welcoming as a polar bear." She nestled more closely into him, again noting how he smelled faintly of peppermint.

"Are you all right?" Daniel murmured, bending to catch her gaze. "It must have been a shock to find those two here."

She absently stroked a patch of stubble Daniel had missed while shaving. "I'm fine. I was more angry than frightened. I don't know what Peter was thinking, coming here at this time of night."

"His motives seemed benign enough, thankfully, but I don't think the same can be said of Anders. Jenny, what the devil happened between the two of you?" It was clear Daniel hoped for them to exchange truths. "He would have kicked the door in tonight if he could have, I could see it in his eyes. Why won't he leave you alone?"

Again, she did not answer.

"Please, Jenny," he said, his voice softening. "I only want to help, if I can."

Shaking her head, she mumbled back, "I ... I don't know why this is so hard to talk about."

Daniel's arms tensed at her sides, as if he were bracing himself for what he was about to hear. The sudden storminess of his countenance, and the telltale throb of a large vein in his forearm, suggested a quickened pulse and troubled heart – the natural result of envisioning worst-case scenarios. If only to protect him from his darkest imaginings, Jenny fixed her eyes on the carpet and launched into her tale.

"Anders asked me out a few times last year. Well, no, that's not quite accurate. To be more precise, he asked me out *many* times last year. I had no idea why, since I didn't know him very well. I'd only just got back from France, and I was busy with my courses, so I kept putting him off. By the end of term I'd become tired of turning him down, so I finally agreed."

"Then what?"

"He took me to dinner at some frightfully expensive place in

Grassby. It was pleasant enough." She let out a hollow laugh. "Even if all he did was talk about his boat."

"And then?"

"After dinner he took me to a film, during which he ... I don't know, tried to exact certain boorish privileges." She emphasized that point by angrily throwing bandages into her bag.

"What kind of privileges?" Daniel said quickly.

Still not looking at him, Jenny began slowly capping and uncapping the antiseptic, just to occupy her fingers.

"He reached for my hand, and I let him hold it. Everyone in our cohort seemed to like him so much, and they kept telling me how mad I was to turn him down, and I supposed I was flattered by his persistence, so I thought ... but then he ... he tried to slide his hand up my skirt, halfway through the picture. I saw it coming, so I slapped him and ran out." Jenny swallowed painfully. "He followed me and began yelling. Stupid things, awful things. About how I ought to remember that he was a Manwaring, and that he didn't take girls out every day, and that I should be grateful someone like him had noticed a girl like me in the first place. A girl from nowhere."

Daniel opened his mouth to speak, but Jenny hadn't finished her narrative. Sharing it was strangely unburdening.

"Then he said that I was wasting my time studying Archaeology, because women never get hired in the field anyway, so 'why didn't I just study secretarial sciences and focus on having a good time,' with *him,* specifically." Jenny scowled. "Hearing that was almost worse. I gave him an earful from across the street, and then I got in a cab and cried all the way home." She took a deep, shuddering breath. "The next Monday I reported him to the administration, but ... not much has been done about it."

Daniel's jaw was set in a firm line, and he said nothing for a full minute after her speech. When he did unclamp his mouth to speak, he sounded as though he'd swallowed a quart of lemon juice.

"Well. I'll be very much surprised if Anders is still a student at Browning on Monday."

"What are you going to do?"

He glared into the distance. "Whatever it takes."

"No. It's too risky," Jenny argued. "I don't think Peter recognized you, but suppose Anders remembers it was you who flattened him? I have a feeling he's quite a practiced drunk. If you make trouble, he'll just come after you."

"I'm not worried," Daniel assured her. "I'll talk to Antony on Monday. As dean of the department, he'll have access to the university's official complaints. We'll find yours."

"I suppose I'd hoped Anders would just get tired of bothering me. I've been trying to avoid him all term."

"Him and someone else, I think?" Daniel said quietly.

She nodded, understanding his allusion to Peter but not feeling up to discussing either young man for another moment. Both had already taken up too much of their preciously short time together. She gave a playful tug on his collar and smiled. "You look nice. Very dashing."

Daniel also seemed relieved by the change of subject. "So do you."

"Don't tease," Jenny protested archly. "Look at the state of me, sitting here in my old robe while you look like something out of a film."

"No, I like it," he chuckled, tugging on her sash. "It suits you." Something in his happy, boyish expression softened the last bit of frustration Jenny clung to.

"Thank you," she whispered in his ear. "For what you did tonight. I know I was waspish earlier, but ... thank you."

Daniel's only response was to shrug and then kiss her. Though still a bit abashed over her appearance, Jenny wrapped both arms about the neck of her quiet, serious defender. A war hero, apparently. An enigma she yearned to unravel, swiftly and completely.

She brushed the tip of her nose against his, hoping for another kiss. Daniel snuck in a second peck, sweet and soft and disappointingly short. With the taste of him still lingering on her lips, she slipped both her hands into his thick hair. Her mouth sought the boundaries of his, and gently parted.

Daniel seemed taken aback at first, but his large hands drifted readily to her waist. They caressed her in small movements, gradually becoming stronger and more confident in their strokes as she signaled her enjoyment of the sensation. She reveled in the pressure of his thick arms about her, and the unfamiliar softness of his tongue as it occasionally brushed her lip. She snuck the tiniest peek at him as they kissed, adoring the way Daniel's dark, diligently closed lashes tickled the top of her cheek.

As she brushed the lines of his chest, his forehead wrinkled with some deep-seated emotion. Without warning, he let out a deep sigh and swept her completely into him.

Jenny let out a muffled sigh of surprise as he tilted her chin upwards and vigorously explored the warmth of her mouth. The slumbering creature behind her navel awoke, leaping and twisting deliciously in response. An embrace as strong and open as this was new to her; it felt almost mythic in its pleasure and power. It was, in her fanciful imagination, a type of talisman. A protective enchantment, guarding them both against the fears of tomorrow and of what they might mutually face.

But she was not long permitted to stay in such a sanctum. With a heavy breath, Daniel slid Jenny off his knee. He stood and began putting on his jacket a few paces away.

"I'm going to tell Dr. Miller on Monday."

"Wh-what?" Jenny stammered, not comprehending his meaning. The abruptness of their separation was disorienting, to say the very least.

"I think I should tell him about us on Monday." Daniel's eyes gleamed strangely in the kitchen's dim light. "Jenny, I have never ...

I don't want to wait a year, Jenny. There must be a way, there just has to be. If there is, then Antony can help."

Jenny did not speak, as her heart was still racing from their kiss. The possibility of walking hand-in-hand with Daniel, in broad daylight, without fear of recrimination, was so lovely, so bewitching a dream, that she had no wish to shatter it by uttering cold realities. But Daniel wasn't thinking clearly. In revealing the truth to Dr. Miller, they would risk compelling him to act. At best, Daniel would be disciplined. At worst, his professorship might be lost. Nothing could be worth that. Nothing.

Her heart sank as the ardor of the moment faded and other risks rose to mind. Even if Dr. Miller responded well and by some *miracle* they were allowed to openly see each other, Jenny's own situation was far from resolved. She hated to admit it, but she had just as much to lose as he. Being romantically involved with a mentor could only complicate her chances of a field placement, if not obliterate them. These were elements they hadn't yet thought through as a couple, and if her own deepening attachment was anything to go by, they needed to resolve them quickly.

"Daniel," she began, "what if he's forced to terminate your employment, or ..."

"I know," he said, with a look that confirmed he'd followed her line of thought. "I know, it's a gamble. For both of us. And if you don't want me to say anything, I won't. I swear it. But for my part, I don't want to continue like this, Jenny. Not knowing when I'll see you, or talk to you, or even how to get in touch. I really think this is our best chance if we ever want to ..."

She gave a reluctant smile. "To 'go steady,' as the kids say?"

"Something like that." He took her hands in his and searched her eyes. "But only if that's what you want? To 'go steady,' that is?"

Jenny's heart soared at his timid invitation. Despite her objections, she heard herself answer, "Yes. That's what I want. If it can be managed."

He let out a little grunt of relief. "Antony's my friend. I trust him. I know he can advise me. And," he finished with a slight frown, "there's a pretty good chance he suspects already."

"Yes, I gathered as much," Jenny replied, glancing at the stack of articles Dr. Miller had loaned her for the weekend.

"I can catch him on Monday, after his last lecture."

"Classical Languages. I'm in that class," Jenny reminded him.

"All the better." Daniel pressed her hands. "Wait for me. Some-where in the building. I'll ask to speak to him alone."

"No. It's my future on the line as well. We'll speak to him together."

"Together?" He raised his dark brows. "Are you sure?"

"This may be the stupidest, most reckless thing I've ever said, but" – she nodded – "I'm sure."

He held her, wistfully, tenderly, and with so much transparent worry and longing that her heart resumed its exhilarating dance. She rested a hand against his cheek, hoping he could feel her reas-surance that whatever was to come, she too was facing it head-on.

"I just wish I knew what was going to happen," he murmured in anguish.

"We'll find a way," she whispered back.

"Monday after class," he said. The corner of his mouth twitched. "Don't skive off this time."

"I promise I won't," she laughed.

He laced his fingers through hers and led them both to the door.

"Goodnight, then," Daniel murmured. Jenny kissed him in farewell, but it soon became evident that both felt Monday to be an eternity away. Their parting kiss took on a life of its own, flatly refusing to part them. It became long and rapturous, slow and sweet, lasting one minute, then two, then three.

Four minutes passed, and still, neither moved to end it.

With a strong step forward, Daniel leaned one hand against the doorframe and placed the other against Jenny's lower back. He drew her steadily upwards and against him, nearly lifting her off her feet. His lips broke from hers and dragged softly along her jaw, coming to rest in the crease below her ear. Jenny let out a little gasp as they slowly danced over her skin.

For a moment Daniel lingered there, just lightly and sweetly kissing. But then he stopped. He fingered the threadbare sash of her robe, staring silently at it for some time.

"... I should go," he whispered, letting it fall.

She nodded faintly, still reeling from the sensation of his embrace. "Goodnight."

He moved to exit.

"Jenny?" Daniel hesitated with his hand on the knob. "Conditions being what they are, I think perhaps I should ... given the situation, I just want to say that ... I'd never ... unless of course, you ...?" He cleared his throat.

"Yes?"

Her prompting yielded no clarifying comment. His countenance remained questioning, almost bashful. She could not fathom its intent.

"It's nothing," he said, with something resembling a flush. "That is to say ... it'll keep." A little smile crossed his face. "Goodnight, Jenny."

He slipped out of her apartment and darted to a nearby fire escape. Jenny watched as he slid down its ladder and crossed into the darkened, slushy street.

"Monday," she whispered, almost as a prayer. It could not come soon enough.

CHAPTER 33

"Jenny?"

"Mmm," she groaned, rolling over as someone repeatedly poked her shoulder.

"Are you all right, Jenny? Are you sick?"

"What?" she muttered, rubbing her eyes and squinting. A concerned, freckled face came into focus above her.

"Margie!" Jenny croaked, struggling to sit up.

"Good morning, sleepyhead." She chuckled. "I just got in. Why are you on the sofa? I thought you might have been ill or something."

"No, no. I just had trouble sleeping, that's all."

Trouble was an understatement. Daniel's parting words had ensured that Jenny tossed and turned well into the morning hours. Around three she had finally moved to the lumpy old sofa, in the hopes a change of venue would allow her to doze for an hour or two. It must have done in the end, for the sun was high in the sky now. Light was streaming through the curtains and gleaming pleasantly upon the entry's cream-colored tiles.

"What time is it?" Jenny asked, rubbing her very sore neck.

"Half-past eight. I was just going to fry a half dozen eggs. Want some?"

"Oh, yes please," Jenny answered hungrily, folding her quilt and thanking her lucky stars it bore no bloodstains or other signs of Daniel's visit. "You're back so early, Marge. Had your fill of skiing already?"

"I'll say," she grumbled. "The hill was so crowded, I couldn't even make it down the practice slope. I ran into the hill monitor, I mean, *really* ran into him, at full speed, and he 'asked' me to leave the place until I got some proper training in."

Jenny chuckled. "Oh dear."

"I was so knackered after the first day, I kissed Mum and Dad goodbye and caught the first bus back this morning. What's on your docket?" she asked brightly. "Want to catch a film later?

"Maybe. I don't know Marge, I—"

"Don't tell me," her roommate moaned. "You've got *loads* of homework and fifteen exams to prep for, and you couldn't *possibly* take any time off at this critical stage of the term without risking the absolute ruin of your academic career. Is that what you were going to say?"

"I ... no," she lied, flushing hotly.

"Ha! I'll bet you ten pounds I'm right," Margie said, storming away. "Is it really school you're up to? You're gone so often, for all I know you might have taken up with Peter at last."

"Margie, where are you going?"

"On second thought, I can't make you any eggs," she said loftily. "I've got some homework myself, and then I'm going dress shopping with Nyra this afternoon. She has a job interview next week at Porter Telephone Company, did you know? Oh no, I don't suppose you would, you probably—"

"Oh, I wish you'd just come out and say it," Jenny cut in sharply.

Margie shot her a glare. "Say what?"

"I know what you've all been thinking," Jenny sped on, as weeks of pent-up frustration, and sleep deprivation, and anxiety spilled into angry speech. "You're mad that I'm always gone, and that I miss all the parties you plan, and that I'm never around for rugby matches or pub crawls or dinner on weekends. You all think I'm batty for spending my evenings in the library or the lab, and that I'm some 'trophy hunter' who's trying to—"

"Hang on, hang on," Margie said, looking genuinely astonished by Jenny's steamroll of a rant. She waved her hands to stop the torrent of words. "Who said anything about being a trophy hunter?"

"Peter," Jenny snapped. "Right after I turned him down. He called me that, he *actually* said that to my face, and I just stood there, silent and weak and stupid. I should have boxed his ear right then and there."

Margie winced. "I suppose that was a bit harsh of him. But he's pretty cut up over you, you know."

"I never ... Marge, I never wanted ..." Jenny stammered. "And with Anders, too, I *never* ..."

"I know, Jen," Margie said with a shrug. "Cheer up, I was only joking about Peter. As for the rest of it, I'm sorry I was a bit snippy earlier. Yes, you're gone a lot, and yes, it's a bit disappointing, but there's no need for either of us to get so worked up about it, is there?"

Margie had spoken calmly enough, but she stood at attention. The two friends had almost never fought, and what might happen next between them was anyone's guess. Fortunately, neither seemed to want to hurl more harsh words into the wake.

"Are you all right?" Margie added shortly.

Jenny simply nodded, hoping her roommate would leave it at that. In moments like these she was always "all right," unless someone asked more persistently whether she was. It was when someone tenderly began digging that tears would start to flow.

Her wish to be left alone was in vain, for with a watchful tilt of her head Margie said, "No, you aren't. You haven't been yourself all term. All this work, the extra research, the skipping classes and dinners and running on only a few hours' sleep at a time – it's madness, Jenny. What's really going on?"

Thoughts of Daniel, and the Amity, and Egypt and Crete and Peter and Anders and a thousand other things spread like wildfire through her brain. She counted to fifteen as a wave of anxiety crested. Though she willed it to recede, it could not be quenched. It crashed with vigor, leaving her thrashing in the break, and with a shuddering, defeated exhale, Jenny sat heavily upon the sofa and strangled a sob.

"Jenny," Margie murmured, rushing to sit at her side. "What is it? What's wrong? You can tell me, you can tell me anything."

"No ... nothing. I'm tired, that's all. I'm being silly."

"I'm not stupid, you know." Margie stubbornly crossed her arms.

She sniffed. "There's the old mother hen again."

"Quite right. Now come on. The truth."

She sifted through her numerous secrets, surprising even herself by lashing out with, "The truth? You want the truth? All right. Here's the truth. Anders Manwaring is more dangerous to a woman than *anyone* here knows or suspects. I *hated* being at his house for my birthday."

"Oh! Oh *Jenny,* I'm so sorry, I didn't—"

"I'd take a job after graduation over an honor from the king," she pressed on. "I'd rather read a thousand books than go to even one rugby match, and I know that makes me strange, but I also don't know how to be any different. I *like* studying and writing and researching, and what's more, I *have* to like it to even stay at Browning. I'm here on academic merit, remember?"

"Right ... I'd forgotten," Margie muttered, looking a little abashed.

"I come from a tiny, tiny village," Jenny continued hoarsely.

"The kind of place people like you, and Nyra, and Anders have never even visited, and probably don't think still exists. No one ever moves there, and no one ever leaves. My father is a country accountant. He could never afford the tuition of a place like this, and I grew up knowing from the age of nine that if I ever wanted to go to university, it would be completely upon my shoulders to make it happen. I needed be top at whatever I did."

"So, you were top," Margie finished, a little sadly.

"I had to be. I *liked* to be."

"Because it was easy?"

"No. Because it gave me a path out of there. Because it was necessary."

"Mmm. And controllable," Margie murmured with a knowing look. "Safe."

"What?"

"Nothing." Margie shook herself. "Go on."

Jenny took a deep breath. "I know I've been a 'friend in absentia' this term, and whether it shows or not, I'm kicking myself for not having been around more for Nyra and Sagan. I'm aware that you all think I'm crazy, or that I'm ... I don't know, missing out on all the good years. It's just I have so many plans, Marge. I *know* what I want to do, and this work – the Amity Scholarship, all the extra research – I can't afford to miss out on any of it. Not for someone like Peter or Anders or Jillian, or anyone else I wouldn't so much as send a Christmas card to after graduation."

Margie let out a single, hearty peal of laughter. "That was a bit harsh, Jennifer Ellison. I'm curious, do I at least make this exclusive Christmas card list?"

"I'm sorry," Jenny said, wiping her streaming nose on her sleeve. "I'm sorry, I know that sounded heartless. Of course you do."

"Good." Margie chewed on her lip, looking as though she were measuring her next words very carefully. "If what you said is true, it looks like we're all better off without Anders. Peter will grow up and get over you. But if you'll let me play mother hen for one more moment ... I worry about who you'll be down the road, Jenny. No one wants you to succeed more than I, but sometimes I think you might actually work yourself to death. When I picture you crouched down, translating hieroglyphs all alone in the desert, it just about breaks my heart. You might not need Anders or Peter; but you do need your *friends*, Jenny. If only because you can get so tightly wound. So single-minded. You never let yourself do anything fun, or silly, or downright reckless."

"You might be surprised," Jenny muttered, glancing to the chair Daniel had occupied last night. Her heart lurched just at the sight of it.

"Answer me this," Margie said quietly. "What's the point of getting everything you ever dreamed of if you don't have anyone to share it with at the end of the day? Someone to celebrate your joys, and mourn all your losses?"

"I ... couldn't agree more," Jenny said, taking Margie's message to heart but applying it to an altogether different relationship.

"The truth is," Margie pondered wisely, "you're probably the sort that will always be happy with a small address book. An intimate circle. That's all you want, isn't it? There's nothing wrong with that. Just ... just keep your close friends close," she finished stiffly. "Keep up with them. Invest in their lives too, for your own happiness as much as theirs."

"Fine words." Jenny gave her a watery smile. "I'm sorry, Marge. About all of it."

"Oh, that's all right." Margie grinned and looped her arm through Jenny's. "You're stuck with me. Best friends forever, whether you like it or not."

"Say!" Jenny snapped her fingers more cheerfully. "I have a terrific plan. Forget the eggs. The town looks so lovely, with all the snow and everything. Let's go window shopping on Main Street and have a late breakfast at The Blue Dragon."

"Ooh! Trying to make amends right away, are we?" Margie grinned. "Go on, then. Are you sure you can spare an hour for breakfast, oh Atlas?"

Jenny laughed merrily. "After that beautiful lecture, I don't think I have much choice. Just give me a moment to change."

Brightened by the prospect of trudging through clean, unbroken snow, Jenny donned a warm wool skirt, white beret, and boots over her black stockings. Slipping on a red coat and scarf, she joined her roommate in the parlor.

"Ready!" she announced. "Now let's go eat a mountain of bacon."

The girls chatted more about Margie's disastrous skiing trip as they crunched though the snow. Both were in high spirits, having left weightier matters behind them. It was so easy to be cheerful this bright morning, especially with Belmont looking something like a Christmas village. The doors of the shops were wreathed in fresh-cut greenery and bright red ribbon, and the brown row houses, with their pillowy blankets of snow, reminded Jenny strongly of iced gingerbread cottages. Chimneys puffed white-gray smoke into the air, and the smell of wood-burning stoves and hot cinnamon cider was everywhere.

"Golly, it's cold," Jenny said, after twenty minutes of walking and window gazing. She rubbed her hands together to warm them, as she had once again forgotten her gloves.

"Why don't we step into The Belmont Arms?" Margie said through chattering teeth. "Maybe get some cider?"

"And hot chocolate," Jenny eagerly agreed. "My treat."

Together they pushed open the heavy oak door. Its bell tinkled pleasantly as a wave of warmth and noise washed over them. The pub was surprisingly crowded for this time of day; nearly every table was full of diners and merrymakers. Jenny cast her eyes about for open seats, with no immediate luck.

"So many people!" she remarked in amazement. "Do you see an open space?"

Margie gasped and clutched frantically at Jenny's arm.

"Look!" she whispered hoarsely. "It's Dr. Carter! Look, Jenny, look, over there!"

Margie pointed across the room, and a white-faced Jenny followed her gaze. It was true. Daniel was sitting at the bar with a short, tawny-haired, pleasant-looking man – presumably a friend, since they were laughing and finishing a large breakfast.

"Oh, I've thought about this," Margie mused dreamily. "Running into him in the village, quite by accident. Falling into conversation, and—"

"*Shh!*" Jenny hushed her in a panic. "They're coming over!"

Daniel had seen them. After staring at Jenny for a moment, he leaned towards the barman to close his bill.

"Golly, is he coming to talk to us?" Margie shrieked. "Oh, my goodness, what will we say?"

"Will you pipe down?" Jenny hissed. "He'll hear you!" She steadied herself as the two men walked over, determined to remain calm at any cost.

"Good morning, Dr. Carter," she greeted him cordially.

"Miss Ellison." Daniel gave her a brief, warm smile, then nodded kindly towards Margie. "Miss Payne."

"Doctor ... Professor ..." Margie mumbled incoherently.

"This is my friend" – Daniel gestured to the shorter man – "Charles Russell. Charlie, these two ladies are students at Browning. Some of the very brightest that we have, as it happens."

Margie giggled shrilly. Jenny kicked her.

"Pleased to know you," Charles said, beaming and shaking hands all around. Jenny had the immediate sense that she was going to like him. He had such an open expression, such hearty manners.

"I suppose you two ducked in here to warm up, eh?" Charlie boomed good-naturedly. "We had the same thought, but then ended up ordering the entire pantry for breakfast."

"Oh, excellent!" Margie blurted out. "Because we were thinking of going to The Blue Dragon for lunch. I mean breakfast. But perhaps we should just stay here? Do you know if the lunch is good? Oh, no, of course you wouldn't. Breakfast, right. And we were going to get breakfast as well. Sorry ..." Margie's voice trailed off in confusion.

"All of the food here is excellent," Charlie confirmed, kindly filling the embarrassed silence. "You can't go wrong with their kippers. Well! I wish we could stay and chat, but alas, duty calls. Daniel – that is, Dr. Carter – is dragging me to some confounded charity auction this afternoon, and then a – what was it?" he grunted. "An opera, tonight?"

"It'll be over before you know it," Daniel said, clapping his friend on the back. "Then we can both get back to more important concerns." His gaze flitted to Jenny for the second time since their greeting.

"It's awfully crowded in here," she remarked after a pause, just for something to say.

"Why don't you take our seats at the bar?" Daniel suggested as he tied on his plaid scarf.

"Better get a move on," Charlie warned, "before someone else does."

"Thank you, Dr. Carter," Jenny said quietly.

"My pleasure." Daniel nodded politely to the space between her and Margie. "Good day, ladies."

The gentlemen departed, and they hurriedly took the bar seats.

"I am a complete idiot," Margie moaned, putting her head in her hands.

"No, you're not," Jenny reassured her, feeling a little unsettled by Margie's infatuation, but not wanting to crush her friend's fantasies for the world. Sitting in Daniel's seat, Jenny moved to take off her coat. She froze as she looked down at the dirty bar counter, where a tiny, hieroglyphic message had been penciled in just moments earlier.

"Monday."

CHAPTER 34

The tick of the clock was like the tick of an armored bomb. In one hour Jenny and Daniel would take Dr. Miller aside to confess their wonderful, terrifying truth.

It was a moment she both longed for – and dreaded.

Jenny shifted uncomfortably in her seat; revealing such a fledgling relationship was starting to feel desperately rash. Yet a secretive approach was even less palatable. At least one person had already seen them together and reported it. The potential fallout of that truth had more than once made Jenny consider stuffing a note of her own under Daniel's door, stating in no uncertain terms that this wasn't going to work, that there was too much at stake for them both, and that although she would always remember him with great tenderness, it was imperative they stop this madness before it got out of hand.

But when she had sat down to compose that short message, she had failed even to pick up the pen. There was a simple reason for this, however hard it was to swallow.

She wanted Daniel.

Powerfully. The precious hours they had spent together at the lab, the concert, and in her home were burned beautifully into her memory. Daniel's pursuit was so different from the boyish, aggressive advances of Anders, and even Peter. His affections were so gently, so hesitantly offered. Somehow the mere fact that he had fought his admiration for so long, had tried to hide it, had *tried* to keep his distance, had given Jenny the confidence to close the gap between them.

It was she who had chosen him.

Daniel seemed to perceive that, and now her trust, like a delicate orchid, was thriving in the hands of a man who perceived its value and fragility.

Abandoning her notebook, Jenny closed her eyes and tried to recapture the feeling of his hands upon her. How lovely it was, and how strange it felt, to crave someone's embrace so completely. How achingly beautiful was the warm brush of his lip, the damp heat of his breath upon her neck. Her stomach swooped deliciously at the mere memory of it, and she savored the more powerful sensations associated with her thoughts.

A natural part of herself was reawakening, a part long repressed but all the sweeter for its emerging at a time when she could both welcome and cherish it. It was born again, this time without shame or fear. Daniel was rooted irrevocably in her heart. Indeed, after his tenderness on Friday night, it felt as though he were living in her very skin. Jenny had no idea what the future may bring, but of one thing she was certain. Daniel Carter was the rarest and best of men.

And she would fight for him.

Opening her eyes, Jenny studied Dr. Miller more intently. Both she and Daniel suspected that he knew the truth. If this was the case, however, the jolly old gentleman did not betray any peculiar awareness of her during the lecture. He plowed through his notes with the same affability and ease he always did, at one point convulsing the class with a truly terrible joke in Latin. The groans and laughter were just fading, when ...

Bang.

The classroom door to her left unexpectedly burst open.

"Dr. Miller, Dr. Miller!" A red-faced and clearly distressed Howard ran into the classroom.

"What the devil—" Dr. Miller muttered.

"I'm sorry, Professor!" the young man gasped. "But I've been sent by Dr. Carter to fetch Miss Ellison, straight away! It's an emergency, sir, and I've not a minute to lose!"

If the roof had blown off the building, Jenny could not have been more aghast. This had not been the plan. What was Daniel thinking, singling her out in this way? She turned to Dr. Miller, whose mouth was hanging slightly agape.

"Well." He gruffly nodded his permission. "I do hope it's nothing serious. Off you go, Miss Ellison."

The class began to buzz with confusion and interest. Blushing violently, Jenny shoved her notes in her satchel and joined Howard in the hallway.

"What is it?" she whispered sharply as she caught up with him. "Why on earth couldn't that have waited?"

"Oh, Jenny, something dreadful has happened, something truly dreadful!"

"What ... what's wrong?" she faltered, taking in Howard's blotchy face. To her astonishment, it was streaming with tears.

"I only just got the message," he wailed. "Spencer fetched me from class, and I said I'd come find you. Dr. Carter has sent for all of us, the entire team. They're waiting for us. You'll see, you'll see it then, but ... oh, Jenny!" Howard wrung his hands in anguish. "It's just awful!"

A cold hand of fear gripped her heart. Leaving Howard to follow behind, Jenny bolted up the stairs two at a time and burst through the lab door.

A confusing scene met her eyes. She had expected to see someone hurt, or at the very least hysterical. What she saw instead was a gravely clustered group of students and Daniel facing them with a stony expression. His arms were folded, and his jaw was clenched so tightly it might have been cemented shut. She had never seen him look so stern.

"What is it?" Jenny cried, her eyes darting frantically around the room. "What's wrong?"

No one answered. Her gaze fell upon Daniel's desk, which was conspicuously out of place. It looked as though it had been shoved into the supply shelf, leaving a pile of glass vials shattered on the floor. Two large bottles of chemicals were tipped onto their side, completely drained and hovering perilously over ...

"The stone," Jenny moaned weakly.

The artifact had been resting on Daniel's desk in its large wooden crate, ready to be shipped out. The wood of the box was soggy and splintered, crumbling in portions as though it had been smashed. Jenny rushed to it, her shoes grinding into the powdered glass covering the floor. What she saw made her stifle a cry of horror.

The stone was mottled and chalky. The precious pigmentation had pooled upon it in murky puddles of orange and blue. The beautifully carved figures were now shapeless lumps of stone, and except for a few dim lines scattered in spidery patches across its surface, the hieroglyphs had been completely effaced.

It was unrecognizable.

"What happened?" Jenny whispered, a sob catching in her throat. She was too desperately upset to ask anything else.

"When Dr. Carter and I came in this afternoon," Max reported in a fury, "we found the lab like this! The Egyptian Ambassador will be *livid*, we've already—"

"Calm down, Max." Jenny thought Daniel's tone was remarkably well-controlled, given the situation, but there was a bitter edge to his words. He glared darkly at each of the students.

"I trust that you all understand the seriousness of what has happened here," he said, his words cutting through the silence like a knife. "A priceless, three-thousand-year-old artifact has been destroyed. The university's relationship with the Amity program, to say nothing of the Egyptian government, is now at risk. And my own reputation has been indelibly compromised."

No one spoke. The group seemed collectively petrified.

"I checked this lab on Friday afternoon," Daniel continued angrily. "At that time, my desk was centered, and the crate was safely stacked on the workbench. Something happened here this weekend. Only the five of you had access to the room. Whoever is responsible for this disaster will kindly step forward. Now."

Again, no one spoke.

"One of you must know *something,*" Daniel said roughly. Then he softened. "Listen to me," he said with an exhale. "This appears to have been an accident, one that could have happened to anyone. I'm not going to rap your knuckles, and I certainly don't have the power to expel you. But if this did happen on your watch, then in order to protect you and this university, I have to know."

"I haven't been here for two weeks," Spencer piped up quickly, his voice cracking under the strain.

"Neither have I," shrieked Howard.

Jenny and Jillian just shook their heads.

"Nonsense," Max sneered. "This wasn't the work of a ghost. They're just too scared to confess, Dr. Carter." His eyes lit up. "Hang on – we have a way of checking who's been in here!" He vaulted to a filing cabinet and unlocked the drawer holding last week's timesheets. He paused, reviewing the most recent page with his back to them. Turning around with a triumphant smile, he read:

"Jenny Ellison. Friday, December fifth, ten forty-five in the evening."

"What?" Jenny cried, as her teammates began to murmur around her. "That's not true! I didn't even come to the lab Friday evening, I was—"

"Then how do you explain this?" Max gloated. He handed her the paper. "That is your signature, is it not?"

Jenny wavered for the briefest of moments. Admittedly, the writing was very like her own.

"Aha!" Max rejoiced, seeing her hesitation. "Proof! Proof!"

"Max," Daniel rebuked him sternly.

"It's plain as day," he chanted. "Jenny was here Friday night, and she tried to pack up the stone alone, but she knocked everything over, and—"

"I didn't!" Jenny returned hotly.

"Well, then prove it! What's your alibi?" Max demanded.

"I was at home, I ..." Jenny quickly bit her tongue, remembering that her "alibi" was not exactly one she could share openly. On Friday evening she had been in her apartment – alone with Daniel.

"Well, that looks an awful lot like your signature, and unless you have a secret twin—"

"That's enough, Max." Daniel unfolded his arms. "If you would all be so kind as to return to your lectures, I would like to question Miss Ellison. Alone."

The students trickled out, wearing various expressions of concern and relief. Only Howard glanced back at her sympathetically. Max, the last to leave, closed the lab door behind him with a smug expression.

Jenny spun about to face him. "Daniel, I swear it wasn't me."

"I know, Jenny." Daniel walked quickly around the room, looking for something on the shelves.

"That log, my signature, I didn't even—"

"That signature is a fake," he replied, opening a cabinet. "A good one, but a fake, nonetheless. I checked the log before I called this meeting."

"A fake?" Jenny repeated in disbelief. "You mean someone forged my signature?"

"Yes."

"You knew it was a fake all along?"

"Of course. Your lowercase 'E's aren't that flat." Daniel was still rummaging frantically in his cabinets.

"Someone *planted* a fake log? To try and pin this accident on me?"

"Oh, this was no accident," Daniel answered bitterly.

"But … but earlier you said …"

"At last," he muttered. He had found what he was looking for: a slim file full of papers. He slammed it on the desk and opened it, rifling through the contents at great speed.

"What do you mean, *this was no accident?*" Jenny pressed him. "You know who did this?"

"Yes." Daniel straightened. "It was Jillian."

"Ji-Jillian?"

He nodded grimly. "And she wasn't acting alone."

CHAPTER 35

"How do you know it was her?" Jenny joined Daniel on the other side of the desk as he quickly thumbed through papers.

"I watched her," he replied simply. "During the meeting. She didn't look at you once, not even once. Not when you arrived, not when Max announced your name on the log – not even when I asked you to stay behind."

"That's why you called this meeting?" she whispered. "To watch her?"

"Partly. I wanted to see how she'd react if it appeared you were taking the fall for it."

"But why would she do something like this?" Jenny cried. "It's horrible!"

"Oh, we'll get to that. Now, where did Max put it?" Daniel muttered.

"What *is* the matter with Max, anyway?" Jenny said crossly. "He seemed positively delighted to see my name on that log!"

"I imagine he's jealous," Daniel replied, poring over another sheet. "You've been an important part of the project, and he's a bit of a kiss-up. Aha! Got it."

Daniel had found his quarry: Jillian's research agreement. Smiling in triumph, he turned to Jenny. "Do you remember Jillian's response when Howard suggested cleaning the stone with acid?"

"No?"

"Oh, right, you were delayed by that blasted Anders." Daniel frowned. "Well, her knowledge that first night surprised me, and it struck me that Jillian was cleverer than I'd supposed. I checked her information sheet the next day, just out of curiosity. Students usually do a terrible job of filling these out," he added, clutching his hair with professorly frustration. "But Jillian's was fairly complete."

"Well?" Jenny prompted, looking at it over Daniel's shoulder.

"I asked everyone to list their schedule," he explained. "To make sure they had enough time to devote to the project. Here's Jillian's course load: Paleography, Advanced Theories of Excavation, Calligraphy, Human Origins, and *Chemistry*."

"The chemicals," Jenny said, catching on quickly.

Daniel pointed to the overturned bottles, which still hung over the mottled stone. "We don't carry anything strong enough to do destruction on this scale." He let out a hollow laugh. "Why would we? It would be conservational suicide. Jillian's clearly emptied the solution of oxalic acid and refilled the bottles with something else. See how the stone looks burned in places? How it's crumbling away?"

Jenny nodded. The sight of it turned her stomach afresh.

"She must have been trying to make this look like a mistake, like the mixing of several chemicals caused some ungodly reaction. I'd bet my life she used a concentrated acid, much more potent. Hydrofluoric, or muriatic maybe."

"Which she could have nicked from the chemistry lab," Jenny finished.

"Exactly. Unluckily for her, Professor McNeil in the chemistry department happens to be a very good friend of mine." Daniel grinned exultantly, and for a moment Jenny caught a flash of intelligence officer Captain Carter. "I know for a fact he uses muriatic acid in one of his mid-term labs. He was just telling me how expensive his materials have been after the war."

"Oh, Jillian," Jenny lamented. "What have you done?"

"That's not all," Daniel said, somberly reaching into his pocket. "I was going to tell you about this later. Earlier today, I found this note stuffed under my office door."

He handed Jenny a crumpled wad of white paper. Unfolding it, she read aloud a simple, typed threat:

I KNOW WHAT YOU'VE DONE.
RESIGN IMMEDIATELY,
OR I'LL GO PUBLIC.

Jenny's head snapped up in shock. "Jillian again? She sent the notes? She wants you fired?"

"Oh, I'm not sure it's what she wants, necessarily." Daniel scowled. "But I know someone else who'd be thrilled to see that happen."

"Chilcott."

"Do you see? If he couldn't be part of the project, his next best move would be to ruin it. He's been using Jillian in order to get to me." Daniel's face fell. "In order to get rid of me."

"I can't believe this!" Jenny fumed. "*Jillian?* And she just stood there, claiming that she hasn't been near the project in weeks, when all this time she—"

Jenny froze.

"Oh no," she moaned, a dreadful idea forming. "Daniel, oh no, this can't ... oh, *please no* ..."

"What's wrong?"

"Oh Daniel, I have the most awful feeling that ..." Jenny shook herself and grabbed his hand. "We need to find Dr. Chilcott," she said, breaking into a run and dragging Daniel behind her. "We need to find him now. Then we have to talk to Jillian, quickly. Before anything else happens."

She led Daniel down the stairs to the second floor, dropping his hand when two students started climbing past them. Together they raced to Chilcott's study and skidded to a stop in front of his office. A shade was pulled tightly over the door's windowpane. Every few seconds, a rattling, scuffling sound could be heard from within it – not at a timbre that would intrigue a casual passerby, but enough of one to make Daniel nod with a groan of understanding.

"No," Jenny moaned. "Oh no, no, *no*."

He and Jenny stared dumbly at each other for a moment. Then, slowly, Daniel pulled a spare paperclip from his pocket and unbent it. Nodding at Jenny, he crouched down and began to pick the lock. Within a few seconds, he had burst it open.

A terrified shriek pierced the air. Jillian was sitting on Dr. Chilcott's lap, barefoot, with her blouse completely unbuttoned and the straps of her pink slip sliding off her shoulders. Seeing Daniel and Jenny, she jumped up and began desperately trying to re-fasten her shirt.

"What do you think you're ... get out!" Jillian screamed, bursting into hysterical tears. "Go away, get out of here!"

"Oh, Jillian," Jenny murmured sadly.

Dr. Chilcott had gone starkly white. "Close the door, do you hear me? Close it!" he seethed.

Daniel slammed the door shut behind them, glaring at Chilcott with unrestrained fury and disgust.

"Go away, just go away!" Jillian wailed. "This is none of your business!"

"Miss Ellison," Daniel said. A muscle in his jaw flinched. "Would you kindly take Miss Stewart down to my study and wait with her there? I have a few questions to ask Dr. Chilcott."

Jenny shrugged off her cardigan and put it around Jillian's poorly clad shoulders.

"Come on," she said gently. "Wear this. We'll go and have a chat."

She picked up Jillian's shoes and extended her hand. The girl was still choking out indignant sobs, but after a helpless glance towards Dr. Chilcott, she followed. Jenny peered nervously behind her before closing the office door. Daniel and Dr. Chilcott stood grimly facing each other.

Neither man was saying a word.

Daniel waited until Jenny and Jillian were out of earshot. Once they were, he pounced. Crossing the room in two steps, he snatched Chilcott roughly by the collar and shook him.

"You lying, sneaking, hypocritical mass of—"

"Let go, let go of me at once!" Chilcott barked, batting his arms with a shrill cry. "Get off! Unhand me, or I'll—"

"Keep your voice down," Daniel warned with a growl. He was quivering with rage, but remembering that there were other professorial offices on this floor, he kept his voice deadly quiet. Despite his inclination to shake Chilcott until his teeth rattled out of his head, he had to know the full extent of what he was dealing with before he acted.

"How dare you!" Chilcott roared, trying and failing to escape Daniel's grip.

"I said keep it down," Daniel said, shoving Chilcott into a chair. He folded his arms and towered menacingly over him. "Talk."

Chilcott was purple with indignation but looked as though he was trying to recover some sense of self. "You're jumping to conclusions, Carter. You don't know what you saw, not really. Nothing happened."

"You dared to accuse me of accepting sexual favors from a student, when all along you've been—"

"I have not accepted any favors, as you call it," Chilcott snarled. "This ... may have been a little underhand, but it was a consensual exchange, based on a mutual—"

"*Liar*," Daniel cut him off. "You knew Jillian was on my team. You targeted her, you used her."

"Now, listen here!"

"I knew you were intent on sabotaging my career!" Daniel shouted, grabbing Chilcott's collar again and completely forgetting to keep his voice down. "I just never thought you'd stoop so low as to seduce a student to do it."

"I have not seduced anyone!" Chilcott barked back.

"Do you have any idea what your actions have cost us? The damage to the stone is irreparable, Chilcott. You and your accomplice have single-handedly put our entire Amity accreditation at risk. Are you happy now?"

"What are you talking about?" Chilcott replied, the blood draining steadily from his face. "W-what's happened? What's wrong with the stone?"

A boiling surge of rage shot through Daniel, and he had to restrain himself from clocking the man then and there. "Don't play the innocent with me, Chilcott," he snapped.

"What are you—"

"It was you who tried to break into the lab in November, and you and Jillian who destroyed the stone. Don't try to deny it! You've been trying to sabotage the project for weeks."

Chilcott held up a shaking hand. "Dr. Carter, I have no idea what you are talking about. Absolutely no idea."

"*Liar.*"

"Daniel, I swear it."

At the use of his given name, Daniel froze. His eyes darted across Chilcott's face, studying his features for any sign of deception. The man's bushy moustache was fluttering in and out with rapid breath, and his quivering hand was extended in a kind of plea. Though he looked terrified, Chilcott's gaze was steady.

Daniel stumbled backwards in shock. As much as he loathed this man, no intelligence training was needed to see that he was telling the truth. Every inch of his desperate countenance confirmed it.

"You didn't ask Jillian to destroy the stone."

"No." Chilcott shook his head vigorously. "I swear on my life, I would never do such a thing. I know nothing about it. Daniel, is it really true?"

"But you *did* forge Miss Ellison's signature," he continued sharply, desperate to pin something on this loathsome creature if it was the last thing he did. "You intended to frame her for the damage. I know your work, Chilcott. I saw at once that it was you."

"I only did that for Jillian as a favor," Chilcott insisted. "As a prank, that's all she said it was! I had no idea what it was all about."

"You also tried to break into my lab."

"Well ..." Chilcott shifted restlessly. "Very well, I admit, yes I did. I wanted to examine the stone. Jillian told me it had turned out to be rubbish, but I found I was still curious. She loaned me her key" – Chilcott held up his other hand, as though worried Daniel might suddenly strike him – "but the door was obviously dead-bolted, and I knew you must have been inside, so I left in a hurry. I haven't tried to get in since. I give you my word."

Seeing that Daniel had backed away from him, Chilcott cautiously lowered his hands. Grief displaced white-hot anger. After weeks of suspicion, intrigue, and slander, Dr. Chilcott was only guilty of an affair with a student and trying to force open a door. It was too much to handle in this moment.

"The notes," Daniel said, secondary anxieties now rearing their ugly heads. "The notes shoved under the door. Your idea or Jillian's?"

Chilcott gulped nervously. "I'm sorry, I don't – notes?"

"Never mind." Daniel sat down wearily. "I'll find out soon enough." He rubbed his temple and groaned. "All right. So you didn't put Jillian up to the destruction. But one mystery remains. How on earth did a man like you coax her into such debauchery? Did you threaten her?"

Dr. Chilcott spluttered in offense. "I beg your pardon? A man like me, did you say?"

"You're finished at Browning, Chilcott. A married man having an illicit affair with a fourth year?" He shook his head. "The board of governors won't hear of it. If you ever want to work again I advise you to give your notice quickly. I'll be telling Dr. Miller what has happened before the day is out."

Chilcott jumped up from his seat, his eyes narrowing to slits. "You wouldn't dare."

"Oh, but I would," he said coldly. "Your girlfriend has just jeopardized my life's work, and I find I'm in a foul mood."

"It's your word against mine, you self-righteous pup!" Chilcott snarled. "Who will believe you? I've been here for sixteen years. I'm next in line for the deanship. Most of the department is on my side, don't you forget!"

"Don't you forget, Chilcott," – Daniel turned his back on the man as he walked out – "that I had a witness."

CHAPTER 36

Jenny led a sobbing Jillian to Daniel's office.

"When you said you had a new boyfriend, I hardly thought you meant Dr. Chilcott!" she whispered sharply. "He's married, Jillian!"

Jillian only sobbed harder.

"Please keep quiet," Jenny hushed her. "People are staring."

It was true. Several passing students cast concerned looks over the barefoot, blubbering young woman. Thankfully, Jillian's open blouse was mostly covered by Jenny's sweater, but the sooner she was out of eyesight the better. Jillian seemed to sense this, for choking back tears she quickened her pace.

At last they reached Daniel's lecture hall, which was blessedly empty.

"What were you thinking?" Jenny demanded while closing the door. "Why would you go up there, why now? Right after the team meeting? I've never heard of anything more reckless!"

"It's none of your business," Jillian sneered, though she was crying again.

"You do realize what all of this means, don't you?"

"Well, how was I to know you lot would come barging through

242

the door?" she cried. "I always meet Will at this time. Dr. Carter's stupid meeting made me late."

"Well, I think you might have skipped the tryst, just this once. Now come on."

Trying to forget that Jillian had called Dr. Chilcott "Will," Jenny pulled her into Daniel's adjoining office and shut the door. Jillian immediately collapsed at a round table and buried her head in her arms. Jenny hesitated, unsure how to proceed with a line of questioning when she was in such a state. Seeing an electric kettle, she plugged it in and began searching out tea things. In no time at all, the water was bubbling away.

"Here." Jenny slid a steaming cup in front of Jillian. "Try to calm down."

"You had no right to break in," Jillian moaned, her frame shaking with sobs. "You've ruined me, you've spoiled everything."

"Drink your tea," Jenny insisted. "It will do you good."

"No!"

"Fine. Don't, then." Jenny plopped down in exhaustion. "The stone, Jillian?" Just saying the words sent a shard of ice to her heart. "How could you?"

At last Jillian raised a tear-stained face. Her black mascara was streaming onto both of her cheeks.

"Who says I did?" she replied defiantly. "What proof do you have?"

Jenny glared at her. "None of our lab chemicals are potent enough to dissolve limestone. Dr. Carter knows you're in chemistry this term. He knows you stole the acid from the chemistry lab."

"*Knows*?" Jillian snarled, though she looked a little pale. "You mean *suspects*. Again, what proof do you have, ickle Jen-Jen?"

"Well, I imagine a quick check of the chem lab would confirm the acids are missing. It would have taken quite a bit of product to destroy so much wood and stone, after all."

"I didn't hurt that stupid stone. I don't know anything about it."

"Dr. Carter could see that you were guilty," Jenny said fiercely. "He knows you tried to make the damage look like an accident. He knows you forged my signature on the log. It's all over. You've been found out."

Jillian flinched. She looked strange – uncharacteristically vulnerable – in her half-buttoned blouse and the ill-fitting sweater. Her red hair was matted, and her nose and eyes were awash with tears. For a moment, just a moment, a flash of pity warmed the shard of ice in Jenny's heart.

"Jillian Stewart, I've just caught you in the lap of a married professor. That and the destruction of the stone are enough to get you expelled. Believe it or not, I want to help you. No, truly, I do," she added, when Jillian opened her mouth to protest. "You may not believe me, but I want to anyway, because I have a feeling there is more to this story. However" – Jenny took a steadying breath – "I cannot help you unless you tell me what happened."

After a long pause, Jillian said with a faint sneer, "I don't see the point of all this fuss. It wasn't even a groundbreaking discovery. That stone's about as exciting as a biscuit recipe."

"Yes, but it was a three-thousand-year-old artifact on loan from the Egyptian government!" Jenny countered, her temper flaring again. "When they find out what's happened, they'll never work with Browning again!"

"They'll never work with Dr. Carter again," Jillian corrected.

"Was that Chilcott's intent? To get rid of him and have full reign of the department?"

"Leave Will out of this," Jillian said, stubbornly smearing her nose. "He didn't know anything about it. I acted alone."

"That can't be true. You would never have done this on your own. What did Chilcott promise you? A better grade? A chance at the Amity, perhaps?"

Jillian laughed scathingly. "Ickle Jen-Jen. Still thinking about school, even at a time like this."

"My name is Jenny," she said, folding her arms coldly, "and you had better start using it, because right now my silence is the only thing keeping you from getting expelled."

Jillian's mouth trembled, and fresh tears spilled out of her eyes. Still, she said nothing.

Jenny sighed. When she next spoke, it was in a voice that was exceedingly gentle, almost silk-like in its inability to harm. "Jillian, as much as you pretend not to care about this work, I know that you do. Destroying an artifact like that ... it's not who you are. What happened? Why did you do it?"

Jenny's tender sympathy only seemed to make Jillian more defensive. Drawing herself up haughtily, the girl snapped, "You've threatened to expose my relationship with Will. Well, what if I were to expose you first?"

It took everything in Jenny's power to remain calm. "What are you talking about?"

Jillian looked as though she had just swallowed castor oil. After throwing a loathsome glance at Jenny, three words burst from her.

"I saw you."

"What?"

"I saw you! You and Dr. Carter, walking out together!" She wiped her smudged eyes with the back of her hand. "I had just met Will in his office. It was late. As I walked back to the bus stop, I saw you and Dr. Carter leaving the campus together. I saw it."

Jenny nodded. "So you reported it to Dr. Miller. Jillian, that night was completely innocent. He walked me home after the team outing. If he hadn't I'd have waited a half hour for a bus, alone in the cold."

"I know. I had to, after I met up with Will," Jillian muttered bitterly.

"He offered to escort me back out of kindness. Why did you report him? Why didn't you just ask me about it?"

Jillian hesitated, tears still streaming from her eyes. "I don't know. I suppose I wasn't sure what I had seen at the time. But I was angry with Dr. Carter, so ..."

"Because he wouldn't give you the time of day," Jenny interjected.

"Fine, if that's how you want to put it, then yes. I admit, I was annoyed, so I turned him in. I hoped he'd be taken down a peg or two."

Another worry surfaced in Jenny's mind. "Did you tell Dr. Chilcott you'd seen us?"

"No."

Jenny wrinkled her nose dubiously. Something about this didn't quite track. Doing so would have given Chilcott the perfect ammunition to use against Daniel, and if Jillian and Chilcott were truly lovers, she felt certain it would have come up.

"Why not, Jillian?"

"Because ..." She swallowed. "I knew if I told Will I'd seen Dr. Carter walking out with a student, he'd ask me who that student was, and I ..." Jillian cleared her throat and looked determinedly away from Jenny. "I know we don't get on, but at that point I didn't truly *hate* you. I thought perhaps ... maybe, just maybe, I might have misunderstood what I saw. I knew you were going for the Amity, and Will is on that committee, so at that point I just ... did nothing."

Jenny stared at her in shock. Jillian had always railed against Jenny's ambitions, teasing her for applying to the Amity and berating her for all the time she spent studying. Was Jenny hearing this correctly? Underneath all that malice, could Jillian truly, secretly, have wanted Jenny to succeed?

"You tried to protect me?" Jenny whispered. "Why?"

"But then," Jillian wailed, unable to hear her, "I heard the truth about you from Anders, and something in me just snapped. I went mad."

The icy shard in Jenny's heart pierced even more deeply at these words. "When did you talk to Anders?"

Jillian threw her a look of the deepest disgust. "At the gala on Saturday. It was some sort of ghastly opera fundraiser, my parents made me attend. Anders was there too, and we got talking." She took a shuddering breath. "He told me that he went to visit you on Friday night."

"Anders showed up uninvited, slobbering drunk, and tried to force his way into my apartment," Jenny fumed. "I called the police, and he was arrested."

"Yes, I know," Jillian said. "Anders told me. But he *also* said that a very tall man had come out of your apartment, and that this man had beaten him. He tried to tell the police and his parents, but no one would believe him, because, yes, I suppose he was a little sauced that night."

Jillian's words were now pouring forth rapidly, as though she could not stop herself from sharing once she'd started.

"Then I told Anders I'd seen you and Dr. Carter walking out together, and I knew you had logged nearly a hundred hours in the Archaeology lab, and I suspected there might have been something going on between the two of you. And then Anders said he was sure his attacker was Dr. Carter, and I felt … I don't know, I felt sort of betrayed, because I had covered for you, and hadn't told on you, and—"

"You and Anders decided to get back at me *and* Dr. Carter, so you left the gala, robbed the chem lab, doused the stone in acid, and smashed everything about to make it look like an accident. Do I have that right?"

Jillian sniffed and wiped her nose, looking utterly defeated. "You're forgetting the part where we tried to pin it all on you."

"Oh, I haven't forgotten," Jenny said bitterly.

"I don't know why I did it!" Jillian shrieked. "Truly, I don't. I just went mad for a moment. I know it was stupid, but it wasn't my idea to destroy the stone, I swear. That was all Anders' plan, I just … gave him the method of doing it."

"So, the rantings of a drunkard and your own anger towards me were enough to make you jeopardize the department, the Amity program, and your entire educational career?" Jenny could hardly believe what she was hearing. "Jillian, think of what you've just sacrificed. You've got loads of talent, you might have become anything. But now—"

"Stop saying that!" Jillian yelled. Her eyes were ablaze with ferocious anger, so much so that Jenny was caught off guard.

"Jillian, I—"

"Stop spinning fairy tales about how women can do anything in this world!" she cried. "That's not how it works, Jenny! Oh, I'm such a fool. You know, I actually thought for a moment that you might have been right. When you got the Amity, I thought, 'Perhaps there is some fairness to this system after all! Perhaps with hard work and dedication, a woman's potential in the field *might* be recognized, might even amount to a work placement. Perhaps *I* could ...' but then I heard that you and Dr. Carter were lovers, and I knew that you had slept your way to the top, and something in me just snapped."

"Jillian Stewart, you take that back," Jenny broke in, her voice quivering with emotion. "I have not slept my way anywhere."

"*Brilliant Jenny,*" she retorted in a harsh, sing-song voice. "Book-worm Jenny, Amity winner Jenny. 'The girl no one can get.' The girl Peter's half in love with but she's too stupidly ignorant to notice. Poor Peter, little did he know that all along she was a scheming, conniving—"

"That's enough," Jenny said sharply. "I'm not conniving. Everything I have I've gotten on my own merit. You're the one limiting yourself, Jillian. Not the university, not the world, you." She threw her a nauseated look. "Is that why you took up with Chilcott? To get a field placement after graduation?"

"There's no need to look so disgusted, Jennifer Ellison." Jillian sniffed and wiped her mascara-stained cheeks. "He's terribly nice, much nicer than you think. And he's not so very old. I know he's married, but he's been very kind to me." At last Jillian took a sip of her tea. Staring at the table, she tremulously asked, "Then you're not lovers? You and Dr. Carter?"

Jenny was relieved that she could answer truthfully. "No. We've never been lovers."

"There really isn't *anything* between you?" Jillian whispered. "Sometimes I thought ... I caught him looking at you a few times, watching you as you worked and such, and I thought ... "

Thankfully, the office door opened at that moment. It was Daniel. Jenny suspected he had been waiting outside, listening to Jillian's confession, and had chosen this opportune moment to interrupt. He looked very grave.

"Ah. I see you've had a chance to calm down, Miss Stewart. If you would please make yourself decent, the three of us will be heading to Dr. Miller's office now."

"No!" Jillian cried, looking desperately between him and Jenny. "You promised you would help me if I told you everything. You promised!"

"I'll try," she said sorrowfully. "But you have to tell the truth, Jillian. You have to report Anders before he can claim you acted alone."

"I can't," Jillian whispered tearfully. "I'll be expelled!"

Daniel nodded somberly. "It's possible. I won't lie to you. But I can assure you that it will be far better for you if you try to make this right. There may yet be a way forward."

"Come on. Let's get you cleaned up." Jenny helped Jillian to rise. "Dr. Carter, if you'll please wait outside, we'll meet you in one minute."

"I can't do this," Jillian moaned as Daniel closed the office door. "Oh, what is Will going to say? I can't, Jenny, I just can't."

"Courage," was all she could manage to reply. "Don't think about Dr. Chilcott. He has his own mistakes to answer for. You won't be alone. I'll stay with you. Courage."

CHAPTER 37

"Oh, good heavens. This is a pickle." Dr. Miller completely undid his bowtie, which Daniel recognized as a sign of the severest distress. The dean began huffing and puffing uncomfortably, and a few beads of sweat broke out on his reddening forehead. "I am sincerely hoping I have misheard you. Did you just say that the stone has been damaged?"

"Destroyed," Daniel repeated, with a painful lump in his throat. He had been pushing that fact out of mind for the last hour, but it now rose horribly to the forefront.

"*Destroyed?* By our own students?"

"Yes, sir," Jillian sobbed.

"And there is no hope of salvaging it?"

"No, sir," Jenny answered sadly. "What's left is in pieces, and the markings have all but vanished."

"Why, oh why, didn't I retire last year?" Antony mumbled, putting his tufty-haired head in his hands. After a minute's pause, he lifted it sharply.

"Well, Miss Stewart. Although it was very brave of you to come and confess, I must tell you that I am extremely displeased by this news. I should never have expected such behavior from you. What can have possessed you to act so violently?"

Daniel glanced at Jillian, who was sitting between him and Jenny. Her hands were folded meekly in her lap, and she was shaking with petrified sobs.

"I ... just went mad for a moment. I bitterly regret it now. I'm ... I'm sorry. I'm so, so, sorry," she wept.

"Yes," Dr. Miller returned coolly. "I assumed you would be. For surely you understand what your actions could mean for your enrollment at Browning."

"Yes," Jillian answered, flushing in anguish.

The crease about Antony's mouth deepened. "I presume you also understand the damage you will have done to Dr. Carter's excellent relationship with the Egyptian ministry, and that Browning's Amity chapter could be shut down when our partners hear of this catastrophe."

Jillian swallowed. "I realize that now, sir."

"Do you also realize that the destruction of international property is a punishable offense, for which the university could face legal action?"

At this last statement Jillian's face whitened. "Do you mean ... would I ..." She burst into fresh tears and buried her face in her hands.

Dr. Miller's stern expression softened, and he let out a gruff sigh.

"Come now, no one's going to prison. At least not yet. Here." He reached into his desk and brought out a gold foil box. "Have a chocolate."

Jillian looked surprised but accepted the box with a shaking hand. She began stuffing chocolate-covered cherries into her mouth with astonishing speed.

"I'm very disappointed in you, Miss Stewart," the old dean said softly. And truly, Antony did look more disappointed than angry. Though Daniel's thoughts were still consumed by the stone, he couldn't help but ponder on how moments like this were what made Antony such an effective dean. The regard Dr. Miller's students had for him made any small expression of displeasure as painful as though he had slapped them in the face. Antony had barely even raised his voice during this meeting, yet Jillian looked as though she wanted to crumble to dust before him.

"The worst of it is, I have thought very highly of your work in the past," Dr. Miller continued gravely. "Now I am unsure I could trust it again."

"Y-yes, sir."

The dean sighed and pulled a memo pad towards him.

"Very well, Miss Stewart. I thank you for confessing, but you should be under no illusions. You will face consequences for these actions. For guidance on them, I shall look to your professor. He will certainly suffer the most from what you have done."

Daniel had expected this, as Antony was always democratic when deciding upon student discipline. He was prepared with his recommendations.

"I move to have Miss Stewart placed on immediate academic suspension for the remainder of the autumn term. I ask that her enrollment at Browning be evaluated by an impartial committee with a decision on her status to be announced by January of next year."

"Granted." Antony scribbled the terms on his notepad. Jillian let out another strangled sob.

"*If* that committee allows Miss Stewart to return to Browning," Daniel said, a note of bitterness seeping through his voice, "I request permission to refuse her entry to my classes."

"Granted." Antony made a further entry on the notepad.

Daniel hesitated. His third request carried unknown consequences for his own hopes with Jenny. But it had to be made.

"I cannot be certain," he said slowly. "But Miss Stewart may have other information for you, Antony. I'll leave you to it."

Antony looked puzzled, and Jillian absolutely mortified, but Daniel was resolute. He stood to leave, and Jenny followed him out into the hall.

"Daniel?" she whispered helplessly, looking up at him. There were tears in her eyes, and he knew she shared his thoughts. Today's events had thrown their tentatively planned future into complete chaos. Even now, Jillian would likely be testifying about her relationship with Dr. Chilcott, and Daniel was sure the man would be fired. How could he follow that conversation with his *own* request for Antony's blessing?

If that were not enough, the new Abu Simbel dig was almost certainly lost. Once the Egyptian ministry found out about the stone, they might remove him from his site altogether. Daniel longed to pull Jenny into his arms, to bury his face in her neck, to rant and rave about the madness of this day, but he couldn't, not here. He whispered an urgent plea.

"Meet me tonight. Somewhere, anywhere."

"Name the place."

Daniel thought for a moment. "Mount Belle. I'll borrow a car."

"No, I will," Jenny said. "What's your address?"

"Number thirty-four, Denby Drive. I'll be waiting out front in an hour."

"I just hate all this sneaking around," Jenny said softly, her brown eyes brimming with tears. "Daniel, I really don't think I can do this much longer."

"I know. We'll think of something. I promise."

His hand twitched, longing to reach for hers, but the door opening made them jump apart. Jillian had finished her confession.

"I told him," she reported, her face blotchy and flushed from crying. "I chose to tell him about me and Will. I've told him everything. He said it will be taken into account during my hearing, and that I can go home now."

Daniel exhaled slowly. "Good evening, then, Miss Stewart."

At last lifting her reddened eyes, Jillian stumbled through an apology. "I-I know what I did was hateful. Unforgivable. I'm ..." She took a tremendous, shuddering breath. "I'm sorry. For everything."

Jenny nodded sadly. Daniel cleared his throat, trying to answer cordially if not kindly. "That's good of you to say, Miss Stewart. Goodnight."

A miserable Jillian left.

"If you would join me in here, Dr. Carter," Antony called out from his office, "we can discuss the case of Anders Manwaring."

"Ought I to stay?" Jenny whispered.

"No. I'll see you soon."

She nodded. "One hour."

Daniel watched as she walked to the stairs, then turned to see the dean pouring out a tall glass of Scotch.

"This is a double," Antony informed him. "And it's well-earned after the day we've had, I must say. Care for one?"

"No, thank you." Daniel collapsed heavily into his chair. "So."

"So. Chilcott." Shaking his head ruefully, the dean swallowed a large gulp of Scotch. "The fool. There have been rumors for years, of course. A liaison with a third year before the war. A graduate student, some years before that. But no one ever had any proof. And now ..." Dr. Miller grimaced as he took his seat. "A firsthand confession."

"What will you do, now that you have that proof?"

The old professor scoffed. "Fire him. Nothing else I can do, I'm afraid. I'm drawing up the paperwork tonight. Poor Alice Chilcott, she's in for a very rough day tomorrow."

Well aware that the fate of his own relationship hung in the balance, Daniel attempted to sound casual as he asked, "Are you firing him because he had a relationship with a student or because he was married while having a relationship with a student?"

Antony grunted. "Does that distinction matter?"

Here was the moment of decision. Daniel desperately wanted to tell Dr. Miller everything, to beg for his help, to solicit understanding. Yet today's events had forced him to delay that request. The risk of having his relationship judged in the same light as Chilcott's (and consequently being ordered never to see Jenny again) was far too great.

"I was simply curious, that's all."

"Browning forbids all instructor and student relationships, Daniel. If you recall, there are about a dozen—"

"A dozen different regulations against it, yes, I know," Daniel interrupted. "Just as a matter of curiosity, have there ever been any exceptions? For any reason?"

He knew that his question was a transparent one. Gratefully, Antony did not press him. Avoiding Daniel's gaze, the old man reached for his box of chocolates. "Blast. The girl has eaten them all." He irritably tossed the box aside. "Yes. One or two exceptions. In very extenuating circumstances."

"Such as?" Daniel asked hastily. Having given up all hope of being discreet, he simply prayed Antony would not ask him outright why he wanted to know.

The old man huffed. "In 19 ... 1928, was it? A graduate student and a professor were allowed to court. This required special permission from the university president, and a great many professional agreements. Paperwork over a relationship, can you imagine? I believe the only reason permission was granted was that she had nearly finished her graduate thesis. Those were very different times."

Regardless, a spark of hope was kindled in Daniel's heart. If such allowances had existed in the past, might not he request permission as well? When the time was right?

"And the other circumstance?" he pressed.

Dr. Miller chuckled. "Oh, but that story is almost legend. In 1906, I think it was. Browning had only one economics professor at the time, and there was a great shortage of them throughout England. The man was allowed to court a student because he insisted that he would quit, otherwise, in order to be with her. Since we had no one to replace him, Browning kept him on out of dire necessity. These have been very rare cases."

"I see." Daniel knew better than to press his luck by asking more questions. He could not risk obliging Dr. Miller to act against him. At least not yet.

"Now about Anders," Daniel said.

"Yes." Antony swirled his Scotch. "Anders."

"I move to have him expelled."

Dr. Miller froze with his glass halfway to his mouth. "What? Expelled, did you say?"

"Yes."

"But ..." Antony moved to pluck at his bowtie, which had long since been removed. "We've only suspended Miss Stewart, at least for the time being. We cannot enact a harsher punishment for Anders, especially since the legal and financial circumstances of the case aren't yet clear."

Daniel's jaw clenched. "Oh, I think we can. As you heard from Miss Stewart's confession, the destruction of the stone was his idea. The boy is an absolute disgrace to this university."

"That may be, but—"

"If you truly need further grounds for dismissal, just look at the other complaints lodged against him," Daniel urged. "I know of at least one, but there may be more. It would seem Browning has so far failed to act on these reports."

Dr. Miller shifted in his seat. "Complaints? What sort of complaints?"

"Reports of predatory behavior towards our female students.

He's a *scoundrel,* Antony. I've seen his type before. He's the kind of man who would stalk a woman across the globe just to salvage his own bruised ego. I witnessed him harassing someone who had turned him down with my own eyes, and he was threatening ..." Daniel stopped. "Antony, are you already aware of this? You ... you don't look at all surprised."

Dr. Miller winced.

Daniel stared at his mentor, his heart sinking. "You *knew*? You knew, and you did nothing*?*"

"The matter was out of my hands," Antony insisted. He stood and paced so vigorously that a bit of Scotch splashed out of his tumbler. "Any Manwaring incidents go directly to President LaTrell, and he has so far chosen not to issue punishment."

"*Why*?" Daniel challenged him. "I don't care how rich or important this family is, if Anders Manwaring is threatening our students and destroying Browning property, then he has no right to be here."

"Yes, but the Manwarings—"

"What Anders did is unpardonable, Antony. If there are no consequences he will only go on!"

Antony held up a hand to silence him. "I agree with you, Daniel. I do. But the fact is, the Manwarings' annual contributions comprise twelve percent of our discretionary budget. Twelve percent. That's a figure that would be impossible to replace. I don't like it any more than you do, but you can see why the president would be loath to act."

There was a long pause. Daniel stood to leave.

"Where are you going?" Dr. Miller cried out in surprise.

He paused with his back still turned. "Have we finished here? I have to place a call to the Egyptian embassy, and I imagine they're not going to like what I have to say."

"My dear chap." Dr. Miller's voice shook with regret. "Any misdemeanor by Anders goes to the president. Those are my instructions. It's a sorry sort of game, I know, but that is the hand we've been dealt."

Daniel shook his head. "You're wrong, Antony. You're the department head. Anders is in your jurisdiction. You have every right to discipline him, but it seems you're content to forfeit that power. It's the easier move, I'm sure. I'm only sorry that playing this game so long has blinded you to the right one. Goodnight, Antony."

Leaving a sputtering Dr. Miller behind him, Daniel left.

CHAPTER 38

Daniel and Jenny spoke very little on the drive to Mount Belle; he suspected both were still processing the horrifying events of that evening. Strangely, he found he did not object to the silence. After such an unspeakable tragedy, the warmth of Jenny's hand in his was all he really wanted. Somehow the consensual quiet felt as soothing as a tonic.

He stared out the window as they drove towards the hills. It was Jenny who was behind the wheel, as their borrowed car was Margie's. A vague interest in where Jenny had learned to drive stirred within him, briefly relieving his melancholy. Few Browning students had cars, to say nothing of formal driving licenses. Perhaps Jenny had trained during the war, driving medical jeeps. Daniel made a mental note to ask her in a better moment.

"I called the embassy," he confessed at last.

"You did?" Jenny replied, clearly relieved he had brought up the subject first. "What did you say? What did *they* say?"

He rubbed at his aching temple, unsure where to start. "I told Ambassador Nassar that two students had sabotaged the project, for reasons that weren't worth his time."

Jenny's grip on his hand became vice-like. "How did he

respond?" she croaked, as Daniel's crushed fingertips pooled with blood and began to tingle.

He stroked his thumb over hers to loosen her grip and cleared his throat. "He was, erm ... pretty furious, to say the least. I begged for forgiveness, of course, and vowed that Browning would offer compensation. That was all I could do. He pretty much took over the conversation from that point."

"Oh, Daniel," Jenny whispered. "What did he say to you?"

"Rejected my permit for the Abu Simbel dig, for a start, and then sorely reprimanded me. Rightly so."

"That's not fair," she objected. "Others are to blame, not you."

"You think so?" he mused. Regrets that had been simmering deeply now bubbled to the surface. "I try to tell myself that, but the truth is, despite my misgivings I let Jillian onto the project." Daniel shook his head. "The stone was in my charge. I should have been more selective of its caretakers. At the end of the day the blame rests with me."

"Share that blame with me, then." Jenny sighed. "I should have expected Anders would make some kind of trouble, but never in my wildest dreams would I have thought Jillian capable of something like this."

"Really?"

"I'm serious," Jenny insisted, picking up on his skepticism. "I'm furious at her, but the odd thing is, as angry as I am about the stone, I'm almost more upset by the thought of her being duped by Anders. She's really so intelligent, and I just ... I just *hate* the fact that she was under his thumb. And Chilcott's, for that matter."

"I imagine 'that matter' will be forgotten eventually," he said, referencing Chilcott but thinking about the stone.

"I'm not so sure. Scandal follows a woman, more than it does a man," Jenny intoned more pensively than Daniel would have liked. He pushed aside the uncomfortable parallels of their own situation.

"Jillian's made of tough stuff. She'll rally," he consoled her.

"But her life will be so different than it might have been," Jenny continued. "*Shame on Chilcott.* I blame him, I really do, when it comes down to it. I had no sense that he could be so manipulative. Anders, on the other hand ..."

Daniel scowled darkly. "Yes."

"What will happen to him?"

He looked out the window. "I believe Dr. Miller is handling it."

Silence fell between them once more.

"Daniel," Jenny whispered after a long while. "What will happen to your site?"

He felt another flash of guilt, as excruciating as molten lead being poured down his throat to his stomach. It hardened into a heaviness he couldn't seem to escape. "I've not been banned from coming back. At least not yet."

She nodded weakly. "That's something to be grateful for, I suppose."

"Yes. I suppose it is."

Jenny's fingers nervously drummed against the steering wheel. "Golly. To say this has been a complicated term would be the understatement of the century. To top it all off, we have finals next week, and I haven't cracked open a book in *days.*"

She said this with such a funny little expression that Daniel burst into laughter. Only Jenny – bookish, adorable, darling Jenny – could move so seamlessly from the destruction of ancient artifacts to the dread of studying for an exam. The laughter she'd caused was medicinal, and the lead weight in Daniel's stomach lessened ever so slightly.

"Why are you laughing at me?" she demanded, though chuckling herself.

"No reason." He smiled. "I was just thinking about how lovely something as normal as exams sounds in this moment."

"That's easy for a professor to say," she countered with a wink. "Hang on – is it left or right at the turn?"

"Left. We're nearly there." The sky was completely dark now, and even with the car's headlights it was difficult to see the path ahead. For a moment, Daniel worried the tiny vehicle wouldn't be able to climb the mountain's slope; there was still plenty of snow on the ground. Thankfully, the way up seemed to have been partly cleared by residents at the mountain's base.

The gravel road wound through a deep, canyon-like expanse, coming out onto a flattish hilltop with a lovely view of the valley. The summit, for which the town was named, was not so much a mountain as it was a set of very steep knolls. It was grassy more than rocky and dotted thinly with trees. Bare-limbed ashes and beeches lined the ridge, and there were even a few Scots pines at its tallest peak. It was a popular place for picnicking in the summer but was predictably abandoned on this wintry night.

Jenny coaxed the car to a level spot and parked it. During its last grumbling movement, Daniel climbed out his side to open her door. She pressed his hand gratefully as she alighted onto the snowy gravel, her brown eyes shining in wonder.

"It's so lovely," she whispered, gazing at the snowy boulders and trees. "I've always meant to come here, but I never have."

"What, never?" he teased. "None of the dozens of fellows who've asked you out in my class have taken you?"

She gave him a playfully berating look. Holding onto her white beret, she arched her neck and surveyed the stars. Hundreds upon hundreds sparkled overhead, as sharp and clear as cut glass.

"So many of them," she murmured. "I think I could stare forever, and never tire of it."

Daniel fetched a bag of blankets from the backseat and closed the car door. Smiling, he held out a gloved hand.

"Come on."

She beamed and took it. Together they walked down a winding path to a clearing, each remarking on the menacing look of the pines. When they reached the overlook, Daniel spread thick layers of blankets upon the snow. The last, largest blanket he wrapped about the two of them as they sat nestled together. Jenny leaned immediately into Daniel's chest – a trusting, intimate gesture that caused his heart to swell with happiness.

"I'd forgotten how nice it is up here," he said, taking in the glimmer of lights from the valley. "I don't even remember the last time I came."

"Perhaps it was with that nice secretary from the first floor?" Jenny suggested, seemingly determined to get in some teasing of her own.

Daniel winced. "So you did hear Antony that day."

"Yes. It doesn't matter, though. I don't expect you to have lived a monastic life. I certainly haven't."

"Right." Daniel had a sudden burning desire to change the subject. "There's Canis Major," he said, gesturing to a constellation. "And Auriga, the Charioteer. Then of course, my personal favorite: Orion the Hunter."

"I like Taurus the Bull," Jenny replied, pointing to its bright cluster. "You can so clearly see the face, the eyes. Most of the other constellations look like triangles or boxes. Sometimes I wonder what the ancients could possibly have been thinking."

He smiled. "That's odd."

"What is?"

"Our favorite constellations. They're right next to each other."

Jenny turned her face shyly upwards. Daniel could just make out her features in the moonlight. His gaze drifted slowly over her forehead, her lips, the waves of her hair. For a glorious moment, Daniel pushed his distress to his mind's back corner. He leaned in to kiss her, his cold lips just brushing hers. Enjoying their warmth and fullness, he moved to do so once more, but Jenny quickly turned her face towards the overlook.

"It was nice of Margie to lend me her car," she said hastily.

"Yes." Daniel settled back into his seat, simultaneously

lamenting this turn of events and kicking himself for his eagerness. He wrapped the blanket tighter around them and watched as their breath formed clouds in the thin, clear air. "You know," he said, "I've always wondered if I could make rings with my breath in the winter, like Antony does with his pipe smoke." He attempted it, with no success.

"You have to sort of tap your cheek and click your tongue," Jenny instructed. "Like this." She demonstrated the motion.

"And what, may I ask, makes you such an expert on smoke rings?" he asked with a chuckle. "Hard at the pipe these days?"

Jenny rolled her eyes. "No. My father used to smoke one. Until my mother said 'trop c'est trop,' and threw them all out."

"What does your father do?" Daniel asked, more curiously. He knew a little of her French mother and two older brothers, but nothing of her father.

"He's an accountant at a small country firm, and he raises sheep on the side, though not in a big way. It's just a small family trade. I've tried to convince him to give it up, since he loses money on it every year, but he won't." Jenny frowned thoughtfully. "I suspect he's keen to honor my grandfather, and my great-grandfather, and his father before him. We've been sheep farmers since the Middle Ages, apparently."

Daniel marveled at how a young woman from an obscure country village had aspired, seemingly without fortune and connections, to attend one of the most expensive private universities in the country. Before he could ask how that had come about, Jenny posed a familial question of her own.

"What about your father? Is he a professor, too?"

"Nope." Daniel shook his head. "He was a private secretary to a diplomat. My mother worked for the diplomat's wife."

"Oh, how wonderful! Your mother was employed? Where do they live now?"

Daniel cleared his throat roughly. "They've ... both passed on."

"Oh." Jenny's face fell. "Oh, Daniel, I'm so terribly sorry."

"That's all right. It was a long while ago now."

"How did they ..."

He cleared his throat again. "Car accident. On assignment in Milan. I was seventeen."

"You've been on your own since you were *seventeen*?"

"Yes, I suppose so."

"Daniel, I ..."

"Well no, not really alone. Antony stepped up quite a bit while I was at Browning. You might say he sort of took me under his wing. Invited me over for holidays and everything." Not wanting to dwell any further on the subject, Daniel shifted in his seat and said, "If I recall correctly, Antony sort of sucks the smoke in before he puffs it out." He took in a tremendous breath of cold air, which immediately dried his throat and set him hacking.

Jenny burst into laughter. Daniel protested, but was secretly delighted by her mirth. He kissed the top of her head as the sound of her chuckles faded into the night air. They sat quietly for a long moment, looking serenely up at the stars. A cloud drifted over the moon, plunging them into darkness.

"I haven't, by the way," Daniel said in a low voice.

"Hmm?"

"You asked if I had brought any other women up here. I haven't."

Jenny did not respond, but settled more deeply into Daniel's chest. He longed to kiss her again, yet didn't dare try it. Words that astonished even him were on the tip of his tongue, and it was taking considerable effort to withhold them.

It was too soon. It was too much.

For now, it had to be enough to hold her lovely form, to breathe in her faint scent of orange blossoms – to listen to the rise and fall of her slow, quiet breath.

Being an analytical sort, Daniel instead occupied himself with an objective, intellectual curiosity about how quickly he'd been captivated by this woman. He'd been in and out of many relationships, and enjoyed romance with several attractive partners. There had been months-long courtships, passionate two-week flings, and some of the exciting, undefined in-between. Yet now, in the most unexpected place imaginable, Daniel had met a woman who was swiftly driving those memories to oblivion. The intensification of his feelings shocked him, but he couldn't deny the truth of what was happening, nor the reasons it had.

Jenny was beautiful, of course. Her lovely figure and pretty legs were, in this moment, making it very hard for Daniel to discipline his thoughts. More than that, however, she approached life with a frankness and sincerity that completely undid him. She challenged him. She cajoled him. She shared openly and sought out Daniel's secrets. If he did not divulge them, she stubbornly deduced them anyway, refusing to let his dismissive, surface-level answers be the end of his sharing.

She was clever, and willful, and ambitious, and kind. Holding her in his arms now, Daniel was overcome by a feeling he felt he'd been in search of for years, without ever really finding. His carefully arranged loneliness, so familiar that it had come to feel like the only space he truly belonged, had been ruptured forever, along with any desire of maintaining its solitude. Jenny seemed to guess the nature of his thoughts, for her breath caught. Shifting in his seat to look at her once more, he found that her expression was both gentle *and* inviting.

Heart pounding, Daniel leaned Jenny back in his arms. She rested her hand against his neck, smiling a little as she stroked the line of his jaw. Then, slowly, she raised her eyes to meet his. Her eyelids fluttered to a close, and lowering his own, he swept her lips softly between his.

For the third time, Daniel was astonished by the strength of Jenny's response. Though she may have been an inexperienced lover, he sensed she was a quick learner with strong desires of her own. She moved into him with bewitching confidence, and he let his body curve firmly against the shape of hers. When she drifted towards the ground, he went with her.

He stroked her cheek, studying her face for a sign of how to proceed.

"Jenny?"

She brushed her icy nose against his in another subtle invitation. Mesmerized, he moved one hand under the small of her back. There was so much that he wanted to say - so much he was too terrified to admit. He kissed her with his heart on his lips, willing her to understand what he could not yet put into words. That silenced longing must have transferred into an urgent, almost frantic energy on his part, for under his ensuing fervor Jenny let out a muffled little sigh.

The sound thrilled him. They were close together now, so tenderly, beautifully close that he wasn't sure where his own chest ended and hers began. The rise and fall of her breath was barely keeping time with his as their mouths wove deeply in a tender exchange. It was bliss. No, it was quickly becoming more than that. It was *fever*. It was euphoria, it was numbness, it was freedom and possibility and glory, until Jenny let out another little sigh and raised a hand sharply to his chest.

Looking deeply into her eyes, Daniel nodded to show that he understood. For a moment he simply lay over her, stroking her cheek.

"Are you all right?" he whispered, trying to slow his heartbeat.

She smiled happily. "Yes."

With a final tender kiss, he slipped to her side and wrapped her in his arms. He held her like that for some time, gazing at the numberless stars.

"Daniel?" Jenny whispered into the darkness.

"Mmm?"

"I'm so cold."

With an apologetic chuckle, he stood and swept Jenny up into his arms. "Come on," he said, winking cheerfully. "Let's get you home."

Trudging through the snow to the car, Daniel had the welcome (if unsettling) realization that although his life and career were fast crumbling around him, he had truly never been happier.

CHAPTER 39

Early the next morning, Daniel stood with his fist hovering uncertainly over Antony's door. He had been up half the night, agonizing over the stone, his site, his professorship, Anders, and most importantly, Jenny. Around dawn Daniel had resolved to throw caution to the wind. There was too much uncertainty in every aspect of his life these days, and if there was anything he could do to lessen it, he simply had to try. For the benefit of all involved.

He had used his walk to campus to form a plan – a plan that now found him standing uncertainly outside Antony's office. Steeling his nerves, he rapped his knuckles against the door and waited.

"Come in," Antony called gruffly.

Daniel pushed his way inside. The old dean was standing behind his desk and filling a pipe with tobacco. Upon seeing Daniel, he stopped.

"Oh. It's you," Dr. Miller said with uncharacteristic coldness. "How can I help you, Dr. Carter?"

It was clear that Antony was still ruffled from yesterday's exchange. In truth, Daniel was scarcely less so. After their conversation about Anders, his sharp disappointment in his mentor had followed him like a dark cloud. The usual ease and friendliness that existed between them was strained, and there was no doubt today's discussion would upset it even further. But Daniel's mission was too important to abandon. He entered the office.

"Hello, Antony." Daniel kept his tone light, attempting to smooth over the awkwardness of the moment. "How has your morning been?"

"Terrible, as it happens," Antony said curtly. He popped the pipe in his mouth and irritably lit a match. "I've just given Chilcott his marching orders. It was quite a nasty scene."

Despite the tension, Daniel felt a surge of concern for Antony. "What did he say?"

"Oh, what you might expect." Antony shook the match to extinguish it. "That I was making a mistake, and that I'd never find a more dedicated servant of this university, or a finer expert on Iran. Then he railed against you for a while, claiming you were a slanderous fool who had paid Miss Stewart to seduce him."

"He's a liar," Daniel muttered in disbelief.

"Yes." Dr. Miller took a long draught of his pipe. "Well, I suppose we always knew that, didn't we?"

"What else did he say?"

Dr. Miller snorted. "He wasn't permitted to say much else. I dismissed him. He's clearing out his office even now."

"You've been through quite a lot this week," Daniel said, wanting to steer the conversation more sympathetically in light of Chilcott's unpleasantness.

Dr. Miller let out a short, barking laugh and pointed a finger in Daniel's face.

"Not as much as you, I should think. Don't try to butter me up, my boy. I still haven't forgiven you for calling me an unprincipled bureaucrat."

"I never said that, Antony."

271

"Well, perhaps not in so many words." Antony puffed grumpily on his pipe. "You did, however, accuse me of being tainted by a corrupt system. I could not have been more offended if you'd spat in my face. I've spent my entire career challenging the idiocy that is bureaucracy, you know."

"Unless that idiocy involves the Manwarings," he said quietly. "To the detriment of at least one female student, who has reported Anders' offenses and is waiting for justice that may never come."

Antony flushed to the tips of his flossy white hair. "Daniel. I know what you must be feeling, but the ugly truth is, without the Manwarings' support, we—"

"I didn't come here to fight about Anders," Daniel interrupted, calmly helping himself to a seat. "I came here to confide and to ask for your assistance."

"Oh?" Dr. Miller replied, his shoulders tensing. "Confide, you say? Yes, well. I would love to be of assistance, Daniel, and I will be if I can, but the fact is with Chilcott's dismissal and the stone damage, I have rather a lot going on today. There are hearings to attend, and reports to be filed. Then there is Miss Stewart's review committee to select, and—"

"I've been seeing Miss Ellison."

The reaction to Daniel's statement was immediate. Antony's shoulders slumped dejectedly, and he suddenly looked ten years older.

"Yes." He sat down wearily. "I suspected as much."

"I'm surprised you didn't confront me about it sooner."

The old professor rubbed his chin, looking more exhausted than Daniel had ever seen him. "Perhaps I should have done. I suppose I hoped it would fizzle out on its own." He heaved an enormous sigh. "So. How long has it been going on, then?"

"Officially? Four days."

Antony threw him a stern look. "Why the devil are you telling me this now? After what's just happened with Chilcott? You do realize I've just had to fire him, don't you? Couldn't you at least have waited until after the term ends?"

"I'm telling you now because if things progress as I hope, neither Jenny nor I can risk speculation about when our relationship began. I don't want her work, or mine, to be tainted by association or scandal. I've realized my case is different enough from Chilcott's to stand on its own, and I want to formally petition the school for permission to court Miss Ellison. I'll fill out whatever paperwork and agreements are necessary. I'm willing to cooperate and work within the university's parameters."

Looking truly exasperated now, Antony replied, "My dear boy, I told you yesterday that there have only ever been two exceptions to our policy, and those were granted under extremely unique circumstances. The school will not look favorably upon your request, especially once they learn that you and Miss Ellison have been meeting secretly, and making love after class, and —"

"We're not lovers. Not in that way, not yet. I swear it. And we've only met in secret a handful of times. Besides, unlike Chilcott, I am unmarried, and I'm openly seeking permission to do this the *right way*, from the very start. Surely the university would look favorably upon that."

Daniel's argument was well-prepared, rational, and carefully persuasive. Dr. Miller seemed not to hear his points, however. He was staring at him in relief, as though he had gotten stuck on a particular item.

"You mean ... the two of you ... you have truly never?"

"I've kissed her three times. Well ..." Daniel flushed and shifted slightly in his seat. "That is, on three separate occasions. Only once on Browning property."

"Where?"

"In my office."

"Oh, Daniel," Antony groaned.

"Again, we've kissed. But that is all."

"On your honor?"

"Yes. You have my word."

Antony evaluated him for a moment, his expression softening. "If what you say is true, that might work to your advantage. Perhaps ... just perhaps, if this were to be framed as the beginning of a courtship, or an exploration of the possibility of one ..." He stroked his chin thoughtfully, but a moment later his jolly features hardened. "*No*. As dean of this department, I must speak my mind. I strongly advise against this, Daniel. Submitting such an application would open you up to malicious gossip on all sides."

"I'm not afraid of gossip."

"There would be repercussions beyond just yourself, Daniel. Ugly prattle about Chilcott is already spreading throughout the department. With a reduced staff and a potentially huge fine to pay to the Egyptian government, I need the administration on our side. We cannot afford another dramatic incident, not now."

"I know it's poor timing," Daniel admitted. "I know it. There may be consequences I haven't considered. But this is my situation, and I am asking for your help. So will you help me?"

Antony tapped his fingers impatiently against the desk. "Listen. Miss Ellison is a very good sort of a girl, and I like her tremendously, but I tell you as your friend, you're not thinking this through. She's young, Daniel. Only nineteen or twenty, if I remember correctly, and—"

"She's twenty-three."

"Nevertheless." Antony plucked nervously at his bowtie. "Despite the relative nearness of your ages, your relationship would be scoffed at by every administrator at Browning. I tell you plainly that most of the professors here are a very conservative sort. They will not welcome this news."

"I'm prepared to make a few enemies, if it means my relationship with Jenny can be out in the open," Daniel rebutted.

"Well, as long as we're being open, I will lay all of my cards on the table." Antony firmly interlaced his fingers. "Daniel, I will make no secret of it. I want you to become dean of this department. Not next year, not in five years, but one day. Once you're fully tenured and have ten to fifteen years of teaching under your belt, you could easily win the deanship. You have it in you to become one of the greatest leaders at Browning. Why, you might even go on to become a university president yourself! But not if you take up with a student. It would be suicide for your career."

"Antony—"

"Think of what people will say!" the old man interrupted, standing and pacing the room. "Even if you take the requisite steps and your relationship is, on the off chance, approved, you and Miss Ellison will face the worst sort of gossip. You'll be accused of seduction, intrigue, secrecy. Your professionalism and personal standards will be cast into doubt. More than that, you'll be forever changed in the students' eyes. They will see you as one of them, Daniel. They'll try to take advantage of your position and exploit your connection to the girl."

"I have no doubt there will be complications, but I'm even more confident that Jenny and I can manage them. Anything would be better than sneaking around under fear of being caught. We both feel that."

"That brings me to my next point. What of Miss Ellison?"

"What about her?"

"I assume you've thought about what all of this will mean for Jenny?"

Daniel said nothing for a long while. He wasn't sure what Antony was getting at, but he had a feeling the man's next point would be an inconveniently good one.

"I'm ... not sure what you're asking."

Antony shook his head soberly and emptied his pipe. "Jennifer Ellison is not just a brilliant student. She's also an ambitious one, with very lofty plans for her future. Did you know that she hopes to attend graduate school herself?"

There was a heavy pause.

"No," Daniel admitted quietly.

"Well, she does. A relationship with you, Daniel, will cast doubt on anything she achieves. If she does get work placement, few would believe it was on her own merit. At best, she'd be accused of favoritism and profiting by association. At worst, she'd be painted as a loose woman and a schemer. Is that what you want?"

"Of course not," he huffed.

"And what of her friendships?" Antony pressed. "Imagine the complications you would face in that arena. Could you accompany her to a housemate's birthday party, or wedding, for example? Could you join her student chums for drinks at the local pub? Certainly not. Miss Ellison wouldn't be just one of the students anymore, and she wouldn't be welcome in a circle of professors, either. She'd be isolated, an 'other.' A spare part."

This was a painfully reasonable argument, and for a moment Daniel was lost for words. Antony looked distractedly out the window, speaking his next thoughts as though to himself.

"Young people in this stage of life can be peculiarly unfeeling, Daniel. I've seen it time and again. She'll be mocked, ridiculed. She'll be called a teacher's pet, and far worse. Miss Ellison doesn't deserve any of that. It would be better, and safer, for you to find some local woman."

Again, Daniel remained silent.

Dr. Miller turned to him sympathetically. "I know this must be hard to hear, my boy. Miss Ellison is very charming, of course, and anyone can see why you might have come to like her very much. But—"

"Not like," Daniel interrupted, his expression deathly serious.

Antony's blue eyes became as round as coins. "Love?"

He gave a short, stiff nod. "Possibly."

After a moment of speechlessness, Antony collapsed into his chair and slapped his forehead. "You mean ... oh, bother." The old man laughed weakly. "I simply cannot believe what I am hearing. Love. You love her. You're in love with Miss Ellison."

"Yes."

"Truly? You *love* her? Are you certain?" The old dean looked positively jubilant. "Gumdrops and goose eggs, love certainly is a flighty temptress. After sixty-four years of living, the only thing I know about it is that I know *nothing* about it. Are you telling me that the man who would not even make time for a dinner date has gone and fallen in *love*?"

"Yes."

"And" – Dr. Miller looked around furtively – "does she know?"

Daniel shook his head. "I suspect I'm a bit further along in my feelings than she is."

"A difficult place to be, my friend," Antony said with a hint of a wink.

He smiled. "It certainly is."

"But this is remarkable!" Dr. Miller said with a look that was at once incredulous and reproachful. "After years of me prodding you to put down romantic roots, you at last find love in your classroom?"

"Believe me," Daniel said apologetically. "It wasn't the plan. No one is more surprised than I."

Antony thumped his empty pipe against his palm and said nothing for a full two minutes. Though Daniel was in agony, he didn't dare risk his good fortune by breaking the silence.

"Oh, good heavens," Antony finally muttered, a shade of his jolly self returning. "This is all most unconventional, but ... oh, dash it all. If I didn't care for you so very much, Daniel Carter, you'd be out of here on your rear end and make no mistake."

"I know."

Antony let out a rough exhale. "Very well. I wish I was sure you knew what you were doing, Daniel. If you are willing to take this risk, then I shall petition President LaTrell on your behalf. I can make no promises, mind. His final word on the matter is law, and if he refuses consent, I cannot go against him."

"Thank you, Antony," Daniel replied, his voice thick with gratitude. "A chance is all I ask." Though his heart leapt with joy, he sobered to deliver his next, most important message. "As for your concerns about Jenny, I swear to you, I would never compel her to give up anything in order to be with me. I would give her the time to nurture her friendships, to enjoy them apart from me if need be, and if anyone mocked her, or attributed her achievements to my influence, then they'd have me to answer to."

"Yes, well, I'm not exactly sure how that would help the situation," Antony replied bluntly. "But you can worry about all that if the time comes. Until you receive notice from me, heed what I say." He lifted a warning finger. "Be on your guard. No sneaking around the campus. No clandestine getaways. And *no* making love to her on your office desk."

"Antony," Daniel said sternly, his face reddening. But the old professor only chuckled.

"Now, don't try to deny that you've thought about it!"

Daniel sputtered indignantly, but couldn't come up with a convincing rebuttal. Of course he had.

"There! It's just as I thought," Dr. Miller said, a merry twinkle in his eye. "You needn't act so shocked, my boy. It wouldn't be the first time it has happened at Browning, as we well know." He hesitated. "Again, I cannot guarantee that you will receive the answer you hope for. But, as your friend, I promise I will try."

He held out his hand, and Daniel clasped it hopefully.

"Thank you, Antony. *Thank you.*"

CHAPTER 40

"I still can't believe it," Margie whispered. "Taking up with a married man! And to have never said a word to me, or Nyra!"

"I know," Jenny said mournfully. "I can't stop thinking about it. It kept me up half the night."

The two girls were sitting side by side in Paleography and working on a review worksheet Daniel had assigned. They had been instructed to study in pairs, and the roommates had quickly taken advantage of the classroom chatter to catch up on recent events.

"It just doesn't make sense!" Margie said, her face contorting in disgust. "Jillian's young, smart, good-looking. She's had a whole string of boyfriends, some of them very nice. She was set to graduate in the spring. Why would she throw everything away for that old beanpole? Could there really have been a physical thing between them? Oh, I think I'm going to be sick just thinking about it," she finished, looking a bit green in the face.

"To be fair, I think Jillian's motives were a little more complicated than that," Jenny said, shifting slightly in her seat.

"You've heard she's transferring schools, haven't you?"

Jenny's eyes snapped up from the petroglyph she was copying. "What?"

Margie nodded. "Jillian said she couldn't bear to wait through her review period when there's a decent chance she'll be expelled at the end of it. She's enrolling in Stanwyck University."

"It makes sense," Jenny mumbled sadly. "She can start over, away from all the gossip. Where is she now? Will she go home?"

Margie shook her head. "I doubt it. Not if she's trying to feel any better. Not a great home life, apparently. Stepdad's a bit of a nightmare."

"Oh."

"It's a shame." Margie sighed. "As much as Jillian rails against this place, you know she'll hate to leave. She's been crying nonstop for two days."

This news sparked a complicated reaction. Despite Jenny's lingering anger, she pitied her. The heartache at leaving Browning was something she could well understand. Though she doubted she could ever forgive the damage done to the stone, it seemed clear Jillian's choices had been been influenced as much by desperation as they had revenge. Perhaps – just perhaps – Jillian's scorn had been a symptom, and not a trait. If there was anything Jenny felt responsible for, it was not perceiving it as such before it was too late.

"Look sharp," Margie breathed. "Dr. Carter's coming this way."

"No, he's not," she answered wearily. "He's helping Solomon and Andrew."

Margie's infatuation was finally striking a nerve. Jenny could admit to feeling a bit ... what was the emotion? Jealous? No. Defensive, she thought. Protective.

Her friend plumped her thick auburn hair. "Quick. Think of a question to ask him."

"I don't have any questions."

"Oh, never mind, he's heading the other way." Margie's face fell in disappointment. "Blast, I thought that was my chance. I've been putting on an air of confusion all morning, just so he'd walk over."

"I can't make out this glyph," Jenny said, tapping her pencil on their assignment. "Will you try?"

"I thought I caught him looking over here once or twice during the lecture." Margie leaned her chin on one hand with a glum expression. "Golly, he's beautiful. It's almost unfair."

Jenny glanced towards Daniel, who was still making his rounds about the classroom. She, too, had been trying to catch his eye all morning. If Daniel had looked her way at all, she had missed it entirely.

Her tension eased somewhat as her own eyes confirmed how extraordinarily handsome Daniel looked this morning, in his favorite navy-blue sweater and dark slacks. Despite the disastrous week, he appeared to be in a fairly good mood. He was cheerfully discussing the school's last rugby match with a group of male students. Jenny's eyes lingered dreamily on his muscular forearms and trim, athletic abdomen. She had a sudden passionate urge to curl into his chest, just as she had on Mount Belle.

The campus bell chimed, signaling the end of the lecture. Startled from her reverie, Jenny knocked over her pencil case. A dozen pens and pencils clattered onto the classroom floor, rolling under desks and chairs in every direction.

"Blast!" Jenny muttered, launching herself onto the cold marble tiles.

"Oh dear!" Margie sprang into action beside her. "There's some under the window, look! Never mind, I'll get them."

Students filed noisily out of the classroom, jostling Jenny as she frantically scooped pencils back into her case.

"Allow me."

Daniel had seemingly crossed the room in two steps and was stooping to help her. He began collecting her things with a quiet, satisfied smile.

"Th-thank you." Jenny stammered, blushing. After their lovely kisses on the mountain, her heart pounded violently just at being near him again. She wondered vaguely if his was doing the same.

"One rolled under the closet door, and I can't get it because it's locked," Margie said, returning with a handful of pencils. "Maybe we ..."

Seeing Dr. Carter crouched so near, Margie flushed and dropped most of what she was holding.

"Dr. Carter!" she cried. "That's very gallant of you to help, Professor!"

"Not at all. It's my pleasure."

Daniel collected the last of the mess and zipped up Jenny's pencil case. He stood and held out his hand, helping Jenny to rise from the floor. Though he did not look at her, he gave her fingers the tiniest squeeze before releasing them.

"Now," he said, smiling cordially at Margie, "if all is well, I'll leave you ladies to it. Have a good afternoon."

Margie turned ecstatically to Jenny.

"You're brilliant!" she mouthed.

"That wasn't intentional!" Jenny hissed under her breath, but Margie wasn't listening. Clearly emboldened by the "accident," she blurted out a blunt, "Dr. Carter? May I ask you something?"

Daniel turned. "Yes, Miss Payne?"

"I was just wondering ..."

Jenny squirmed as Margie's freckled face turned scarlet. Whatever was about to happen, it was certain to be uncomfortable for all parties involved.

"I was wondering if, after the term is over ... that is, do professors ever socialize with students?" Margie spoke very quickly. "Because my parents have an annual Christmas party, you see, and they always invite several Browning administrators. Dean Anderson usually comes, and so does Dean Williams, and sometimes even President LaTrell if he's not too busy. I know my parents would be simply delighted if you came too."

Daniel paused. "Well, I ..."

"It's just a quiet affair, but it's always a laugh," Margie sped on. "There's a dinner, and then a game or two of snapdragon or billiards. Truly, my mother and father would be delighted if you joined us. Mum's always saying we could use some fresh faces around the table," she said with a puttering laugh.

There was a brief silence, in which Jenny actually smiled at this endearingly rushed offer. She turned to Daniel, curious to see his response. Bafflingly, a deep frown had creased his brow.

"That's very kind of you, Miss Payne. Unfortunately, I'm afraid I prefer not to socialize with students outside of the classroom. I do apologize."

Jenny widened her eyes in astonishment, but Daniel, having set his feet in motion, did not witness her response to such a brush-off.

"I hope you'll thank your parents for their kind invitation and wish them a very happy holiday. Good day." He walked to his office without so much as a backwards glance.

"Oh dear," Margie groaned, looking as if she would have welcomed the crush of a falling boulder. "Why did I even say anything?"

"Because you're a kind and generous person," Jenny said, taking her friend's arm consolingly. Her thoughts were buzzing over Daniel's perplexing dismissal.

"Of course he can't socialize with students," Margie anguished. "I don't know what I was thinking! What could have possessed me, Jenny?"

"I'm sure he thought it was very nice of you. It *was* nice. Marge, can you head to lunch without me? I just ... I need to check something with Dr. Carter."

"All right," Margie said miserably. "See you in class."

Jenny busied herself with her pencil case, waiting until the hall had completely emptied before approaching Daniel's office. Taking a deep breath, she rapped softly on his door.

There was no answer.

Composing herself, Jenny entered to see Daniel sitting in his deep green armchair, one hand clutching an open book, the other thoughtfully rubbing his chin. His face was etched with all the usual marks of concentration; he looked miles away.

"What's the book?"

Daniel jumped up from his seat in surprise.

"Jenny." He smiled at her wistfully. "Hello."

"*Nomadic Tribes of The Arabian Peninsula*," she read aloud, walking towards him. "Sounds interesting."

"Yes."

"But you weren't reading it."

"No."

Jenny softly lifted the book from his hands. "What's wrong, Daniel?"

He cleared his throat. "What do you mean?"

"Your conversation with Margie just now." She gave him a searching look. "Would it have been so wrong for you to attend her party? You wouldn't have been the only professor there."

"Yes, but she's your friend," Daniel replied, as though the problem should have been obvious.

"So?"

His expression was impassive, unreadable. "I've just ... got to be a bit more careful than most other professors, that's all."

He turned his head and looked past her. Jenny's eyes moved swiftly over Daniel's sharp profile and somber, vacant eyes.

"Something's happened. What is it?" she pressed. "Tell me."

"Nothing."

"Something's changed," Jenny insisted. "I can feel it. What's wrong?"

Daniel hesitated. "Nothing's wrong, exactly. But I've spoken with Antony, and he made me aware of certain ... certain complications that might arise from our being together. I'm just trying to head off any of those problems."

"You've told him about us?"

"Yes."

She stepped backwards in a panic. Although they had discussed confessing their plight, she was not prepared to hear that it had already taken place. Without her.

"We were supposed to tell him *together*, Daniel!"

"I'm sorry, I—"

"Why did you ... what did he say?" she cried, wringing her hands. "Tell me quickly. Did he fire you?"

"No, it wasn't like that," Daniel explained hastily. "He listened to me, he heard me out. I asked for permission to date you publicly, and he promised to petition the university president on our behalf. Apparently there's an application, a set of forms that can be filled out for cases such as these. If the university approves, then we could pursue a relationship without fear of a rebuke. He thinks there's a chance."

"A chance?" she repeated, her heart burning with something that felt like hope – and residual fury that he'd pursued these arrangements on his own.

"Yes. A chance. It won't be long now." Daniel smiled, yet his own expression was far from hopeful. His blue eyes were empty, mask-like in their manner; they held back feelings he hadn't shared, and that she could not yet name without his assistance.

"Daniel," she prompted warily. "There's more. I can feel it. What else is wrong?"

He turned his attention back to the spot over her head. "I suppose Margie's invitation made me think about something else Antony said."

"*What* did he say?" Jenny urged, dearly hoping he wouldn't make her ask that question a third time.

He pressed his lips together in a firm line. "He gave me a highly logical list of obstacles. Most of which involve negative consequences for you."

"Such as?" she whispered.

Daniel took one of her hands into his own; his palm was clammy with perspiration. He looked at their clasped fingers and carefully stroked her wrist. "Jenny ... I think I've been a selfish fool. The worst sort of academic, too, because I ignored the truth. I didn't want to see it. I never admitted the harm that this – that *we* – could do."

"What harm?" she rebutted. "If Browning consents, why should there be any harm done?"

"Even if we get their permission, what future would we have?" Daniel argued. "Think about it. We'd be in a relationship, yes, but with what support? I couldn't bring you to a university event, and I couldn't go to Margie's holiday party with you on my arm. You'd be left alone and partnerless."

"Why couldn't you come with me?" she challenged him. "You really didn't need to turn down Margie's invitation. After this term you won't be her professor any longer, and you won't be mine."

Daniel closed his eyes and squeezed her hands more tightly. "Jenny, if I begin spending time in your circle of friends, I'll quickly forfeit any authority as a professor. I'll lose all control of my classroom." He gazed at her sadly. "More than that, you'd be set apart from your own peers. You'd be the 'professor's girl.' You'd be notorious. Anything you achieve academically would be made suspect, Antony made that very clear."

"What do you mean 'suspect'?" Jenny said shortly. She wasn't at all worried about consequences for her social circle. If her recent argument with Margie had made her aware of anything, it was that she only needed a handful of close friends to be perfectly content. After all she and Daniel had been through to get to this point, his sudden wave of doubt felt unforgivably feeble.

"If you go to graduate school," he stressed, "or make a major discovery of any kind, people could attribute it to my influence and connections. They'd accuse you of profiting by unfair means."

"Is that what this is all about?" Jenny groaned. "I don't need you to worry about that, Daniel. I know what I'm up against, but I'm not going to wither if someone questions my achievements. I've dealt with that my entire life."

"Yes, but Jenny—"

"As a woman bent on becoming more than a secretary, I've had to defend my dreams more than once," she said flatly. "Believe me, I'm quite good at it by now."

"You'd be dismissed by every professional in our field," he emphasized. "That's the greatest risk of our being together, Jenny. I can't be a part of anything that would take away your credibility or opportunities."

"But you can't take away what you haven't given!" she fumed. "Everything I have I've earned. I know it, and you know it. Who cares what the rest of the world thinks?"

"Yes, but—"

"I know the risks," she said. "I've weighed them, time and time again, but I also know what I want." She swallowed, hard. "I want *you*, Daniel Carter. I've decided that much. I told myself that we can make all the naysayers eat their words, once they see what I'm capable of. I told myself we could face anything, if we chose to take it on together." Jenny took a deep, shuddering breath. "But if you're already giving up on this fight, then it's clear I've selected the wrong partner." She snatched away her hands and began marching from Daniel's office.

"Jenny!"

"What?" she demanded, turning to him with blazing eyes. Daniel paused, then crossed to her without a word. Pulling her in for a deep, swelling kiss, he locked the office door.

CHAPTER 41

Across campus, Dr. Antony Miller sat outside of President LaTrell's highly burnished office entrance. His foot tapped impatiently against the black marble, as his meeting with the president was meant to have started at twelve sharp. It was now almost half past.

Groaning over the precious time being wasted, Antony straightened his papers and mentally sorted his talking points. There was much to discuss with the president, and each new task weighed more heavily on his mind than the last. The strategy of the pending conversation eluded him, yet it was always wisest, he thought, to begin with good news. He would first report on the successful termination of William Chilcott. Then, he and the president would undoubtedly digress for a few minutes into strategies of containing Chilcott's affair. It was imperative to reduce the damage done to his department, and to Browning, insofar as that was possible; Antony had a few very good talking points prepared on that score.

When it came to the stone's damage and the punishment of the two perpetrators, however, his arguments thinned out considerably. To be frank, he was still wrapping his head around the whole ghastly debacle.

At least the girl, Jillian, had chosen to transfer universities. This was a most fortunate development. Having her out of sight, and consequently out of mind, would hopefully ensure that gossip over Chilcott's affair died down quickly. When it came to Anders, he could only pray that a timely solution satisfying all parties involved might somehow, magically, present itself. What the sum of all this drama would mean for Antony's third task – informing Dr. LaTrell of Daniel's extraordinary wish to begin seeing a student himself – was anyone's guess. With the memory of his young protégé's hopeful face burned sharply in his mind, it was perhaps the duty he was most dreading.

Dr. LaTrell's office door opened, but to Antony's unpleasant surprise, it was young Anders Manwaring himself who came walking out of it. The boy was expensively dressed in a well-tailored suit and impeccably polished black shoes. He wore an expression of the utmost contrition, but thirty-plus years of teaching warned Antony these manners had been rehearsed. He could detect the slightest trace of a smirk lingering beneath the boy's fair features.

"Dr. Miller!" Anders walked over to him and extended his hand. "What brings you here this afternoon?"

"Oh, I think you might hazard a guess at that," Antony replied coldly, without extending his in return. Anders had clearly been having a meeting of his own with the president. Given how lazily the lad's tie was positioned, their discussion had not been a stressful one.

Anders arranged a mournful wince. "About that. I am truly, truly sorry about the stone. I give you my word that my parents will make it right. They're organizing a sizable donation to Browning even now."

"Not everything can be put right with a donation, young Mr. Manwaring. That stone was a priceless artifact that can never be restored." Antony's anger bled into his tone more than was probably wise, but something in the boy's patronizing expression had inflamed his temper. He had to resist an urge to box the lad smartly across the ear.

"The whole thing was such a horrible misunderstanding. I really thought I was acting for the greater good."

"The *greater good*, you say?"

"Please let me explain, Dr. Miller. You're a swell chap, so I'd hate to think you'd got the wrong end of the stick. You see" – the boy lowered his voice – "I went to visit my girl last weekend. I found a man in her flat, bothering her, and I tried to stop him, but he knocked me out. I could have sworn it was Dr. Carter, but no one believed me. My girl was in danger, I could feel it, and I had to watch out for her. Damaging the stone was the wrong move, perhaps, but I thought getting rid of Dr. Carter was the best way forward at the time. As misjudged as my actions were, I never meant to hurt the school. Truly."

Dr. Miller's eyes narrowed. "Is this what you told Dr. LaTrell?"

"Yes," Anders replied, the corners of his mouth lifting slightly. "He advised me to come directly to him next time. And so I shall. But you must excuse me, Dr. Miller. I'm late for a rugby match. So sorry again for all the bother." Without another word the boy removed his tie, pocketed it, and walked languidly away.

Just then Dr. LaTrell, a tall, graying man with a foxlike face, poked his head out from his office door.

"Antony? Aren't you coming in?"

"Yes, yes, just a moment." Antony gathered up his things, determined after this exchange to pin something on Anders if it was the last thing he did.

The president led him in and shut the door. "Help yourself to a seat, Antony. I desperately need a brandy. Care for one? Or perhaps some sherry?"

"No thank you," Dr. Miller replied. He needed his wits about him for this conversation. While the president poured himself a tumbler full, Antony nervously took in the opulent room. He had been here only a few times before, and never at midday. Despite the brightness of the hour, the large office was cast with long shadows. Valuable works of art graced the room, but its black marble walls and floor were quite cheerless. He let out an involuntary shiver.

"What a week," Dr. LaTrell said heavily, sitting down with his glass of brandy. "So. You've fired Chilcott, have you?"

"Yes," Antony replied, grateful that the president was not wasting time with pleasantries.

"The evidence against him was watertight, I trust?"

"Absolutely. I had a firsthand confession from the young woman herself."

"Really?" Dr. LaTrell raised his brows. "How unusual."

"Yes, well, there were two eyewitnesses who happened upon the lovers in the act."

"Good heavens. My condolences to them both." He sipped thoughtfully at his drink. "Did Chilcott go quietly?"

"Not so quietly, no. But he's gone, and that's the main thing." Antony paused, overtaken by a sudden idea. A risky, but potentially wonderful, idea. "What a fool William has been," he said with a dramatic shake of his head. "If only he'd gone about this relationship in the right way, then none of this unpleasantness would have happened."

"The right way?" Dr. LaTrell's brow creased. "What right way could there have been in this situation?"

"Well, if he had been a single man, for example—"

"But he's not."

"Yes, but if he had been," he continued hurriedly. "If Chilcott had petitioned the school, for example, he could have had his relationship with Miss Stewart approved. That would have been a far more honorable path. Why," he continued with a warm chuckle, "contrast Chilcott's actions with the highly respectable motives of another professor in my department. Just the other day I received a relationship application from a fine young instructor who wishes to court a student after the term has finished. Now, there's a young man who is bound and determined to go about this business honorably. He's—"

"I hope you refused him, Antony," Dr. LaTrell cut in with a strange look. "You know our policy. No instructor and student romances. We have at least a dozen different—"

"A dozen different regulations against it, yes I know," Dr. Miller interrupted, his anxiety rising. He decided to change the subject, at least for the time being. A momentary delay was better than an immediate no.

"Returning to our original subject," Antony said lightly, "I am happy to report that Dr. Chilcott's – erm – that is, Miss Stewart – has withdrawn from Browning, and opted to attend another university. We no longer need to evaluate her case."

"Good. That's one less fire to worry about, at least."

"Speaking of fires" – Antony plucked anxiously at his bowtie – "I imagine there will be some form of legal action against Browning as a result of the stone's destruction. We must prepare ourselves."

"That we must," the president grunted. "This morning I received a phone call from Ambassador Nassar himself. The Egyptian government is threatening to sue Browning for property damages and negligence. As you might guess, the compensation they request is not an insignificant sum."

"How much?" Antony whispered hoarsely.

"You don't want to know."

"Please," he urged. "How much?"

Smiling wryly, Dr. LaTrell handed him a slim brown file. With shaking hands, Antony opened it and read the estimated figure.

He looked up at the president weakly. "This would be impossible to repay."

"Indeed." LaTrell drained the last of his brandy.

Dr. Miller almost couldn't bear to ask his next question. "What of Dr. Carter's site? Will they ban him from returning?"

"That's the odd part of the business." The president stood to pour himself a second glass. "The Egyptian ministry has agreed to allow Dr. Carter to return to Egypt, on two conditions."

"What conditions?"

"The first is that the fine be paid before site work resumes next summer. Very understandable. The second is that Dr. Carter agree to forfeit leadership of the Abu Simbel site and work under one of the Egyptians' own men. A Dr. Abasi Fahrut, I believe."

Dr. Miller's heart sank on behalf of his friend. "A demotion."

"Yes," the president said crisply, recapping the brandy bottle. "To be honest, I was quite shocked they'd let him come back at all. As enraged as they are, they seem to like him."

"Of course they do," Dr. Miller replied stoutly. "They're not fools. Dr. Carter is one of the best in the field, and they're lucky to have him. I'm determined that he not be held responsible for the deplorable actions of our students." Antony tossed the file onto the desk. "There's only one possible course of action. The Manwarings must pay the fine, and Anders must be expelled."

The words were out of Antony's mouth before he could think what he was saying. Dr. LaTrell paused, then threw back his head with a roar laughter.

"Don't trouble yourself over Anders. I've taken care of it. All is in hand."

"And?" Dr. Miller urged. "Will the Manwarings make this right?"

Dr. LaTrell nodded thoughtfully. "After a manner of speaking, yes. Silas and Patricia have consented to double their annual donation, on the condition that young Anders be allowed to remain in school. I have agreed to their terms."

"You have agreed to their terms?" Antony said in disbelief. "Are you hearing yourself, Phillip?"

MINDY LAWRENCE

Dr. LaTrell was beginning to look more irritated than placating, but he pressed on in his typical crisp, dry manner. "In the meantime, I intend to phone the Egyptian embassy and inform them that, unfortunately, Browning is not in a sound enough position to compensate them at this time. I'm drawing up a repayment schedule this weekend, but they'll have to be satisfied with a ten-year plan. Since we cannot immediately meet their conditions, our Amity chapter, at least at the Egyptian location, will have to be closed, and all projects temporarily—"

"You cannot do that," Dr. Miller broke in, leaping to his feet in dismay. "This is not Browning's fault, or Dr. Carter's! Anders Manwaring is responsible, and he must bear the consequences. The Amity program is a peaceful, prestigious international cooperation, and we need it now more than ever, after the war. You cannot—"

"We have no choice," Dr. LaTrell interrupted loudly. "If I punish Anders, the Manwarings will withdraw their support from Browning entirely. Is that what you want? To cut corners, to defund our arts, our athletics, to freeze our hiring? I simply cannot allow that to happen."

"But ... but ..."

"I'm sorry, Antony. My decision is final. Anders will remain at Browning, and the Amity program – at least the Egyptian site – will close. For the good of the university."

Antony's brain felt as though it had been doused in petrol and flame. Summoning all his courage, he said, "You mean for the good of Phillip LaTrell."

The president raised a single, silver eyebrow. "I beg your pardon?"

Now that Antony had made his sentiments known, there seemed little point in backing down from them. He took a deep breath.

"I know what you're doing, Phillip. You're unwilling to face leaner times. You don't want to make unpopular cuts. Why would

294

you? It's so much more comfortable to keep things as they have always been, bankrolled and effectively run by people like the Manwarings. Far better to let the programs and professors you deem irrelevant suffer. Tell me. Have the Manwarings bribed you personally, as well?"

The president rose from his chair, quivering with anger. "How dare you accuse me of—"

"Cordelia Adams," Antony cut him off. "Penelope Smith." He swallowed painfully. "Jenny Ellison."

Dr. LaTrell flinched. "What did you say?"

"The names of three young women who I happen to know have accused Anders Manwaring of unwanted sexual advances, without any response to their cases." Dr. Miller set his jaw. "The local papers might be very interested to hear that you have overlooked these reports and kept Anders on at the school without consequences. A good journalist might easily assume – just as I have – that you ignored these complaints to preserve your revenue stream, and keep your popularity intact."

LaTrell's face darkened.

"Chilcott's scandal, the stone's destruction, and a presidential cover-up?" Antony quietly spouted off. "That would be a lot of bad Browning press in quick succession, Dr. LaTrell."

"Are you threatening me, Antony? Am I to understand that you intend to go to the papers?"

"I'm inviting you to do the right thing," Dr. Miller said firmly. "We've known each other for a long time, Phillip. As a professor you were a man of truth and integrity. Tell me. Do you enjoy taking orders from a spoiled young poodle like Anders?"

The president glowered. "I don't take orders from any of the Manwarings."

"Then prove it. Hold the lad accountable. Kick him out. Force Patricia and Silas to pay the fine in full, immediately, so that Dr. Carter may safely return to his site. Threaten them with legal action if they resist, for goodness sake! Make an example of them, make an example to all the wealthy families who think they run this place." He hesitated. "I beg of you. Don't let the Amity program suffer for the sake of your own pride. If the Manwarings withdraw their support from the school, so be it. We can find other ways to fill the deficit. I'm sure of it."

The president roughly stroked his chin, scarlet with fury but evidently stewing over Antony's words. The old dean could sense that the implication LaTrell had been taking orders from Anders, mixed with the threat of bad publicity, had proved to be an effective cocktail.

"Suppose, just suppose, that I were to do as you say," LaTrell said slowly. "How far would you be willing to go to help fill that deficit?"

Antony's heart sank. "I assume by that you mean ..."

Dr. LaTrell raised one hand in a sort of shrug. "You're the longest tenured dean here, Antony. Getting your salary off my payroll would free up quite a bit of capital. I could easily replace you with Dr. Jones or Dr. Christiansen. Either man would be a much, much cheaper dean of the department." He scowled. "To be frank, I'm really not sure I want you around much longer, Antony. Not after the threat you've just leveled against me."

Dr. Miller attempted a polite smile, but he felt as though he had been punctured somewhere under his left rib; all his hot air seemed to be slowly seeping out of him. Despite his many jokes about longing for retirement, being faced with it so suddenly was a crushing, crushing blow.

"Well." He weakly cleared his throat. "If this week has done anything, it has shown me how ready I am for some peace and quiet. Consider it done." With a sudden stroke of inspiration, Antony added, "On one last condition."

CHAPTER 42

Admittedly, Daniel got a bit carried away. Jenny's forceful assertion that she didn't need him to succeed, she merely *wanted* him, come hell or high water, had left him too spellbound to speak.

He'd seen glimpses of this part of her nature over the past week; hints of an iron-like will, forged in the furnace of opposition. Yet never had there been such a clear, demonstrable force of it. Her brown eyes sparked with an energy capable of consuming everything in its path. It had proven impossible to resist basking in that warmth, that unquenchable heat. Pressing his body firmly against Jenny's, Daniel thrust his hands into her hair and explored her lovely, stubborn mouth more boldly than he had ever dared.

Jenny accepted his kiss rigidly at first, but soon abandoned her thorny defenses. With a little utterance that was half a sigh, half a sob of relief, she soon responded in kind. Looping both her hands firmly around his neck, she drew herself up on tiptoe and pressed her elbows hard into his shoulders. When he moved to sweep her off the floor, she leaped instinctively into his arms.

Though in a haze of feeling, Daniel had managed to keep some semblance of self-control. With Antony's warning resounding loudly in his head, he carried her to his comfortable old chair, seating them at a respectable distance from the desk. They cuddled comfortably, an intimacy that felt almost as glorious as the rapturous kissing that followed. Jenny's fingers tenderly stroked his Adam's apple and jawline; his, meanwhile, could not find a place in which they were content to rest. They tangled themselves joyfully in her hair, or wandered up and down her back, or skimmed the top of her bare knee.

When she gave an involuntary shiver, he pulled off his own favorite blue sweater and draped her in it, gallantly insisting that his office ran cold and rejoicing in the thought of something so close to him being closer still to her.

"Thank you." Jenny smiled as she pulled the article over her head. "Well. I suppose it's sink or swim together, now."

Daniel rested his lips on her wool-clad shoulder, too happy to speak. The words she had spoken kept resurfacing in his mind: "I want you, Daniel Carter."

A quiet resolution seemed to have passed between them. Jenny was right. Now was not the time to worry; it was the time to work.

"I'm sorry I wavered," he murmured in her ear. "I wasn't certain either of us really understood what this could mean, in the end. I was trying to give you a chance to get away, if that was what you wanted."

"Well, I tried," Jenny replied with a melodramatic sigh, "but then you locked the door."

Daniel let out a short burst of laughter. "I suppose I did. Sorry."

"I'm not. Someone recently advised me to keep my close ones close." Her beautiful brown eyes glistened with feeling. "I intend to, Daniel."

He gave her shoulder another grateful kiss. "Now that we are 'sinking or swimming' together, I have to tell you something."

She tensed. "About Egypt?"

"Yes."

"What is it? Do you have more news? Will they let you return?"

"If certain conditions are met, then yes, I can go back."

"Oh, Daniel!" Jenny gave him a quick little kiss. "Oh, thank heavens. Conditions, you said? What conditions?"

"Browning will pay a sizable fine for the damage." He cleared his throat. "And I will no longer be head of the Abu Simbel site."

"*What?*"

"I'll be working under one of their own scholars, Dr. Abasi Fahrut. He's a very well-respected Egyptologist. I've met him once or twice at the odd conference. He knows what he's about."

"They're replacing you?" Jenny cried indignantly. "But it's your site, Daniel! You're the one who opened the area, and applied for the original permits, and planned all the preservation work, and everything. This wasn't your fault, don't they understand that?"

Daniel shrugged, hoping he looked less disheartened than he felt. "Their officials have lost trust in my judgment. I can't fault them, really. But I know I can win them over again in time. Right now they want consequences, and a period of penance." He straightened his shoulders. "I can give them that."

"So you're being punished for trusting your students and giving them the opportunity of a lifetime?" Jenny said incredulously. "You're being punished for Anders' betrayal?"

"No," Daniel replied gravely. "I'm being held accountable for not keeping better watch on the artifacts in my care. I suppose, under the circumstances, I'm lucky to come back in any position."

"What about the map? The tomb?"

Daniel had almost forgotten it. The hidden tomb of Ahrunset seemed such a distant memory, given everything that had happened since.

"Will you tell the new site leader about it?" she prompted.

Before he could answer, Daniel's office telephone rang. Jenny sprang up from his lap, and he reluctantly rose to answer the call. As Jenny smoothed her rumpled hair, Daniel's eyes flitted shyly over her lovely form. He took a peculiar pleasure in how at home that old sweater looked upon her shoulders, though it hung comically long overall. Smiling, he lifted the receiver to his ear.

"This is Dr. Carter."

"Daniel? Hello, Daniel, can you hear me? *Hello, hello?* Are you there, Daniel?"

Daniel smothered a laugh. It was Dr. Miller. Antony always shouted over the telephone.

"Yes, I can hear you. What is it, Antony?"

"You can? You can hear me? Excellent, because I have such news! I've done it, I've actually done it! I gave the president a piece of my mind, and what do you think? He listened, he actually listened! I have so much to tell you – Daniel, can you still hear me? Are you still there?"

"Yes, I'm still here." Daniel held the receiver a few inches away from his ear. "What's this all about, Antony?"

"Now, don't leave your office, I'm coming to tell you in person. I'm in the administration building, but I'll head over directly. Did you understand that last bit? Don't move, I'm coming your way. Stay where you are. Such marvelous, marvelous news, Daniel!"

He heard the click of Antony's telephone as the line went dead. Replacing his own receiver, he looked quizzically at Jenny.

"What was that all about?" she asked, through a mouthful of hairpins.

"Apparently Antony has good news. The kind that he insists on telling me in person." Daniel glanced at his desk, which was still blessedly tidy. "Why don't you stay, Jenny? You might as well hear it too."

"Are you sure?"

"Absolutely." He crossed to her and took her hand. "Any news I hope to hear involves you, after all."

Jenny looked immensely gratified. Daniel wondered if she

shared his relief that at least one person knew of their romance. It would be a blessing not to have to hide it for a moment.

She pulled off his sweater and held it towards him. "Do you ...?" She gestured wordlessly over it.

"Keep it."

Beaming, she hugged the item to her chest. "If he's coming," she whispered, "then you had better unlock your door."

"Yes. Right."

They waited for him a surprisingly short time. Antony was over sixty, yet his burgeoning enthusiasm seemed to have quickened his pace. Within just a few minutes, he was huffing and puffing through the entrance of the study.

"Daniel!" he exclaimed happily. "I – oh!" Dr. Miller started upon seeing Jenny. "And Miss Ellison, too! What a pleasant surprise. Very good, very good. This is a fortunate meeting."

Antony helped himself to a seat, grinning like a Cheshire cat at the pair of them. "Well. Daniel Joseph Carter, I must admit, I never thought this day would come. I feel, to quote Dickens, 'as giddy as a drunken man'!"

Daniel stared at his mentor suspiciously. "What are you up to, Antony? Are you well?"

"Never better!" The old man chuckled heartily. "I feel as though I have the strength of a lion, my boy! Why, I wonder, didn't I do this years ago?"

"Do what, Professor Miller?" Jenny gently inquired.

"Stand up to LaTrell, of course!" Antony rubbed his hands together eagerly. "I told him what was what and no mistake. I insisted that right is right, and wrong is wrong. Oh, Daniel, it felt simply glorious. After years of careful diplomacy, of internal politics, of bowing and scraping and kissing up, I said to myself, 'enough is enough.' I said my piece. Before I even knew what was happening, I just came right out with it!"

"With what, Antony?"

"Why, I warned LaTrell that justice would prevail with or without him, so he had better get on the right side of the argument. I have, Daniel, effectively 'thrown the moneychangers' out of this temple of learning! Well, almost. Oh dear." The old man chuckled. "I imagine I'll shortly be struck down by God for that comparison. Heaven help me."

Dr. Miller rubbed a silk handkerchief over his glistening forehead and beamed. He was clearly too caught up in excitement to provide more concrete details. Jenny looked helplessly at Daniel, who attempted to re-start the conversation.

"Did you discuss Anders' punishment? What is the president's decision?"

"Ah! Yes! We will begin there." Dr. Miller tapped his nose joyfully. "Against all odds, Dr. LaTrell has consented to punish Anders with a two-week suspension. His enrollment will then be evaluated during a formal hearing, at which all accusations made against him to this date will be brought to light. It is not quite expulsion, at least not yet, but it is more than I ever dared hope for!"

The old man's eyes misted over, and he regarded Jenny with unexpected pain.

"This hearing should have taken place long ago. I am so very sorry, Miss Ellison, that your ... your own complaint was not acknowledged sooner. I only hope you can forgive me."

Jenny seemed unable to speak for a time. At last, she nodded, with an expression of such intense emotion that Daniel could not begin to fathom its full meaning; he thought he could detect gratitude and sorrow, but the rest was mingled and indiscernible.

"Thank you, Dr. Miller," she said. "I can't tell you how happy I am that something is being done at last."

Antony sniffed into his handkerchief. "The best part is, the prospect of Anders' hearing seems to have put the fear of God into Patricia and Silas Manwaring. They have agreed to pay the fine to the Egyptian government in full! I believe they are writing it out even as we speak. Who could have foreseen that turn of events, I ask you? One resistant act on Browning's part and the power of the Manwarings topples. It appears that their influence was only ever a castle in the air! They are cowards at their core, truly."

Daniel found an outlet for his happiness by embracing Jenny, twirling her high above him in the air while she laughed and kicked her heels.

"My second piece of good news," he said, beaming fondly at the pair of them, "is that I have secured permission for the two of you to court. Openly. With Browning's full blessing and approval. The terms are being drawn up today."

The couple froze mid-spin, unable to believe their ears.

"What?" Jenny whispered as Daniel let her slide to the ground. "Can this be true?"

"Antony," Daniel said in disbelief. "How—"

"There are conditions, of course," Dr. Miller continued gravely. "Reasonable ones, I have to admit. Miss Ellison will never be able to take a class from you again, Daniel. That much should be obvious. And – oh, blast!" Antony slapped his forehead. "I never thought! She may even have to re-take Paleography from another professor next term. There will be no way to prove that you haven't unduly influenced her grades through favoritism. I didn't consider that. Blast, that's most unfortunate."

"I haven't marked any of Jenny's papers since the first week of term," Daniel said hastily. "I asked Max to grade them all."

Antony slapped his knee and roared with delight. "Didn't trust yourself to be impartial, eh? Knew she'd be a favorite early on? Splendid, splendid! Well, I see no reason why her original grades should not stand, then. But mind you don't mark her exam papers," Dr. Miller said, pointing a warning finger.

"Of course." Daniel's heart soared with happiness, and Jenny actually giggled in rapturous delight.

"What are the other conditions?" she asked, pressing Daniel's hand in both of hers.

Antony sobered. "Though he has given his consent, Dr. LaTrell requests that your relationship remain private. For the time being, at least. He wants to distance Browning from the scandal of Dr. Chilcott. Therefore, and I realize this might be difficult to hear, he is giving you a choice, Daniel. If you wish to go forward with this, he requires that you participate in our professorial exchange program next term. You will be temporarily reassigned to Radwyth University."

"Radwyth?" Daniel repeated, his heart sinking to his toes. "Leave Browning, and Jenny? Now?"

"Yes. For a term, Daniel. Just one term, until all of this settles down. He was quite insistent upon that point, but I have one last piece of news to soften the blow. If Daniel completes the exchange program, and the two of you agree to be distanced for the spring term, then Dr. LaTrell has agreed to allow Jenny to accompany you in Egypt this summer." Dr. Miller grinned rather mischievously. "That last bit was my doing. Evidently Phillip does not care whether the two of you are together, so long as you are far out of sight of this town and university."

Jenny's brows shot up her forehead. "The Amity committee would let me change sites? Truly?"

"Oh yes, I think so, seeing as Browning's Amity committee currently consists of Dr. Carter and myself," Dr. Miller chuckled. "I really feel it ought to have been this way from the beginning. Any objections, Dr. Carter?"

"None," Daniel said quickly. "But what about Mark Phillips, my other candidate?"

Dr. Miller waved his hand. "Oh, Mark will be simply delighted to exchange! He always preferred Crete. I have arranged to mentor both him and Solomon – Chilcott's candidate, you know – at my site. They are fine boys who get along well together. The three of us shall have a very merry time." Antony busied himself with his cuff-links. "I can think of no better way to end my career at Browning."

Daniel's smile froze.

"What did you say?" Jenny whispered.

"I said I can think of no better way to end my career." Antony looked up again and smiled.

Daniel stared at his old mentor. "What are you talking ab—"

"The formal announcement will come out next week," Dr. Miller cut across him. "I'm retiring at the end of the summer. Dr. Christiansen will be taking over as dean next autumn term. After nearly forty years of teaching, I will settle into my country house for a decade or two – hopefully two – of peace and quiet. I am very much looking forward to it."

"No ... no, Antony," Daniel whispered. Jenny had begun softly crying at his side.

"What's this?" Dr. Miller laughed. "Tears? Come, come, my dear girl. There's no need for all that."

He handed Jenny his silk handkerchief with a touchingly paternal look. "You forget that this is my choice, dear Miss Ellison. I've had a good run. It's time to make way for the younger talent; to pass the torch to those with clearer, and stronger, and braver voices. Such as your own."

This little speech did nothing to stop Jenny's tears. Accepting the handkerchief, she walked over to Dr. Miller and kissed him softly upon the cheek.

"I don't know what to say," she whispered. "Thank you. For all your kindness."

Dr. Miller could not have looked more surprised if the roof had caved in. Blushing rosily, he stammered and stood. "Yes, well. You've got a good young man there, Miss Ellison. I know that four months apart may seem like an eternity now, but in the grand scheme of life, that's but the blink of an eyelash. If you'll take my advice, Miss Ellison ... Daniel Carter is worth the wait."

"Antony." Daniel had found his voice at last. Walking over to his friend, he held out a shaking hand. "This isn't ... this is all my ... how can I ever ..." Yet again, his speech left him. His grief was still too sharp to trust himself with words.

The old man took Daniel's hand in both of his own.

"Daniel, my boy," he whispered throatily. "When you returned ... thank the heavens above ... when you returned *alive* from the war, I thought to myself how terribly, horrifically unjust it was that someone so young had already been made to survive loss, a global conflict, and unspeakable personal violence before the age of thirty. I've said it before, and I'll say it again. You deserve the best that life and love have to offer. I wish you – I wish you *both* so much joy. God bless you, Daniel Carter." Looking around the room, he smiled affably. "I've always loved this office. It could use a slightly bigger desk though, eh?"

Chortling to himself, Dr. Miller trotted from the room before the couple could even call after him. Daniel turned to face Jenny, who was still sobbing in bewilderment.

"What did he say?"

"Nothing." Daniel reddened.

"Why is he leaving? Why now?"

Daniel only shook his head, suspecting the awful truth but not feeling ready to own it, even to himself.

"Was it because of us?" Jenny moaned. "First Chilcott's scandal, then us. Did we make it look like Dr. Miller had lost control of the department? Is this our fault?"

"I-I don't think so." He exhaled roughly, his thoughts a tangled mess of grief and guilt. "He's been talking about retiring for a while now. Perhaps it just felt like the right moment."

She gazed at him sadly. "The way he spoke to you, Daniel. As if you were his ..."

Daniel nodded, his throat constricting with emotion. Hot tears brimmed in his eyes, and he blinked them back furiously.

Jenny weakly ran a hand over her face. "I need things to stop changing, just so I can catch my breath. First your demotion, then the Radwyth proposition, and now Dr. Miller is leaving us?"

"Speaking of leaving ..." He cupped her face in his hands. "Four months. *Four months,* Jenny?"

"I know," she lamented. "Daniel, how could you leave Browning for that long? You can't go. You belong here."

"But think." He softly stroked her cheek. "At the end of spring term, we'd be in Egypt."

"Together," Jenny said dreamily. "Searching for a tomb under a sacred temple."

"Exactly. We can write and telephone each other in the meantime. Perhaps we could even visit on weekends and bank holidays."

"That's what you want?" Jenny asked, searching his eyes for answers. "Truly?"

"To be in Egypt with you?" Daniel shook his head incredulously. "I can't think of anything I've wanted more. But is it what *you* want?"

"It's as I keep telling you, Dr. Carter," Jenny murmured with a loving smile. "I want you." Looking deeply into his eyes, she sealed their agreement with a long, slow, tender kiss.

END

ACKNOWLEDGMENTS

Thank you so much for picking up this book. Time is a precious and finite resource, and I don't take for granted a single minute you have spent with this story. Thank you from the bottom of my heart. (If you were entertained, I hope you will consider leaving a review!)

I wrote this novel during a global pandemic, and there is a touching irony in the fact that I have people all over the world to thank for its existence. While sharing an early version of the story online, I met amazing friends from Australia, Canada, Scotland, England, Egypt, Russia, France, Brazil, Hong Kong, Norway, Spain, and all over the United States, among other places. These relationships have enriched my life more than I could ever express.

The final product wouldn't have come together without the support of my loving family, friends, and the #SanditonSisterhood. I also want to give special thanks to Nunya, who has done so much to help raise awareness of my stories. Thank you, thank you, thank you!

I'm exceedingly grateful to Ashley Santoro for her beautiful cover design; to Katherine for her editing; to Jessica for her honest feedback and design assistance; and to my beta readers for their advice and critiques, all of which have raised the tone and quality of this work beyond what I could achieve alone.

Lastly, to my loving husband: you'll always be my #HotProf.

ALSO BY MINDY LAWRENCE
BOOK TWO IN THE ADVENTURES OF THE HEART SERIES

In the summer of 1948, Dr. Daniel Carter and aspiring archaeologist Jennifer Ellison must navigate professional obstacles, shocking betrayals, and the joys (and challenges) of a quickly-deepening love as they search for the tomb of Ahrunset.

ABOUT THE AUTHOR

Mindy Lawrence is a period drama fanatic, a dark chocolate advocate, and a night owl. More than anything, she adores dreaming up stories of great loves and awe-inspiring places. Readers of Mindy's books can expect lots of twists and turns, a dash of intrigue, and plenty of tender, thrilling romance. She lives in the United States with her husband and two darling children.

For book updates, you can subscribe to Mindy's newsletter and connect with her on Instagram. She hopes you'll join her for an adventure or two.

NEWSLETTER: WWW.MINDYLAWRENCEAUTHOR.COM
INSTAGRAM: @MINDYLAWAUTHOR

1. Jenny and Jillian have several important clashes throughout the book. In what ways are the two women alike, and in what ways are their characters foils of each other? How is Jillian a sympathetic character?

2. Anders pursues Jenny throughout the term, even though she has rebuffed him numerous times. What is driving his attraction to her, and why does he continue to target her?

3. Margie is quite protective of Jenny throughout the story. Consider Jenny and Margie's friendship and the boundaries that exist between them. Do those boundaries need to be adjusted, or is Margie justified in calling out Jenny's lone wolf behavior?

4. Daniel's character vacillates between fastidiousness and informality. In what areas is he a rule keeper, and in what areas is he a rule breaker? How might this fluidity have guided him in his military career and his choices with Jenny?

5. Daniel has been on his own since he was seventeen. How has his background influenced his feelings about love? What is it about Jenny that finally touches his heart?

6. Jenny's feelings for Daniel develop much more gradually than his. When did you first suspect her romantic attraction to him?

7. What factors have contributed to Jenny's own hesitation to love? Ponder the influence of trauma and anxiety on Jenny's own romantic choices. How is Daniel able to overcome these barriers?

8. What are Daniel and Jenny's strengths as a couple, and what are their weaknesses? What challenges and blessings might they encounter as a result?

REFERENCES

Ancient egyptian royal titulary. (2021, November 18). In Wikipedia. https://en.wikipedia.org/wiki/Ancient_Egyptian_royal_titulary

Antiquity. (n.d.). Pigments through the ages. Retrieved November 18, 2021, from http://www.webexhibits.org/pigments/intro/antiquity.html%7CWebexhibits-Pigmentsthroughtheages-antiquity

GCT. (2019, November 2). Archaeologists discover new treasures from flourishing minoan settlement on crete. Greek City Times. https://greekcitytimes.com/2019/11/02/minyan-settlement-crete/

George, N. (2012, December 31). Egyptian sweetmeat. Pass the garum. Retrieved November 18, 2021, from http://pass-the-garum.blogspot.com/2012/12/egyptian-sweetmeat.html

Lane, J. (2017, November 18). Abu simbel, egypt. Art now and then. Retrieved November 18, 2021, from http://art-now-and-then.blogspot.com/2017/11/abu-simbel-egypt.html

Limestone reacting with acid (n.d.). Science photo library. https://www.sciencephoto.com/media/594776/view/limestone-reacting-with-acid

Literacy. (n.d.). Digital egypt for universities. Retrieved November 18, 2021, from https://www.ucl.ac.uk/museums-static/digitalegypt/literature/literacy.html

Literacy in ancient egypt. (n.d.). Www.worldhistory.biz. Retrieved November 18, 2021 from https://www.worldhistory.biz/ancient-history/67600-2-5-literacy-in-ancient-egypt.html

Mark, J. J. (2016, February 14). The step pyramid of djoser at saqqara. World history encyclopedia. Retrieved November 18, 2021, from https://www.worldhistory.org/article/862/the-step-pyramid-of-djoser-at-saqqara/

Maya script. (2021, November 18). In Wikipedia. https://en.wikipedia.org/wiki/Maya_script

Millmore, M. (n.d.). Egyptian hieroglyphic alphabet. Discovering egypt. Retrieved November 18, 2021, from https://discoveringegypt.com/egyptian-hieroglyphic-writing/egyptian-hieroglyphic-alphabet/

Nebu. (2021, November 18). In Wikipedia. https://en.wikipedia.org/wiki/Nebu

Norman (2018, June 2). Visiting abu simbel temple (from luxor or beyond). Annees de pelerinage. Retrieved November 18, 2021, from https://www.annees-de-pelerinage.com/abu-simbel-temple-egypt/

Norway World War II. (n.d.). Brittanica. Retrieved November 18, 2021, from https://www.britannica.com/place/Norway/World-War-II

Norwegian resistance movement. (2022, January 5). In Wikipedia. https://en.wikipedia.org/wiki/Norwegian_resistance_movement

Phoenician alphabet. (2021, November 18). In Wikipedia. https://en. wikipedia.org/wiki/Phoenician_alphabet

Serra da capivara national park. (n.d.). Unesco. Retrieved November 18, 2021 from https://whc.unesco.org/en/list/606/

The Editors of Encyclopaedia Brittanica. (n.d.). Abu simbel. Brittanica. Retreived November 18, 2021, from https://www.britan nica.com/place/Abu-Simbel

The Editors of Encyclopaedia Brittanica. (n.d.). Altamira. Brittanica. Retrieved November 18, 2021, from https://www.britannica.com/ place/Altamira

The Editors of Encyclopaedia Brittanica. (n.d.). Phoenician alphabet. Brittanica. Retrieved November 18, 2021, from https:// www.britannica.com/topic/Phoenician-alphabet

The social structure of ancient egypt. (n.d.). Ancient egypt online. Retrieved November 18, 2021, from https://www.ancient-egypt-online.com/ancient-egypt-social-structure.html

Urry, W. G. (n.d.). Paleography. Brittanica. Retrieved November 18, 2021, from https://www.britannica.com/topic/paleography

Wadjet. (2021, November 18). In Wikipedia. https://en.wikipedia. org/wiki/Wadjet

Wilson, S. (n.d.). Rationing in world war two. Historic uk. Retrieved November 18, 2021, from https://www.historic-uk.com/CultureUK/ Rationing-in-World-War-Two/

World war II and its aftermath. (n.d.). Brittanica. Retreived November 18, 2021, from https://www.britannica.com/place/Egypt/World-War-II-and-its-aftermath

Phoenician alphabet. (2021, November 18). In Wikipedia. https://en.
wikipedia.org/wiki/Phoenician_alphabet

Serra da capivara national park. (n.d.). Unesco. Retrieved November
18, 2021 from https://whc.unesco.org/en/list/606/

The Editors of Encyclopaedia Brittanica. (n.d.). Abu simbel.
Brittanica. Retreived November 18, 2021, from https://www.britan
nica.com/place/Abu-Simbel

The Editors of Encyclopaedia Brittanica. (n.d.). Altamira. Brittanica.
Retrieved November 18, 2021, from https://www.britannica.com/
place/Altamira

The Editors of Encyclopaedia Brittanica. (n.d.). Phoenician
alphabet. Brittanica. Retrieved November 18, 2021, from https://
www.britannica.com/topic/Phoenician-alphabet

The social structure of ancient egypt. (n.d.). Ancient egypt online.
Retrieved November 18, 2021, from https://www.ancient-egypt-
online.com/ancient-egypt-social-structure.html

Urry, W. G. (n.d.). Paleography. Brittanica. Retrieved November 18,
2021, from https://www.britannica.com/topic/paleography

Wadjet. (2021, November 18). In Wikipedia. https://en.wikipedia.
org/wiki/Wadjet

Wilson, S. (n.d.). Rationing in world war two. Historic uk. Retrieved
November 18, 2021, from https://www.historic-uk.com/CultureUK/
Rationing-in-World-War-Two/

World war II and its aftermath. (n.d.). Brittanica. Retreived November 18, 2021, from https://www.britannica.com/place/Egypt/World-War-II-and-its-aftermath